A VOICE FROM OUT OF THE DISTANT PAST . . .

A vague shape developed, a sculpture of fog—except that it was glowing, and the energies of this place were definitely centered around it. Now that Elspeth knew what to look for, the lines of force were as clear as ripples in a pond. This—thing—was a part of the forest—of the energies that lay under the forest.

But it was still changing; it blurred, or perhaps her eyes blurred for a moment. And then, the figure solidified. It was not at all what she had expected.

It was a handsome man, silver-haired, silver-eyed, handsome enough even to cast Firesong into the shade, of no determinate age.

And he was dressed in an antique version of Herald's Whites. He looked like a glowing statue of milky glass, or like—

Oh, gods. Like a ghost, a spirit . . .

The hair on the back of her neck rose with atavistic fear, and she backed up another pace, holding out one hand as if to ward the thing off.

As if she *could*! This was not the first spirit she had encountered, but how could she know what this spirit could do? How could she hope to hold it off if it chose to attack her?

A crisp, clean breeze rose and fell. It sounded like the forest was sighing.

:Bright Havens!: said a cheerful, gentle voice in her head. *:You all look as if you'd seen a ghost!:*

WINDS OF FURY

WINDS OF FURY

Book Three of The Mage Winds

MERCEDES LACKEY

DAW BOOKS, INC.

DONALD A. WOLLHEIM, FOUNDER

375 Hudson Street, New York, NY 10014

ELIZABETH R. WOLLHEIM
SHEILA E. GILBERT
PUBLISHERS

For color prints of Jody Lee's paintings, please contact:
The Cerridwen Enterprise
P.O. Box 10161
Kansas City, MO 64111
Phone: 1-800-825-1281

Interior illustrations by Larry Dixon.

All the black & white interior illustrations
in this book are available as 11″ x 14″ prints;
either in a signed, open edition singly, or in
a signed and numbered portfolio from:

FIREBIRD ARTS & MUSIC, INC.
P.O. Box 14785
Portland, OR 97214-9998
Phone: 1-800-752-0494

Time Line by Pat Tobin.
Maps by Victor Wren.

DAW Book Collectors No. 921.

DAW Books are distributed by Penguin USA.

First Paperback Printing, August 1994
1   2   3   4   5   6   7   8   9

DAW TRADEMARK REGISTERED
U.S. PAT OFF. AND FOREIGN COUNTRIES
—MARCA REGISTRADA.
HECHO EN U.S.A.

PRINTED IN THE U.S.A.

DEDICATED TO THE
TEACHERS OF THE WORLD.

OFFICIAL TIMELINE FOR THE

by Mercedes Lackey

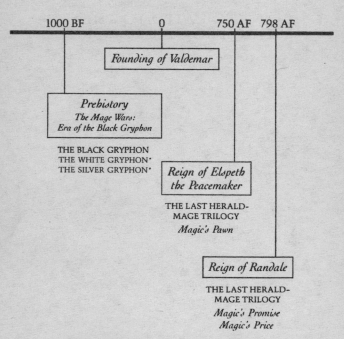

1000 BF   0   750 AF   798 AF

Founding of Valdemar

Prehistory
The Mage Wars:
Era of the Black Gryphon

THE BLACK GRYPHON
THE WHITE GRYPHON*
THE SILVER GRYPHON*

**Reign of Elspeth
the Peacemaker**

THE LAST HERALD-
MAGE TRILOGY
Magic's Pawn

Reign of Randale

THE LAST HERALD-
MAGE TRILOGY
Magic's Promise
Magic's Price

BF   Before the Founding
AF   After the Founding
*   Upcoming from DAW Books in hardcover

HERALDS OF VALDEMAR SERIES

Sequence of events by Valdemar reckoning

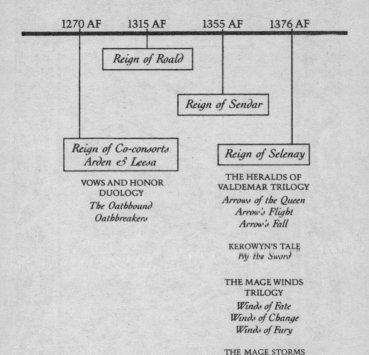

1270 AF	1315 AF	1355 AF	1376 AF

Reign of Roald

Reign of Sendar

**Reign of Co-consorts
Arden & Leesa**

VOWS AND HONOR
DUOLOGY
*The Oathbound
Oathbreakers*

Reign of Selenay

THE HERALDS OF
VALDEMAR TRILOGY
*Arrows of the Queen
Arrow's Flight
Arrow's Fall*

KEROWYN'S TALE
By the Sword

THE MAGE WINDS
TRILOGY
*Winds of Fate
Winds of Change
Winds of Fury*

THE MAGE STORMS
*Storm Warning
Storm Rising*
Storm Breaking

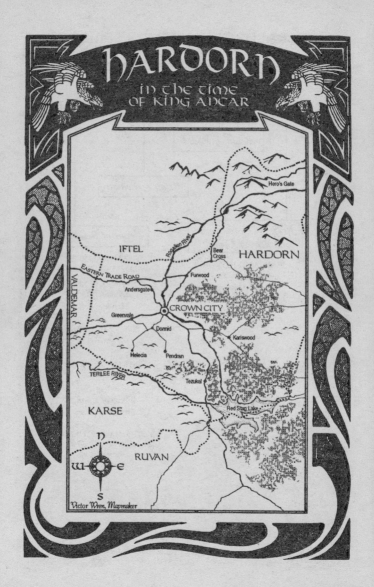

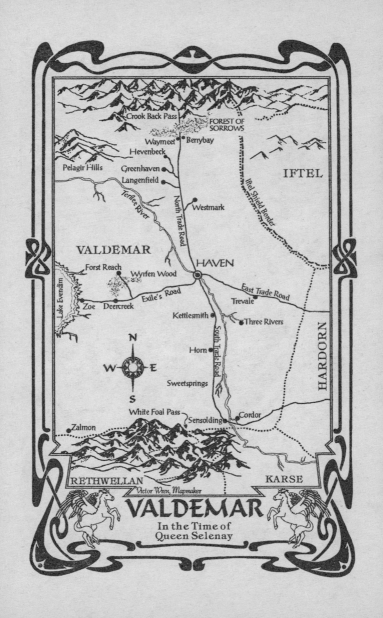

VALDEMAR

In the Time of
Queen Selenay

Victor Wren, Mapmaker

Crook Back Pass
FOREST OF SORROWS
Waymeet Berrybay
Hevenbeck
Pelagir Hills
Greenhaven
Langenfield
Terilee River
North Trade Road
Westmark
IFTEL
Ilel Shield Border
VALDEMAR
Forst Reach
Wyrfen Wood
HAVEN
Lake Evendim
Zoe Deercreek
Exile's Road
East Trade Road
Trevale
Kettlesmith
Three Rivers
South Trade Road
Horn
HARDORN
Sweetsprings
White Foal Pass
Sensolding
Cordor
Zalmon
RETHWELLAN
KARSE
N W E S

Chapter One

Ancar, King of Hardorn, slumped in the cushioned embrace of his throne and stared out into the empty Great Hall. Empty, because he no longer bothered with holding audiences. He was not here to listen to the complaints of the people of Hardorn. When he wished *them* to learn of his will, there were better ways to inform them than to gather them together like a mass of milling sheep and declaim it to them.

He did not *serve* them, as one petty bureaucrat of his father's reign had whined that he must—just before he had ordered the man given to his mages. They served *him;* his pleasures, his will, his whims. That was what his mother had taught him before she died, and Hulda had simply confirmed those lessons. Now, after all these years, they were finally learning that. He was their ruler by right of arms and strength; he had the power of life and death over them, and all that lay in between.

It had certainly taken them long enough to realize that.

The servants had lit the candles ensconced along the birch-paneled walls, and the dancing flames reflected from the polished gray-granite floor and the varnished maple beams above. Wavering spots of flame twinkled at him from gilt trim and gold fittings, from crystal ornaments and the metal threads of battle flags hanging from the beams. This had been a court of weaklings, once. His few decent enemies had been subdued or annihilated, and their families and lands with them. Now all that remained of them were the flags of their conquered holdings, and a few trophies Ancar kept to remind others of his grasp.

Echoes of his movements came back to him like a whisper. He found a peculiar irony in this empty chamber; a poignancy, yes. He found all of his pensive thoughts poignant. He had run out of challenges. This hall was as empty as his own conquests.

Oh, of course, he had all of Hardorn trembling at his feet—but he could not extend the borders of his Kingdom more than few shabby leagues in any direction. Even he dared not look Eastward, of course; to the East was the Empire, and the two-hundred-year-old Emperor Charliss. Only a fool would challenge Charliss—or someone who was stronger than Charliss. Ancar knew better than to think that *he* could boast of that.

To the North was Iftel, and he frowned to think of how his single attempt to invade *that* land had ended: with his armies transported bodily back to the capital and deposited there, and not a memory of crossing the border among them—and with his mages vanished utterly, without a trace. There was an invisible wall stretching along the Iftel-Hardorn border, a wall that would allow no one to pass. No, whatever guarded Iftel was as powerful as the Emperor, and there was no point in making It angry.

To the South was Karse. Ruled by priests, at war with Valdemar for hundreds of years—he would have said that Karse was a plum ripe for his picking. Except that he had been unable to gain more than those few leagues; after that, it seemed as if the very land itself rose up against him, and the Sun-priests certainly called up demons against his armies, for scores of men would vanish every night, never to be seen again. And it had become worse since the Priesthood had been taken over by a woman; he had lost even those few leagues he had gained.

But he could have coped with the losses in Karse. It

was all hill country, rocky and infertile, of little use. He could have even coped with the humiliation of Iftel. If it hadn't been for Valdemar.

If he lowered his eyes, he would see the map of Hardorn inlaid in the granite of the floor just in front of the throne. The Empire in black terrazzo, Iftel in green marble, Karse in yellow marble, and Valdemar in its everlasting white. Valdemar would be at his left hand; the hand of sorcery, or so the old-wives' tales had it. Valdemar, the unconquered. Valdemar, that should have been first to fall.

Valdemar, the ripe fruit that Hulda had promised him from the beginning.

He felt his lips lifting in a snarl and forced his face back into his mask of calm. And if the truth were to be admitted, he could not have told whether the snarl was meant for Valdemar and her Bitch-Queen, or for Hulda, the Bitch-Adept.

He shifted uncomfortably and the echo whispered back at him, a phantom rustling of fabric. Hulda had promised him Valdemar from the time she began to teach him black sorcery, had promised him the pretty little princess Elspeth, had vowed that he would have both within moments of seizing the throne of Hardorn from his senile old father. He *liked* tender little girls; at sixteen, Elspeth had been a little riper than he preferred but was still young enough to make a good plaything. At a single stroke, he would have doubled the size of his kingdom, and created a platform from which to invade not only Karse but Rethwellan as well. Then, with both those lands firmly in his fist, he could have challenged the old Emperor or simply consolidated his power, making himself Emperor of the West as Charliss was of the East. Hulda had *promised* him that. She had sworn she was the most powerful Adept in seven kingdoms! She had pledged him her help and her teaching; she had certainly not been backward in teaching him the secrets of her body! He had had no reason to doubt her at the time—

Except that it had never happened. *Somehow* the damned Heralds sent to negotiate a marriage with Elspeth got word to their Queen of his plans and the death of his father. *Somehow* one of them even escaped Ancar's prison cell, warned the Queen, and stopped him and his hastily-gathered army.

But it got worse with his second attempt. *Somehow* the Queen managed to raise a mercenary army that was capable of defeating his mages as well as his troops. *Somehow* they had cobbled up an alliance with the fanatics of Karse.

Somehow all of this had happened without Hulda, "the most powerful Adept in seven kingdoms," ever becoming aware of what was going on until after the fact. Bitch-Queen Selenay was still firmly on her throne. Another bitch, a mercenary Captain named Kerowyn, now held the border against him, and there didn't seem to be a single trick any of his commanders or mages could work that she hadn't seen before—and countered before. The Herald-Bitch Talia had been made a Sun-priest herself, and vested with the authority of the Arm of Vkandis by yet another bitch, the High Priest Solaris. And Bitch-Princess Elspeth had simply vanished, on some other quest for help, and he had to assume, given the absence of panic, that *she* was succeeding, even though not one of his agents could locate her.

And Bitch-Adept Hulda sat and twiddled her thumbs.

He was beginning to grow very tired of women. He had already grown tired of Hulda.

He was not aware of the fact that he had spoken her name until the echoes sent it back to him. This time he did snarl.

Yes, he was growing very tired of Hulda. He was tired of her whims, her eccentricities, her pretenses. What had been charming and exciting when he was sixteen now bored him—when it didn't disgust him. She was too old to play the coquette, too old for girlish mannerisms. And when she cast them off, she acted as if *she* was the monarch here, and not he.

That galled him almost as much as her consistent failure, and he would have tolerated the former if she had not brought him the latter. But she had the attitude without producing results, and if she weren't an Adept, he'd have had her slow-roasted alive by now.

When he was younger, he had accepted the fact that she virtually ruled him without a thought. But then, he had accepted many things back then without a thought. He was older now.

And wiser.

She treated him exactly as she had when he had taken the throne. She spoke, and expected him to listen attentively; she issued orders, and expected him to fling himself into whatever she ordered him to do.

I could have tolerated all of this if she had only done what she had promised. Out-thinking her was a challenge then. . . .

She had pledged him before he took the throne that he would soon be an Adept to rival her; she swore he would have power beyond his wildest dreams, power enough to level mountains if he chose. She swore that she would teach him everything she knew.

But the power never materialized, and the training she gave him never went beyond the level of Master. She had never taught him how to use all the powers he could Sense, and all the training she had given him until that moment had made it impossible for him to touch them. Or at least he had not been able to touch them during the time that she had been his *only* teacher.

He had encountered this reluctance on Hulda's part to give him any more real teaching two years ago, shortly after he had turned Master. He had been certain at that moment that the powers of an Adept were almost in his grasp, that it would only be a matter of a little more training.

That was when the excuses began. Hulda suspended his regular training sessions, telling him that he was beyond such things. That had made him elated, briefly—until he realized that there was no way other than regular training to achieve his long-sought goal. And when he began to seek her out, asking for more teaching, she was always busy. . . .

And at first, her excuses had seemed plausible. After so many defeats from the west, they were taking no chances. Hulda had mustered a cadre of mages of relatively low power to watch the border for any weaknesses in the force that protected Valdemar from magic. She needed to organize these people, to make certain that the coercion spells upon them were powerful enough to keep them at their work no matter what temptations and opportunities to defect were placed before them. But after weeks of such excuses, they began to wear thin.

After a few months, he took matters into his own hands.

He had been collecting mages since his first, ill-fated attempt to take the Valdemaran throne. Now he began doing more than collecting them and placing them under his coercion spells; now he began finding out, in a systematic sweep through his mage-corps, just what they knew.

He had been collecting and recruiting every kind and type of mage that showed even the faintest traces of power—from hill-shaman to mages of no known School. By aggressively pursuing a course of forced-learning, he had picked up every bit of knowledge, however seemingly inconsequential, from any of his "recruits" that had teachings he had not gotten. He had also been collecting every scrap of written information about magic that he could lay his hands on; every grimoire, every mage's personal notebook, every history of ancient times, and *anything* concerning magic to be had from within the Empire. Much of it had been useful. Some of it, he was certain, Hulda herself did not share. But none of it brought him the prize he was trying to reach—

At least, not to his knowledge. As he understood it, only an Adept could use the power of "nodes," those meeting places of the lines of power that he *could* use. Every attempt he had made so far had resulted in failure. He was still not an Adept, and he had no idea how far he was from that goal.

He had been trying to find an Adept to teach him, with no luck. Of course, Adepts could be avoiding Hardorn; everything he had ever heard or read indicated that the kind of Adept willing to teach *him* would also be the kind unwilling to share power, and that was precisely the problem he had with Hulda. Hulda might be warning them off, somehow. It would not surprise him much to discover that she had been working against him, preventing him from locating an Adept so that he would always be her inferior.

But she had underestimated him, and his willingness to tolerate a position as ruler in name only. There could be only one Ruler of Hardorn, and it would not be Hulda.

A servant appeared at the door, waiting silently for him to notice her existence. He admired the woman for a moment—not for her own looks, but for the new livery he had ordered. Scarlet and gold: the scarlet of blood, the gold of the wealth he intended to grasp. The livery matched his new device, now blazoned above his throne, replacing the insipid oak tree of his father. A winged serpent in gold, upon a field of blood-red, poised to strike.

Hulda should have taken note of that new device, and thought about what it meant.

Hulda thought that she had him under control, but she had not counted on the more mundane methods of dealing with an enemy. He had placed spies among her servants, loyal only to him, their loyalty ensured not by spells, but by fear. He had chosen these people carefully, finding those for whom death would be preferable to losing someone—or something. For some, it was a family member or a lover that they would die to protect. For others, it was a secret. And for a few, it was a possession that made life worth living. Such passion meant control—and such control could not be revealed by magical means.

These servants followed Hulda's every move, and let him know when she was so deeply engrossed in some activity that he would be able to act without her guessing what he was up to. She was not infallible—for instance, she did *not* possess a spell that he had read about, one that permitted the caster to see into the past. Whatever he did while she was occupied, she would not know about. She also did not possess the mind-magic that enabled one to read the thoughts of others. Well, neither did he, but that was of little matter at the moment. What was important was that she could not detect his control of her servants from their thoughts. So as long as she did not torture their secrets from them, he would always know where she was and what she was doing.

She might have servants of the same sort watching him; in fact, he had planned on it. His propensity for taking young, barely post-pubescent girls was well known—as was their regrettable tendency to not survive such encounters. He still enjoyed such pleasures, but as often as not, the girl was incidental to something magical he wished to achieve. There was great power in a painful death—something about a life being ended prematurely released incredible power. He did not think Hulda knew that *he* knew this; after all, his preferences had been well established long before he learned of the power these acts released. So he would wait until Hulda was occupied, then select one of the little lambs in his private herd and repair to his own chambers for an enjoyable and profitable candlemark or two.

His hand-picked servants watched Hulda, and guarded his secrets against her.

The woman waiting for him to acknowledge her, for instance, was Hulda's personal maid, and privy to her comings and goings. She was common enough to attract no notice; middle-aged, neither plain nor pretty, neither fat nor thin. And well-trained; she would not have slipped away, she would have waited for Hulda to dismiss her—and yet, at the same time, she would have arranged to be so attentive that Hulda would not dismiss her unless the mage wanted privacy. What a shame she wasn't younger.

He raised his eyes and nodded. The servant crossed the floor silently, her eyes lowered, and prostrated herself at the foot of the throne.

"Speak," he said quietly.

"Hulda has retired to her chamber in the company of the muleteer I told you of, Majesty," the servant replied, in a voice carefully pitched so as not to carry beyond the immediate vicinity. He had not chosen this chamber as a place to sit and brood without thought; it was impossible to be spied upon effectively here, and impossible to be overheard, given the acoustics of the place. It had been built to enable a semi-private audience in the midst of a crowded court. Such clever design gave him true privacy without making it obvious.

He raised his eyebrows in sardonic surprise; the muleteer must be a remarkable man, for this would be the fourth time he had graced Hulda's bed. Then again, Ancar had heard that the man had the strength and stamina of one of his mules . . . and perhaps shared more with them than Ancar had guessed.

The King had no fear that this muleteer might be an agent of Hulda's own; he knew everything there was to know about the man. Gossip in the kitchens had first alerted him to the muleteer's unusual abilities, although none of his excellence was in the area of intelligence. Hulda's muleteer was as dense as a rock and possessed of very little wit, only one short step above absolute simpleton. And Ancar had, in fact, *arranged* for his erstwhile tutor to hear about the muleteer's physical attributes. It had been no surprise to him when she immediately found an excuse to go down to the secondary stables to see the man for herself. As he had expected, once Hulda had ascertained that there was no hook attached to this very attractive bait, she had taken it.

Yes, well. The "hook" is the man himself, and his ability to keep a woman occupied and heedless of anything else for several candlemarks at a time. Not something Hulda would be looking for.

So, once again, Hulda and her new toy were amusing themselves. He wondered how long this toy would last. She tended to be as hard on her playthings as he was on his.

"Very good," he said in reply. "You may go."

The servant got slowly to her feet and backed out, closing the door behind her. Ancar did not immediately rise from his throne; he would wait, and give Hulda the opportunity to become completely engrossed in her lover before he moved.

No, there could be only one ruler in Hardorn. He was going to find a way to rid himself of Hulda, sooner or later.

That was, in a way, something of a pity. She was the only woman above the age of fifteen that he found desirable; perhaps that was because her sexual experience was so vast, and so unique. She constantly found new ways to amuse him. And it would be *very* pleasurable to somehow reduce her to the level of one of the servants; to strip her of all ability to challenge him, and yet leave her intelligence and her knowledge intact. *That* would be a triumph greater than conquering Valdemar.

No, I don't think that will ever happen. No matter how powerful I became, there would be no way I could strip her mind bare without fearing she would find a way to release herself. She would never accept any kind of role as an underling. It would be a waste of power I could better spend elsewhere. Once I am an Adept, once I have defeated her, that defeat must be followed by her death.

Finally, when he was certain he had given Hulda enough time to put everything except the prowess of her muleteer out of her mind, he rose and took his slow, leisurely way to his own chambers.

And not to his official chambers either.

"Keep watch," he told one of the guards outside the chamber—another of his hand-picked armsmen, but this one controlled directly, as all his personal guards were, by spells controlling his mind. He turned to the other. "Tell my chamberlain I am not to be disturbed unless there is an emergency."

Then he turned just outside of the double doors of the audience chamber and entered one of the corridors of the sort used by the servants. The guard followed him, walking about three paces behind. This was not a heavily trafficked corridor, either; in fact, it was likely that no one walked it except to keep it clean and keep the lights burning along it. It led to a set of dark stairs, which led downward, directly to one of the oldest parts of this castle; one of the round towers that had once anchored this building against siege. Seldom used now, but he found the round shape of the rooms very useful.

He held the only key to the door on this level; he unlocked it, after first making certain the spells and physical devices meant to insure his privacy were still intact. The wooden door had a copper lock; very useful in that copper retained the traces of *any* magic that might be used on it. He let himself into the bottom room of the tower and relocked the door behind him.

This room held his collection of peasant girls, gleaned

from the countryside by his troopers, all housed in neat little cells built about the exterior wall of the room. They were carefully chosen by his chamberlain and himself; he looked for deep emotional capacity, and his chamberlain looked for a lack of awkward relatives who might miss them. A spell of silence ensured that they could not speak to one another, nor communicate in any other way. Every day he had food and water delivered to them by a servant; each cell had all the facilities of one of the finer guest rooms in the castle itself, even if the space was a bit cramped. No vermin here, and no dirt either. He was quite fastidious about his person, and what he permitted in close proximity to it. Every girl here was under a minor coercion spell, set by one of his tame mages, that forced her to eat, drink, and keep herself neat and bathed.

The aura of terror in this room was quite astounding, and wonderfully sustaining. The spell of silence only made waiting more frightening to his captives.

Hulda assumed that this was the only purpose of the tower; she had never looked beyond this chamber and the one immediately above. She had no notion of what lay in the windowless third-story room, under the round, peaked roof.

He would not be availing himself of the services of any of the girls today. He had already charged himself with as much power as he could handle yesterday, and the little that had leaked off in the interim was insignificant.

He crossed the chamber to the spiral staircase that rose through the middle, taking it up to the room above. He ignored this room as well; he had no use for the couch, the rack, the chest of instruments. Not today. He permitted the room to remain in darkness, lit only from the chamber below, as he crossed to the staircase that curled up the stone wall and rose to the third and final room.

It, too, lay in near total darkness. He lit a lantern at the head of the stairs—without the use of magic. He would need all the power he had for what lay before him; the manuscript he meant to follow today had made that much quite clear.

Once the lantern gave him some light to see by, he made a circuit of the room, lighting every burnished lantern within it, until it was as bright as possible in a room with no windows.

This wood-floored room was ringed with bookcases, exactly as the ground-floor room was ringed with cells. And here lay the prisoners of his intellectual searches, the captives of his quest for knowledge. Hundreds of books, of book-rolls, of manuscripts; even mere fragments of manuscripts. All of them were handwritten; the kind of knowledge contained in *these* words was not the kind that anyone would ever commit to a printer. He had been collecting these for more than the two years of his disenchantment with his mentor, but it was only within the past two years that he had begun studying them and trying the spells described in them without supervision.

He fully intended to try another of them today.

He did not know what this spell was supposed to do, but he had some hopes that it might be the long-sought way to tap safely into the power of nodes, the spell that would finally make him an Adept. It was in this very manuscript that he first *found* the word "node," and realized from the antique description that these knots of energy at the junction of two or more ley-lines were the same energy nexus-points that he had been, thus far, unable to tap himself.

This was one of the incomplete manuscripts, and it was the many pages missing and paragraphs obliterated that had made him hesitate for so long before trying anything contained in it. The real purpose of this spell was in the pages that were missing, and the pages he possessed were riddled by insects and blurred by time. Still, this was the closest he had come in all the months of searching, and for the past week or so, he had felt ready to attempt this "spell of seeking." For some reason, today *felt* right to try it.

He had managed a week ago to restore some of the manuscript at least; a clear description of the level of Adept that could tap into the "nodes," though *not* the safeguards that would make such tapping less hazardous. This was the first time he had seen such descriptions, or the directions on how to use the node-power once he obtained it.

Hopefully, if he were strong enough, the safeguards would not be necessary. He had never once seen Hulda using any such safeguards when *she* accessed the power of "nodes."

Then again, his more cautious side chided, *she could have established those protections before you were in a position to watch her. She could have been hiding them from you.*

The spell described was not the same one that Hulda used, of that much he was certain. This spell required the construction of some kind of "portal"; he could only assume that it was a portal to the node-power. That made sense; he already *knew* that he, at least, could not touch these things directly.

He settled into a chair he often used for his meditations and suppressed a shiver. He recalled only too well the first and last time he had attempted to touch the nodes directly.

He had been able to see these power nexus-points, as well as the lines leading to them, from the time he reached the level of Journeyman. From the time he was first initiated by Hulda into the world of magic, he had been able to see the power that all things created, all the colors and intensities of it. But until Hulda drew power from those points during an attempt to pierce the sky above one of the Valdemar border towns with magic and let loose a plague of poisonous "insects" there, he had not known they were useful for anything. That was when she had told him—a little *too* proudly, he thought—that he would not be able to copy her example until he was an Adept.

He had tested that himself, when he realized that she was never going to assist him to achieve that status.

The power had been wild and startling; he had known immediately that he did not have the ability to control it at all, much less do so safely. It had felt as if he were suddenly juggling red-hot stones, and he had quickly released his tenuous contact, suddenly grateful that it *was* so tenuous. He had felt "scorched" for days afterward, and he had never again made the attempt.

But this time—perhaps through this "portal"—

The manuscript had been very clear on one point; that the only energy he would be able to use to form this portal was the energy he contained within himself. A pity, but he saw no reason to doubt it; hence the conscientious effort to fully charge himself, as if for a battle. Now he was as ready as he would ever be.

This room was perfect for use as a mage's private workroom; the wooden floor could be inscribed with chalk for diagrams, the peaked roof allowed a great deal of clearance in the center, and the only furniture was the bookcases, two chairs, and one table. There were no windows that needed to be shut or barred, and the stone walls were thick enough that very little sound penetrated. The old tower had been relegated to storage until he took it over, and most of the servants were unaware it was being used for anything else.

The portal required a physical foundation; he used the frame of one of the bookcases, an empty one, since he did not know what would happen to the contents once the portal was complete.

He sat bolt upright in a chair, took a deep, settling breath, and began.

He raised his hands and closed his eyes. He did not need to see the bookcase; what he wanted was not within the level of the visible, anyway. Within the framework of the bookcase he built another framework. Its carefully spun energy intertwined with the grain of the wood. The new framework was composed of energy taken from Ancar's own reserves.

I call upon the Portal—

Those were the words the spell called for; within the structure of those words he built up his frame of power, building it layer upon layer, making it stronger, spinning more and more of himself into it. The words were a mnemonic, a way of keeping track of the anchoring points for the spell; one for each syllable, there, there, and there, seven points. He concentrated on manipulating the energies exactly as the manuscript had described.

Then he reached the place where the manuscript had ended. From this moment on, he would be working blind. He hoped that at the proper moment the portal would extend to one of the nodes, and enable him to take in the node's wild power without harm. In fact, he thought of that as he built up his portal, hoping that the thought would be echoed in the power, as often happened in higher magery. It was yet another reason why complete control was paramount to an advanced mage; stray thoughts would always affect the final spell.

Steady now; control and command. You rule the power. Shape it to your will, keep it in your hands.

The interior of the bookcase warped away from him and vanished, leaving behind a lightless void. He began to lose strength, as if his life were bleeding away into the void.

No reason to panic. The manuscript said this would happen. I just have to keep it from taking everything.

Then came the unexpected.

The portal's edges pulsed, then extended tendrils in all directions! Lightninglike extrusions of power began spinning out from his carefully-wrought framework, waving aimlessly, as if they were searching for something.

Then, as a thread of fear traversed his spine, they reacted as if they felt that fear, and began groping after *him!* And he was paralyzed with weakness, unable to move from his chair!

Gods and demons! No!

He couldn't tell what had gone wrong, or even if this was somehow what was supposed to happen—

No, this couldn't be what was "supposed" to happen; if those tentacles touched him, they would suck the rest of the power from him before he could even blink. He could tell by their color, they *had* to be kept from him. Something had gone wrong—very, very wrong. This was worse than when he had touched the node—for this *thing* he had created was part of him, and he could no more cut himself off from it than he could cut off an arm. What now?

The life-energy tentacles reached blindly for him, threatening to create a power-loop that would devour him. All he could think of was that an Adept would know what to do if this spell was going wrong. At this point, he would gladly have welcomed *any* Adept; Hulda, an Eastern mage, even one of the disgustingly pure White Winds

Adepts. *Anyone,* so long as they knew what this thing was and how to save him from it!

At that moment, the groping tendrils stopped reaching for him. They hovered and flickered, then responded to his panicked thoughts and reached instead into the void, growing thinner and thinner. . . .

What—?

Suddenly there was no strength to spare even for a thought; his strength poured from him as from a mortal wound, and he collapsed against the back of his chair. His head spun, his senses began to desert him, and it was all he could do to cling to consciousness and fight the thing he had created.

Then, between one heartbeat and the next, there was a terrible surge of energy back *into* him and through him. Soundless light exploded against his eyelids; he gasped in pain.

That was too much; he blacked out for a moment, all of his senses overloaded, all of his channels struggling to contain the power that had flooded back into him.

Finally, he took a breath. Another. His lungs still worked; he had not been burned to a cinder after all. He blinked, surprised that he could still see.

And as his eyes focused again, he realized that he was no longer alone in his tower room.

There was something—some kind of not-quite-human creature—collapsed at his feet. The portal was gone, and with it, the back and shelves of the empty bookcase.

His first, fleeting thought was that it was a good thing that he had chosen an *empty* bookcase for his experiment. His second, that whatever it was he had created, it had *not* been the means to tap into the nodes that he had thought it would be.

His third—that he had somehow *brought* this creature here. Was that why the manuscript had called the construct a *portal?* Was it a door to somewhere else, not the nodes? If it was, this creature he had somehow summoned through it was from a place stranger than he had ever seen or heard of. It was unconscious, but breathing. He turned it over, carefully, with his foot.

It? No, indisputably "he," not "it."

Whatever he was, this strange creature, he was in very bad condition; in the deep shock only handling too much mage-energy could produce, the shock that Ancar himself had only narrowly escaped just now. He was manlike, but had many attributes of a huge and powerful cat—a golden pelt, manelike hair, the teeth of a carnivore—and the more Ancar examined him, the more certain he became that those "attributes" had been created. This being had somehow been involved in changing his own shape, something that Ancar could not do, and had only seen Hulda do once. This was a more useful ability than a spell of illusion, which could be detected or broken.

Wait a moment, and think. He might have been born this way, and not something changed by magic. Or he could even be a different race than mankind altogether. This could be the creature's natural shape.

That thought was a trifle disappointing, but if it was true, it still meant that the creature was from so far away that Ancar had never even picked up a hint of anything like it before. It had to be involved in magic to have gotten into that void between the Planes. And together, those two facts meant that it must know many things that were not in the magic traditions that Ancar had been using.

And that meant things entirely outside Hulda's scope of knowledge.

Ancar smiled.

He drew upon the energy of his imprisoned girls below, and gained the strength to rise and examine the creature sprawled across the wooden floor of his tower room.

Carefully, warily, Ancar knelt beside him and touched him, extending his own battered probes to the mind and the potentials within that mind.

Whatever shields the creature had once possessed were gone; all of his remaining energies were devoted to simply staying alive. That left him completely naked to Ancar's probes, and what the King found as he explored the creature's potentials startled him into a smothered shout of glee.

The odd half-beast was an Adept! It was clear for anyone of Master rank to read, in the channels, in the strength of his Gift. And a powerful Adept as well . . .

that much was evident from the signs all over him that pointed to constant manipulations of mage-energy on a scale Ancar had only dreamed of.

And with his shields gone, his mind open, he was entirely within Ancar's power. Here it was, exactly what he had been longing for. The power of an Adept was what Ancar wanted; whether it was within himself or in another, it did not matter—as long as it was in his control.

The beast stirred and opened his eyes. Slitted eyes, with rings of gold and green, blinking in a way that could not be counterfeited. The creature was dazed, disoriented, and so weak he could not even manage a coherent thought.

Quickly, before the strange creature could do anything to orient itself, he flung the simplest controlling spell he could think of at it, sending it to sleep. Clumsy with excitement, he lurched to his feet and ran down the two staircases to the room at the base of the tower.

There was no time for finesse, and no time to worry about subtlety. He unlocked the first cell with a touch of his finger, and dragged the shrinking, terrified girl huddled inside out into the light.

She wore a collar and nothing else; a red collar. Good, she was still a virgin.

He snapped a chain onto her collar, and hauled her up the staircase behind him.

Ancar flung the knife aside, to lie beside the lifeless body of the girl he had brought up from below. He had been a little disappointed in the amount of power he had been able to drain from her before she died. He hoped it would be enough.

He raised his hands and held them palm-down over the creature at his feet. The runes of coercion gleamed wetly on his golden pelt, drawn there in blood while the girl's heart was still beating. This, at least, he had done many times.

He recited the spell under his breath, and chuckled in satisfaction as the runes flared up brightly, then vanished, along with the girl's body. He stepped back a pace or two, then settled himself in his chair again, without once taking his eyes off the body of his new acquisition.

Once he was comfortable, he banished the spell that held the creature unconscious, and watched as the golden eyes flickered open again.

This time there was sense in them; sense, and wariness. But no strength; the creature tried to rise and failed, tasted the strength of the coercive spells binding him, but did not even attempt to test them. Ancar had taken a small risk with one of his spells; he had substituted the glyph for "sound" for the one of "sight" in the only translation spell he knew. He hoped it would enable this strange creature to understand him, and be understood in return.

"Who are you?" he asked carefully.

The creature levered itself into a sitting position, but did not seem able to rise any farther. The man-beast stared at him for a long moment, while Ancar wondered if the spell had worked, or if he should repeat the question.

Then he saw the flicker of sly defiance in the eyes.

. . . or perhaps a little coercive pressure.

He exerted his will, just a trifle, and had the satisfaction of seeing his captive wince. The sensuous mouth opened.

"Falconsbane." The voice was low, and Ancar had the feeling it could be pleasant, even seductive, if the owner chose. "Mornelithe . . . Falconsbane."

Oh, how pretentious. At least the creature understood him. "Where do you come from?"

A very pink tongue licked the generous lips; Ancar stared in fascination. This Falconsbane had tremendous powers of recovery! He had gone from comatose to speech in a much shorter time than Ancar had expected, even with the magical assistance of the girl's life-force. But the question seemed to confuse the creature.

Well, of course it does, fool! If he does not know where he is, how can he know where he is from?

"Never mind that," Ancar amended. "What are you? Is that your natural form?"

"I am . . . changed," Falconsbane said slowly. "I have

changed myself." The words were dragged out of him by the coercion spells, and Ancar clutched the arms of his chair in glee. This had tremendous potential, oh yes, indeed.

Ancar spent as much of the creature's strength as he dared, extracting more information. Some of it he did not understand, although he expected to at some point, when he had time to question Falconsbane in detail. What was a "Hawkbrother," for instance? And what was a "Heartstone?"

But the initial information was enough. Falconsbane was an Adept; he understood the spell that Ancar had botched, although it was fortunate that he *had* botched it, and Ancar had no intention of revealing his inexperience. It was called a "Gate" and Falconsbane had somehow gotten caught in the backlash of a spell that had sent him into the void between Gates. Ancar had hauled him out of there, with his very wish for an Adept to come to his rescue! Falconsbane was not only an Adept, he was probably more powerful and knowledgeable than Ancar had dared to imagine. He had enemies—the "Hawkbrothers" he had mentioned, and "others from his past." He had a vast holding of his own, and Ancar guessed from descriptions that it was to the south and west of Rethwellan, out in the lands purportedly still despoiled by wild magic. He sometimes referred to himself as a "Changechild," and had said things that made Ancar think that what Falconsbane had done with his own body he could do with others. That was an exciting possibility; it meant that Ancar could infiltrate spies anywhere, simply by substituting his own changed men for people in positions of trust.

And Mornelithe Falconsbane was Ancar's entirely.

He was, however, not in very good condition. Even with Ancar's sorcerous support, he had begun to waver during the last few questions. His strength was giving out, and he was still very disoriented. His answers had all come from memory; in order to have an effective servant, he would have to be able to think, and that would require a certain amount of physical recovery.

I am going to have to get this creature back on his feet—and hide him from Hulda. If I am very, very lucky, she will have attributed the tremors in the fabric of mage-energy to her own passions. If I am not, I shall have to think of something else I could have done that would make the same ripples in the energies.

He had no doubt that if Hulda got wind of Falconsbane's existence—at least up until the Changechild was capable of defending himself—the creature would either vanish or end up in Hulda's control. It was *much* easier to break coercion spells from outside than it was from within them, and Hulda was still stronger than Ancar.

Now, where can I hide this little guest of mine?

He left Falconsbane slumped in the middle of the floor, and hastened down his staircase to summon more of his hand-picked servants. More members of his personal guard; men Hulda never saw, who masqueraded as stable hands and acted as spies among the lowest servants. On his instructions, they brought with them robes and a litter, bundling Falconsbane into it and covering him as if he were sick or injured. Their eyes showed not even a flicker of curiosity at the strange creature. Ancar smiled in satisfaction.

"Take him to the house of Lord Alistair," Ancar told them. "Tell Lord Alistair that he is to take care of this man, and see to it that he receives the best possible care, under constant guard." He pulled off his ring and handed it to the ranking officer. "Give him this; he will understand."

"Lord" Alistair was one of Ancar's own mages, a man he had recruited himself, and on whom he had so many coercions he did not think that Alistair would even be able to use the guarderobe without permission.

He's not powerful enough for Hulda to worry about, not attractive enough for Hulda to care about, and I doubt she's going to try to manipulate him. Even if she does, she'll leave her mark on my coercions, and I will have ample time to move my little prize before she learns about him.

The officer accepted the ring and slipped it into his belt-pouch with a bow. He waved to the others to begin the awkward task of taking the litter down the staircase as Ancar stepped back to give them room. But before they had gone more than a step, a voice emerged from the pile of robes on the litter.

"Wait—"

The men stopped, confused. Ancar moved closer to the side of the litter. A pair of feverishly bright eyes looked up at him from under the shadows of a hood.

"Who—are you?"

Ancar grinned, his spirits buoyed up by his new-found feelings of power. This was too great an opportunity to resist.

"King Ancar of Hardorn," he said, softly; then, with steel in his voice that showed he would not be trifled with, added, "But you will call me—'Master.' "

The bright eyes flashed in impotent anger, and Ancar laughed, waving to the litter bearers to be on their way. He had the upper hand here, and he was not going to give Falconsbane a chance to regain it.

Chapter Two

Herald Elspeth, Heir to the Kingdom of Valdemar, Adept-Mage-In-Training, Wingsister to Tayledras clan k'Sheyna, was in hot water up to her neck—again. She was immersed in a steaming pool, surrounded by Hawkbrother scouts and mages, and members of the legendary Kaled'a'in clan k'Leshya, not all of whom were human. . . .

"This feels marvelous. I say it every day, but I'll say it again: We don't have *anything* like this back in Valdemar. *Yet!*" Elspeth smiled to her counterparts in the hot-spring grotto. "I got word from Gwena there were inventors in Haven working on a water heating system using the fires from forges. If they can make it work, I am definitely going to encourage them to make something like this."

Iceshadow k'Sheyna twisted a few strands of his waist-length, winter-white hair around his finger, and looked thoughtful. It was difficult to tell how old he was, despite the white hair; older than Elspeth, but that was about it. His smooth, sculptured face showed little sign of age, and only a few worry lines creased Iceshadow's brow as a sign of past troubles. He stretched out his arms, popping his joints softly. "You'll be taking many new ways of thinking back to your people. However," he continued, "k'Sheyna will always be a home to you."

"Very true. And while I am proud to be a Wingsister ... well, as much as I love the Vales, I would like to see my old familiar surroundings. I like to travel, but I'm not really nomadic. Even people I couldn't stand back at the palace seem pleasant once I've been away from them for a while."

"I feel the same way about our Clan. Those few I disliked in person, I have come to feel affection for when away. Distance and time can do that. But I must admit," he said to Elspeth, "that despite being thrilled at the thought of seeing the rest of k'Sheyna again, this whole Gating business makes me very nervous. Making a Gate, in the heart of this Vale. . . ."

It wasn't Elspeth who answered him. Firesong, who seemingly had not been paying attention to anyone but his black-haired companion Silverfox, grinned back over his shoulder at them. "Ah, there is no unstable Heartstone here, elder cousin. You have no reason to be nervous. Well, not because of Gates, anyway."

When Firesong smiled, it was difficult not to smile back. The supernally handsome Adept from the North could charm just about anyone or anything if he exerted himself, and Iceshadow was no exception to the power of that charm. "Only a node here, and another in the gryphons' ruins. Nothing to fret over. There are more than enough mages here to keep the effects of a Gate Spell balanced, and prevent a spring storm from dropping down upon us."

The older Hawkbrother laughed shakily, returning Firesong's grin. "It is difficult to convince my insides of this, youngling. We lived too long in the shadow of power we dared not trust. It can make anyone wary."

Firesong scowled a little but nodded. He, of all of them, knew best the chill of that shadow, for he had been the one most directly involved in confining it. Elspeth understood Iceshadow's meaning only too easily herself. The little time she had spent in the presence of the rogue, unstable Heartstone of k'Sheyna Vale had been more than enough to convince her that Iceshadow's fears would be hard to lay to rest.

And yet, the real damage that power had done had all been beneath the surface. This Vale had looked to her—and still did—like a little corner of the Havens itself, the realm of the gods. She looked about her, at the luxuriant life of the heart of k'Sheyna, at the incredible beauty of the flowering bushes and vines everywhere, the fluted, sculptured rocks surrounding the hot-spring-fed pool—

Then her senses took in the things that did not fit in a scene from a Valdemaran fantasy or Bardic play.

The huge trees, each supporting as many as a dozen *ekele,* the Tayledras treehouses. The silver-haired mages and mottled-haired scouts taking their ease in the warm waters of the pool, their exotic birds in the branches above them. Hummingbirds drifting by and hovering. The Kaled'a'in, who were clearly some kin to the Tayledras, but of more diverse breeding, some with round faces, some with green or brown eyes instead of silver-blue, and here and there a blond or a redhead. The swirl of silk and the hushed scrape and creak of well-worn leather amidst the calls of immense birds of prey.

And last of all, the gryphons lounging about in the warm sun—gryphons gray and golden-brown, peregrine-patterned and cooperi-striped, purring or cooing, and talking with Hawkbrothers—

She had a sudden feeling of disorientation, and shook her head. If, a year ago, anyone had told her that she would be soaking in a pool with a half dozen Hawkbrother mages, numbered as a Wingsister to a Hawkbrother Clan, and watching the antics of a score of legendary gryphons, she would have been certain that whoever asserted this had been severely intoxicated.

If they had told her she would be instrumental in the overthrow of a marauding evil Adept, and have a Hawkbrother lover—while her fellow Herald Skif would have an even stranger lover, the half-feline Nyara, daughter of that Adept—and that this same Nyara, and not Elspeth, would be the holder of Elspeth's sword Need—

I would have carefully caught that person off-guard,

tied him up, and put in an urgent call to the MindHealers, that's what I would have done.

But MindHealing comes in many forms, and experience is the best of them. Time had passed. She'd experienced all of that and more, and still the future was wide open.

A blazingly white figure appeared at the far side of the pool, just at the edge of the spray from the tiny waterfall that cooled one end.

And right on cue, a beam of sunlight penetrated the clouds and illuminated Elspeth's Companion Gwena, framing her in a rainbow's refracted light, making her look like a horse from the home of the gods, or a Companion-illustration in some book of tales.

Several of the Hawkbrothers gazed appreciatively.

"Good entrance," Firesong laughed, approvingly. "I could not have managed better myself." Silverfox chuckled, and continued to braid the man's waist-length silver hair in an elaborate Kaled'a'in arrangement. Firesong spent most of his time with the Kaled'a'in, and surprisingly, not all of that was with the Kestra'chern Silverfox. Evidently, the Kaled'a'in had explored the usages of magic along much different lines than the Tayledras, and what he was learning from them both excited and fascinated Firesong. Among other things, they had learned how to build Vales without needing a Heartstone; old chronicles spoke of this, but the Tayledras had lost the knack. Elspeth was interested in learning this trick as well, since if it could be managed in Valdemar, it would be possible to create some very comfortable safe-havens in inhospitable territory for, say, Healer's enclaves.

Or Heralds' Resupply Stations . . . what a lovely thought.

"You look fine today," Firesong continued.

:Thank you for the compliment, my dear,: Gwena replied, winking at the Adept, her calm completely unruffled. *:From you, that is high praise indeed.:*

Elspeth giggled. Gwena was much easier to live with these days, now that she had given up on steering Elspeth to some "destiny," and had resigned herself to the fact that Elspeth was going to make her own way whether or not Gwena liked it. *:So, dearheart, have you finished gossiping with Rolan?:*

Gwena had been giving Rolan—the Queen's Own Companion—daily reports for the past several weeks now, as winter turned to spring, and matters in k'Sheyna Vale were slowly settled. The original plan, made in the euphoria of victory, had been to return to Valdemar immediately, and then, if their enemies gave them a chance, to explore just what, exactly, was going on with the Forest of Sorrows. Several times during their struggle with Mornelithe Falconsbane it seemed as if some power up there was interfering on their behalf. But that plan had to be amended; there were many things she needed to learn from Firesong before he returned to his own Vale, and in the end there seemed to be no real urgency in getting back to Valdemar before winter ended. Ancar had been well confined by the combined armies of Valdemar, Rethwellan, and—miracle of miracles—Karse. His mages seemed to be doing nothing, except waiting and watching. And Elspeth really didn't *want* to go home until the last of winter was over—

—and until memories had faded of the hideous headache that had hit every Herald and Companion in the capital city of Haven, the day that control of the Heartstone's power had been wrested from Mornelithe Falconsbane. The day that same power had come to rest *somewhere* in the Palace/Collegium complex, giving Haven what appeared to be a small, new and, so far, quiescent Heartstone of its own, as if it were to be a new Tayledras Vale.

Elspeth had not known this until after the fact, but as that power snapped into place, every Herald within a few leagues' radius of the capital had been struck down with a blinding, incapacitating headache. So had their Companions. For most, the worst pain had lasted no more than a few hours, but for several others, it had taken days to recover. Elspeth didn't *think* they were going to blame her for it—after all, no one knew the power-locus would go there! It had been intended to go to where most of k'Sheyna Clan waited, to the prepared node and carefully anchored proto-Heartstone they had waiting for it.

K'Sheyna had been very gracious about the theft of their power-source, much more gracious than Elspeth had any right to expect, and quite philosophical about it all.

Still, she didn't think that was going to soothe the ruffled feathers of those Heralds who had found themselves facedown in the snow—or the soup—or otherwise collapsed with indignity and without warning. She absolutely dreaded having to answer to Weaponsmaster Alberich and her own teacher, Herald-Captain Kerowyn. And they were both going to demand answers. They might be contemplating retribution. It would be hard to convince them that *she* had nothing to do with it, and that she had no idea that it was going to happen. It would be even harder to convince them it seemed to be due to some nebulous force living in the Forest of Sorrows. Neither Alberich nor Kerowyn believed in ghosts, not even Herald-Mage ghosts.

Fortunately, Rolan had been mostly immune to what Gwena later said must have been a magical backlash as the great power landed in the middle of the "Web" that connected all Heralds. He had helped calm the panic, had helped Healers and the rescuers find Heralds who had simply dropped, all over Haven. Talia had been one of the first to recover, and she had organized those who bounced back into caring for the rest until the pain passed. And Gwena passed word to Rolan that this was *not* some new and insidious attack from Ancar, that it was—well—an accident.

Since then, Gwena had been in daily contact with Rolan, by order of Elspeth's mother, Queen Selenay. The order had sounded less like an hysterical mother, however, and more as if it had come from Her Majesty the Queen. An hysterical mother was not something Elspeth could handle, but duty to the Queen and Realm was the first order of any Herald's life. Since Falconsbane's banishment into the Void between Gates—and highly probable death—life at k'Sheyna had been *much* less eventful, it was an easy order to fulfill.

The shaft of sunlight faded; still bright but no longer illuminated like the gods' own Avatar, Gwena surefootedly made her way around the pool to where her Chosen was soaking. Elspeth had been spending a great deal of time with the Kaled'a'in as well, not only to learn magic, but to learn new fighting skills. They had a number of bare-handed combat techniques that could allow one who was skilled in them to take on a fighter with a weapon in his hands. Useful techniques for someone who had already faced one assassin.

But occasionally painful to learn. . . .

:It wasn't entirely gossip, dear,: the Companion said, in Mindspeech pitched only for Elspeth to catch. *:Although we've been doing more of that than exchanging any real news lately. Things haven't been all that interesting around Haven or k'Sheyna Vale.:* She chuckled mentally. *:I haven't even had to edit for your mother's consumption once during the last two weeks!:*

Elspeth laughed out loud. "Just remember, heart of mine, that 'may your life be eventful' is the worst curse the Shin'a'in know!"

Iceshadow looked over at her quizzically.

"Oh. I was talking to Gwena. She said things weren't as interesting around here as they used to be."

"Ah. Indeed," Iceshadow agreed. "I will be glad, after all, to see this Gate built to the new Vale, and find myself living in times *much* less interesting!"

He climbed out of the pool; before he had done more than stand, a little lizardlike *hertasi* appeared with a speed that was close to magical. Iceshadow nodded his thanks, and accepted the thick towel the lizard handed him. Again, Elspeth was forced to confront how much she had changed.

Not only in accepting something that looked like an overgrown garden-lizard as an intellectual equal, but in other ways as well. Iceshadow wore nothing more than his long hair; in fact, no one soaking in this pool seemed terribly body-shy. A year ago she would have blushed and averted her eyes. Now she was so much more aware of what each of the Hawkbrothers and Kaled'a'in here *were,* their bodies were simply another garment for the spirit within.

Iceshadow wrapped the towel around himself, and the *hertasi* looked down at Elspeth. The little lizard-folk who had come with the Lost Clan were much bolder than the *hertasi* native to k'Sheyna; she hardly ever saw the latter, while the former bustled about the Vale, undoing the overgrowth of nearly a decade, as oblivious to watchers as a hive of bees. Except, of course, when someone needed something. They seemed to thrive on tending others. Silverfox had said something about that being "part of" them, but hadn't elaborated except to say that it was due to their "recovery" from a long-ago trauma. She wished she knew more; there was such knowledge to learn, and so little time!

"Need towel?" it said to her. "Need drink?" While the *hertasi* seemed to have an instinctive ability to anticipate the needs of the Tayledras and Kaled'a'in, they were at a bit of a loss with her. Gwena and Darkwind had both tried to explain why; she was still at a loss after both explanations. The Lost Clan lizards were perfectly willing to talk to her, sometimes in Mindspeech, and often in audible speech. Even if their speech was a little difficult to understand, if they didn't mind, how could she?

"Thank you, no," she replied. "But when Darkwind gets in, he'll want food and drink, please."

The *hertasi* hissed, "Of course!" and vanished again. Iceshadow gave her a farewell smile, and wandered off to his own *ekele* barefoot. She turned to Firesong, who was leaning back against the stone of the pool's edge and enjoying the massage Silverfox was giving to his long and graceful hands.

It was hard to get her mind on business, but in the next couple of days it *would* be time to leave, and she had better get her mind set about doing so. "Have Treyvan and Hydona made up their minds what they want to do first?" she asked. "I'd be perfectly happy to have them come to Haven as ambassadors, but if there are more Kaled'a'in out there wanting to come back, they *really* ought to go to k'Treva first, as you suggested."

Firesong made a small sigh of utter contentment, and answered without opening his eyes. "I believe that I have talked them into my scheme, cousin," he replied. "K'Treva will not be long in moving on to a new Vale; there have been no troublesome outbreaks of any kind for better than a year now. Indeed, we would have moved on this winter, had it not been for your request for help. And if I may boast—k'Treva Vale is second to none. I think that our Kaled'a'in brethren would be most happy there, taking it after we have gone."

"Is that fulsome description for my benefit, *shaya?*" laughed Silverfox. "I promise you, there are not many who would require convincing. We had not expected to find ourselves offered safe-havens and homes, ready to our hands—yet another miracle of Treyvan and Hydona's doing. And I think that none among you will find fault with our stewardship of what you will leave behind."

The Kestra'chern tossed his dark hair over his shoulder, and moved his graceful fingers along the tendons of Firesong's wrists. Firesong sighed with content.

It was still very hard to think of Firesong as a relative, however distant. She had not even known that Herald-Mage Vanyel had left any offspring—much less that she and a Hawkbrother Healing Adept were descendants of two of them! Really, she had learned more about herself in the time she had been here than she had learned about magic. . . .

"On the whole, I think it's a better idea," Elspeth told him. "I'm glad you talked them into it. My people are going to have enough trouble with Darkwind and a Changechild appearing on their doorstep. I'm not sure I want to subject them to gryphons and gryphlets as well."

"Ah," Silverfox said shrewdly, "But with gryphons and gryphlets, a Changechild and a Hawkbrother Adept might well look less strange. Hmm?"

"The thought had occurred to me," she admitted. "But—well, let's just leave things the way they are. The gryphons can always change their minds when Darkwind and I are ready to Gate out of k'Treva."

"And gryphons are wont to do *just* that," Darkwind said from behind her, where he had already begun undressing.

She turned quickly with a welcoming smile, and he slipped out of the last of his scout gear and into the warm water of the pool. "Gods of my fathers!" he groaned. "That is wonderful! I thought I had become naught but a man of ice! I have never found anything colder than a spring rain."

Elspeth could think of several—such as the snowdrifts that she and Darkwind had collapsed into in the aftermath of Falconsbane's banishment—but then, she hadn't been out on the border all day, either. Temperature seemed to depend on context.

"Just be glad that we're going to k'Treva by Gate, then," she replied. "Skif and I got here the hard way. It's a lot colder outside the Vales up north!"

She tapped his shoulder to get him to turn his back to her so that she could work on his shoulders, and his skin was still cool to the touch. He must have gotten quite thoroughly soaked and chilled while out patrolling the boundaries of k'Sheyna territory for the last few times. Soon, that would be the duty of the Kaled'a'in, and indeed, Kaled'a'in scouts were making the patrols with the Tayledras to learn the lay of the land that would soon be theirs. Darkwind had gone out alone, and come back late; she didn't even have to ask why. She knew that he was gradually saying his farewells to the hills and trees he'd known for so long.

"The gryphons are envious of Treyvan and Hydona," Darkwind continued, with an inquiring glance at Silverfox. "Apparently there's something special about the lake near k'Treva. The one the Valdemarans call Lake Evendim?"

Silverfox nodded. "It is the site of the Black Gryphon's defeat of the Dark Adept Ma'ar. They wish greatly to see this."

Elspeth laughed. "I tried to tell them that they won't *see* anything, that it's all under water, but they didn't care. They are still excited about the whole idea, and every other gryphon is dying for a chance to get up there, too. You'd better be careful about how many of them you let come at once, Firesong, or you'll be up to your eyebrows in gryphons!"

"I shall remember that, cousin. And warn the rest of k'Treva," Firesong replied lazily. "Not that I think such an eventuality would be altogether bad. I find them delightful company, and I'm sure the rest of my Clan will feel the same."

Darkwind snorted. "*You* haven't been responsible for keeping those feathered eating machines fed! Talk to me after you've been hunting for hours, trying to find something larger than a rabbit!"

Silverfox chuckled. "If you think that this is difficult," he pointed out, "think about how it must be in a Vale full of breeding gryphons. The gryphlets eat three times their body weight a day until they are fully fledged!"

Elspeth tried to imagine that, and in the end just shook her head. "No wonder you wanted to move here. How do you keep them from stripping the countryside bare?"

"We have herds," Silverfox replied. "Fear not; we have learned how to manage our own needs and balance them against the needs of the land. We have beasts that are quick to grow, and eat nearly anything. We shall start the herds as soon as you are gone."

As soon as you are gone. Darkwind turned his head to smile into Elspeth's eyes, a glint of anticipation in his, and suddenly she was impatient to get back home. *He* was certainly excited about the prospect of leaving his Clan and kin, and seeing new lands. And there had been so much going on that she had missed out on—the twins getting older, the alliance with Karse, Talia being made a titular Priestess of Vkandis—

Home. . . .

It seemed to beckon her, for all the drawbacks of life there, under a kind of siege.

And now she could hardly wait.

Elspeth folded one of the scarlet silk shirts that Darkwind had designed for her; it rolled up into a surprisingly compact bundle, as did most of her Tayledras clothing. She was certainly going to cut quite a figure when she returned. She had the feeling that a lot of eyebrows were going to go up and stay up.

Things had not been as simple to take care of as they had seemed in the aftermath of the victory over Falconsbane. It had taken most of the winter for the party in search of k'Sheyna to journey overland to the new Vale and return. The very first order of business after everyone had recovered from that last confrontation with Falconsbane had been to *find* the new Vale again. That had taken a great deal of searching by mages who had near relatives or dear friends that had been sent on with the children and artisans. In the end they had found it by sending hummingbirds in the right general direction, keyed to those friends, and waiting for the reply.

Finally, after nerves had been strained to the breaking point, they had found the place, and then with the help of gryphon warriors aloft, two mages, the k'Sheyna Adept Silence and the Kaled'a'in Adept Summerfawn, had gone to find it and return with a mental picture of the place. No Gate could be built without knowing what the destination looked like, which made the things rather limited in practicality, so far as Elspeth was concerned. On the other hand, she was deeply grateful that this *was* the case; she did not even want to think of the Gate Spell in the hands of Ancar, if it made it possible for him to go and come at will to any place he cared.

Silence had returned, thin and travel-worn, but smiling and no longer silent. And now bearing the name "Snowfire," which told everyone that Silence had finally been healed of the emotional trauma that the shattering of the Heartstone and the deaths of so many of k'Sheyna had inflicted, years ago.

With that good omen, it was simply a matter of letting Snowfire rest, and then the Gate between the two Vales, old and new, could be built, and k'Sheyna would be a whole Clan once more. The Kaled'a'in had another trick up their ornamented sleeves as well; not one Adept, but two would build the Gate; Summerfawn from the new Vale and Snowfire from the old. They would build two Gates in parallel, and fuse them into one; halving the fatigue and doubling the strength.

Tomorrow. So many things would begin and end tomorrow—though there would be more endings for Darkwind than for Elspeth.

Now, with the culmination of many weeks of work at hand, Elspeth carefully packed away everything she would not need over the next two or three days. She had been a little dismayed at how much she had accumulated, but now that she had begun, she realized that most of it was clothing, and that packed down into an amazingly small volume. Probably because it was mostly silk, or something like silk. . . .

Darkwind seemed unusually silent, although he was packing just as busily as Elspeth.

I wonder if Gwena made it plain to Mother that I'd been sharing quarters with one of my mage-teachers. Probably not. No point in giving her another thing to get hysterical about. It had seemed rather stupid to keep two *ekeles* when they really only needed one, especially after the arrival of the Kaled'a'in had made things suddenly rather cramped. She had moved in with him, since the *ekele* he had was nearer the entrance to the Vale and had more room than hers.

Perhaps they should have reversed it. Perhaps he would feel the loss less if he had already left his "home."

He tucked a folded garment into the top of a pack and laced the whole thing shut. "I am very glad that I had already left the other *ekele* that I had built before all this happened," he said into the silence. "That was my home—for all that it leaked cold air all winter long. Built by my hands. But it seemed foolish to be living outside the Vale once the Heartstone was shielded, so—" He shrugged. "This place we have shared is dear only because we have shared it. It gives me no great wrench to leave it for another, especially after they have had a long journey."

She stifled a sigh of relief. "I saw how packing up affected Starblade, when he and Kethra had to abandon the place Falconsbane wrecked. It was very emotional for him, and I couldn't help think that leaving your home and your Vale both at once was going to give you some problems."

He made a face and threw a shirt at her; she caught it and began folding it. "Father's emotional condition is a bit less stable than mine, I dare to think."

She nodded agreement. "Well, I for one am truly glad that Kethra is going with your father. I was afraid she might do one of those typically Shin'a'in things and declare she couldn't leave the Plains!"

Darkwind grinned, and this time tossed a pillow at her. She ducked. "You are being silly. How could she do anything like that with one of Hyllarr's feathers, beaded and braided into her hair for all to see? They are mated, silly Herald. She could no more leave him than Hyllarr can."

"Silly Herald, yourself," she retorted. "How am I to know what all these beadings and braidings mean? And how in Havens am I to know one feather from another?"

He shook his head sadly. "Barbarian. Barbarian and ignorant. *How* could you not tell that the feather was from Hyllarr? From where else would such a great golden primary have come? There are no other birds the size of a crested hawk-eagle here!"

She cast her eyes up at the ceiling, as if praying for patience. "Just wait," she replied. "Just *wait* until I get you home, and you complain about not being able to tell Companions apart! Revenge will be so-o-o-o sweet!"

He only grinned and went back to his packing, and she to hers and her thoughts. Thinking about the Shin'a'in Healer Kethra made her a great deal happier than worrying about Darkwind. There were going to be problems when she got home that she'd rather not think about right now. . . .

She and Kethra had struck up an odd friendship over the winter, and a bond forged by their love for Darkwind and Darkwind's father Starblade, cemented by the new bondbird that Darkwind and Elspeth had found for the weakened Adept. From the very moment that charming Hyllarr had come into Starblade's life, his recovery from the terrible damage Falconsbane had done to him had been assured. For that alone, Elspeth suspected, Kethra would have been inclined to like her, although Hyllarr's discovery was still sheer good luck in Elspeth's mind. But they were surprisingly alike, and that helped; Kethra had been able to deliver authoritative conversations on caring and partnering that would have been a lecture coming from anyone else, but seemed no more than good advice from Kethra.

It was due to Kethra's suggestions that Darkwind, Skif,

and Elspeth, together and separately, had urged Starblade and Wintermoon—Darkwind's half brother—to begin simply *talking* to one another. Wintermoon had long envied Darkwind's favored-son relationship with his father, and had withdrawn from Starblade when quite young. Kethra felt that the time was long past when they should have reversed that withdrawal.

Now—with Kethra, Darkwind, Elspeth, and Skif urging and encouraging, Starblade and Wintermoon had begun building the father-son relationship they had never really enjoyed. Another sign of healing, perhaps, but just as importantly it was a sign that Starblade felt worthy of having relationships at all.

Darkwind had said at one point that he thought in some ways this was the easiest of the relationships for Starblade to establish. There had been so much that had been warped and destroyed of the relationship between Darkwind and his father, that even trying to reestablish it was painful. And so much about loving had been tainted by Falconsbane that simply to permit Kethra into his heart must have been an act of supreme and terrible courage for Starblade.

Yet another thing Falconsbane has to answer for, whatever hell he's in, Elspeth thought angrily. *The beast.*

In many, many ways, it was a good thing that Darkwind and Starblade would be separated for a while. That would give emotional scars a chance to really heal without constant contact irritating them; give Starblade time to find a new way to think of his son—as something other than a little copy of himself that had been his pride.

And it would give Darkwind time to reconcile everything that *he* had endured.

I think emotional damage is harder to heal than physical damage. . . .

Well, tomorrow would put that distance between them. And if it had not been for Clan k'Leshya and the gryphons, instrumental in helping to find the exact physical location of the rest of k'Sheyna, the healing process would have been put off a lot longer. That alone had succeeded in convincing the last diehards of k'Sheyna that the Kaled'a'in *deserved* the stewardship of the old Vale. If they had not generously volunteered their help, it would have taken months to locate the Clan and get an Adept in place who could handle the Gate Spell from the other end.

She looked around for something else to pack, and realized that there was nothing left. Darkwind's collection of feather-masks had been carefully packed up by one of his *hertasi,* and the walls were bare. Books and furniture would be left behind for the next occupant. Small keepsakes and jewelry had been tucked into odd corners of packs; feathers likewise. The few papers and notebooks Darkwind meant to take with him were already in the last pack. That left only the clothing they would need for the next couple of days.

Elspeth was not even taking her old Whites, nor was Skif. The *hertasi,* particularly the Kaled'a'in *hertasi,* had made their disdain of those plain, utilitarian garments very obvious. She had finally given in to their unremitting pressure to let them "make something better." She had only specified that the resulting clothing must follow the same general lines as the old Whites and *must* be completely *white.* Not ecru, not eggshell, not ivory, nor pearl-gray, nor pale pink. *White.* The clothing must be functional; ornamentation must not be any color but white, and it must not catch on things, tear off, or glitter in the sun to give her away—

"As if big white target in green field not give you away," one of the k'Leshya *hertasi* had replied in scorn.

She suspected that in the end the *hertasi,* frustrated, had appealed to Darkwind for help; certainly the new Whites had his touch about them. And it was possible to see the pattern of the originals in the new uniforms. But there the resemblance had ended.

Flowing sleeves caught in long, close cuffs at the wrists, white-on-white embroidery and even beadwork, leathers softer even than deerskin with cut-out patterns as elaborate as lace and long fringe that fell like a waterfall, beautifully tooled and fringed boots and half-boots, and more of the ubiquitous silk so beloved of the Tayledras— the clothing was far more exotic than she could have imagined Whites would be. And, somewhat to her own surprise, she liked them. Even more to her surprise, so did Skif, who asked the *hertasi* to make him something suited to his size and frame—and style.

So the *hertasi* had their hearts' desire, and took apart the old Whites to be used as scrap material and cleaning rags. And the two Heralds would be returning not only splendidly garbed themselves, but with matching gear for their Companions, who gloated that they would be the envy of the Collegium.

"We will do well wherever we go. Home should be in your heart, the Shin'a'in say. Worry not about me," Darkwind said, breaking the silence of Elspeth's thoughts.

"I'll always worry about you. At least a little. I guess we're done," she said, uncertainly. Darkwind laced his pack shut and stood up, smiling.

"Not quite yet, I think," he replied—and before she could react, he caught her up in his arms and tumbled her into their bed.

"We have all evening, and no duties, *kechara*," he said, between kisses. "And *I* at least, had plans—or at least, hopes. . . ."

Given all the unexpected disasters that had followed them, Elspeth more than half expected something to interfere with the opening of the Gate the next morning.

But nothing happened. Those among the gryphons and humans that were relatively low-level mages, or even simply mage-apprentices, contained and smoothed over the power-fluxes caused by diverting the energy-flows at both ends of the Gate. Elspeth had not, in fact, been aware of such work until months ago, after the attempt to move the Heartstone power. Firesong had pointed it out to her with his usual seriousness.

"Never underestimate the importance of even an apprentice," he had told her. "Their work goes on constantly, so that *we* do not so greatly upset all the balances of power and nature that we drive the weather and the ley-lines wild with our actions. If they were not at work, every time an Adept reached out with some major spell-casting, we would be plagued by at least one terrible storm, and perhaps more; the effects tend to be cumulative. Sometimes Adepts forget to thank their so-called 'lesser' cousins, but if it were not for them, we would be greatly handicapped, and everyone for leagues about would curse our names!"

Even so, it was wise to make certain of the weather before attempting a Gate. If there had been any storms in the neighborhood, the attempt would have been delayed.

The appointed day dawned clear and bright, and all of k'Sheyna except Darkwind, Skif, and Elspeth gathered in a pack-burdened crowd before a carved arch, created by the *hertasi* expressly for the purpose of giving the new Gate its physical frame. That it stood on the exact spot where the old Heartstone had been was an irony that was not lost on anyone.

Snowfire stood before the arch, her eyes closed in concentration. A half dozen Hawkbrothers in blue robes cast a carefully-prepared, bright-feathered bundle of incense and aromatic leaves into the brazier that honored the Tayledras lost over the years the Vale had been in existence. The entire group bowed their heads in a silent prayer, and the blue smoke from the brazier dwindled down as Snowfire prepared the Gate.

There would be no physical signs of the powers being called into play until the Gate opened, but Elspeth was watching with what Firesong called "the Inner Eye," and the sight was quite impressive.

Snowfire built up the framework of the Gate with power spun from her own resources; she was connected to the Gate by a scintillating cord of energy, multicolored and shining, energy that spun out from her like spider-silk, and came to rest in a continuously shifting pattern laid over the arch. And spinning out from the Gate, reaching off into the void, were more little threads, exactly like the "flying threads" of baby spiders, catching the wind of the void and seeking their anchor.

There was a moment's transition between this Gate-form and the finished Gate. Suddenly, it felt to Elspeth as if the ground dropped out from beneath her for a moment.

Then, instead of the other side of the clearing, there was another side of—something else. Summerfawn k'Leshya stood framed inside the archway, and behind her was a crowd of Tayledras, strangers to Elspeth, who cheered and beckoned.

There might have been sentimental reluctance to leave on the part of some, but at the sight of all those k'Sheyna, a half dozen seized packs and flung themselves through the portal, into the arms of those who awaited them; the rest picked up their belongings and proceeded in a more orderly, but nonetheless eager, fashion. Through it all the two mages holding the Gate stood like rocks, impervious and oblivious.

Starblade came toward Darkwind, with Hyllarr waddling along the ground behind him. The hawk-eagle walked whenever speed was not a factor; his wing never had healed so well that he could fly strongly, and he would have been a terrible burden even for someone like Wintermoon to carry. So he walked. It was not a graceful gait, for no raptor is terribly graceful on the ground, but it served, and it kept Starblade from having to carry him very often. Starblade was the strongest he had been in months, but the weight of a carried raptor seemed to multiply with each passing minute.

Hyllarr leapt to a low branch with only three wingbeats, and regarded the departing Tayledras. Starblade stood on his own before Darkwind, without resting on his walking stick.

"It is time to go, son," the elder Tayledras said quietly, as more of k'Sheyna filed through the arch. "I have not said so until now, but what you are about to do is more important than a single Clan, Darkwind. You carry the bravery of all our ancestors with you, not just k'Sheyna. I am proud of you, and where your mother is, she is proud of you as well."

Darkwind swallowed audibly. Although he had been determined to remain stoic, his throat tightened and his jaw twitched. His father had not spoken to him of his mother with anything besides a tone of self-pity and grief. Now, he spoke of her memory as something factual, not as something that was a knife through his heart. He was healing, and becoming better than he was before. The simple bravery of speaking plainly what was in his heart brought back early childhood memories of how Starblade was invincible and unshakable in Darkwind's eyes.

"I send my prayers with you, my son." Starblade smiled crookedly, and for a moment, many of his years dropped away. The creases of worry and pain changed to become smile-lines, something that hadn't crossed Starblade's face in recent memory. "When you return, you will surely have more tales of life in the Outlands than any scribe will ever be able to pen. And some of them *might* even be true!"

Darkwind laughed, and embraced his father with none of the hesitancy that such embraces had caused before. His own tears touched his father's. "And I expect to hear many tales of your own adventures in dealing with a wild Shin'a'in and a crafty hawkeagle! I think that between them, they will give you no end of excitement!"

:I?: Hyllarr replied, in feigned innocence. *:Not I! Am only meek, crippled bird.:*

A shadow and rustle of cloth announced Kethra's approach. "I most certainly shall keep his days and nights active," the Shin'a'in Healer said firmly, taking her turn to embrace Elspeth and Darkwind. "Take care of each other, children," she added giving them each a penetrating glance. "Remember, together you are far stronger than you are individually. I think that is something that no enemy will ever be prepared for."

Starblade took Elspeth into his arms, and whispered into her ear, "Watch over my son, dear lady. He is unused to having someone to guard his back, and may not ask for help. Give it anyway, unasked."

"I will," she promised fervently, and kissed him, an act that surprised them both and clearly delighted Starblade.

Starblade lifted his walking stick, and Kethra took the other end onto her shoulder as he did the same. Hyllarr glided down from the branch and alighted between them. His talons closed firmly on the walking stick and he folded his wings, accepting a caress from Starblade. Then it was time, and they took their places as the last in the line.

"Clear skies, Father."

"Wind to thy wings, my son. I love you."

And then they were gone.

Snowfire seemed to wake from her trance; she glanced around the clearing to make certain that there were no stragglers. She saw that Summerfawn already stood on *this* side. Her eyes took in the smoldering embers of the brazier. Then without a single backward look, she strode across the threshold of the Gate.

With a flare of energy, the Gate collapsed.

And for the first time, Darkwind, Elspeth, and Skif were the only k'Sheyna left in the heart of what had been k'Sheyna Vale.

Chapter Three

The Kaled'a'in clan k'Leshya had been in possession of the Vale for less than a day, and already the place had taken on an entirely new personality.

The Kaled'a'in had waited politely for the former owners to leave before so much as changing a single bush; now they swung into action, taking plans that had been made weeks ago and turning them into reality. The highest *ekeles* were to be converted for use by gryphons after appropriate strengthening, and gryphons and *hertasi* were checking the hillsides around the Vale, and the cliffs at the rear, for suitable lair locations above, and *hertasi* and *kyree* dens below. There were more birds in the air now; not only raptors of bondbird breeding, who had come to the Vale in answer to some unspoken call, but small, colorful creatures in feathered harlequin coats of red, blue, green, and yellow, with raptorial hooked bills and an uncanny ability to mimic human voices. A trio of Kaled'a'in mages began setting up new defenses and Veils to protect the place from the weather as the old Veil faded; rather than receiving power from the nonexistent Heartstone, these defenses would take their energy from a webwork of ley-lines the Kaled'a'in would arrange around the perimeter, lines which would in turn be fed from the node under the ruins where Treyvan and Hydona had nested.

Tervardi and *kyree,* creatures Elspeth had seen only rarely, were part of Clan k'Leshya; considered to be full members and not merely allies. So were the *hertasi,* who bustled about, full of energy, rearranging things to the new Clan's liking now that the old owners had gone.

One thing they were doing was trimming back much of the vegetation. While Elspeth had enjoyed the wildly overgrown Vale with its many shroudings of vine curtains and maskings of flowering bushes, she had to admit that it was a bit difficult to get around in. Every time someone had stormed off in a temper, or had to run somewhere in an emergency, he (or she) had usually wound up with minor scrapes and cuts, leaving behind shredded vegetation. The *hertasi* were taming all that, opening up sunny clearings, making it possible to travel down arched paths without risking strangulation. All the while, those places that needed a certain amount of privacy were left with their surrounding bushes and vines relatively intact. But as Elspeth saw, when she poked her head into the work-in-progress around one of her favorite small hot springs, they were trimming away growth inside the area, so that leaves and dead flowers no longer dropped into the pool to foul it.

Nets were being strung for vines to creep through until they could support themselves and provide more privacy in strategic places. Poles were planted by the *hertasi,* for the greenery to grow against. Dust kicked up by the work filtered through the sunlight as dancing motes of light. Nothing would be quite the same when they were done.

They were scrubbing the stones of the edge, and sifting debris out of the sand at the bottom. Already the water ran clearer. She left the area of the spring much impressed.

The little that Elspeth knew of the Shin'a'in she had learned from Kethra, but it seemed to her that these people were very different from both the Shin'a'in and the Tayledras. They were less solitary than the Tayledras,

though more so than the Shin'a'in. They were certainly
noisier than the Tayledras. Every job was accompanied by
the murmur of human voices blended with *hertasi* hisses,
tervardi trills, *kyree* growls, *dyheli* chuckles, and the bass
rumblings of gryphons. The Vale as populated by the
k'Sheyna had seemed deserted; the Vale as populated by
k'Leshya was as full of activity as the Palace/Collegium
complex.

Not all of k'Leshya would live inside the Vale. Some
would take over the lair begun by Treyvan and Hydona in
the ruins overlooking the Dhorisha Plains. They had
brought the books that Darkwind had helped build
shelves for so long ago.

Others would take the *ekeles* that had been made by the
k'Sheyna scouts, surrounding the Vale. Most of the artisans and craftspeople, scholars, and those families with
young children would live in the Vale itself—those who
were most vulnerable, and most in need of protection.
Silverfox had told Elspeth that they hoped to begin a
thriving trade with the Shin'a'in, and even with Outsiders. "We use very little magic in everyday things," he had
told her. "Mostly for self-defense. But we are fine crafts-
men, and trade is how we would prefer to make our Clan
prosper."

Even the gryphons? she had wondered. She couldn't
see how the gryphons, with those massive talons, could
craft anything. Treyvan had needed Darkwind's help just
to install a simple set of shelves. But then again, perhaps
there were things those talons were good for. Piercing
practically anything that needed a hole in it, for one
thing. . . .

And gryphons were strong. She'd already seen a
gryphon dragging a man-sized log in its beak. Treyvan
and Hydona were mages; a little magic went a long way
when it came to crafting things. Maybe all the gryphons
were mage-craftsmen.

*Maybe I just shouldn't worry about it. They hardly
need my help or approval!*

There seemed to be less activity up near the waterfall,
so that was where she went. Everywhere else she got the
feeling she was in the way. Perhaps not everything in the

Vale would be changed; the k'Leshya had not touched the waterfall and the pool below except to trim back some branches. It was possible to watch several groups hard at work from here without getting underfoot.

She settled down on a sculptured stone, fascinated by the coordinated working party of two gryphons, two humans, a *tervardi,* and three *hertasi* who were opening up an *ekele* for use by gryphons. They were taking out partitions and creating landing platforms on the roof. The gryphons pulled massive coils of twisted cord with their beaks from the corners of the platforms. Steadying themselves with their wings, they increased the tension as a *hertasi* directed them. *Tervardi* scrambled over the construction and reported to the *hertasi,* and holding pins were hammered in by the humans. Elspeth had never taken much notice of construction workers around the Palace, but these workers fascinated her.

Darkwind found her still gazing almost a candlemark later.

He sat down beside her, shaking his head, as his forestgyre Vree winged in and took a perch in a nearby bush. "They confuse me," he said without prompting. "I like them, indeed, but they confuse me deeply. Here— they make so much noise, and yet when we are outside the Vale even the largest gryphon makes no more sound than a leaf falling. They move like they are dancing. And their customs—"

Again he shook his head; Elspeth took his hand and squeezed it. "It's just because they are really *like* your people, but not quite identical," she said comfortingly. "That's all. For you, it's kind of the way I felt when I was learning your tongue. I already knew some Shin'a'in, and it was very confusing when you said something that wasn't *quite* what I knew. It was just similar enough that I felt I ought to know it, and different enough that I couldn't understand."

His puzzled look cleared. "Exactly. That is what I could not put into words. It is very strange to find those who are not human as full Clan members, for instance. I think it a good idea, but I find it strange. They are planning even their homes with that in mind, for instance—

rebuilding the stairs to suit not only human feet but *kyree,* and reinforcing the floors and adding landing porches for gryphons. The lower floors even have ramps for *dyheli.* All their thoughts run like that. We built to accommodate our bondbirds, but not to suit anything else other than humans. They consider first how any decision will affect *all* the beings of the Clan."

Elspeth nodded, understanding now what he meant. As considerate as k'Sheyna had been, they would never have considered modifying their homes to suit other creatures. And they would never have taken the needs of the nonhumans into consideration when making any kind of major decision.

Not only the needs, but the abilities— she thought, watching two of the gryphons hovering, holding a thin beam aloft so that it could be set into place and pegged there. Darkwind had seen that they had strengths the humans did not—and his former lover Dawnfire had *used* those often-discounted abilities of the nonhumans. But k'Leshya counted on them; the nonhumans were integral to any plan.

The unfamiliar as an ally.

Darkwind watched the construction work for a moment, and nodded with admiration, his pale blue eyes candid and open. "It is amazing," he said at last. "In a few weeks' time, I shall not know this place." He brushed a strand of silver hair out of his eyes. "In a few years, it will look like nothing that Tayledras built."

"Do you ever want to come back here?" Elspeth asked hesitantly. "I know Firesong is talking about doing so."

But Darkwind shook his head. "I do not think so. I think that no matter what the next few moons bring us, we will be too busy to even consider such a thing. Firesong has good reason to come here, for he is a Healing Adept and k'Leshya has many new magics he wishes to learn. But I am not even well-practiced in our own magics."

"You aren't exactly inept, lover," she smiled.

"Heh. Thank you, bright feather. I would prefer to wait on the learning of new magics until I am more comfortable with the known."

She laughed a little ruefully at that. Over the past several weeks she had found it much easier to admit her own shortcomings since Darkwind had become so open about his. And her shortcomings were many—not the least of which was that she had come so late into her mage-training. She still felt like a stone skipping across ice when she thought about magery in general. "That sounds like something I would say! I had no idea there was so much to learn—nothing I ever read in any of the histories said *anything* about needing lesser mages to take care of the things unbalanced by Adept spells. The histories just said that a great mage did—*thus*—and said nothing about what went on behind the spell-casting."

Darkwind leaned back against the sun-warmed rock. "Not all Adept spells require such a thing," he corrected. "Only those which cannot be performed from within proper shielding—or which *are* not performed from within proper shielding. And then, only those which manipulate great amounts of energy. There are different ways of accomplishing the same result."

She saw the differences, and nodded. "And anything that changes the force-lines, or creates nodes, or whatever, right? Darkwind, just what *is* the difference between a node and a Heartstone?"

He blinked at her, as if he wasn't certain he had heard her correctly, then instead of answering, asked her a question. "Where does the energy go when it flows into a node?"

She was used to that now; if she didn't know the answer, he asked her a question that would make her see the answer for herself, rather than simply telling her. It had been infuriating, at first, but she had to admit that the answers stuck with her much better when she had to deduce them for herself. "It flows right back out on another—oh! Now *why* didn't I see that before?" She shook her head, annoyed. "How could I be so stupid? The difference between a node and a Heartstone is that the energy *doesn't* flow out of a Heartstone. It all stays there. I can't imagine why I didn't see that; it's like a lot of rivers flowing into a sea, and who ever heard of a river flowing *out* of a sea?"

"Well, at least it does not flow out on another ley-line," Darkwind amended. "Power is taken from a Heartstone, of course, or it would build up past the point where it could be contained. It is used to provide the power for all the things in the Vale that require such power. But that is our great secret, the construction of such a thing. Even had Falconsbane succeeded in stealing the proto-Heartstone, I do not think he could have turned it into a real one. He would *have* to have given it an outflowing ley-line, however small, and all he would have had would have been, in the end, no more than an exceptionally strong node. Not that such a node would not have granted him great power! But it would not have been the power of a Heartstone, which has no known equal to my people. It is the fact that a Heartstone has no such way to relieve the pressure of the contained power that makes a Heartstone so very powerful."

"But the one in Haven now *is* a Heartstone, and not a node, right?" she asked anxiously.

He shrugged. "It appears so, yes, but I cannot be certain until I can view it myself. At the moment it is a guess, an assumption, based on some signs we can See at this great distance. If it is—well, that means that whatever force sent it there knows how to create Heartstones, or cause a waiting one to settle. And what that could portend, I do not know."

"I don't either," she replied. Although that was not strictly true, since the force that had sent the proto-Heartstone to Haven instead of the new k'Sheyna Vale had come from the North of Valdemar, and in the North of Valdemar was the Forest of Sorrows. . . .

"Well, Firesong has cloistered himself away for a day and a night, to rebuild his own energy levels, so we cannot ask him," Darkwind said with a hint of unease in his blue eyes. "I suspect he would only shrug and look mysterious, though."

"Probably," Elspeth chuckled, trying to remove the unease. "You know what a showman he is, he can't even drink a cup of *chava* without making a production out of it. At any rate, in two days we'll have some of our answers, when we get to k'Treva, and we can consult the mages there. The rest can wait until we reach Valdemar. Certainly whatever is under Haven can wait until then."

They had all decided that the first step on their journey would be to return to k'Treva with Firesong. Elspeth had hoped that this would make the change from Darkwind's home in the Vale to Valdemar less of a shock. Only Firesong could create the Gate for this journey, but the Gate would not have to be held open for so great a span of time, so only one Adept would be needed. And while the creation of a Gate was no small task, it was one that Firesong had undertaken so many times that with due preparation, he would emerge into his home Vale in fairly good shape, not as drained and exhausted as Darkwind. Besides, once there, he would have his own Heartstone, keyed to the mages of k'Treva, to draw upon to replenish his resources.

Darkwind remained silent after that last comment, and Elspeth wondered now if she should have left all mention of Valdemar out of the conversation. She had been very reluctant to discuss anything past their departure from k'Treva, and she had sensed a corresponding reluctance in Darkwind. He *was* going with her; that much was absolutely certain. But she would no longer be simply Elspeth k'Sheyna k'Valdemar at that point; she would be a princess, the Heir, and on her home ground, with responsibilities to Valdemar that went far beyond personal feelings. For that matter, *she* hadn't thought much about those responsibilities of late.

I should. I need to weigh them all out, and decide what is important and what isn't. And what I am actually able to do. And, a little reluctantly, she decided one other thing. *I need to talk to Gwena. If there's anyone that can discuss where my responsibilities end and stupid customs begin, it's her.* She nibbled her lip uneasily. Gwena had been very agreeable lately; maybe too much so. On the other hand, the Companion had sworn she was not going to attempt to manipulate her Chosen any more.

But did she say she would do so any less? *Hmm. . . .* On the other hand, she admitted she had no real control over her Chosen. And Gwena's disposition lately had been as cheerful as this sunny day. Whether it would continue to be so, if Elspeth did something totally against her Companion's advice, was a good question.

Well, there was no point in getting worked up over something that was days, weeks, perhaps months away. But it might be a good idea to drag Gwena off for a long heart-to-heart talk now.

She squeezed Darkwind's hand again, and he smiled at her. "I'm going to make a round of the Vale to make sure I haven't forgotten anything we might need," she told him, as an excuse to get Gwena alone for that long talk. "It won't take more than a candlemark or two. Where shall I meet you?"

"Right here?" he offered. His expression lightened considerably, and his eyes crinkled at the corners as he smiled. "It's about the least-busy place in the Vale at the moment; I was half afraid to go to our *ekele* lest I be thrown out by a work crew!"

She laughed, and tossed her hair over her shoulder—now it was long enough to toss, for the first time in years. "I think they'll be polite enough to wait until we're gone, but you ought to take Vree outside the Vale for a hunt. Maybe you and I have been working our tails off, but I think he's been bored."

Nearly invisible in the bush, Vree made a chortling sound. *:Good Elspeth,:* he Mindspoke—more in images than in words. *:Keep this mate, Darkwind. Elspeth bright/clever/wise.:*

Darkwind flushed, but Elspeth only chuckled and made a mock bow to the forestgyre in the branches. "Thank you, Vree, for your unvarnished and candid opinion."

Darkwind rose and offered her his hand to help her up. "I expect I'd better, before he offers any more unvarnished opinions. A good chase followed by a full crop should keep him quiet—so he doesn't lecture me as often as Gwena lectures you!"

Nyara separated her hair with clawed fingertips and began braiding it as she watched Skif from a corner of their shared *ekele*. She had considerably less to pack than anyone else, other than, perhaps, the gryphons. Just herself, two changes of clothing, a set of armor made by the *hertasi,* and a very large and vocal sword. . . .

:I'll thank you not to think of me as baggage, young lady,: Need said dryly, but softened it with a chuckle. *:Baggage can only hinder, after all.:*

:Oh, you can hinder, too, my teacher—when you choose to,: Nyara replied saucily, as she bound off the little braid she wore at the side of her head with a thin strip of twine.

"Is Need putting her point in again?" Skif asked, looking up from his own packing. Nyara watched him with a great deal of admiration; she could not for a moment imagine how he was getting so many things into those small packs.

"Why, yes!" she said in surprise. "How can you tell?"

He chuckled and put one gentle finger right between her eyebrows. "Because you get a little crease *here* when you Mindspeak with her, and you only get it then." He raised a bushy eyebrow at the sword, and addressed Need directly. "Well, dear lady, do you think you are prepared for Valdemar?"

:Is Valdemar prepared for me, might be the real question, insolent brat,: Need countered. *:I'm not at all certain that anyone there is.:*

"Well, I'm entirely certain that they're *not,*" Skif replied, with a laugh. He ran one hand through his curly dark hair and waggled his eyebrows at both the sword and her bearer. "You're not the same sword that left. I think Kero is going to be quite happy to have you at someone else's side, all things considered. I don't even want to contemplate the clash of personalities that would ensue if you went back to her."

:I'd win,: Need stated arrogantly.

But Skif shook his head. "With all due respect, my lady, I know you both and I think it would be a draw," Skif told her. "Kero is just as stubborn as you are. What's more, that would just be if the confrontation was one-on-one. With Sayvil on her side, you wouldn't stand a chance."

:Hmm.: The sword thought that over for a moment, then turned to a more impartial judge, one who was crop-

ping grass beneath the *ekele* Skif and Nyara shared. *:Cymry? What do you think?:*

Skif's Companion shook her head noisily, and glanced up at the open windows of the *ekele*. Skif had yet to figure out how the sword could talk to both Cymry and Gwena, when Companions were only supposed to be able to Mindspeak their own Heralds.

But then, Need was a law unto herself. How else to characterize a kind of ghost bespelled into a magical blade, an artifact of such age that the places she had known as a woman didn't even exist on maps anymore?

:I think even you would be no match for Kero and Sayvil together,: Cymry said decisively. *:And your magic would give you no edge—pun intended—if Sayvil were to bend her will against yours.:*

If a sword could be said to sigh, Need did so. *:No respect,:* she complained. *:Now silly white horses are punning at me. Ah, well. At least my bearer appreciates me, even if she does think of me as* baggage.*:*

Nyara giggled, and Skif smiled at her. The sound that she made rather surprised her; she had not done much laughing in her short lifetime, and it seemed as if all of it had been occurring in the last year.

Since Skif. The conclusion was as inescapable as her feelings for him. And his feelings for her. When the plans for their departure from the Vale had been discussed, Nyara had entertained no doubts; she would go with Skif, even into a place that had never seen anything like her kind before, and endure whatever came.

Whatever came—it could be some formidable opposition from his own people. She did not look very—human. Her father, Mornelithe Falconsbane, had used her as a kind of experimental model of himself, working the changes he wished to make on his own flesh upon hers first. She had no illusions about herself; she knew there was no disguising her strange, catlike features. What would people who had never seen anything that was not completely human think of her?

What would they think when they learned that Skif, one of their precious Heralds, was her lover?

:Don't lose that smile, Kitten,: Need said, as she tensed

unconsciously. *:Remember, you have Cymry favoring you, and you have* me. *These Heralds listen to their horses, and the horses don't give advice so often that they can afford to be ignored. And as Skif pointed out, I'm not the sword that left. I'm better. In fact—:* Need produced another one of her dry mental chuckles, like the creaking of forge bellows. *:—in a sense, you will have them by the proverbial short hairs. They can't afford to offend Skif by treating you poorly; he'll leave. They can't afford the loss of a single Herald right now, not with a war on the horizon. That Ancar character is not going to give up, and we're just lucky he's been so busy stewing his own little pot that he hasn't come roaring up to the Border before this. But besides Skif, they certainly can't afford to do without me! I may not be an Adept by the current standards, but I can do a great many things that an Adept can do, and some that I suspect no one knows how to do anymore. I'm a mage that is utterly unpredictable and unexpected. I can shield my powers and yours; I can look like nothing more than an ordinary sword if I try hard. No one else that I know of can do that. We're too valuable to lose, my dear. Remember, where you go, I go.:*

Nyara considered this seriously; it was an advantage she had not put into her calculations. *:Do you mean you would be willing to coerce all of Valdemar—:*

:Blackmail them to be certain you are happy?: Need finished for her. *:In a moment. Without a second thought. I don't have any stake in their little war, and now that I'm awake, I don't send my bearer rushing to the side of whatever female is in trouble. What happens with Ancar is not necessarily my concern. If Selenay wants me fighting on the side of Valdemar, she's going to have to make certain* you *are treated well.:*

Nyara was taken aback, but in a flattered and delighted way. She had not expected such a strong response from her teacher; she hadn't let herself expect any backing at all. Need had taught her to be self-sufficient, at the cost of many hard and bitter lessons. To *depend* on no one but herself—while at the same time learning to give another her trust as a partner.

:Yes, you could *face them alone,:* Need said, answering

her unspoken thoughts. :*You have the strength to do so. You are willing to. That's what matters, and if you hadn't been ready, I'd have taken steps to make you ready before you got there, and then I would have backed you. You've earned it. Skif will back you; you've more than earned his trust, as well as his—yes, I'll say it—love. And Cymry will back you because she knows you're one of the best partners Skif could have. Kitten, you are a fine person. And we'll give that fine person the support she deserves.*:

Nyara blinked back tears from burning eyes, quickly, before Skif could see them. :*I do not know what to say. . . .*:

:*Kitten, don't think this is going to be easy,*: the sword cautioned. :*I can't change people's minds or attitudes, nor can Skif or Cymry. People have to change their minds because they want to. You are still going to be the strangest thing they have seen in a long time. But at least I can make certain that you know what a brave child you are. Anything else, you're just going to have to deal with.*:

Nyara nodded, slowly. :*I think I can do that,*: she replied. :*It can be no worse than life in my father's fortress. And I will have Skif, and you, so it will be better, for I will have no chance to be lonely.*:

Again, the dry chuckle. :*I'm glad you remembered to put me in there somewhere!*:

There was not a large gathering at the carved arch the next morning; only a few gryphons, one or two of the Kaled'a'in mages that Firesong had been exchanging techniques with, and of course, Silverfox. That was something of a relief to Elspeth, since she had hoped to slip out of k'Leshya Vale with a minimum of fuss. The less fuss, the better for everyone. She was hoping Darkwind could continue to keep up his eager interest despite leaving everything he had ever known.

She hoped. There was no real way to tell, after all, how he was likely to react.

But he seemed cheerful enough, as the *hertasi* brought the last of their packs to be loaded on the two Companions, Firesong's blazingly white *dyheli* stag, and (temporarily) on the gryphons, who were willing to bear the burdens through the Gate to save strain on Firesong.

And, as usual, the young Adept looked as if he had been groomed to within an inch of his life by an entire troupe of *hertasi*. His long hair flowed down his back in a deceptively simple arrangement. His sculptured face wore an expression of interest and amusement. Although it was warmer, he had donned pristine white robes of exotic style and cut—exotic even by Tayledras standards. His ice-white firebird sat on his shoulder and regarded the company with a resigned silver-blue eye. The snow-white *dhyeli* stag that had brought him to the Vale waited beside him, as still as any marble statue. As usual, he looked magnificent.

"Well, I have had converse with my mother and father," Firesong said, as soon as Skif and Nyara arrived and took their places. "I have warned them that I am about to Gate to k'Treva, as we discussed, and that I will have four of k'Sheyna, Companions, gryphons, and a *most* gallant *kyree* with me."

He bowed gallantly to Rris, who wagged his tail and grinned with his tongue lolling out of his mouth. Rris had agreed to come along both to act as guardian and teacher to the gryphlets, and to chronicle whatever happened as an "impartial" observer. That was Rris' chosen function, after all; the *kyree* had an extensive oral history, and Rris was one of their historians. Although his specialty seemed to be the tales of his "famous cousin Warrl," Elspeth knew that he would rather have had his tail pulled out than miss a chance to see what happened in this new alliance of Tayledras, Kaled'a'in, and Valdemaran.

"So, my ladies and lords, if you are all prepared to depart?" Firesong indicated the arch that would contain the Gate with a nod of his statuesque head, and everyone present made some indication of agreement.

Elspeth had long since gotten over being surprised at how little time it took Firesong to accomplish anything magical. Between one heartbeat and the next, he had established the Gate itself. In the next heartbeat, he had sought out the terminus in k'Treva Vale. In the third, he had anchored it, and the Gate stood open, ready to use, the greenery of k'Treva showing through on the other side, looking disconcertingly like and unlike k'Sheyna Vale.

"After you," Skif said to Elspeth a little nervously, eying the portal which had been empty one moment, then black as pitch, then filled with scenery which was *not* the same as the clearing they stood in. She hid her smile, took Darkwind's hand, and together they stepped through—

She had been told she would feel something like a little jolt; a shock as she passed across the intervening "real" distance. But instead of a shock, she felt a moment of disorientation—

She clutched at Darkwind's hand; there was something pulling and twisting, rippling across the power that held the Gate! He stared at her, his eyes wide—then he and everything else blurred and faded for a moment. Vree spread his wings and mantled in alarm; his beak opened, but nothing emerged.

She might have screamed; it didn't matter, for in that moment that they hung in the Void between Gates, no sound she made would be heard.

Then, just as suddenly, they dropped down with a lurch, safely on the other side. Vree was screaming, still agitated.

They were through. Except—it was not where they were supposed to be.

She looked around wildly, for there was no expanse before a carved archway; no wild and exotic foliage, and no waiting Tayledras. They stood on a dense mat of browned evergreen needles, in a tiny clearing. Behind them was the rough mouth of a cave. Before them was a northern forest, with no one at all in sight. The air was sharp and cool, spicy with pine-scent and mountain-odors. This was upland country; *northern* country—farther north than most of Valdemar.

Darkwind seized her elbow as she stood there aghast, wondering what had gone wrong, and hurried her out of the way. Just in time; first Skif and Nyara emerged, followed by the Companions, then the gryphons and their young, then Rris, the *dyheli,* and Firesong. All of them emerged with the same shocked, puzzled look on their faces.

Firesong was more than shocked, he was startled into speechlessness.

Darkwind seized him, jarring the firebird on his shoulder, which flapped its wings and uttered a high-pitched whistle of distress. "What happened?" he demanded harshly. "This is *not* k'Treva!"

Firesong only shook his head numbly. "I—" he faltered, at a loss for the first time since Elspeth had known him. "I do not know! I might err in just where a Gate opens, any mage might—but it *must* go to some place that I, personally, know! *And I do not know this place.* I have never seen it in my life!"

Skif looked around wildly, as Nyara took a wary grip on Need's hilt. "Where are we, then?" he demanded.

No one had an answer for him.

Chapter Four

Mornelithe Falconsbane lay quietly in his silk-sheeted bed and feigned sleep. He was still uncertain of many things. His memories were still jumbled, but the bonds upon his powers told him the most important facet of his current condition.

He was a prisoner.

Still, it could be worse. He might be a captive, but at least his captivity featured all the luxurious appointments and appearance of being an honored guest.

But it was captivity nonetheless.

Falconsbane was not the master here; that young upstart puppy called "Ancar" was. That alone rankled, although he endeavored not to show how much.

He spent most of his time in sleep, either real or feigned. He was not at all prosperous at the moment, and he was only too well aware of the fact. Merely to rise and walk across a room cost him more effort than summoning an army of *wyrsa* had when he was at his full powers. And as for working magic—

At the moment, it was simply not possible.

How long had he hovered in that timeless Void? He did

not know; it was more than mere days, more like weeks or even months. He had been snatched from that dark and formless space before he had gone quite mad, and he had drained his magical power just to keep his physical body barely alive. Now both were damnably slow to return to him. He had become used to recovering swiftly, taking the lives of his servants to augment his own failed powers. That was not an option open to him at the moment, and his recovery was correspondingly slow.

In fact, even as he lay in his soft, warm cradle, he knew that it was weakness that kept him here rather than his own will. It would be very hard to rise and force his body into some limited form of exercise; very easy to drift from feigned into real sleep. And very attractive as well, for sleep held far more pleasant prospects than reality.

Sleep—where he would forget where he was and the bonds that had been placed upon him, the coercions that now ruled his mind and powers. Where he would forget that it was a mere stripling of a usurping King that he must call "Master."

He had learned his captor had given him his real name quite by accident, during one of those bouts of pretended sleep. The annoying hedge-wizard who played host to him had entered with the servant that had brought him food, and had ordered the frightened man to wake Falconsbane and see that he ate and drank. The servant had objected, clearly thinking Falconsbane some kind of wild beast, half man and half monster, fearing—he little knew how rightly—that Falconsbane might kill him if he ventured too near. The wizard had cuffed his underling, growling that "the King wants him well and what Ancar will do to both of us if he is not is worse than anything this creature ever could do to you!"

At the time, Falconsbane had come very close to betraying his pretense by laughing. Clearly, this foolish magician had *no idea* who and what he was entertaining!

And if he had? Likely he would have fled the country in terror, not trusting to anything but distance to bring him out of Falconsbane's reach. The silly fool; even that would not help him if Mornelithe became *upset* with him.

He still had no real idea why it was that Ancar had placed him under magical coercions—other than the obvious, that the upstart wanted an Adept under his control. Why he wanted and needed an Adept—what purposes he wanted that Adept to serve—that was still a mystery. But at least, after listening covertly to the conversations between the sniveling hedge-wizard and his Master, he now knew *how* Ancar had brought him here.

By accident. Purely and simply, by accident and blundering.

The thought that he, Mornelithe Falconsbane, Adept of power that puny young Ancar could only *dream* of, had been "rescued" entirely by a mistake was enough to make him wild with rage—or hysterical with laughter. It was impossible. It was a thing so absurd that it never should have happened. No mage of any learning would have ever given credit to such a story.

Nevertheless. . . .

It was logical, when analyzed. The backlash of power when his focus had been smashed, his web of power-lines snapped back on him, and the proto-Gate had been released from his control had sent Falconsbane into the Void. No ordinary Gate could have fetched him back out again, for ordinary Gates were carefully constructed, and the terminus chosen, long before the Gate energy was set in motion. No Gate *could* be set on the Void itself; to attempt such a folly would be to court absolute disaster as the Gate turned back on itself and its creator and devoured both. But Ancar had not created an ordinary Gate; he had not been creating a Gate at all, so far as *he* knew. He had thought then—and *still* thought now—that he had been constructing some safe way for a lesser mage to handle the terrible powers of node-energies, energies only an Adept could safely master. Ancar did not have Adept potential, for all his pretensions; Master was the most the whelp could ever aspire to. But whoever his teacher was, that teacher had evidently chosen not to inform him of this, and he had been searching for a way to make himself an Adept for some time now.

His collections of spellbook fragments must be quite impressive—and the fact that he was willing to risk himself using only fragments proved either that he was very brave, or very stupid.

Or both.

The directions for the Gate had come from one of those fragments, one that had not included the purpose of the spell he had decided to try. As a result of incomplete directions and the utter folly of following them, he had set up a Gate with no terminus. But at the time, at the back of his mind, he had been concentrating on something he wanted very much.

An Adept. If he could not *be* one, then he *wanted* one. Actually, he had probably hoped for both, to become an Adept and to control one, or more than one. A suicidally stupid plan, one that Falconsbane would never have tried. Dark Adepts, the only kind Ancar would be likely to attract, were jealous of their powers, unwilling to share them, and would never stop testing any bonds that were put upon them. And when those bonds broke—

—as eventually, Falconsbane would break his—

—then revenge would be swift and certain.

Falconsbane had known of some of Ancar's activities from his spies; he had been interested in the young King purely because the boy was the enemy of those blasted allies of k'Sheyna, the ones with the white horses. He had briefly toyed with the notion of an alliance himself—with him as the superior, of course. He knew that Ancar had longed for Adepts for some time, and it was logical to assume that he had been concentrating on the need for an Adept at the time the Gate began to fold back in on itself.

Falconsbane knew everything there was to know about Gates, except the few secrets that had disappeared with the Mage of Silence. Oh, *him* again. He could make some deductions now, with the information that he had gleaned from his covert listening, that were probably correct. The energies making up Gates were remarkably responsive to *wants,* as Falconsbane had every reason to know now. Especially when those wants were triggered by fear as the Gate began to reach for its creator.

Ancar wanted an Adept, and no doubt wanted one very badly when his spell went awry; as it happened, the Void had one. Falconsbane, still caught in nothingness.

And once the Gate had a goal, it "knew" how to reach that goal, given the strength of Ancar's need.

So, taking Ancar's desire as *destination,* the Gate had stopped folding back upon itself, and had reached out to bring Ancar what he wanted.

Falconsbane wondered, as he had wondered before this, what would have happened if the Void had *not* contained what Ancar had wanted. Possibly the Gate would have completed its attempt to double back, and would have destroyed itself and its creator with it. Well, *that* would have been entertaining to watch, but it wouldn't have saved Falconsbane.

Possibly Ancar would have thought of some place he considered safe, and it would have read that as a destination, creating the terminus and thus showing Ancar what it was he had *truly* called into being. It was impossible to say, really, and hard thinking made Mornelithe's head hurt.

Ancar's first Gate had collapsed for lack of further energy. And Ancar still was not aware of what he had created.

Falconsbane had no intention of telling him. He intended to keep as many secrets as he could, given the coercive spells that Ancar had layered on him. He was aided by the fact that Ancar was not aware how much Hardornen Falconsbane knew, or that he had a limited ability to read the unguarded thoughts of the servants to increase his vocabulary. As long as he pretended not to understand, it should be possible to keep quite a bit from Ancar.

He stirred restlessly, clenching his jaw in anger. When he had awakened to himself, he had found himself constrained by so many coercive and controlling spells that he could hardly breathe without permission. And for the first time in a very, very long time, Mornelithe Falconsbane found himself trapped and moving only to another's will.

It was not a situation calculated to make him cooperate with his captor and "rescuer." Not that anything would be, really. Falconsbane was not used to cooperating.

Falconsbane was used to giving orders and having them obeyed. Anything less was infuriating.

In his weakened and currently rather confused state, he often lost track of things. At the moment, he was fairly lucid, but he knew that this condition was only temporary. At any moment, he could slip back into dreams and semiconsciousness.

So while he was in brief control of himself, he laid his own set of coercions on his mind, coercions that would negate the effect of any drugs or momentary weaknesses. He would not answer anything except the most direct of questions, and he would answer those as literally and shortly as possible. If asked if he knew who he was, for instance, he would answer "Yes," and nothing more. If asked if he knew what spell had brought him here, he would also answer "Yes," with no elaboration. If Ancar wanted information, he would have to extract it, bit by painful bit. And Falconsbane would do his best to confuse the issue, by deliberate misunderstandings.

It would be an exercise in patience, to say the least, to learn anything at all of value.

Let Ancar wear himself out. Meanwhile, Falconsbane would be studying him, his spells, and his situation. Let Ancar continue to believe that he was the Master here. Falconsbane would learn to use Ancar even as Ancar thought he was using Falconsbane. He would not remain this fool's captive for long.

Falconsbane had forgotten more about coercion than this piddling puppy King had learned in his lifetime! It would only take time to undo what had been done, or to work his way around what Ancar had hedged him in with. Falconsbane knew above all that any spell created could be broken, circumvented, or twisted.

Even his own, he remembered with some bitterness.

True unconsciousness rose to take him under a blanket of darkness, even as that last sordid thought cut through his mind.

As Falconsbane drifted from pretended slumber into real sleep, An'desha shena Jor'ethan watched from his own starry corner of the Adept's mind.

When Falconsbane's thoughts clouded and drifted into dreams, An'desha opened his shared eyes cautiously, alert to the possibility that such an action might wake Falconsbane again.

But Falconsbane remained asleep, and An'desha reveled in the feeling that his body was his own again—however temporarily that might be. Once Falconsbane woke, he would have to retreat back into the little hidden corner of his mind that Falconsbane did not control, and did not even seem to be aware of. Even his ability to view the world through Falconsbane's senses was limited to the times when the Adept was very preoccupied, or seriously distracted. Any time there was even the slightest possibility that Falconsbane could sense An'desha's presence, An'desha kept himself hidden in the "dark."

He was not certain why he was still "here." The little he had read in Falconsbane's memories indicated that whenever the Adept took over one of his descendants' bodies, he utterly destroyed the personality, and possibly even the soul, of that descendant. Yet— this time both had remained. An'desha was still "alive," if in a severely limited sense, thanks only to his instincts.

Not that I can do much, he thought with more than a little fear. *And if he ever finds out that I'm still here, he'll squash me like a troublesome insect. He may think he's too weak to do anything, but even now he could destroy me if he wanted to. He'd probably do it just to sharpen his appetite.*

If I'd accepted becoming a shaman ... none of this would have happened. There wouldn't even be a Mornelithe Falconsbane, if I hadn't tried to call fire. If only.

If only ... easy to say, in retrospect. Half Shin'a'in as he was, would the Plains shaman have even accepted him? There was no telling; the shaman might just as easily have sent him away. Shin'a'in shaman did not practice magic as such—but did they have anything like the fire-calling spell? And if they did, would it have been similar enough to bring Mornelithe out of his limbo? And if it had been—what would have happened then?

If, if, if. Too many "ifs," and none of them of any use.

The past was immutable, the present what it was because of the past. An'desha *had* been gifted with mage-power. He *had* chosen to run away to try to find the Tale'edras and master that magic, rather than become a shaman as the custom of Shin'a'in dictated. He *had* become lost, and he *had* tried to call fire to warm himself the first night he had been on his own. That had been his undoing.

An'desha was a blood-descendant of an Adept called Zendak, who had in turn been the blood-descendant of another and another, tracing their lineage all the way back to the time of the Mage Wars and an Adept called Ma'ar. That Adept had learned a terrible secret; how to defy death by hiding his disembodied self at the moment of his body's death in a pocket of one of the Nether Plains. And Ma'ar had set a trap for every blood-descendant of Adept potential, using the simple fire-spell as the trigger of that trap. A fledgling mage shouldn't know much more than that fire-spell, and so wouldn't be able to effectively defend against the marauder stealing his body.

An'desha, all unknowing and innocent, had called fire. Mornelithe Falconsbane had swarmed up out of his self-imposed limbo to shred An'desha's mind.

But this time, the theft had not taken place completely. An'desha had studied what being a Shin'a'in shaman entailed, and was familiar with some of the ways to control one's own mind. He fled before the Adept's power into a tiny space in his own mind, and had barricaded and camouflaged against the invader. And Falconsbane was completely unaware of that fact.

Sometimes I wish he had gotten rid of me . . . how can I still be sane? Maybe I'm not . . .

An'desha had been an unwitting and terrified spectator to far too many of Falconsbane's atrocities—appalled at what was happening, and helpless to do anything about what was being done. And he knew, from stolen glimpses into Falconsbane's thoughts, that the little he had been witness to was only the smallest part of what Falconsbane had done to his victims. His existence had all the qualities of the worst nightmare that anyone could imagine, and more than once he had been tempted to reveal himself, just to end the torment.

But something had always kept him from betraying himself; some hope, however faint, that one day he might, possibly, be able to get his own body back and drive out the interloper. He never gave up on that hope, not even when Falconsbane had changed that body into something An'desha no longer recognized as his.

He had welcomed the embrace of the Void, at least as an end to the madness. He had no more expected release from the Void than Falconsbane had.

He had not been as weakened or as confused as his usurper when that release came, but caution made him very wary of trusting anyone with his secret. He had remained silent and hidden, and that, perhaps, is what had saved him.

The coercions on Falconsbane had not taken hold of *him,* and he had come through the ordeal in far better shape than Falconsbane had. And to his surprise and tentative pleasure, he had discovered that the damage done to Falconsbane had permitted *him* some measure of control again—always provided that he did not try to control something while Falconsbane was using it.

Falconsbane did not seem any more aware of An'desha's presence than he had been before, not even when An'desha, greatly daring, had taken over the body, making it sit up, eat, and even walk, while Falconsbane was "asleep."

What all this meant, An'desha did not dare to speculate.

But there had been other signs to make him hope, signs and even oblique messages, during the time that Falconsbane had waged war on the Tale'edras.

The Black Riders. He had known who and what those mysterious entities were, even though Falconsbane had not. When they had appeared, he had nearly been beside himself with excitement. They were as much a message to him—or so he hoped—as they were a distraction to Falconsbane.

And there had even been an earlier sign, at Falconsbane's battle and subsequent escape from the ruins where the gryphons laired. *He* knew why the Kal'enedral had failed to slay Falconsbane, even if no one else did. They had not missed their mark—nor had they been concerned with sparing the Adept. Their later actions, in the guise of Black Riders, luring Falconsbane into thinking that he was being "courted" by another Adept, only confirmed that.

They—or rather, *She,* the Star-Eyed, the Warrior—knew that An'desha was still "alive." She would; very little was lost to the deity of both the Tale'edras and the Shin'a'in, so long as it occurred either on the Plains or in the Pelagirs. When the Black Riders sent the tiny horse and the ring to Falconsbane, An'desha was certain that they were also sending a message to him. The black horse meant that he had not been forgotten, either by his Goddess or by Her Swordsworn. The ring was to remind him that life is a cycle—and the cycle might bring him a chance to get his body and his life back again.

The question was, now that he was far from the lands that he had known, could *they* act this far from the Plains? The Goddess was not known for being able to do much far from the borders of Her own lands. She had limited Her own power, of Her own will, at the beginning of time—as all the Powers had chosen to do, to keep the world from becoming a battleground of conflicting deities. She would not break Her own rules.

And yet ... and yet ...

She was clever; She could work around the rules without breaking them. If She chose.

If he proved that he was worthy. That was the other thing to keep in mind; She only helped those who had done *their* part, who had gone to the end of their own abilities, and had no other recourse. If he were to be worthy of Her help, it was up to him to do everything in his power, without waiting for the Star-Eyed to come rescue him.

He would, above all, have to be very, very careful. Just because Falconsbane was damaged now, it did not do to think he would continue to be at a disadvantage. If there was one thing An'desha had learned from watching the Adept, it was this; never underestimate Mornelithe Falconsbane—and always be, not doubly, but *triply* careful whenever doing anything around him.

But—he dared, just for a moment, to send a whisper of prayer into the darkness of the chamber. To Her.

Remember me—and help me, if You will—

Then the sound of footsteps outside the chamber door made him flee back into his hiding place, before Falconsbane was awakened, or woke on his own.

He reached that safety, just as the door opened, and Falconsbane stirred up out of the depths of sleep.

The sound of his door opening and closing roused him from slumber. Falconsbane opened his eyes a mere slit.

It was enough to betray him to his observer.

"I see you are awake." The smooth young voice identified the speaker at once, even before Ancar moved into the faint light cast by a shadowed lantern near the bed. "I hope you are enjoying my hospitality."

Falconsbane refused to allow himself to show any emotion. He simply studied his captor, committing every nuance of expression to memory. Falconsbane knew well the value of every scrap of information, and the more he knew about Ancar of Hardorn, the sooner he would be able to defeat the boy.

He was a handsome young man, showing few signs of the dissipation that Falconsbane suspected. But if he had achieved the position of Master, he surely knew all the tricks by which a mage could delay the onset of aging, strengthen the body, and even make it more comely. Only an Adept could actually *change* the body, as Falconsbane had done with both his own form and that of others. But a Master could hold his own body in youth for a very long time, if he had sufficient energies. Life-energies would serve the best, the life-energies of others. One could steal years, decades, from other lives and add them to one's own. Or one could steal the entire remaining lifespan. Easily done; very tempting and a very useful skill to learn. For Mornelithe, in days long ago, it had approached being a hobby.

Ancar of Hardorn was certainly a young man that women would find attractive; his straight, black hair was thick and luxuriant, his mustache and beard well-groomed. Neither hid the sensual mouth, a mouth that smiled easily, if falsely. The square face was pleasantly sculptured, the dark eyes neither piggishly small nor bovinely large. But the eyes did give him away, for they were flat, expressionless, and dead. The eyes of someone who sees others only as objects—as things to use, destroy, or ignore. A more experienced man would have learned how even to manipulate the expressions of his eyes, as Falconsbane had. Mornelithe fancied that he could convince anyone of anything, if he chose to. He was certainly convincing this Ancar that his "Master" had him cowed and under control.

Falconsbane considered his answer carefully before making it. How much to reveal? If he seemed *too* submissive, Ancar might suspect something. A mere touch of defiance, perhaps. A faint hint of rebellion. "I cannot say that 'enjoy' is the term I would use."

Ancar laughed, although there was no humor in the sound. "I see you have regained some of your wits at last. Good. I will ask you some questions that have puzzled me."

Since that was not a direct question, Falconsbane made no answering comment. Ancar waited for a moment, then said sharply, "What is your *true* name? And where do you come from?"

The coercions tightened about his mind, forcing answers from him, but he made them as literal as he could. "Mornelithe Falconsbane. I came from the Void, where you found me."

That last was enough to confuse him. Falconsbane preferred that Ancar not learn his true place of origin. Not yet, at least.

Ancar's brow furrowed as he considered this. "Are you an Adept?" he asked at last. "Are you a demon?"

"Yes," Falconsbane replied quickly. "No."

"But you are not human—" Ancar persisted, but since it was not a question, nothing compelled Falconsbane to answer, and Ancar glared at him in frustration. Falconsbane kept his own expression bland and smooth.

"Do you know who I am?" Ancar asked at last—then, finally realizing what game Falconsbane was playing, changed his question to an order, backed by the coercive spells. "Tell me what you know of me!" he demanded.

Mentally cursing, Falconsbane did as he was told. That Ancar was a ruler and a mage, and that his enemies were the Outlanders who rode white horses as a kind of badge. That the king was the one who had cast the spell that had brought Falconsbane out of the Void, and had cast coercive spells to make Falconsbane his captive. Ancar listened to the little that Falconsbane could tell him, then stroked his beard for a moment in thought.

"I am going to give you some information I wish you to think about," he said at last, "because I am certain that once you are aware of who and what you are dealing with, you will be disposed to cooperate. I am Ancar, King of Hardorn, and the most powerful mage in this kingdom. I am, as you surmised, the enemy of those you called 'Outlanders,' the folk of Valdemar who ride those white witch-horses you described. They are known as 'Heralds,' and they possess a certain mastery of mind-magic. I intend to conquer them, and to that end, I require the abilities of an Adept, for their Kingdom has protection against true magic. Not only does it not operate within their border, but mages who attempt to cross that border are driven mad within a short time of trying to exercise their powers. So, you are both useful and necessary to me—but *not* so necessary that I cannot do without you. Keep that in mind."

He smiled, and Falconsbane refrained from snarling. The boy's rhetoric was incredibly heavy-handed. How he had managed to keep himself on his throne, Falconsbane could not imagine. Luck, the help of someone more skilled than he was, or both.

"Now," Ancar continued silkily, "I have every intention of seeing that you are brought to your full health. If you cooperate fully with me, I shall be certain that you are rewarded. If you do not—I shall force your cooperation, and dispose of you when I no longer need you. The situation is just that simple."

He did not wait for an answer this time, but simply turned and left, and Falconsbane felt mage-locks clicking into place behind him.

Slowly, Falconsbane pushed himself into a sitting position, his anger giving him more energy to move than he had thought he possessed. There was food and drink on the table beside the bed; Falconsbane helped himself to both while he still had the strength to do so, and then, when his head began to swim a little, lowered himself back down again.

But although he was prone, his mind continued to work. Ancar had revealed more than he had known, for although he was wearing a mage-constructed shield protecting his thoughts, his expression was perfectly open, and his body had revealed things his words had not.

His hold upon his throne was by no means as secure as he would like Falconsbane to think. There was someone else in the picture—another mage, Falconsbane guessed—who kept the boy in power. That was why Ancar needed Falconsbane. Oh, it was true enough that he also needed an Adept to help defeat these "Heralds" as he had claimed; his body had proclaimed that much also to be true. But his hidden agenda was to rid himself of this other person's influence, if not, indeed, the person.

Now that had a great deal of potential, so far as Falconsbane was concerned. Perhaps when Ancar had first mounted the throne, his people would only have accepted a ruler of the proper lineage. But by now, Falconsbane suspected that Ancar had been foolish enough to mistreat his people very badly indeed. There was only so much mistreatment that a populace would put up with, and after that, they would welcome *any* ruler marginally better than the current despot.

Perhaps this other mage had already calculated precisely that. Perhaps not. It would certainly enter into Falconsbane's calculations.

He would play along with Ancar—perhaps continue to feign weakness, perhaps simply feign complete cooperation. He would work at the coercions until they were no longer a hindrance. Then, when the time was right— Falconsbane would turn the tables on the arrogant brat.

Then this kingdom would be in Falconsbane's hands. That would give him a new base of operations from which to work. He could then discover exactly how far from home he was—and determine if he actually wanted to return home. It might not be worthwhile. After all, one thing he lacked was a decent population base. Such things made real, human armies possible. Add human armies to the armies of his image-born creatures, and he might well prove to be the most powerful ruler this area had ever seen.

Those Outlanders whose interference had so undone his own plans were almost certainly on their way home. And *now* he knew where that home was. So by furthering Ancar's plans, he would be furthering his own revenge. Then, when *he* was the one in control, he would be able to exact a more complete form of vengeance.

Vengeance again; how it comforted him! It was simple and elegant, however messy or convoluted its execution might be. As it had so many times before, vengeance would pull him through troubles—no, *inconveniences*—like a bright lantern seen through stormy darkness.

Taking their land would be a good start. Finding the girl and the man would complete that particular facet of his revenge.

And from there, with two lands under his control. . . .

Well, it would be much easier to attack the Bird Lovers with a conventional army at his call. They were not prepared for such things. He could take them with little personal effort.

After that—

After that, he might well think about all the blighted ambitions of Leareth and Ma'ar. All the plans he had laid that could actually be brought to fruition. He could become more than a mere "king"—even more than an Emperor. He could have the world calling him Lord and Master.

He closed his eyes, picturing himself as Master of the World, and drifted again into pleasant dreams.

An'desha emerged from hiding as soon as Falconsbane was truly asleep again. This time, although he took care not to move Falconsbane's body, he took a few moments to get some idea of his surroundings.

He was in what seemed to be a very luxurious bedroom. The bed itself was canopied, with heavy curtains that were now pulled back and held against the posts of the bed with straps of fabric. There was a fireplace, although there was no fire burning at the moment. Beside the bed was a table with the remains of Falconsbane's meal still on it. Shadows against the wall hinted at more furniture, but the light from the two heavily-shaded lamps beside the bed was not enough for An'desha to make out what kind of furnishings were there.

So much for the physical aspects of the room. As for the nonphysical—

He paused for a moment, then used the Mage-Sight that had become second nature over the years of Mornelithe's dominance.

The door is mage-locked. There are protections on the bed and wards and shields everywhere—baffles and misdirectors. Ancar doesn't want anyone to know that he has a mage in this room.

An'desha hesitated for a moment, trying to decide if he should probe those protections further, or try to investigate the locks on the door.

An odd stirring in the energies surrounding the room alarmed him. Something was coming!

He readied to bolt back into hiding again, when the gentle touch of a thread of Mindspeech touched *his* mind. His—and not Falconsbane's! Was this the madness he had feared? Was his remaining consciousness having fever-dreams of its own now?

:Do not fear, An'desha. We are here to help you.:

He paused in frozen amazement, too shocked at hearing his own name to even think of what to do next. It was the kind of wish fulfillment he had always mistrusted, but it seemed real. Would madness seem so real? Would a madman know?

A sparkling energy coalesced in the room, then formed a rotating center and swirled around it. A column of twisting, glowing mist formed in the center of the room, spreading two wide wings, raising a head—

The image of a ghostly vorcel-hawk, many times life size and made of glowing amber mist, mantled its wings and stared at him for a moment.

A vorcel-hawk—*Her* hawk! This was no trick. Falconsbane knew nothing of Her creatures, nor would the foreigner Ancar have any notion of what a vorcel-hawk meant to a Shin'a'in!

The Hawk gazed at him with star-flecked eyes for three heartbeats. Then it pulled in its wings and became a mist-cloud; the mist swirled again, split into two masses, and began taking shape for a second time.

Not one hawk, but two stared at him, one larger than the other—

Then the hawks folded their wings and the mist clouded; not two hawks, but two people stood there. One, a woman, so faint and tenuous that An'desha could see nothing clearly but her eyes and the vague woman-shape of her. But the other was male.

The other was a man of the Shin'a'in.

He very nearly cried out—but the man motioned him to be silent, and with many years of control and caution behind him, he obeyed instantly. He took a tight rein on his elation and his confusion as well, lest they wake Falconsbane out of slumber. Whoever, whatever these were, they could only be here to help him—but they could not help him if Falconsbane learned of his existence.

:I am Tre'valen shena Tale'sedrin, An'desha,: the spirit-man said in his mind. *:We have been sent to help you as much as we can—but I must warn you, although we come at the order of the Star-Eyed, we are far from our forests and plains. Both we and She are limited in what we can do. She is bound by rules even as we are.:*

There was a little disappointment at learning they would not simply invoke a power and banish Falconsbane, but far more simple relief. He was not alone at least, he had not been forgotten! He nearly wept with the intensity of his emotion.

But like lightning, his relief turned to bewilderment. What, exactly, was this Tre'valen? He didn't *look* anything like one of the Swordsworn . . . could he be spirit-traveling in some way, and was his real body somewhere nearby? If An'desha had a real, physical ally somewhere, it would be more than he had hoped for. A physical ally *could* free him from Ancar. But on the other hand, wouldn't someone who was *leshy'a* be better suited to free him from Falconsbane?

:What are you?: he asked timidly. *:Are you a spirit?:*

Tre'valen smiled ruefully. *:I am not precisely a spirit— but I am not precisely "alive," either. I was, and am still, a shaman of Tale'sedrin. I do not believe that the term "Avatar" would mean anything to you—:*

An'desha dared not shake his head, but evidently Tre'valen "read" the intention.

:We are "Avatars," for what that is worth. We serve Her a little more directly than the Kal'enedral do. We go where She cannot and where the Kal'enedral are un- suited. As now, when a shaman is needed, and not a war- rior.:

A shaman? He couldn't help himself; he had gotten into this mess by trying to *escape* the shaman. He shrank back a little, both afraid of Tre'valen's censure, and ashamed. Surely, since She knew so much, She knew of his foolish attempt to flee, and her—Avatar—knew it, too.

Tre'valen sensed his shame, and Sent him a feeling of reassurance. *:An'desha, you need not fear me because of your past. Would She have sent us to you if She thought you deserved punishment? Would She punish you because you chose to flee instead of being forced into a role you didn't want?:*

A good point. He breathed a little easier.

:And think on it, An'desha. She takes no one who is not willing—Kal'enedral or shaman. She also punishes only those who have betrayed that which they promised. Why should She be angered at you because you were not will- ing?:

Now he felt twice as stupid. All this could have been avoided if only he had thought before he acted.

Tre'valen shook his head. *:An'desha, I learned to think long before I acted—and when I was young, that broody thoughtfulness became inactivity. I was shocked out of it in my own way, even as you have been shocked. I became what I am now because of a moment when I did not have* *time to consider hundreds of options. I believe the choice I made was the right one. And perhaps, so was yours.:*

Now he was confused. And what on earth did Tre'valen mean by saying that he was not precisely a spirit, but not precisely alive?

Oh, it didn't matter. What mattered was that he had been forgiven. Tre'valen seemed to be able to follow that thought, for he nodded.

:You were not thinking, An'desha, to run off like that. A better choice would have been to go to another sha-man, one of some other Clan, who would have been more objective about you and your life-path. But you were also very young, and being young and stupid is not supposed to open one up to consequences quite as serious as you suffered. We all learn. That is why we live.: Tre'valen smiled a little and the woman-form behind him took on more substance. And to An'desha's surprise, it was not one of the Kal'enedral as he had suspected it might be, nor was it even another Shin'a'in. Instead, the woman matched all the descriptions of the Tale'edras that he had ever heard! She was very beautiful, and it was clear to An'desha that these two were bound by more than similarity of form and purpose.

:This is Dawnfire,: Tre'valen said, confirming his guess by giving the woman a Hawkbrother name. *:She and I are your friends and your helpers. You know what you want most—:*

:My body!: he cried involuntarily. *:My freedom!:*

:We can free you of your body—permanently, but I suspect that is not your first choice,: Dawnfire replied wryly.

No. For all that he had wished for oblivion and death before, he truly did not want it now.

:In that case, you will have to earn your body and your freedom,: Tre'valen told him. The mist-forms glowed, like dust in a sunbeam, sparkling and dancing. *:And even if you do all that we ask, there is no guarantee that we can grant what you want. We will do our best, but we are very limited in power. There are many other forces at work here.:*

But it was a chance; it was more than he had ever had

before. Even a chance was worth fighting for, and especially a chance for freedom.

Both of the spirits nodded encouragingly. *:An'desha, what we want from you is relatively simple. Watch. Listen. Learn. And tell us all that you have learned.:* Tre'valen's mind-voice was earnest. *:This will not be easy, because we will be asking you to do more than simply observe what happens. We will be showing you how to see into Falconsbane's thoughts and memories without him being aware that you are doing so. As you have been, brave one, when Falconsbane is fully aware, you are in limbo. We will show you how to protect yourself so that you are part of everything he thinks and does. Eventually, you will be an unseen witness to what goes on within him and outside of him. Eventually, you will invade his memories and learn the answers to questions we shall ask in the future:*

An'desha writhed with indecision and discomfort for a moment. He had *not* liked the little he had seen; he knew very well that Falconsbane had done horrible things, much more horrible than An'desha had ever been aware of. As Mornelithe had become more intent on his depravities, An'desha had been pushed back into limbo. He had awakened to the aftermath when Mornelithe came down from his twisted pleasure. Could he bear to see and know these things that had been done with *his* body?

:You will not like any of what you find,: Dawnfire warned soberly. *:Falconsbane is a monster in every sense. What you discover for us will bring you pain. But these are things that we must know in order to help you. And—to help others; those Falconsbane would harm.:*

In that case—if they meant to *stop* Falconsbane from hurting anyone else—how could he refuse? How many times had he prayed for a way to stop the madness that he had seen? How many times had he cursed his inability to save even one creature from Falconsbane's evil? The old Shin'a'in proverb of "Beware what you ask for, lest you receive it" seemed particularly apt. . . .

Wordlessly—even though he was full of fear, and already shrinking from what he knew he would find—he gave his assent.

By the time they left him, they had shown him as much

as he could encompass in a single lesson. They had coached him through making his little corner of Falconsbane's mind more secure, and even more invisible to the Adept. They had taught him how to gain access to Falconsbane's memory without the Adept being aware that he was doing so. They had shown him how to extend his reach into areas of Falconsbane's waking mind, so that now he would be able to see and hear whatever Falconsbane did, and to read the Adept's waking thoughts at all times, and not just when Falconsbane was extremely preoccupied. And they had gently praised him, something he had not experienced in what felt like eons. He quivered at how it made him feel.

When they took wing into the night, he withdrew again, buttressed up the walls of his defenses, and assimilated everything they had taught him. As Falconsbane continued to sleep, he made his first overt move. He sent the Adept into deeper slumber.

It worked.

Falconsbane descended into a sleep so deep that not even an army marching by would have awakened him. It would not last for long, but it was the first time that An'desha had *dared* do anything directly *against* the Adept.

Encouraged by his success, he thought for a moment.

He did things to my body; I know he did. More things than just changing the way it looks—and I don't even know how far he went with that. I ought to find out.

And the memories of how Falconsbane had done those things were likely to be some of the least noxious.

That would be a good place to start, then.

He settled down, made his own thoughts very quiet, and began his work.

Chapter Five

Elspeth stared at the enormous conifers surrounding them. Their trunks and branches were not "enormous" by Tayledras standards, but they were huge when compared to the trees around Haven.

If the air had not been so cool, she would have thought they had been transported into a miniature Vale, or part of a larger one. They stood in a pocket-valley, with the cave that had formed the terminus of the Gate behind them, a small, grassy meadow in front of them, and those huge trees climbing up the steep slopes to either side of them. Any place where sunlight might penetrate the canopy, there were bushes and other low-growing plants clustered thickly about the bases of the trees. And yet, the meadow here had nothing taller than a few weeds, and while it was not exactly symmetrical, it still felt artificial— arranged somehow. There were no exotic flowering plants, and no signs of a Veil or other protections. But for all of that, it still reminded her strongly of a Hawkbrother stronghold. There was something about the placement of the trees that gave her the sense that this place had been touched by the hand of man.

Could trees grow that tall without something nurturing them? She didn't think so . . . but then she was not exactly an expert. Hadn't Darkwind once told her that the trees in the Pelagiris Forest were this tall?

Could they somehow have come out into an *old* Vale, one abandoned long ago? How did they get *here* instead of k'Treva? Certainly Firesong did not seem to recognize this place either. If he had targeted an old Vale by mistake, wouldn't he know it? Wouldn't he *recognize* it, if it was an old k'Treva Vale?

The group moved so their backs faced each other, with the gryphlets in the middle of the circle. Darkwind and Skif had dropped all burdens but their weapons, and Vree was already ranging up onto station to scout. Firesong stood with the most perplexed expression Elspeth had ever seen, one hand to his scalp, pulling his white hair back.

"I have no *clue* how we got here!" he cried, and received a gesture to be quieter from Darkwind, Skif, and Nyara.

A bird called off in the distance somewhere. It sounded like a wood thrush. There weren't any wood thrushes around k'Sheyna, at least not that she had ever heard. She had always thought they were a northern bird . . . were there other birds that sounded like wood thrushes? Scarlet jays mimicked other birds, so perhaps it was a jay. But would a jay mimic a bird that didn't live in the same region?

"We are definitely far north. I think we can calm down, though—if we were meant to be killed, it would have been done as we exited the Gate. Still," Firesong continued, "this seriously annoys me."

Something about the light shining down into the center of the clearing was unusual. Its color—and the angle at which it fell.

Light in the center of the clearing? But the sun isn't high enough—it's early morning—there can't be a shaft of light in the middle of the clearing!

But there was—only it wasn't a shaft of light coming down through the treetops, but a column of light, taller than a man. Silver-gold light, the kind of light that shines over snow on a winter morning. Everything developed odd double shadows as the light became brighter still.

A ripple in the energies of the place made her redouble her shields quickly, and join them with Darkwind's, in a move that was near-instinctive now. Gods only knew what this thing was, but it surely had something to do with whatever snatched them away from k'Treva.

A vague shape developed, a sculpture of fog—except that it was glowing, and the energies of this place were definitely centered around it. Now that she knew what to look for, the lines of force were as clear as ripples in a pond. This—thing—was a part of the forest—of the energies that lay under the forest.

But it was still changing; it blurred, or perhaps her eyes blurred for a moment. And then, the figure solidified. It was not at all what she had expected.

It was a handsome man, silver-haired, silver-eyed, handsome enough even to cast Firesong into the shade, of no determinate age.

And he was dressed in an antique version of Herald's Whites. He looked like a glowing statue of milky glass, or like—

Oh, gods. Like a ghost, a spirit. . . .

The hair on the back of her neck rose with atavistic fear, and she backed up another pace, holding out one hand as if to ward the thing off.

As if she *could!* This was not the first spirit she had encountered, but how could she know what this spirit could do? How could she hope to hold it off if it chose to attack her?

A crisp, clean breeze rose and fell. It sounded like the forest was sighing.

:Bright Havens!: said a cheerful, gentle voice in her head. *:You all look as if you'd seen a ghost!:*

A quick glance showed her that everyone else had heard that mind-voice as well. Darkwind looked startled; the gryphons were mantling and the little ones hid under their wings. Skif was white—and round-eyed with astonishment, for he was *not* a strong Mindspeaker, and it would take a powerful Mindspeaker indeed to make him Hear. Nyara simply looked frightened and puzzled. The

Companions—there was no reading them. They stood as stock still as if they had been carved of snow.

Firesong was as pale as his hair—or the apparition. This was the first time that Elspeth had ever seen the Hawkbrother truly frightened. She'd seen him worried, yes. Anxious and even apprehensive. But never frightened.

Still, it was Firesong who recovered first. He regained a little more color, drew himself erect, and approached the—man.

The apparition simply smiled. For a revenant, this one was remarkably good-natured. Weren't ghosts supposed to rattle chains and moan curses or warnings? But she had never heard of a Herald coming back to haunt anyone before.

"And have we not?" Firesong asked, stopping within touching distance of the spirit and looking challengingly into its "face." "Have we not seen a ghost, Forefather?"

Forefather? "Firesong, what are you talking about?" Elspeth asked in a whisper, as if she really thought the thing wouldn't hear her if she kept her voice down.

Firesong's voice shook, and he was clearly having a hard time keeping it steady. "Don't *you* recognize him, Elspeth?" he asked tremulously. "Have you never seen those features before? Are there no portraits in your home in Valdemar of your ancestor and mine?"

The spirit folded his arms over his chest. It looked, perversely, as if he was enjoying this. It was hard to feel frightened of someone who had that kind of mischievous twinkle in his eyes—or whatever passed for eyes.

"My ancestor?" she repeated, feeling remarkably stupid. "I mean, it looks like he's wearing old Herald's Whites, but I don't—I mean, there isn't anyone in the royal family who looks like—there's no one in the Royal Gallery who—"

Firesong regained a little more color. "Elspeth, have you no eyes in your head?" he asked, in a much steadier—and rather impatient—tone. "Look at him. Look at me! This is *Vanyel*. Your great-great-many-times-great grandfather, and mine. *Herald* Vanyel. The last Herald-Mage, Elspeth. Ally of the Clans."

Her mouth dropped open. The apparition winked broadly. *:Very good, Firesong,:* he said.

:Close your mouth, granddaughter,: said a voice she knew was only in *her* mind this time. *:You look very pretty, but not overly bright that way. There is no Veil to hold insects out; something might fly right down your throat.:*

She snapped her mouth shut and blushed in confusion.

She was not the only one with a reaction to the identification. "If *that* is Vanyel," Skif said, and gulped, "then *this* must be—the Forest of Sorrows!"

She knew even as he said it that Skif was right. But how? How had they gotten here? Skif might well gulp, for she had thought there was a reasonable limit on how far one could Gate—and this was well beyond that limit. As nearly as she could reckon, they were more than the length of Valdemar off-course, and *none* of them had ever been up here before, not even Skif.

This was insane. Or else, *she* had gone insane. Or it was a dream—

:It's not a dream,: Gwena said, lipping her to prove it.

:No, it's not a dream,: the spirit said, still smiling. *:And you haven't all gone mad. This is Sorrows and I am Vanyel Ashkevron. I am still in the service of the Goddess and Valdemar. I brought you here.:*

She could only blink. If this was Vanyel—no, who else could it be? It must be. If her mage-senses weren't supporting his claims, she would have thought he was just someone playing a trick on all of them. "Ah, I'm sorry, but—I've never seen a ghost before—I—" she stammered in confusion.

Firesong continued to stare at the spirit, but there was a certain expression of growing accusation on his face. And well there might be, since this ghostly Vanyel had just run roughshod over their plans with this little excursion.

Elspeth tried to shake her thoughts loose. If this was Vanyel, then *this* was the spirit of one of the most pivotal Heralds of all time. His death had ended the age of Herald-Mages. And if her researches in the Archives were correct, he was also personally responsible for the fact that it was impossible for magic to be performed or even *thought of* inside the borders of Valdemar. She had a million questions in her mind, and was afraid to ask any of them.

But another thought occurred to her suddenly. What if this was still some kind of trick? Just because he was a Herald, *then.* . . .

:It is *Vanyel,:* Gwena repeated, in reply to the unvoiced suspicion. Elspeth could sense that she was seriously shaken. *:And this is not a trap or, at least, not a trap of an enemy. Trust me in this.:* Then, as if to herself, she added, *:This was not in the plan.* . . .*:*

Before Elspeth could react to either statement, the spirit himself replied—his smile fading, and being replaced with a look of stern seriousness. *:There have been many things done that were not in the "plan," sister,:* he said, without apology. *:And for the better. I have many reasons to be less than fond of predestined paths. And it would be wise for you and Rolan to recall that plans seldom survive the first engagement with the enemy. A plan that has been in operation as long as this one of yours should never have lasted as long as it did.:*

Gwena's head came up, and her eyes widened, as if she had not expected to be chided. She staggered back a step.

Vanyel's smile returned, this time for Elspeth. *:Personally, I think you have been doing well, especially for someone who had to constantly fight "plans" that had been made without her consent or knowledge.:* He glanced from Elspeth to Darkwind and back. *:I think you will upset a few more plans before you're through. Things should be very interesting for you, at any rate, once you reach Haven. For what it's worth, you have my sympathy.:*

"This is a fine family chat. I'm having a delightful time. May I interrupt and ask how in the silver skies did you bring us here?" Firesong demanded.

:Ah. I'm sorry I had to interfere with your intended destination and your Gate—but this was my only chance to intercept all of you, together. There are forces marshaling now that you need to know about, or Valdemar will be

worse off than I can affect. Much worse than what King Valdemar's people fled.:

Elspeth felt a chill run up her back at his words. There were some who had held—sentimentally, she had always thought—that Vanyel somehow protected Valdemar, haunting the Forest of Sorrows. It seemed the sentimentalists were right.

Treyvan's feathers were slowly smoothing down; he clicked his beak twice, and said—with remarkable mildness, Elspeth thought, considering the circumstances—"I did not know you could change the dessstination of a Gate." He cocked his head to one side, and continued, making no secret of his surprise, "I know of no one alive who can do ssso—"

Then he stopped short, as he realized that he was not precisely talking to someone who was *alive*.

"Urrr. Apologiesss."

:No need to apologize, Treyvan. I've had a great deal of time to research the subject,: Vanyel replied, actually sounding a bit sheepish.

As he spoke, Elspeth noticed that he faded in and out, as if the amount of power he was using to maintain himself, or his control over it, fluctuated.

:I would imagine you have, youngster,: Need's dry mental voice replied. *:Although Gates are not precisely my specialty, I recall someone in* my *time learning how to kidnap the unwitting by interfering with their Portals.:*

:Ah. So I have not discovered anything new.: Did he sound a little disappointed? *:Well, that means that the rest of you can uncover this "secret" for yourselves, later. Right now, you need to hear some things, and I am the one to tell you. That is why I diverted you.:*

:Kidnapped us, you mean,: Need interrupted. *:There are people in k'Treva Vale who are probably tearing their elaborately braided white hair out with anxiety right now! Never thought of that, did you, boy?:*

Vanyel did not exactly sigh, but Elspeth did get a sense of impatience. *:Then perhaps Firesong ought to send a message telling them you will be all right, shouldn't he?:*

Now it was Firesong's turn to look impatient. "You

haven't exactly given me a chance to, Forefather!" he snapped. "If you all don't mind, I shall do exactly that!"

He turned and stalked off into the forest, the white *dyheli* following. His firebird flapped its wings a little to keep its balance as he turned, and favored Vanyel with a contemptuous look and a chitter.

:Oh, dear. I seem to have put my foot in it—and he's as touchy as I used to be,: the spirit said, chagrined. *:I hope he'll accept an apology.:*

"Oh, don't worry too much about it," Darkwind said unexpectedly, giving Vanyel a half grin. "I think he's more upset by the fact that he *isn't* the most powerful Adept around anymore. And it doesn't matter whether you really are what you claim you are, the fact that you played with his Gate proves you're stronger than he is. Besides—you made a better entrance than he did."

Elspeth favored her lover with an odd look. He was certainly taking this apparition rather well—better than she was, in fact. She still wasn't entirely certain that this spirit was who and what he said he was.

No matter what Gwena said. Companions weren't infallible. Could they be fooled?

:Still, I seem to be as bad at handling people's feelings as I was back in my own time. . . . : This time the spirit *did* sigh. *:Shall we take this from the beginning? I need to speak with all of you, but the ones I need to speak with the most are Elspeth and Darkwind—:*

Some of her growing skepticism must have shown, for he stopped and looked only at her.

:You still are not certain that I am genuine, or of my motives. I think you've gotten much more cautious than you once were,: the spirit said at last.

:She's had a good teacher,: Need said gruffly. *:Me. I wouldn't believe the spirit of my own mother if she showed up with as little proof of who she was as you've given us. "Trust me" doesn't fly. If you want her to believe you're what you say you are, you'd better give her some proof she'll recognize.:*

The spirit actually laughed, then turned to Elspeth. *:Will it constitute proof if I answer some questions?*

Things no one outside of Valdemar could know the answers to except me?.:

She nodded, slowly. It would certainly be a start, anyway.

:The thing that is most on your mind is the "banishment" of magic from Valdemar, and the fact that not only is it impossible for mages to remain, it isn't even possible for magic to be thought of for very long. The two are related, but not from the same cause. The first is my fault, a spell I created. It wasn't supposed to work that way,: he added ruefully. *:I was interrupted by emergencies before I could complete what I'd planned, and I never got back to it. What I did was to set the* vrondi *to watching for mage-energy in use. You know what* vrondi *are, I hope?:*

She did, although she hadn't ever heard the name before she came to k'Sheyna. "The little air-elementals that we call to set the Truth Spell," she replied.

Vanyel nodded vigorously. She noticed then that although his feet touched the ground, the grass stems poked right through them. Hard to counterfeit that effect. . . .
:Exactly. And before you ask, even though it is true magic, since you are Heralds they know not to pester you when you cast the spell that calls them. Heralds casting true magic will never be bothered; I couldn't have them swarming every Herald-Mage in the Kingdom, after all! My aunt would never have let me hear the last of that.:

Considering what the Herald-Chronicler of the time had to say about Vanyel's formidable aunt, Herald Savil, Elspeth had to chuckle a little at that. She had apparently been a match for Kerowyn.

:So, when the vrondi *saw magic, if it hadn't been cast by a Herald, they were supposed to tell the nearest Herald-Mage, then keep an eye on the person using the mage-energy unless the Herald-Mage told them differently. I was going to change the spell, later—to ask the* vrondi *to "light up" the person who was using the mage-energy the way they do with a Truth Spell, to make the mage rather conspicuous. I thought that was better than having them simply watch the mage, especially since there might not be a Herald-Mage anywhere nearby—:*

"Unfortunately, after you, there weren't *any* Herald-Mages at all," Elspeth said dryly.

:Well, that's true. No active ones, anyway. So now they just watch. The longer the mage sticks around, the more of them come to watch. It's horribly uncomfortable, since mages can sense the vrondi, *and it's rather like being stared at by an increasing crowd all the time.:* The spirit shook his head. *:The borders have changed since I set the spell, and so far as the* vrondi *are concerned, the "border" really ends where the presence of active, on-duty Heralds ends. They don't always notice where Heralds are unless one of them has invoked Truth Spell lately in that area. So the "borders" are changing all the time, and sometimes mages on the Rethwellan or Karsite borders, or the borders on the west, can get fairly far in before they're stopped. I'm afraid that, enthusiastic as they are, well,* vrondi *just aren't too bright themselves.:*

Elspeth nodded; that made sense. The *vrondi* did not seem to be terribly reliable outside of exact instructions, although they were like puppies, and very eager to please. "But what about the way people simply can't *think* about magic?" she persisted. "The *vrondi* couldn't possibly be responsible for that!"

:No, I am. It was something we decided on after Van and I got together again.:

This was a new mind-voice, and after a moment, Elspeth saw the second, misty figure beside the first. It was nowhere near as well-defined, but if this was Vanyel—

:Yes, that was Stef's idea,: Vanyel said, confirming Elspeth's guess. *:Tell them why,* ashke.*:*

:Because we still had a problem with people refusing to give up the notion that Herald-Mages were somehow superior to Heralds with other Gifts,: the new voice sighed. *:It seems to be an inherent weakness of people to think magic cures every ill. The Bards did their best, but there were still those who felt that the young King was hiding the Herald-Mages away somewhere, keeping them for "special purposes" of his own, or reserving their powers for his own personal friends and favorites. So—we decided it would be best for people to simply "forget" that*

any magic but mind-magic had ever existed in Valdemar,
except in old tales and songs.:

There was a third and larger figure forming behind the
other two, and this one was as strong or stronger than
Vanyel—and there was no mistake that it was horse-
shaped.

Yfandes—Elspeth thought, and as she recognized
Vanyel's Companion, the spirit tossed her head in an unmistakable motion of summoning. Without a single word,
Gwena and Cymry walked toward her; she led them off
into the forest.

:They—ah—need to talk,: Vanyel said delicately. *:Your
Gwena, for all that she is Grove-born, is just as fallible
as any other mortal.:*

"She's *what?*" Elspeth yelped. Darkwind squinted and
scratched his ear to recover from her cry. Grove-born?
And no doubt Elspeth had been made to forget *that* as
well! This passed everything for sheer, unadulterated
gall—

And oddly enough, it was what actually convinced her
that Vanyel was Vanyel. No creature born outside
Valdemar would know what a Grove-born Companion
was. Few inside it would know, for that matter. And no
one else would have dared to make such an incredible
statement.

:She's Grove-born,: Vanyel repeated. *:So, they "forgot"
to tell you that, too, hmm? Doubtless "for your own
good." It's simple enough, Elspeth; you were going to be
the first of the new Herald-Mages, so I suppose they
thought you needed something a little more than the ordinary Companion.:* Vanyel's mind-voice dripped irony. *:It
never fails to annoy me how little faith people can have
in each other, Herald or no. Ah, well. Now that 'Fandes
has her away from you, I'll tell you what she may "forget" to tell you about the Grove-born. Be gentle on her,
Elspeth; as Companions go—when compared to, say,
Sayvil—she is very, very young. No older than you, in
fact. She makes all the kinds of mistakes any young thing
makes, but because she is Grove-born, she thinks she will
always make the right decision.:* He shook his head. *:She
forgets that she has no real, human experience to base*

her decisions on. It is like dictating music when you your-self have never learned to play an instrument.:

If this was supposed to mollify Elspeth, it didn't work. But on the other hand, she had gotten used to Gwena, and her "habits"; by now she had a fair notion how to figure out what was going on from what Gwena *wouldn't* tell her. Gwena wasn't going to change, so there was really no point in getting upset with her at this late a date. And despite her faults, Gwena had been a good friend for a long time.

:Actually, it would be a good thing if I could have a word with the two adult gryphons along with Elspeth and Darkwind. Since there are magics to talk of, it would be best to discuss things with all the mages at once.: Vanyel looked hopefully at Treyvan and Hydona, as the little ones watched the spirit solemnly from behind their parents' wings. *:This valley is quite well shielded and pro-tected; nothing can get in or out unless I permit it. The gryphlets could get some exercise.:*

"While we adultsss ssspeak of thingsss that would bore them into missschief," Hydona laughed. "Well, if Rrisss isss willing to take charge of them—"

The *kyree* nodded his head in a way that made it look like a bow. *:Of course, lovely lady. I can continue hunting lessons if you like.:*

Both gryphlets perked up their ear tufts at that, and suddenly the little round baby faces looked as fierce as the adults'. Elspeth kept forgetting that they were carni-vores. They were so baby-fluffy and, well, *cute*. But they were raptorial, like Vree, and like him they enjoyed the hunt and the kill—when they actually succeeded at the latter, which wasn't often.

"Yesss," Hydona replied thoughtfully. "Hunting lesssonsss would be mosssst appreciated."

:Then come along, younglings,: Rris said, trotting off with his tail high, looking surprisingly graceful for a creature the size of a young calf. The gryphlets bounded off after him, with a great deal less grace. Treyvan winced as Lytha crashed into a bush, tumbled head-over-tail, and kept right on going without even a pause. And

Jerven was no more coordinated than his sister, blundering through the remains of the bush.

:*This is not secret or private,*: Vanyel said then, looking at Skif and Nyara, .*But—much will be very technical. You may stay if you wish* ·

"I don't think so—thank you, but I'm not in the least interested. Really. I think I'd be better off not knowing," Skif said hastily. "And I wouldn't have Mage-Gift if you offered it to me. I wouldn't have it if you paid me Cymry's weight in gold to take it!"

He glanced at Nyara, who shrugged. Elspeth hadn't thought she would be interested, and she was not proven wrong. "My abilities are at the level of Journeyman in a school, or so Need tells me. I would be wasting my time with higher magics. The mage who knows how to use simple spells cleverly is just as effective as the Adept with no imagination. I should enjoy simply being with my friends in this lovely place."

And putting off the encounter with more strangers, Elspeth thought. *I can't blame her, either.*

:*I'm too old to learn another style of magery without a long time to study it,*: Need said. :*To be honest, youngsters, there's things I know you people have forgotten. Simple stuff, but sometimes simple is better. We'll run along, and you'll have your conference without me going "What?" every few moments.*:

Darkwind snickered.

:*Van, I can show them the springs,*: Stefen offered.

At Vanyel's nod, Skif and Nyara followed the little wisp of mist that was Stefen out of the clearing. Firesong came back a moment later, face impassive and unreadable, but eyes sparkling.

"Mother says that this was quite discourteous and inconsiderate of you, even if you are our forefather," he announced. "She told me to tell you that you are old enough to have better manners, especially by now. The only way she is prepared to forgive you is if you teach me what you did. And how to defend against it, if there is any defense."

The spirit rippled, and Elspeth got the distinct impression Vanyel was either laughing or stifling laughter. :*Very well,:* he said after a moment. *:It is, after all, the least I can do. Now if you could make yourselves comfortable. . . .:*

That was not difficult to do, here. In fact, Elspeth suspected Vanyel *had* taken a leaf or two from the Hawkbrothers' book, and had constructed this place along the lines of a Vale.

The gryphons reclined on the soft grass, and Darkwind and Elspeth used them as backrests. *:The first thing I need to tell you about is what I call the Web,:* Vanyel said. *:I created it because there were too few Herald-Mages left—originally there were four we called Guardians who remained at Haven and kept up a constant watch on the Borders. I changed that; I tied all Heralds and Companions into a net of completely unconscious communication. Now when there is danger in any direction, Heralds with ForeSight who are in a position to alert those who can do something about it have a vision or dream. That's how everyone knows when a Herald dies. And it's one way for the* vrondi *to know where Heralds are.:*

"We have done such things, but only for ssshort periodsss of time," Hydona offered. "Becaussse we did not know how to make it an unconssscious ability."

:The Companions are the key,: Vanyel told her. *:Because they are already linked. I couldn't have managed otherwise.:*

"Hmm." Treyvan nodded thoughtfully.

:I never meant anything but the Web to have to last as long as it has,: Vanyel continued. *:The* vrondi-*spell has eroded near to nothing, and constant attacks on it from Hardorn are taking their toll. I'm going to have to take it down in a controlled manner before someone breaks it and harms the* vrondi *in the process. Whether or not it goes back up again will depend on your choices later.:*

It was a good thing they were well-fed and well-rested, or Elspeth would have asked for a recess to think all this through. This was not precisely what Elspeth had expected to hear—but it was logical enough. Harm to the *vrondi* might mean that they would flee Valdemar altogether, and that would cause more problems than taking down the spell would.

"If you remove the warn-off, then mages will be able to enter Valdemar," Darkwind pointed out, as a light breeze stirred his hair. The breeze was from Vree stooping on Treyvan's head and crest-feathers, then angling up to perch in a tree and preen. "Many mages, in fact, through Valdemar's unfortified borders."

:Precisely.: Vanyel was clearly pleased. *:Now I plan to do several things, besides removing the spell. First, I will need to build a Gate to send you home. This will deplete me seriously for a time, and I do not know how long that will be. I will have to concentrate all my attention on this Border, and I will not be able to even offer such paltry distractions as I did against your Falconsbane—along with the Shin'a'in—to make him think that another Adept was courting him for an alliance.:*

Darkwind raised an eyebrow at Elspeth. She nodded; she had already known about the Shin'a'in Kal'enedral being involved. Vanyel's help was probably why the ruse had been so effective; Falconsbane would have seen the traces of real magic at work and if the suspicion that the Shin'a'in were running a trick on him had even occurred to him, he would have dismissed it immediately, since the Shin'a'in didn't use magic.

"What about Ancar?" she asked. "He'll know when that spell comes down."

:Ancar, yes. And others. You will have to warn your people through Gwena and Rolan that the barrier is coming down. I will do this just before I send you home. That way they will be prepared for magical incursions— although I do not think that Ancar will be able to react immediately. He is disposed toward grandiose plans, and those take time to prepare.:

"Hmm." Elspeth replied, after a moment of thought. "Even if he's watching for it to break, he likely won't have anyone strong there to do anything. He doesn't trust his powerful mages out of his sight."

:Once the barrier is down and you are home, there is nothing else I can do,: Vanyel said. *:Now, about the new Heartstone in the Palace at Haven. . . .:* Firesong looked

up alertly, interest immediately captured. *:I anchored the power in the stone I used to center the Web. You will find it in the old Palace in one of the old mage workrooms, and it is on the middle of a table that seems rooted to the floor. It is not yet activated, and I left it that way, keyed only to Firesong. . . . :*

Fortunately for Skif's mental comfort, as they left the clearing, Stefen became gradually less ephemeral and more solid, until at last he seemed almost normal—so long as you ignored the fact that you could see right through him. He seemed a cheerful young man, although his hair couldn't quite seem to make up its mind whether it wanted to be blond or red.

:Here we are—: Stefen announced proudly. *:I thought you'd like this place. It's very romantic.:*

Romantic? Hardly an adequate description for a place where trees overhung a mossy cup of a valley, where delicate flowers bloomed at precisely the right spots, and where a tiny waterfall trickled musically down the back wall of the valley, to fill a perfect, rock-rimmed basin just big enough for two if they cared for a little waterplay. In a candlemark or two the sun would be above the trees, warming this valley and the tiny pool.

Skif had the suspicion that Stefen had a hand in somehow creating this idyllic little hideaway, and was waiting for a reaction.

"This is . . . this is lovely," he said, finally. "I haven't seen anything prettier even in k'Sheyna Vale."

Stefen looked pleased as Nyara nodded agreement. *:I've been training the trees and the plants,:* he said diffidently. *:Not in the way of a Hawkbrother or anything, but—I'm glad you like it. Van likes it, but he's rather biased on my behalf.:*

"If you don't mind my asking," Skif said hesitantly, "Why have you two—you know, *stuck around* all this time?"

:Gods.: Stefen looked embarrassed. *:Responsibility, I suppose. I mean, we finished off magic in Valdemar, and until people were ready to accept Mage-Gift as just one more Gift,* someone *had to make certain that another*

wizard-lord like Leareth didn't come down out of the mountains with a mage-army. Van didn't trust his barriers against someone with Adept strength. So—: he shrugged, *:—here we are.:*

"And I suppose you planned on doing something to educate the next Herald-Mages?" Skif persisted.

:Well, only if there was no other way. We hadn't counted on Gwena getting things mucked up with all her grand plans and predestined paths. If there's anything that Van hates, it's a Glorious Destiny.: Stefen chuckled. *:If he's said it once, he's said it a hundred times. "Glorious Destinies get you Glorious Funerals." Anyway, mostly we're too busy watching for idiot fuzzy barbarians or mages with ambition trying to cross this border to pay too much attention to what's going on down south. Until Elspeth started flinging levin-bolts around, that is.:*

"So you have been aware of that?" Skif asked.

Stefen laughed silently. *:I should say, Van couldn't help but notice, she's in his bloodline, and he put that other spell on all his relatives so he'd know if anyone was trying to turn them into frogs or flatten them or something. That kind of thing persisted a lot longer than he thought it would, too.:*

"Perhaps your Vanyel is a better mage than even he gave himself credit for being," Nyara observed quietly.

Stefen favored her with a sweet smile. *:Once Elspeth started working magic in the Vales, that got his attention and he found out what was going on down there with you folks. He wanted to do something, but he knew his powers were pretty limited that far away. Eventually he started helping the Shin'a'in distract that nasty piece of work, Falconsbane. Sent mage winds to break all his windows, then replaced them with red glass, sent him black roses using a firebird as the carrier—we had a lot of fun with that. And the crystal paperweight with the castle and snow. Even 'Fandes enjoyed that.:*

"I imagine," Skif said dryly. "So now what do you plan for us?"

:Well, Van wanted me to talk to you two, actually. He says I'm better at emotional things, and he's afraid that— well, he knows that you two are not going to have an easy

*time of it. You know that, but it's still just an intellectual
exercise for you. You aren't really prepared for what's going to happen.:*

"It would help, Skif, if you tell me who these people
are—or were—" Nyara said plaintively, sitting down on a
rock and curling her legs underneath her. Skif took a
place beside her. "It is obvious that you and Firesong
trust them, but—"

Skif hit his forehead with the heel of his palm. "Oh,
hellfires. I'm sorry, Nyara—"

:There wasn't time,: Stefen reminded him. *:Why don't
you tell her, and I'll fill in what you don't know.:*

*:So, there it is. You've seen for yourself that the stories
about Van and 'Fandes and me being up here in Sorrows
are true,:* the spirit said cheerfully. *:It's been fun, actually. Maybe there are people who the Havens just won't
have!:*

Skif chuckled. Stefen was making it very easy to simply accept all this, acting quite like an ordinary human
and not at all like something out of legends. Perhaps he
was making a deliberate effort to do so; to Skif's mind
that was a great deal easier than having the two spirits appear, ten feet tall, carrying flaming swords, thundering
"Fear not!" There was a vitality and a lightness about the
spirit; in fact, there was something about him that kept
Skif from feeling worried or anxious when he had every
reason to.

For that matter, there was also a feeling of familiarity
about Stefen, as if he and the Bard had been old friends
of the kind that can say anything to each other, and forgive anything. . . .

"Skif, it seems to me—perhaps I am being forward,
but—" Nyara hesitated, then continued as Stefen nodded
encouragingly. "What he and Vanyel faced—between
them—there is a great deal in common with our situation."

:I think so,: Stefen agreed. *:So does Van. That's part
of why I wanted to talk with you.:* He shrugged. *:You'd
have thought that once we were a pair, everything would
have been lovely, but things kept happening that could*

have ruined it all. He spent a lot of time away from me. Not everyone accepted it. There were always things coming from outside of us that put strains on us, no matter what we did. Things were never perfect for more than a day at a time. Really—I think you would only harm yourselves if you expected perfection. You'd both just be unhappy when you didn't have it.: Stefen's attention was all on Nyara. *:And there is something else Van wanted me to tell you, Nyara. Your father is not sane by anyone's definition. What he did to you—wasn't sane. Insane people do things no one can anticipate.* Nothing that happened to you is your fault. *You didn't "deserve" it, or ask for it, or cause it. And what he did was not right. A parent who does that is a monster, and nothing more.:*

Skif and Need had been trying to tell her the same things, but it was as if a light had suddenly been kindled inside her. And Skif knew why. This was a total stranger, affirming what people she knew cared for her had been saying. And this was a spirit as well, who presumably had a little more insight into things than a still-living mortal. . . .

He shouldn't be jealous, just because it was Stefen who brought that light to her face and not him. And he knew he shouldn't be. But he couldn't help suffering a sharp stab of jealousy anyway.

:This won't be the last time you're jealous, old man,: said Stefen, and he somehow knew Stefen spoke only to him. *:She can't help what she is. There are those who will find her desirable only because she is exotic, and others who will be certain she cannot resist them. She was built for a single purpose, and it still marks her. You have hard times ahead.:*

Skif's jealousy turned to despair; how could he ever hope to hold Nyara once she entered Valdemar and began to meet others? Why should she wish to stay with him? There were people of wealth who had far more to offer than he did. He couldn't even offer her protection from the curious and the unkind. He was a Herald and had duties; he couldn't be with her every moment.

:Don't be a bigger ass than you have to be,: Stefen said sharply. *:She loves you, for one thing. And for another—*

you will likely be the only creature she ever encounters who sees and desires her for her, herself, and not as an object to be possessed. She has had quite enough of that in her life, and believe me, she knows how to recognize it when she sees it.:

Skif blinked as a bee buzzed near his face. He also would have blushed, if Stefen had not resumed the conversation as casually as if he had not interrupted it to talk to Skif alone. *:There's no great virtue in being lifebonded, you know. It's a lot like having a Predestined Fate; often uncomfortable, frequently inconvenient, usually hazardous.:*

Skif shook his head, and waved the bee away. He had often envied Talia and Dirk—how could Stefen say something like that? Wasn't being lifebonded the ultimate love?

"I thought lifebonding was something to be sought above all else," Nyara replied dubiously.

:That's the poets' and Bards' interpretation,: Stefen said with a grimace. *:It has far more to do with compatibility than with love, and the match is more random than, say—finding two people from different countries with exactly the same eye color. When you're lifebonded, your choices are limited to the things you both want, because if your lifebonded is unhappy, so are you. It takes two very strong, well-established personalities to make a lifebonded pair work, because if one is passive, he'll be eaten alive by the other.:*

"That doesn't sound very pleasant," Skif put in. "In fact it doesn't even sound—romantic. It sounds like a disease."

Stefen laughed. *:I don't know about a disease, but it isn't love, that's for certain, even though love usually cements the bond. Van thinks that it's likelier that someone with an extremely powerful Gift of some kind and a tendency to deep depression will be lifebonded than someone who is not so burdened and hag-ridden. That's so the Gifted-and-suicidal half has someone outside of himself to keep him stable and give him an external focus. But— all we know is that while it's rare, it isn't something to yearn after.:*

"To think I've envied Talia all this time—" Skif mused. And at Stefen's puzzled look, he added, "That's the current Queen's Own."

:Of course, the one with all the Empathy! 'Fandes al most swatted her once, when she thought the girl was going to lose all control.: Before Skif could express his surprise, Stefen went on. *:I liked her, though—so, she lifebonded? You shouldn't be too surprised. I'll bet I can describe her lifemate. Strong, kind, thoughtful, intelligent, tends to keep his feelings to himself, the kind of man everyone knows they can depend on. Little children and animals love him immediately.:*

"That's Dirk!" Skif exclaimed.

:So, that illustrates my point. Love now—a good, solid love is something infinitely rarer and more difficult to maintain, because you don't *know everything your partner is feeling. Love takes work. Love means being able to apologize and mean it when you blunder. Love is worth fighting for!:* Stefen sounded absolutely fierce. *:One of the very things that made what Van and I have a lovematch as well as a lifebonding was that we were so different. It is like a marriage—you marry who you* think *your beloved is, and then discover who they really are over the years. It's that discovery that makes a marriage work.:*

:We did have things in common, lots of them, but you would never have assumed that from first seeing us. It made hunting and finding them all the sweeter. And it gave us chances to introduce each other to something new. You two have that same opportunity. Van and I took pride in being different—we enjoyed the diversity to be found among people of all kinds, and we enjoyed the diversity in the two of us.:

Before Skif could react to this, Need spoke up. *:All very pretty, I'm sure,:* she said scathingly. *:But this is Skif we're talking about. You're assuming the young lout has enough imagination to recognize diversity.:*

"Of course he has imagination!" Nyara exclaimed immediately. "How can you say something so stupid?"

:Oh, he has about as much imagination as he has sensitivity,: Need continued as if she hadn't noticed Nyara's

angry exclamation. *:Frankly, I think both of you are giving him more credit than he deserves.:*

Skif wisely kept his mouth shut. He thought he saw what Need was up to. Furthermore, Stefen, after all his impassioned speeches, was keeping quite, quite silent—

And Nyara had taken his hand in a most unmistakably possessive manner. With her other hand, she drew Need from her sheath. Need rasped on. When she insulted Skif's sexual prowess, Nyara pitched the sword away with a hiss.

Skif held Nyara closer. She glared at the discarded sword.

:Well, I've tried to shake you before, but this is going to be the last time,: the sword said, sounding pleased. *:If I can't rattle your faith in each other, no one can.:*

:Exactly so, you crafty woman,: Stefen replied. *:You see, Skif? If her heart doesn't lie with you, then I know nothing of the heart—and as a Bard that has been my special study for a long time. And Nyara—he trusts you enough to allow you to fight your own battle and win, even when he is the target. Love is as much trust as it is devotion.:*

Nyara's face relaxed, then she snorted a tension-breaking laugh and picked up Need. "You fooled me again, you chunk of lead. But—I was not perfectly sure—I—"

Skif smiled. Life was very, very good at the moment.

:Oh, there is no such thing as perfection, or a "perfect" love—Van and I still argue and even become angry with each other,: Stefen countered. *:It annoys the birds and small animals to no end when we do. I doubt there is even perfection in the Havens. Wouldn't perfection be a bore?:*

:Build on what you have, children,: Need said gruffly. *:The foundation is a good one, so now see what kind of a house you can raise. And don't worry if the windows aren't the right size, the door is too tall, or there's dust on the mantelpiece. Just make sure the walls and the ceiling are sound, and make certain your home holds laughter. The dust will take care of itself.:*

"I think we can do that," Skif told Need, feeling much

better about the entire relationship than he ever had before "We'll certainly try." He squeezed Nyara's hand, not
noticing the claws. "And we'll succeed. Won't we?" he
finished, looking into her eyes.

"Oh, yes," she answered, smiling. "I know we will."

Chapter Six

Treyvan curled his tail around his haunches and waited beside the cave for his mate. He needed to have a discussion with her that he did not want anyone to overhear. Especially not certain interfering spirits. . . .

It had been two days since their unexpected arrival in the Forest of Sorrows. The gryphlets had taken it all in stride, as they always did, and found excuses to chase things and chew on them at every opportunity. Rris had been as faithful as a *hertasi* and infinitely patient. Firesong had apparently come to grips with his changing status—that is, not being fawned over—and his *dyheli* companion remained nonplussed. And Vree—well, Vree had resumed hunting crest-feathers. Treyvan tolerated that. It was something familiar in an unfamiliar environment.

It had taken that long to make certain everything was ready for the Gate to go up—and for Vanyel's protective spells to come down. When the moment came, it would feel to the gryphons like the magical equivalent of a change in air pressure before a storm, then all would be calm. Valdemar had been alerted, and there would be an escort waiting for Elspeth and her friends at the terminus of the Gate.

That would be at the entrance to the family chapel at Ashkevron Manor. It was the only place still standing intact that Vanyel knew well enough to make into a Gate-terminus. The chapel in Companion's Field was a ruin, and Elspeth could not honestly assure him that the Palace still looked the way it had when he was still alive. Doors had been sealed up, new doors had been cut—trim and decorations had been added and taken away.

But nothing ever changed in the core building of the Ashkevron home. Elspeth had told them all she recalled hearing some of the family actually boasting about just that. There was even a story that if anyone ever did anything besides add to the buildings, the ghost of some long-dead ancestor would rise out of the grave to haunt the one who dared change what he had wrought.

Firesong had been of two minds about going on with Elspeth, until Vanyel had brought out an argument the spirit had held in reserve. It had been on the afternoon of the first day, when the Hawkbrother had said, dubiously, "It is all very well for Darkwind to follow Elspeth into her land, but what ties have I to such a place? Especially when I have duties elsewhere. And while it is true enough that I have experience with a living Heartstone, well, so does Darkwind. He knew enough before he became a scout to be counted among the Adepts."

Vanyel had nodded, acknowledging the truth of that. But then he had countered that argument. *:It is the duty of the Tayledras to heal places where magic has gone wrong,:* he pointed out. *:And that is doubly the duty of a Healing Adept, such as you. True?:*

"True enough," Firesong had replied, warily.

:Well, then, is it not the duty of a Tayledras Healing Adept to prevent the misuse of magic that could poison the earth?:

"I—" Firesong had begun, even more warily. "I suppose so—"

:Then what of the consequences if the Heartstone beneath Haven fell into the hands of Ancar and his mages? What if its power were to be mismanaged through igno-

rance? Isn't it the duty of a Healing Adept to be as concerned with prevention as with results? Shouldn't, in fact, a Healing Adept be more concerned with prevention?: Vanyel had simply looked at Firesong, as a teacher looks at a student who has failed to study.

Treyvan had seen Elspeth suppress a smile. He knew that she wouldn't be able to resist the opportunity to pay Firesong back. "My stepfather has the earth-sense that a lot of the rulers of Rethwellan have," she had put in. "He says that Ancar does horrible things to the earth-magics in Hardorn—that during the last war he rode through a place where the magics had been so misused that the area was dying, and it made him ill just to ride across it."

Vanyel had nodded, as if to say, "There—you see?" and had turned his unwavering gaze back to Firesong.

The young Adept had grumbled something under his breath. "This is blackmail, you know," he had retorted at last. But when Vanyel did not reply, he had shaken his head, and finally given his reluctant agreement to go. "It may be blackmail, but it is also true," he had admitted, and had gone off to tell his Clan of the change in plans. "I shudder to think how fickle my home Vale will regard me after all these changes of plan."

Now it was Treyvan's turn to make a similar decision. Or rather, Treyvan and his mate, together, for he would make no such important decisions without her. They were explorers by choice. They had chosen, together, to be adventurers until the day fortune dashed them on the rocks. Their names would already live on in the stories told by their Clan, Treyvan knew, and perhaps even become legendary after a few more generations. Hadn't they done enough, after all?

Hydona came winging in from above, fanning her wings to break her dive and landing with practiced ease on the grass beside him. "Do not tell me," she said, snatching playfully at his crest-feathers. "I think I can guesss alrready. You wisssh usss to go with young Elssspeth and Darrrkwind."

He felt his eyes going round with surprise, and his beak gaped. "But how did you know?" he exclaimed. "Sssurely I sssaid nothing—"

"No, only you have hung upon everrry worrd of thisss Vanyel, and your earrrtuftsss have twitched each time sssomeone hasss even hinted of the grrryphonsss in the Norrth of Valdemarrr." She shook her head vigorously, and a loose feather flew off and drifted down like a leaf to land in the grass beside her.

He was chagrined, but he had to admit that she was probably right; he *had* been that transparent. But how could he not be? Every Kaled'a'in gryphon knew that of all of the gryphon-wings flying for Mage Urtho, fully half of them had never reached the Gate that had taken the Kaled'a'in safely away before Urtho's stronghold fell. Most of those had been out on the front lines with the army. Of those, some must have died—but surely others had escaped to live elsewhere. There were more than enough mages in Urtho's army to have set up Gates enough to take those fighting to safety as well, before or after the blast that obliterated Urtho's stronghold and Ma'ar's together.

The only way to find out—or at least the only way that would satisfy Treyvan—would be to try to find these gryphons themselves.

"We arrre magesss," Hydona pointed out thoughtfully. "And both the little onesss have Mage-Gift alssso. We will need to trrrain them—ssso why not trrrain otherrrsss at the sssame time?"

"What, like Herrraldsss?" The idea had already occurred to him, but he was pleased that Hydona had thought of it as well. "It isss trrrue that it would do the little onesss a grrreat deal of good to have sssome competition bessidesss each otherrr. And it could gain usss valuable alliesss."

Her beak gaped in a gentle grin. Oh, how beautiful she was! "My thought prrrecisssely. Thisss issss why I have alrrready told Vanyel that if you wisshed to go, I would not arrrgue with sssuch a change in plansss."

He mock-snapped at her. "Imperrrtinent! Making asssumptionsss—"

"Perrrfectly valid onesss," she pointed out, reaching out to preen his ears. He submitted to her readily, half-closing his eyes in pleasure. "I, of all alive, know you besssst."

"Verrry well, then," he said, with feigned reluctance. "I will misss going to Evendim, but perrrhapsss anotherrr time. If you will have it that way, tell thisss Vanyel that we will be going with Elssspth and our otherrr ssson." He sighed. "I sssupposse it isss jusst asss well. With the way Gating hasss been lately, who knowsss where we might end up otherrrwissse?"

"Mmm," she agreed, mouth full of his feathers.

He closed his eyes completely, and gave himself up to her ministrations.

Ancar started, as a huskily feminine and far-too-familiar voice startled him in the midst of searching through a chest of documents in the war-room.

"Well. What a pleasant surprise. I had *not* expected to find you here."

The silky-smooth tone of Hulda's voice sent a shiver of warning up Ancar's back. She only sounded this sweet when she wanted something—or when she was about to confront him over something, and she knew she had the upper hand.

He straightened, slowly, schooling his face into an impassive mask. He should not fear this woman. He had already subdued a powerful, half-human Adept to his will. She was no greater in power than this "Falconsbane" creature. He had no reason to fear her anger.

But her appearance was not reassuring. She was impeccably gowned and coiffed, looking as near to demure as she ever got. That meant she had found out something that she didn't like, and she was going to have it out with him, here and now.

While he smiled and granted her an ironic little bow, his thoughts raced behind his careful shields. Could she have discovered Falconsbane? But how? He had been so careful. No one came near the creature but those servants he himself controlled.

"Why, my dear teacher, how pleasant to see *you,* after so very long," he replied carefully. "I had thought that your new young friend was occupying all your time—"

"Enough fencing, child," she snapped at him. "We both know you've been up to something, meddling with energies you shouldn't have touched! And so does every mage sensitive to the flows of power! Your fumbling created some unpleasant echoes and ripples that are *still* causing me problems with my own spells, and I wonder how any of your pets are getting anything at all done!"

"My fumblings?" He felt sweat trickling down his back beneath his heavy velvet tunic, and he hoped that he wasn't sweating anywhere that she would notice. "What are you talking about?" Could it be that she actually didn't know what he had done?

"Don't try to toy with me, boy!" she growled. "You were playing with some kind of odd spell or other, and it was either something you made up yourself, or something you got out of one of your damned scraps of half-literate grimoires! Which was it?"

Before he could answer, she cut him off with a gesture. "Never mind," she said. "Don't bother to lie to me. I'll tell you what it was. You were trying to build a Gate, weren't you?"

He stared at her dumbly as she continued, her strange violet eyes flashing with scorn.

"You haven't even the sense to *fear* a Gate Spell, you fool!" she snarled. "Don't you know what the thing would have done if you hadn't broken it first? It would have turned back on you and eaten you alive! Building a Gate without knowing *where* you want it to go, precisely and exactly where, is the kind of mistake that will be your last! You must have used up a lifetime's worth of luck to escape that fate, you blithering idiot."

She went on and on at some length in the same vein; he simply hung his head so that she could not see his eyes and nodded like the foolish child she had named him. He stared at his feet as his sweat cooled, and his flush of fear faded. But beneath his submissive behavior, he was wildly excited and he did not want her to realize what she had just told him.

She had answered his every question about the so-called "portal" he had created! It was not a way to pull in node-energy, but was instead something entirely different, a way to create a doorway that would lead him instantly to any place he chose!

She had given him a weapon of incredible power and versatility, without knowing what she had done. Already he could imagine hundreds of ways to use such doorways.

He could simply step through such a door and into the very heart of a citadel. He could move entire armies without wearying them. He could use these doors to obtain anything or anyone he wanted, without worrying about such pesky complications as guards, locks, or discovery. . . .

As she railed on, pacing back and forth like a restless panther in her black velvet, he also realized from what she did *not* say that she was completely unaware that he had brought anything through his Gate.

She mentioned nothing of the sort, in fact, not even as a horrible possibility. She seemed to be under the impression that he had sensed the Gate turning back on him and, in a panic, had broken the spell, collapsing the Gate upon itself.

He kept his face stiff and expressionless. He answered her, when she demanded answers, in carefully phrased sentences designed to maintain that fiction. The longer he could keep Falconsbane a secret from her, the better.

At least, until the moment that the Adept had recovered enough to bring him openly into the court as a putative ally. That way he would be able to work with Falconsbane without fear of Hulda's reactions.

She has her friends, the ambassador and his entourage from the Emperor . . . I should introduce Falconsbane as an envoy from the West, beyond Valdemar. She may even try to win him over. He'd appeal to her, I expect. Perhaps I should even let her seduce him—or him, her. I'm not certain which of the two would be the quicker to take the other. . . .

As she used up her anger, wearing it out against the rock of his submission, her voice dropped and her pacing slowed. Finally she stopped and faced him.

"Look at me," she demanded. Slowly, as if he were afraid of her continued wrath, he raised his eyes. "Do not *ever* attempt that spell again," she said, in a tone that brooked no argument. "It is beyond you. It is far more dangerous than you can guess, and it is *well* beyond your current ability and skill. Furthermore, it is obvious that you do not have the whole of the instructions for such a spell. Half-understood spells are more dangerous to the caster than to anyone else. Is that understood?"

He nodded, meekly. "Yes, Hulda," he replied softly. She gave him a sharp look, but evidently did not see anything there to make her suspect his duplicity.

"See that you remember it, then," she said, and turned on her heel and left in a swirl of velvet skirts.

Ancar could hardly contain his excitement. If Hulda knew enough to identify this Gate Spell simply by the effects it had on the mage-energies of the area, how much more could his captive know? He burned to find out.

But he did nothing. Not immediately, anyway. Hulda almost certainly had someone watching him; she might even be watching him herself. If he ran off now, he would lead her to his captive.

So he continued with the task that had brought him here in the first place; unearthing a long-ignored map of the west and south, which included Valdemar and what little was known of the area beyond that land. If Falconsbane came from anywhere about there, he might be able to identify the spot on this map.

The map lay at the very bottom of the document chest, amid the dust and dirt of years of neglect. Ancar unrolled it to be certain that it was still readable, then rolled it back up and inserted it in a map tube for safekeeping.

Even then he did not hurry off to where his captive waited for him. Instead, he tended to several small problems that needed his personal touch, heard the reports of his seneschal and the keeper of his treasury, and looked over the written reports of those mages watching the border of Valdemar. He stuck the map tube in his belt and pretended to forget it was there.

Only then did he leave the central portion of the palace and stroll in the direction of the wing to which he had moved his captive once the creature began to recover properly.

As far as he could tell, there was no one observing his

movements at that point, although there had been at least one guard and two servants covertly keeping an eye on him right up until the moment he began looking over the written reports from his mages.

He allowed himself a small smile of victory and put a little more haste into his steps.

The new quarters were an improvement over the old, which had been reasonably luxurious, although not what Falconsbane was used to. This was clearly a suite in Ancar's palace, albeit in a very old section of the palace. Age did not matter; what mattered was that it bore all the signs of having been unused for some time, but it had not been cleaned and refurbished hastily. Some care had been taken to clean and air the place thoroughly, and to ensure that everything was in proper order for the kind of "guest" that the King would consider important.

This somewhat mollified Falconsbane, but only in part. Ancar had not removed or eased the coercions, and his own body continued to betray him with weakness.

He sat now in a supportive chair, padded with cushions. A table within reach bore wine and fruit. Soft light from candles set throughout the room provided ample illumination—making up for the fact that the windows were closely shuttered, and no amount of threat or cajolery on Falconsbane's part would get the servants to open them. Ancar had delivered his orders, it seemed, and they were not to be disobeyed.

The King had arrived for his daily visit, and there seemed to be much on his mind, not all of it satisfactory. He immediately plunged into a flurry of demands for information, demands which had little or no apparent relationship to each other.

"I cannot properly answer your questions," Falconsbane said, with more far more seeming patience than he truly felt, "unless you explain to me what your situation is."

He kept his tone even and calm, pitching it in such a way as to do no more than border on the hypnotic and seductive. He had tried both seduction and fascination a few days ago, in an effort to persuade the upstart to release some of the coercions—and had come up against a surprising wall of resistance. After contemplating the situation, he had come to the conclusion that this resistance to subversion had not come about by accidental *or* true design.

No, there was someone in Ancar's life who had once wielded these very weapons against him to control him, someone he no longer trusted. Thus, the resistance. Falconsbane would have to use a more subtle weapon than body or mind.

He would have to use words.

An exasperating prospect. This sort of thing took time and patience. He did not wish to take the time, and he had little love for exercising patience.

However needful it might be.

However, the fact that Ancar had this core of resistance at all told him one very important fact. There was someone in this benighted place that had once controlled the little fool, and who might still do so.

That someone—given Ancar's biases—was probably female and attractive. That in itself was interesting, because attractive females seldom lost power until they lost their attraction.

He needed to find out more about this woman, whoever, whatever she was. And he needed to discover who had taught the King enough so that the boy was able to command the power of a Gate, however inexpertly and briefly.

Ancar looked away uneasily, as he always did when Falconsbane fixed him with that particular stare. It was as if the youngster found even the appearance of patience unnerving. The soft candlelight touched the boy-King's face; it was a handsome face, with no hint of the excesses fearfully whispered about among the servants.

Had his own servants whispered? Probably. Had their whispers mattered? Only in that rumors made them fear him, and fear made them obey him. Small wonder the child held the reins, given the fear his servants displayed.

"I don't know what you mean," Ancar said. He was lying, but Falconsbane did not intend him to escape so easily.

"You ask me many questions about magic, in a most haphazard manner, and I can see no pattern behind what you wish to know. Yet there must *be* one. If you will simply tell me what drives these questions, perhaps I can give you better answers."

Ancar contemplated that for a moment, then rubbed his wrist uneasily. "I have enemies," he said, after a long moment.

Falconsbane permitted himself a slight snort of contempt. "You are a King. Every King has enemies," he pointed out. "You must be more specific if I am to help you. Are these enemies within your court, within your land, or outside of both?"

Ancar moved, very slightly.

Falconsbane could read the language of body and expression as easily as a scholar a book in his own language. Ancar had winced when Falconsbane had said, "within your court." So there were forces working against the King from within. Could the woman Falconsbane had postulated be one of those forces?

"Those within it are the ones that most concern me," he finally replied, as Falconsbane continued to fix him with an unwavering gaze.

The Adept nodded shrewdly. "Those who once were friends," he said flatly, making it a statement, and was rewarded once again by that faint wince. And something more. "No," he amended, "*More* than friends." Not relatives; he knew from questioning the servants that Ancar had assassinated his own father. "Lovers?" he hazarded.

Ancar started, but recovered quickly. "A lover," he agreed, the words emerging with some reluctance.

Falconsbane nodded, but lidded his eyes with feigned disinterest. "Such enemies are always the bitterest and most persistent." Dared he make a truly hazardous statement? Well, why not? "And generally, their hate is the greatest. They pursue revenge long past the point when another would have given over."

Slight relaxation told him his shot went wide of the mark. So, this woman was not aware she had lost her powers over the boy!

He made a quick recovery. "But she is foolish not to

recognize that you are the one who hates, and not her. So she has lost her power over you, yet thinks she still possesses you." He smiled very slightly as Ancar started again. Good. Now ask a revealing question. "Why do you permit her to live, if you are weary of her?"

His question had caught the King off-guard, enough that the boy actually answered with the truth. "Because she is too powerful for me to be rid of her."

Falconsbane held his own surprise in check. Too powerful? The King could not *possibly* mean that she had secular power; he ruled his land absolutely; and took what he wanted from it. Servants had revealed that much, quite clearly. He could not mean rank, for Ancar had eliminated any other pretender to his throne, and anyone who had force of will or arms to challenge him.

There was only one thing the boy *could* mean, then. The woman was a more powerful mage than Ancar. Too powerful to subvert, too powerful to destroy. Hence, his desire for an equally powerful ally.

Many things fell into place at that moment, and Falconsbane decided to hazard all on a single cast of the dice. "Ah. Your teacher. A foolish thing, to make a lover of a student. It blinds the teacher to the fact that the student develops a will and a series of goals of his own, eventually; goals that may not match with that of the teacher. And it causes the teacher to believe that love or lust are, indeed, enough to make one blind, deaf, and dumb to faults."

Blank astonishment covered Ancar's face for an instant, then once again, he was all smoothness. "I am astonished by your insight," he replied, as if a moment before he had not had every thought frozen with shock. "Is this a power every Adept has?"

"By no means," Falconsbane replied lazily, picking up the goblet of wine on the table beside his chair, and sipping it for a moment. "If your loving teacher had such ability to read people, she would never have lost your affections, and we would not now be having this conversation. You would still be in her control."

Ancar nodded curtly as if he hated having to admit that this unknown woman had *ever* held him under control.

And he did not contradict Falconsbane's implication that his teacher was an Adept. Not surprising, then, the bitterness that crept through his careful mask. This young man was a foolish and proud man, and one who despised the notion that *anyone* could control him, much less a mere woman.

Foolish, indeed. Sex had much to do with power, but little to do with the ability of the wielder to guide it. Falconsbane had seen as many female Adepts in his time as male, and had made a point of eliminating the female rivals as quickly as possible, before they realized that he was a threat. It was easier to predict the thoughts and intentions of one's own sex, and that unpredictability was what made one enemy more dangerous than another.

This changed the complexion of his plans entirely, however. Ancar was not the dangerous one here; this woman was.

"Tell me of this woman," Falconsbane said casually. "All that you know." And as Ancar hesitated, he added, "If I do not know all, I cannot possibly help you adequately."

That apparently decided the boy. Now, at last, the information Falconsbane needed to put together a true picture of the situation here began to flow into his waiting ears and mind.

He felt a certain astonishment and startlement himself, several times, but he fancied he kept his surprise hidden better than Ancar had. This woman—this *Hulda*—was certainly an Adept of great power, and if she had not underestimated her former pupil, he would have granted her the accolade of great cleverness as well.

She was, at the minimum, twice, perhaps three times as old as she looked. This was not necessarily illusion; as Falconsbane knew well, exercise of moderation in one's vices, and access to a ready supply of victims to drain of life-forces, permitted an Adept to reach an astonishing age and still remain in a youthful stasis. One paid for it, eventually, but as Ma'ar had learned, when "eventually" came to pass, all those years might grant one the time needed to find another sort of escape from old age, death, and dissolution.

She had first attempted to subvert the young Heir of Valdemar, that same child he had seen and desired. Had she been aware of the girl's potential? Probably; even as an infant it should have been obvious to an Adept that the girl would be a mage of tremendous strength when she came into her power. Small wonder that "Hulda"—if that was her real name, which Falconsbane privately doubted—had attempted the girl first, before turning to Ancar as a poor second choice.

Ancar was not entirely clear how and why Hulda had been thwarted from her attempt to control the girl. Perhaps he didn't know. There was no reason for Hulda to advertise her defeat, after all, or the reasons for it. Ancar had been given the impression at the time—an impression, or rather illusion, that he still harbored—that Hulda had given up on the girl when she had become aware of *him*.

Falconsbane hid his amusement carefully. There was no point in letting the boy know just how ridiculous a notion that really was. It would gain him nothing, and might lose him yet more freedom if Ancar tightened his coercions in pique. One *might* choose a handful of wild berries and nuts in preference to a feast of good, red meat, but it would be a stupid choice. So, too, would choosing to subvert Ancar in preference to the young woman.

But apparently she had no options. So, after being routed from Valdemar, Hulda had turned her eyes toward Hardorn and had found fertile ground for her teachings and manipulations in the heir to *that* throne. She had promised, cajoled, and eventually seduced her way into Ancar's life, and had orchestrated everything he did from the moment she climbed into his bed until very recently.

But she had been incredibly stupid, for she had forgotten that all things are subject to change, and had grown complacent of late. She neglected her student for other interests. She promised, but failed to deliver upon those promises. Meanwhile Ancar tasted the exercise of power, and he found it a heady and eye-opening draught. He began to crave more of it, and that was when he realized that Hulda held more of it than he did—or ever would, while she lived.

So, although they had once been allies and even partners, they were now locked in a silent struggle for supremacy that Hulda had only now begun to recognize.

Falconsbane toyed with his goblet, listened, and nodded, saying nothing. Certainly he did not give voice to the contempt that he felt for this petty kinglet and mageling. Under any other circumstances he would have been able to crush Ancar like an overripe grape. He still *could,* if the coercions were eased sufficiently.

He learned also how little Ancar truly knew; how effective Hulda had been in denying him any training that might make him a threat to her power. His obsession with Gates now—if Falconsbane were not certain that the coercions binding him would probably cause the destruction of his mind if Ancar came to harm, he would have encouraged the fool's obsessions and illusions. The boy did not realize that he had no *chance* of ever controlling a real Gate. He simply did not have the strength. He had not figured out that a Gate could only go to places he himself had been, and not, as he fondly imagined, to any place he chose. He didn't really believe, despite the way he had been drained and the warnings in his fragment of manuscript, that Gate-energy came from *him* and not any outside sources of power like a node or energy-reserves.

Continued experiments would be certain to get him killed, and in a particularly nasty and messy fashion. Despite how much fun it would be to watch as his body was drained to a husk, there was the possibility that the royal whelp could tap Falconsbane's energy to save himself. That would be difficult to survive in his present state. So Falconsbane dissuaded Ancar from the idea, gently but firmly, pointing out that Hulda had known that he had been tinkering with the spell, and that she would certainly be on the watch for anything else of the sort. "Patience," he advised, as Ancar frowned. "First, we must rid ourselves of this aged female. *Then* I shall teach you the secrets of Greater Magics."

The power struggle between these two held far more promise of turning the tables on Ancar than anything else Falconsbane had yet observed. He noted how Ancar brightened at his last words, and smiled lazily.

"You can rid me of her?" the boy asked eagerly.

Falconsbane waved his hand languidly. "In time," he said. "I am not yet recovered; I must study the situation—and her. It would assist me greatly if you could manufacture a way to bring me into court, where I could observe her with my own eyes, and see what she is and is not capable of. I may note weaknesses in her armor, and I may know of ways to exploit those weaknesses that you do not."

Ancar nodded, his face now betraying both avidity and anticipation. "I had planned to introduce you as a kind of envoy, an ambassador from a potential Western ally. You must mask your powers from her, of course—"

"Of course," Falconsbane interrupted, with a yawn. "But this must wait until I have recovered all of my strength." He allowed his eyelids to droop. "I am—most fatigued," he murmured. "I become weary so easily. . . ."

He watched from beneath his lids and Ancar was taken in by his appearance of cooperation. Good. Perhaps the boy would become convinced that the coercions were no longer needed. Perhaps he could be persuaded to remove them, on the grounds that they depleted him unnecessarily. Perhaps he would even remove them without any persuasion, secure in his own power and the thought that Falconsbane was his willing ally.

And perhaps Falconsbane would even *be* his willing ally.

For now.

Chapter Seven

An'desha felt sick, smudged with something so foul that he could hardly bear himself. It was a very physical feeling, although, strictly speaking, he no longer had a body to feel any of those things with. The spirits had warned him that he would encounter uncomfortable and unpleasant things in Falconsbane's memories. But neither they nor his own brief glimpses during his years of desperate hiding of what Falconsbane had done with his borrowed body had prepared him for the terrible things he confronted during that first look into Falconsbane's past.

For most of the day after his first foray into the Adept's memory, he had withdrawn quickly into his safe haven and had figuratively curled up there, shaken and nauseated, and unable to think. But his "haven" was really not "safe," and nothing would make the images acid-etched into his own memory go away. Still, he remained knotted about himself, tangled in a benumbed and sickened mental fog, right up until the arrival of some of King Ancar's servants. It seemed that the King had new plans for his captive; they had come to move the Adept to different quarters.

That move shook him out of his shock, although he had not paid a great deal of attention to Ancar before this. It occurred to him that he did not really know much about the Adept's captor. Ancar wanted something of Falconsbane—knowledge, power—but he might simply be ambitious and not evil. That made him think that he might be able to find some kind of ally among these people, someone who could help him to overcome Falconsbane and restore him to control of his much-abused body again.

After all, the spirits had not said he would be unable to find help here, they had simply offered him one possible option. And it was a Shin'a'in belief that the Goddess was most inclined to aid those who first put every effort into helping themselves.

So when Falconsbane was settled into his new, and to Shin'a'in eyes, bewilderingly luxurious suite of rooms, An'desha kept his own "ears" open to the gossip of the servants, hoping to learn something about the young King who had them in his possession. After all, if the King was a strong enough mage to put coercions on Falconsbane and keep them in force, he might be strong enough to overcome the Adept. Mornelithe Falconsbane's contempt of Ancar of Hardorn notwithstanding, the young King might very well have knowledge that would give him an edge even over someone like Mornelithe.

But watching and listening, both to the servants' gossip and to the questions that Ancar put to Falconsbane, dashed An'desha's hopes before they had a chance to grow too far. Ancar was just another sort as Falconsbane—younger, less steeped in depravity, with fewer horrific crimes to his account. But that was all too clearly not for lack of trying.

Ancar cared nothing for others, except to determine if and how they might be used to further his own ends. His only concern was for himself, his powers, and his pleasures. If he learned of An'desha's existence, he would only use that knowledge to get more of an edge over his captive. He might even betray An'desha's presence to the unwitting Adept in the very moment that he learned of it, if he thought it would gain him something. And he would do so without a second thought, destroying a soul as casually as any other man might eat a radish.

He had brief hopes again, when he learned of the existence of the mysterious woman rival in Ancar's life—how could a woman who was Ancar's rival be anything but Ancar's very opposite? But then Ancar's own descriptions destroyed the vision of a woman of integrity opposing the King and his henchmen. Even taking Ancar's words with a great deal of leaven, this *Hulda* was no more to be trusted than Ancar himself.

He learned far more than he cared to about her, nevertheless. Once he had admitted Hulda's existence and their former relationship, Ancar answered all of Falconsbane's questions with casual callousness, describing their relationship in appalling detail, and the things she had taught him, often by example, with a kind of nostalgia. And the woman was just as much a monster as her pupil—perhaps more, for Ancar had no knowledge of anything she might have done before she came into his father's employ. So ducing the young child she had been hired to teach and protect was the least of her excesses. . . .

It was a horrible education for An'desha. His uncle had claimed that the so-called "civilized" people of the other lands were the real barbarians, and at the moment An'desha would vouch for that wholeheartedly. No Shin'a'in would ever sink to the depths that Ancar described, and as for Falconsbane—

No Shin'a'in would ever *believe* anyone would do what the Beast had done.

These people were *all* scum!

He longed, with an intensity that made him sick, for the clean sweep of the Dhorisha Plains and the simpler life of a herd guard. What matter if his kin were sometimes cruel, sometimes taunted him for being a halfbreed? What matter if he had been forced into the life of a shaman? He would *never* have had to experience any of this, never *know* that his body had done *these things,* had performed *those acts.* He would never have been forced to look into the depths of Falconsbane's soul and realize that no matter what he saw now, there was probably something much worse in the Adept's memory that he simply hadn't uncovered yet.

The most evil men in recent Shin'a'in history were those men who had slaughtered Clan Tale'sedrin, down to the last and littlest child—except for the famed Tarma shena Tale'sedrin who had declared blood-feud, been taken as Swordsworn, then tracked them down and eliminated them all. But compared to Mornelithe Falconsbane, all of the crimes of all of those men combined were a single poisonous weed in the poisoned lands of the Pelagir Hills, or a grain of sand in the glass-slagged crater that had in the long-distant past, become the Plains at the Hand of the Star-Eyed.

The young Shin'a'in huddled inside Falconsbane's mind—*no, it is* my *mind*—as the conversation with Ancar went on and on, trying to hold in his revulsion and mask his presence, and expecting at any moment to be discovered. And An'desha had never in his entire life felt quite so young, petrified with fear, and quite so helpless. Despite the protections the Avatars had taught him, if Falconsbane found him, he would have no way to prevent the Adept from crushing him out of all existence.

But somehow, those protections held. Either Falconsbane was not as all-powerful as he *thought,* or else the Avatars were more powerful than they claimed.

Ancar left at last, as Falconsbane's feigned weariness became real weariness. And when he dozed off in the chair, An'desha crept out of hiding, to stare at a candle flame and try to think out his meager options.

Ancar was repulsive, but an old Shin'a'in proverb held that anything could be used as a weapon in a case of desperation. *You can kill a man who wishes to destroy you with a handful of maggots if you must.* Could An'desha possibly deceive the King long enough to win himself free? *I could reveal myself to Ancar as an ally, and think up some story that makes it look as if I have more power than I really do.* Well, yes. That was a possibility. And if everything worked properly, he *might* get his body back *if* Ancar could overwhelm Falconsbane. But Ancar had no reason to trust An'desha, and every reason to want one more hold over the Adept. What did An'desha have to offer? The knowledge contained in Falconsbane's memory, assuming it was still *there* after Falconsbane was gone— yes, he did have that. But he had no practical experience as a mage; no idea how to handle all these energies. And truth to tell, he was terrified of them. If Ancar asked for proof of his power, what could An'desha offer? Not much. Nothing that would convince Ancar, who was a suspicious man and saw deception everywhere.

Well, what went for Ancar also went for the woman. More so, actually, since Ancar wanted Falconsbane to increase his own power, and the woman would naturally want to eliminate *both* of them once she discovered the conspiracy against her. He would need to offer nothing more than access to Falconsbane—he could turn the tables on both Ancar and Falconsbane, and reveal himself to this "Hulda." But *she* was an Adept as well, and she would be just as likely to use An'desha to destroy Falconsbane, then proceed to finish the job by ridding herself of An'desha. What did *she* need him for, after all? She had power of her own, and no fear of using it. And she was just as depraved as her former pupil. More; after all, she had schooled him in depravity.

There was a last possibility, as disgusting as it was. He could reveal his presence to Falconsbane, and strike a bargain with him. The "coercions" Falconsbane kept thinking about had been put on the Adept, not on An'desha. If Falconsbane cared to remain in a passive mode and simply instruct An'desha, the Shin'a'in might be able to use their powers to free both of them. . . .

Yes, he could try to strike a bargain to that effect. Offer Falconsbane the way out of this gilded trap in return for simple survival; taking no more than he already had, a little corner of the Adept's mind.

Except that such a bargain would make him no better than Falconsbane; to *know* everything the creature had done and turn a blind eye to it in the hope of staying "alive" was as nauseating as anything Falconsbane himself had ever done. It would be a betrayal of all those Falconsbane had destroyed. Further, such a plan assumed Falconsbane would actually keep any bargain he made,

and nothing of what An'desha knew of him gave any reassurance the Adept would do any such thing.

He felt tied into a hundred knots by conflicting emotions. Only one thing really seemed clear. None of these
folk were worth helping. If any of them had ever done a
single decent thing in all their lives, they had certainly
take pains to insure it went undiscovered.

I must listen to the Avatars and remain quiet. That was
still not only the best plan, it was the only plan. *I must
help the Avatars as they ask; I must hope they can help
me. That is the only plan, the only decent course to take.*

:Wise choice, little one.: Tre'valen's voice rang in his
mind, so clearly that he glanced around, startled, looking
for another physical presence in the room. But there was
no one there; Tre'valen and Dawnfire rarely made physical manifestations since their first appearance. He understood why now; such things made a disturbance that
could be sensed, if one were looking for it with the inner
eye.

:Let the Falconsbane sleep,: the shaman-Avatar continued. *:Meet us upon the Moonpaths, where we cannot be
overheard or overlooked.:*

With relief, An'desha abandoned his hold on the body
he and Falconsbane shared, and turned his focus in the direction Tre'valen had taught him, *within and without.*
There was a moment of dizziness, a moment of darkness,
and a moment in which he felt he was falling and flying
at the same time. Then he found himself standing upon a
patch of pristine white sand, in a world made of mist and
light, and all that had transpired in the time it took to
draw a quick breath.

Tre'valen and Dawnfire were already there, looking
quite ordinary, actually, although they glowed with a soft,
diffused inner light. It was easier to "see" them here;
Tre'valen looked like any of the younger shaman of the
Clans, as familiar as his horse or saddle. Lovely Dawnfire
on the other hand was garbed in odd clothing that made
her look like a slender birch tree wrapped in snow—her
hair was long and as white as a snowdrift—and she was
as exotic as he had imagined the Hawkbrothers to be
when he had first run off to seek them. But her smile and

her wink made her still enough like a young scout of the Shin'a'in that he felt comfortable around her.

Except when he looked directly into the eyes of either of them . . . for they shared the same eyes, eyes without pupil, iris, or white; eyes the same bright-spangled black of a starry night sky. The Eyes of the Warrior . . . and the single sign that they were truly Her creatures. Those eyes made him shiver with awe and not a little dread, and reminded him that whatever they *had* been, these two Avatars were not human anymore.

So he tried to avoid looking into their eyes at all; not at all difficult, really, since he tended to keep his own glance fixed firmly on his own clasped hands whenever he spoke with them on the Moonpaths. Strange, how his body *here* looked like the one he had worn before he left his Clan and home, and not like the strange half-beast creature that Mornelithe Falconsbane had twisted it into.

"We have a new teaching for you, An'desha," Tre'valen said matter-of-factly. "It should help you seal your control over Falconsbane's body so that when he sleeps you will not awaken him by moving the body about."

Even as he spoke, An'desha felt Dawnfire's mental "hand" brush the surface of his own mind, and he absorbed the lesson effortlessly. And he even managed to smile shyly up into those two pairs of unhuman eyes, in thanks.

He took all the time he needed to study the implanted memory, to examine it and walk its pathway until he was certain he could follow their lesson exactly. And it was a most welcome gift. Such an ability *would* make things easier for him, for if Falconsbane's healing body demanded food while he slept, or made other needs known, such things would eventually wake the Adept so that An'desha must quickly and quietly retreat into watchful hiding. Now he would be able to silence the needs of the body before Falconsbane woke, and that would give him more uninterrupted time in full control. It was only when Falconsbane slept soundly, for instance, that An'desha dared to walk the Moonpaths. He feared, and so had the Avatars warned, that if Falconsbane woke while An'desha was "absent," An'desha would not be able to rejoin his body without the Adept noticing that something was different.

"Be patient, An'desha," Tre'valen said, but in a voice full of sympathy and kindness. "We know how tempting it must be to try to find some other, quicker way to rid yourself of the beast. But truly, our way is the surest, and even it is uncertain. We give you only a *chance,* but it is a chance with honor. There would be much less honor in any of the other paths you have contemplated. None of these people are worth the backing, as you yourself thought, much less worth making even temporary allies of them. Even trying to deceive them would be fraught with both peril and dishonor."

He hung his head in embarrassment and a little shame. Tre'valen was right, of course. And it had been making a choice with no concern for honor that had gotten him here in the first place, a fact that Tre'valen kindly omitted to mention.

"If you are very, very careful," Dawnfire continued in her high, husky voice, "you will even have ample opportunity to undermine *all* of them. *She* knows; She has faith in your good heart. Remember the Black Riders."

He looked up again and nodded. *The Swordsworn seldom miss their marks. The Leshy'a Kal'enedral, never.* That was a Shin'a'in proverb as old as the Swordsworn themselves. And yet, in shooting at Falconsbane, ostensibly to kill, they *had* missed, and had left the body holding both An'desha and Falconsbane alive. Then the Black Riders had appeared, bringing gifts that Falconsbane had thought were for him, but were truly for An'desha—a tiny black horse, the kind given to a child on his birthday, the token that he was ready for his first *real* horse and would be permitted to pick out a foal to train on his own. And the black ring, the ring Tre'valen had told him was worn only by those sworn to the service of all *four* faces of the Goddess. An'desha now knew, as Falconsbane did not, that if the Adept had ever held the ring up to strong sunlight, the seemingly opaque black ring would show a fiery heart that contained every color of earth, air, sky and water, a fitting symbol for those sworn to every face of the Shin'a'in Goddess.

And then, after the Black Riders had shown their tokens, Tre'valen and Dawnfire had appeared.

They would not lie. They came to help him; *She* meant to help him save himself, if it could be done. He must not let this fear and uncertainty break him; must not let the filth of Falconsbane destroy his own soul and all his hopes. There was honor in the world, and kindness, and decency.

He must help those who brought those virtues to his aid, even if it meant that he—

He froze for a moment, as the thought ran on to its inescapable conclusion.

Even if it meant giving up his own chance at life and freedom.

There were things worse than death, after delving into Falconsbane's mind he knew that. He would be worse than a rabid animal if he chose his own survival over taking the opportunity to *stop* something like Falconsbane.

And this was a thought that would never have occurred to the "old" An'desha.

Old. . . . He suddenly felt old, a thousand years old, and weary—and very frightened. But quite, quite sure of himself now.

A faintly-glowing hand touched his; it was joined by another. He looked up to see the Avatars standing one on either side of him, clasping their hands over the ones he had locked in front of himself. The warmth of their care and concern filled him; their friendship warmed the cold heart of him.

"Thank you, An'desha." That was all that Tre'valen had to say, but An'desha knew that the Avatar had read his internal struggle and his conclusion and approved. He looked down again, but this time it was with a glow of pride. Whatever else came of this—*Her* chosen servants had given him their own accolade—

"We did not wish to prompt you into that decision, but now that you have made it, we can be more open with you," Dawnfire told him. She took her hand from his, although the warmth that had filled him remained, and she cupped some of the mist that eddied about them in her hands. "Look here—" she continued, and the handful of mist glowed, and vague figures formed and sharpened within it. He recognized most of them, both from Falconsbane's memories and from stolen glimpses through Falconsbane's eyes.

Two young Hawkbrothers; one ruggedly handsome, though a trifle careworn, and one that he did not recognize, but who was so beautiful that his breath caught. The first was Falconsbane's old enemy, Darkwind k'Sheyna, the son of the Adept he had corrupted. The second—

"He is Firesong k'Treva, a Healing Adept," Dawnfire replied to his unvoiced thought. "He is an ally of yours, although neither of you knew it. It was he that came to the aid of k'Sheyna."

An odd feeling stole over him for a moment, as he stared at that flamboyantly beautiful face. He would like to be more than an ally with *that* one. . . .

He shook his head dismissively as the two figures faded and two more replaced them. One also, he knew. The Outlander from Northern lands, the young woman whose potential Falconsbane desired to devour. Both dressed in white garments, and both with blue-eyed white horses.

"Elspeth and Skif, both what are called 'Heralds' out of Valdemar. The Heralds are Clan-allies to Tale'sedrin," Tre'valen added, in a decisive tone, and An'desha nodded. That was all *he* needed. Anyone who had won acceptance of any of the Clans had won it from all. And if they were Clan-allies, An'desha was honor-bound to assist them.

Honor. There it was again. It became easier to understand when one lived it, rather than looking at it from outside.

A single figure took their place, one that could have been a fragile, feminine version of Falconsbane; a young woman with a feline cast to her features, carrying a sword. And, oh, he knew *this* one from many, many of his worst moments, both within Falconsbane's memories and as unwilling witness to atrocity. "Nyara," he said, biting off the word. His gorge rose at the sight of her, but not because she repulsed him but because what had been done to her by her own father repulsed him.

She is my "daughter" as well, because the body that sired her is mine—but I had nothing to do with it. I did not torture her mind and body. And yet her blood is mine, she is of outClan and Shin'a'in breeding as I am. How much responsibility do I have to her? It was not the first time he had asked himself that question, but it was the first time he had felt there was any chance he could *do* something about the answer.

It was something he would have to think about for a long time. If he had felt old before, he now felt terribly young. His body might be over half a century old, but *he* often felt as if he were still the boy who had run from his Clan and his responsibilities. His "life," such as it was, had been lived in moments and glimpses.

"Yes," Dawnfire replied, "and free of her father. You would find her willing to aid you to the end of her powers. She has a score to settle with Falconsbane."

Lastly, two other creatures crowded the first out of the mist. Gryphons and Falconsbane harbored a hatred for gryphons that was quite, quite insane, but these two in particular were apt to trigger rages, for they had eluded and defeated him time and time again, and he would likely do *anything* for a chance to destroy them.

"Treyvan and Hydona, and you would find them as apt to your aid as Nyara," said Tre'valen. "They have as much to call Falconsbane to account for as Nyara does. He violated their young, among other things."

Dawnfire opened her hands and the mist flowed away, losing its colors and dispersing into the starlight that surrounded them.

"These are your allies, An'desha," Dawnfire said, her face grave and her night-starred eyes looking somewhere beyond him. In that moment she looked like a beautiful but impassive statue. "They approach this land even now, coming to the land of Ancar's enemies, the land of Valdemar."

An'desha shook his head, puzzled. How could this mean anything to his situation?

"Ancar wars upon Valdemar and plans another attempt

to crush them even now. This is what he wishes Falconsbane's powers and teachings for, since he has been unable to defeat their defenses in the past." Tre'valen also looked somewhere beyond An'desha, and he was just as statuelike. "He wishes to become a great emperor, a lord of many kingdoms, but Valdemar stands in his way, by an increasingly lesser margin. These folk we have shown you come to help defend Elspeth's land. We will speak to them, through an intermediary that they trust, letting them know that Falconsbane has come to roost here."

An'desha considered that for a moment, seeing something of what their reaction might be to that unwelcome information. "They will know that Falconsbane is their chiefest enemy. So—what am I to do in all of this? What is it that I can do for them that will help them defeat Ancar and Falconsbane? I can do nothing to prevent him from helping Ancar if he chooses."

"Watch," Dawnfire said immediately. "Delve the depths of Falconsbane's memories. Learn all you can of him and of Ancar and Hulda and *their* plans. We will pass this on as well. You will be the spy that no one can possibly detect; the ideal agent, who is even privy to thoughts. Somewhere, in everything that you learn, there will be a way for your allies to defeat not only Ancar, but Falconsbane as well."

But that did not necessarily mean that they would be able to help him . . . and he noticed a curious omission. Neither Dawnfire nor Tre'valen had said anything about mentioning *his* existence to these "allies". . . .

And, feeling a little alarmed, he said so. "You say nothing of me—"

Now Tre'valen looked away, and it was Dawnfire who said, with a peculiar expression of mingled apology and determination, "We cannot tell them of your existence, although we will inform the intermediary, who suspects it already. If we let the others know that you live in Falconsbane's body, they might hesitate to—"

Here she broke off, and An'desha continued, bleakly, with the inescapable. "They might hesitate if it becomes necessary to slay Falconsbane, even if there is no other choice. Is that what you wished to say?"

"The intermediary will know," Tre'valen pointed out, but a little hesitantly. "She can judge best if *they* should know as well . . . but at the moment, she thinks not."

She thought not, hmm? An'desha pondered that for a moment. How likely was it that these "allies" would come face-to-face with Falconsbane?

But at least three of them were Adepts. When was it necessary for an Adept to come face-to-face with an enemy in order to attack him?

"An'desha, we pledged you that we would do our best to free you and save you. We did *not* mean to 'free you and save you' by slaying you," Dawnfire said, quickly. "You know we cannot lie to you in this. You have already accepted the risk, have you not?"

He sighed. He had. And word once given could not be taken back without becoming an oathbreaker. They were quite right, and besides, what choice did he have? He either faced a lifetime—presumably a long one—of being a prisoner in his own body, forced to watch Falconsbane commit his atrocities and being unable to do anything to prevent them, *or* he could retreat into his "safe haven" in Falconsbane's mind, make himself blind and deaf to all that passed while Falconsbane was awake, and live a kind of prison existence in which he would still *know* what Falconsbane was doing, even if he refused to actually *see* it.

Neither was any kind of a life; a living hell was more like it. He had a *chance* now. . . .

And he certainly did not want Falconsbane making free with his body anymore. The creature must be stopped.

"No matter what happens, we will be with you," Tre'valen said softly.

That decided him. At least his loneliness and isolation were at an end. These two were friends already; it would be no bad thing to come to an ending, if it were in the company of true friends.

"Well, then," he said, steeling himself against the horrid memories he must once again face in order to pass the information on to his protectors. "I must begin my part of the bargain. Here is what I have learned of Ancar. . . ."

It took a surprisingly short time to relate, really. It was astonishing how simply sordid those terrible acts Ancar had recited became, when they were told, not to an avid audience of Mornelithe Falconsbane, but to the impassive witnesses of the two Avatars. They seemed neither disturbed nor impressed; they simply nodded from time to time as if making special note of some point. He added his impressions of what Falconsbane had thought, once he came to the end of that recitation. It had not been flattering, for although Ancar had done his best to shock the Adept, Mornelithe had not been impressed either. He had, in fact, considered Ancar to be little more than a yapping pup, barking his importance to an old, bored dragon.

"Things could be worse," Dawnfire commented, when he came to the end of the recitation. "Falconsbane is still far more interested in regaining control of himself and gaining control of the situation than he is in helping Ancar. He does not know that the Valdemarans are returning to their home, so his thirst for revenge has not yet been awakened against Valdemar. And I suspect he will be investigating this woman Hulda as a possible ally against Ancar, simply because he is not the kind of creature to leave any opportunity without at least looking into it. And meanwhile, Ancar has learned nothing useful from him, which is a good thing, and he intends to withhold real information for as long as possible, which is even better."

An'desha sighed. "Better than you know. The things that Falconsbane has done to gain his powers—"

He shuddered without really intending to. Tre'valen touched his shoulder with sympathy. "I can soften those memories, if you wish," he said quietly. "Make them less—immediate. Give you some detachment."

"Give you the real sense that they are *past*, and there is nothing that you can do to help or hinder now—but that you can learn from them to prevent such things in the future," Dawnfire added, when he looked up in hope. "You must *never* forget that those terrible things were done to other living creatures, An'desha. When those poor victims become only icons, when they lose their power to move you, you will have lost something of your soul."

"I will only see to it that there is that distance," Tre'valen said, with a glance at Dawnfire as if he was amused by her preaching. "Your heart is sound, An'desha, and I have no fear that the plight of others will ever cease to move you. If that is what you want—"

"Please!" he cried, and with a touch, some of the feeling of sickness left him, and some of the feeling of having been rolled in filth until he would never be rid of the taste and smell and feel of it.

It was a blessed, blessed relief. He almost felt clean again, and his nausea subsided completely. Now those memories he had stolen from the Adept were at one remove . . . as if they were things from very distant childhood, clear, but without the terrible immediacy.

"As if they belonged to someone else, and not to you," Tre'valen said, with a slight smile. "Which they properly do, An'desha. The problem is that they come from your mind, and not Falconsbane's, and that is what made it seem to you as if they were yours."

He sighed, and closed his eyes. "Can you—" he began, and then realized that Tre'valen had already shown him what he needed to do to put any new memories at the same distance.

"You are a good pupil, An'desha," Dawnfire said, a bare hint of teasing in her voice. "You are a credit to your teachers."

He ducked his head shyly, but before he could reply, an internal tug warned him that he must return to the body he and Falconsbane shared before the Adept awakened.

The others understood without a word; they both touched him again, briefly, filling him with that incredible warmth and caring, and then they were gone.

And he closed his eyes, and sought *without, and within*—

And opened the very physical eyes of Mornelithe Falconsbane, who still slept in his heavily-cushioned chair. Without even consciously thinking of doing so, he had implemented the new lesson even as he returned to the body. Now *he* was very much in control, although he must make certain that he did nothing abruptly, or made any motion or sound that might wake the Adept.

Still, Falconsbane slept very heavily—and people often walked, talked, and did many other things in their sleep without awakening. An'desha should at least have a limited freedom.

For the first time in years, he had full command of all of his body. He now wore it, rather than being carried by it as a kind of invisible passenger. Senses seemed much sharper now; he became aware of vague aches and pains, of the fact that he was painfully thin, most of the body's resources having been devoured in that terrible time between the Gates. Small wonder Falconsbane ate much, slept much, and tired easily!

The warning that had brought him back was thirst; alive and growing quickly. Moving slowly and carefully, he reached out for the watered wine on the table beside him, poured himself a goblet, and drank it down. He then settled back again with a feeling of triumph. *He* had done that, not Falconsbane—and for the first time, he had done so without feeling Falconsbane would wake while he moved!

An'desha marveled at the feel of the goblet in his hands—*his* hands, at last, *his* arms and body. And now, he had many, many things to think about. He did not feel up to another swim in the cesspool of Falconsbane's memories. Not now.

Later, when Falconsbane truly slept; that would be time enough. But for now—now he had another task in front of him. He had felt very young, a few moments ago. He had *been* very young, a few moments ago.

It was time, finally, to grow up.

By his own will.

Chapter Eight

Elspeth's head felt full-to-bursting, the way it had when she first began learning mage-craft from Need and Darkwind. Or, for that matter, the way it used to feel back when she was still a Herald-trainee, and had been cramming information on laws and customs into her memory as quickly as she could. She had a wealth of information bubbling like a teapot in her mind, and she still hadn't sorted it out yet. But she would; she would. It was all a matter of time.

For now, the best thing was to make as simple a plan as possible and go from there—knowing that even simple plans could go awry. *First we go through the Gate, then Vanyel dispels his protections on Valdemar so that mages can use magic without going mad, then we pelt for Haven as fast as we can. Seems simple enough.* But Elspeth was not inclined to think it would stay simple for very long. There were too many things that could complicate their situation.

Just after the vrondi-*watch is dispelled—that's when Valdemar will be at its most vulnerable. I'd better ask*

Vanyel if he can make the eastern border protections go down last.

But risk was part of life. She went through some other things that would be trouble. Communication, for one. She was passing plans on to Gwena, who relayed them to Rolan, who presumably told Talia—a complicated chain in which there were any number of chances for a break in that communication.

They were to return to the Ashkevron estate. Right there, possible problems arose.

Supposedly there were already two Heralds waiting for them at the Ashkevron family manor, who supposedly knew everything that Elspeth had passed on to Gwena and Rolan. They were expecting the Gate, were to have warned the family what was coming.

But just how much were the Heralds really told, how much did they understand, and how much were they able to get the Ashkevrons to believe?

Even if they knew *all* about the Gate, they might not understand what it was. And as for the Ashkevrons believing in magic—that in itself was problematic. Elspeth had on occasion crossed horns with some of the stubborn Ashkevron human oxen, and she knew very well that having been warned and actually doing something about it were two different things.

They were still horse breeders, something that came as no real surprise to Vanyel when she had mentioned it. *:They always have been rather set in tradition,:* was all he had said. He called it "tradition," but she and the Queen had another thing or two to call it, when Ashkevrons showed up at court to protest some edict or other simply because *"We've* never done it that way, and we've never had a problem."

Whether it was sticking younglings with needles dipped in cowpox sores to prevent the Great Pox, or creating a common grazing ground for those folk with single livestock (so that the beasts were not inclined to break free of their tiny yards and roam off to larger and presumably greener pastures), if it was something new and different, the Ashkevrons usually opposed it. Most of them stayed on or near the family property even after marriage, although they were no longer as *prolific* as they had been in Vanyel's day. Most of them were stolid and stubborn, and had to be *shown* why something worked, in detail, and with exhaustive explanations, before they would return home to implement it.

There were no Heralds in this generation of Ashkevrons, although there were two Ashkevron officers in the Guard, one apprentice Bard, and one very ancient Healer. And although the stolid Ashkevrons were always mystified that *anyone* would ever want to leave home, thanks to Vanyel, it was now a *tradition* (and so, unquestioned) that if you didn't feel that you fit in, you left.

Still, Elspeth could just imagine what the two Heralds that had been dragged off their circuits to meet them had gone through, trying to explain to the Ashkevrons just what, exactly, was going to happen. Most likely they themselves didn't even understand it!

The brown-haired, brown-eyed, huskily-built current Lord would blink in puzzlement and say, "You say they're gonna be a-comin' through the chapel door? How in Havens they get in there?" And the Herald in question would have to scratch his head and answer that he really didn't know how, but that they were really going to come through that door—

And then, when the Gate opened—

Gods, it would be a royal mess . . . she only hoped that everyone would at least keep clear long enough for the Companions to get through. And then the gryphons, both young and old. . . .

Just thinking about what could go wrong gave Elspeth a headache. She closed her eyes and rubbed her temple, then opened them again to meet Darkwind's concerned glance. She smiled slightly, and he squeezed her hand in reassurance.

Ready or not, it was all about to become moot. They gathered once again in the clearing in front of the cave-mouth that had first served as their portal to Vanyel's forest—or his current body, it could be argued. Vanyel's image stood to one side of the Gate he was creating, so thinned and tenuous that he looked like nothing more than a human-shaped wisp of mist. Almost all of his power was going into the building of this Gate—a Gate to a place so far away that Firesong admitted he didn't think *anyone* had the temerity to try such a distance. The only feat that dwarfed it was the one that had brought them here, over an even longer distance. But the energy forming that Gate had come from two Adepts, Vanyel and Firesong; this was coming from Vanyel alone.

Then again, Vanyel had resources no merely human mage could command. . . .

The cave-mouth darkened, blackened—and just as suddenly, gave out on a stone-walled corridor, lit with oil lanterns, filled with strange people gaping in slack-jawed amazement.

"It's up! Go *now!*" Firesong shouted. Gwena and Cymry didn't need any urging. They all knew that the strain of this undertaking, even on a being such as Vanyel, was tremendous; he would only be able to hold the Gate open for a limited time.

The Companions bolted across the portal, hooves kicking up great clods of earth from the soft turf. Elspeth and Skif were right on their heels, followed by Darkwind and Firesong with their bondbirds clinging to their shoulders for dear life. Then came Nyara, Firesong's *dyheli,* and Rris, and bringing up the rear, the four gryphons.

Gwena and Cymry simply kept moving as they passed through, recovering from the disorientation of Gating much more quickly than Elspeth could. Sound did not travel across the barrier of the Gate, and as Elspeth dove through, she saw mouths moving as if people were shouting, although there was nothing to hear.

She passed into blackness, and through that moment of extreme dizziness that made her feel as if she was falling forever and would never touch the ground. There was nothing to concentrate on; no contact even with her own body. She could be screaming and waving her arms around, and she would never know—and if something went wrong with the Gate, wouldn't she be left that way forever?

But her momentum carried her forward, out of the complete silence of the Void and into pandemonium. People shouted, hooves clattered on the stone of the corridor, and all of it echoed so much it made all the sounds into meaningless noise. She glanced around, her eyes still blurred, trying to make sense out of the confusion.

She needn't have bothered. By the time she and Darkwind staggered onto the stone of the Ashkevron corridor and shook their heads clear, the Companions had shoved everyone out of the way and had made enough room even for the gryphons.

Even so, there wasn't a *lot* of room. There was a kind of anteroom in front of the chapel door, and that was what the Companions had cleared. Now there was a horde of people jammed into the corridor itself, beyond the anteroom, all of them jabbering. A strange, faintly unpleasant smell struck Elspeth's nostrils, and she sneezed, wondering what the odd, heavy odor was. Then she remembered; it was fish oil, used for lanterns. She hadn't had fish oil lamps inflicted on her for nearly two years—no wonder the smell made her sneeze!

It appeared that their arrival had been deemed something of a carnival, and the Ashkevrons were always prone to pounce on an excuse to see a marvel. Everyone on the estate had turned out to see just what was supposed to happen.

Or at least, that was the way it seemed to Elspeth. There were three Heralds in the front of the mob, their Whites gleaming in the light from the lanterns, and not the two that she had been told would be here. She didn't recognize any of them, not that she necessarily would; Field Heralds seldom came to Haven, and when they did, they would only be one more stranger in Whites to her. But she had hoped that at least one would be a friend; Jeri or Sherril, even Kero. Her heart sank a little, and she hoped she didn't show her disappointment.

Crowded behind the three Heralds were what appeared to be a hundred other people. All three tried to get past Gwena for what she assumed was a greeting; certainly the relief on their faces spoke volumes for their feelings. Even if her feelings were mixed, theirs certainly were not!

But at that moment, Darkwind and Firesong came

stumbling through—then, before anyone could blink, Nyara, the *dyheli* and Rris—

And *then* the gryphons, plunging through the Gate as if they were charging an enemy line, then skidding to a halt just past the threshold.

And the crowd went insane with panic.

A crash of thunder that shook the stones under her drowned out most of the screams, but not all, by any means.

I guess someone forgot to tell them about Treyvan and Hydona—

Thunder faded, but not the shrieks. People stared for a moment, then, like cattle, bolted in the direction of freedom and safety.

That was all she had time to think, before the Ashkevron clan snatched up children, turned tail, and fled the scene, leaving behind three white-faced Heralds to guard their retreating backs.

Crashing thunder covered the sound of their retreat for the most part. All Elspeth could do was stand there, torn between laughter and hysteria.

Meanwhile the three Heralds were apparently convinced they were all about to die at the claws of the strange beasts. All three groped after weapons they weren't wearing, as people shoved and stumbled behind them and thunder crashed again.

Impasse. They were unarmed, but the gryphons weren't moving. And at this point, they must have been wondering why the two Companions didn't do anything! The Heralds stared at the gryphons, paralyzed with indecision, as the Gate vanished behind the winged apparitions, and another blast of thunder deafened them all for a moment.

No one moved.

The gryphons stared back. Elspeth was about to say something to break the deadlock—then stopped herself. Treyvan was an envoy. Let him deal with the situation. If she intervened now, it might look as if he *needed* her intervention. If the Heralds had been armed, it would have been a different story—

In the silence that followed the thunder, Treyvan

opened his beak and the three Heralds stepped back a pace as if they expected him to charge them.

"I take it we werrre not exsssssspected?" he said, in clear, if heavily accented, Valdemaran.

Eventually, everything was sorted out as the thunderstorm rolled on outside. The Heralds—Cavil, Shion, and Lisha—recovered from their terror very quickly in the face of Treyvan's civilized politeness and sunny charm. As she had expected, he soon had the situation under control, and even had the three Heralds laughing weakly at their own fear.

The antechamber and hallways were too crowded a venue for any kind of discussion, however. As soon as the atmosphere settled for a moment, Elspeth suggested they all move into the chapel.

Like most private chapels, this one was devoid of permanent seats and much in the way of decoration. It was basically a simple stone-walled room, empty at this moment, with a stone altar at one end. More lanterns lit it, but these were candle lamps rather than the fish oil, and the honey scent of beeswax was a great deal easier on Elspeth's nose than the odoriferous oil.

Gwena and Cymry picked their way carefully over the stone floor, leading the way, followed by the *dyheli*. They took places near the altar. The bondbirds flew up to the rafters and began a vigorous preening, oblivious to whatever their bondmates were up to for the moment. And the gryphons herded the young ones into a window alcove that no longer looked out on the outside, as evidenced by the lack of glazing and the view of another fish oil lamp lighting yet another corridor.

At that point, Lord Ashkevron reappeared, armed to the teeth and wearing a hastily-donned, antique breastplate. Elspeth would have laughed if she had not been so amazed at his temerity.

She ran quickly to the front of the room, placing herself between him and the gryphons.

"My Lord!" she shouted, pausing for thunder to die down. "My Lord, there is no danger! These are guests of

Valdemar. You were supposed to have been warned they were coming!"

His sword point, held in defensive posture, wavered for a moment, then dropped. He raised the visor of his helm.

"The hell you say!" he exclaimed, regarding the gryphons in puzzlement.

She hastened to assure him that there was no danger, and briefly explained the situation.

He in his turn went cautiously to the doorway and peered in.

Treyvan looked up at just that moment. "Hel-lo," he said, in a voice that sounded friendly to Elspeth—although who knew how it sounded to Lord Ashkevron. "May we impossse upon your hosssspitality and rrremain herrre, good sirrr? I fearrr we would frrrighten yourrr horrrsesss if we went nearrr yourrr ssstablesss. I would not rrrissssk panic to the horssssesss."

That was enough for Lord Ashkevron; whatever this monster was, it had just demonstrated that it cared not to disturb his precious horseflesh. The gryphons were invited to take over the chapel.

He went off to start collecting the terrified members of his household and explain to them that these were not monsters—or at least, these were monsters that were on the side of Valdemar. Lisha wasted no time in seizing on Elspeth and filling her ears with complaints about how little preparation they'd had.

That was when Elspeth discovered that her worries had been dead on the mark. No one had said anything about the gryphons. In fact, no one had told these three that anyone but Skif and Elspeth were going to arrive—and certainly those assigning them to this task had not been able to explain the manner of Elspeth's arrival in any way the three Heralds were able to understand.

Meanwhile, the storm raged outside, its fury no doubt further frightening everyone who had fled, who must be certain that in the howling wind they heard the hungry cries of man-eating monsters. Finally Elspeth called a halt to further explanations until they helped Lord Ashkevron collect and calm his household.

It took candlemarks to soothe the nerves of the terrified

Ashkevrons, who had been certain that they had just witnessed terrible monsters following their Heir—that she and Skif had, in fact, been *fleeing* them when they dashed across the threshold of the Gate. The poor folk had been certain that these monsters came from whatever strange place she had been, and were going to eat them all alive as soon as they caught and devoured the Heralds. People had to be hunted out and reassured, one by one; they had fled to every corner of the manor, hiding under beds and behind furniture, in closets and attics, and even cowering in the cellars. Only the storm outside, pouring so hard that it was impossible to see, had kept them from fleeing the building altogether.

Even now, a good half of the inhabitants were still walking softly and fearfully, expecting at any moment that the monsters would show their true nature. Nothing Lord Ashkevron or any of the Heralds could say would convince them otherwise.

Predictably, it was the gryphlets who eventually won over the rest. Lytha and Jerven had begun a game of pounce-and-wrestle as soon as they were settled, including Darkwind in their fun. There was nothing even remotely threatening in their kittenish play, and they soon had Lord Jehan Ashkevron convulsed with laughter. Now those who dared the chapel soon found themselves engaged in cheerful conversation with one or the other of the adults, while the youngsters continued to entertain themselves and anyone else watching them.

With that crisis out of the way, Elspeth and Skif went back to finding out just how things stood—both here, and in the Kingdom as a whole. She could quite cheerfully have shot whoever had made that particular set of omissions. Fortunately, after the gryphons, even the *dyheli* and Nyara didn't seem to cause too much consternation. Rris was simply assumed to be a very large dog, and neither he nor Elspeth saw any reason to enlighten anyone on that score—although his occasionally acidic comments had her choking down laughter she would have been hard put to explain if anyone had noticed.

By the time everyone had been found and calmed, and all misunderstandings sorted out, it was well into night.

Elspeth was tired, hungry, and in no mood to deal with anything other than a meal and a warm bed.

"But like it or not," she said to Darkwind—in Tayledras, so that no one would overhear and be offended—"I'm back at home, which means work, lots of it, starting this very moment. You don't have to sit through this if you don't want to, but I *have* to have a meeting with these Heralds. If *they* didn't get the message about the gryphons, there are probably a hundred equally important messages we haven't gotten."

"I came to help," Darkwind said softly, the lines of worry in his face softened by the light from the candle-lamps. "If you do not object to my presence."

Object? "Not likely," she said with gratitude. "You probably won't understand half of what they say, but you should get the sense of it all if you link with my mind."

Link with my mind—I never thought I would ever say that to anyone, I never thought I would be willing to. She smiled at him, a little shyly. She was so used to linking with him now that it never even caused her a moment of uneasiness; she did it as easily as she opened her thoughts to Gwena.

He smiled, and touched her hand lightly. She gave him a slow wink, then paused for a half breath to settle her thoughts. After speaking only Tayledras for so long, it seemed odd to speak her own tongue again; the words felt strange in her mouth.

Darkwind waited as she attempted to assume an air of authority. At her nod, he followed, as she went right to the corner to interrupt the low-voiced conversation all three Heralds were having with Lord Jehan.

The Heralds started and looked guilty as she cleared her throat. She was struck, at that moment, by how plain and severe their Whites looked, and spared a flicker of thought to wonder if she and Skif looked as outlandish and exotic to them as they looked plain to her.

Although the three Heralds seemed embarrassed—which meant that they had probably been discussing *her*—Sir Jehan, evidently, was just as blunt and forthright as any of his line, and turned to her immediately.

He was a brown and blocky man; brown eyes, hair, and

beard, with a square face and a square build, all of it muscle. He looked nothing like Vanyel. She remembered something her mother had said once, though: "The Ashkevron look usually breeds true, and when it doesn't, the poor child generally runs off to Haven!"

"Cavil was just saying that no one told *him* that anyone was coming except you and the other Herald," he said, with a hearty chuckle. "He keeps insisting that I ought to complain to someone. Can't understand why. *I* know how it is. You tell someone, 'I'm coming and bringing an entourage of a hundred,' he tells the next fellow, 'Jehan's bringing an escort,' it keeps getting pared down until your host thinks you're only bringin' a couple of servants, and when you show up with your hundred, there's no place to put 'em all." He shrugged. "It happens. Happens all the time, and no one to blame for it."

She sighed with relief. There was one good thing about dealing with people like Jehan; once they calmed down, they were usually able to take anything in stride, from gryphons in their chapels to Gates in their doorways.

"Thank you for being so understanding," she said. "Could I steal Cavil and the others from you for a little? There's a great deal I have to catch up on."

"Oh, no fear, no fear," Jehan replied affably. "I have to go round up the aunties again and let 'em know they aren't goin' to be eaten in their beds." He grinned hugely, showing very white teeth in a very dark beard, then added. "I never believed 'em when they all said you were dead, Lady. Kept telling 'em they were actin' like a bunch of silly hens, flutterin' around over nothing."

And with that odd comment, he sketched a bow and took his leave.

Elspeth turned to Herald Cavil, who looked profoundly embarrassed. He was an older man, thin and harried-looking, with brown hair going gray at the temples. She had a feeling that after today, there would be a lot more gray there. "Just what in Havens was *that* all about?" she demanded. "About my being dead, I mean."

He flushed; his cheeks turned a brilliant crimson. "Some of what we need to brief you on, my lady," he said, quickly, while the other two Heralds nodded. "There have been rumors over the last several months that you were dead and the Council was trying to conceal that fact. Nothing the Queen or Circle could say or do seemed to calm the alarm. We need to proceed back to Haven at all speed, and as openly as possible—"

"We aren't going to be able to proceed *quietly* with this menagerie!" she pointed out, interrupting him. "But apparently, that's going to be all to the good, from what you're saying. The more people that see me, the better, right?" She shook her head for a moment, and caught Darkwind's eye. He was rather amused by something, although she couldn't imagine what. Perhaps it was the notion of trying to conceal the gryphons.

As what? Statuary?

"Of course, with four gryphons along, I wonder if anyone is going to notice *me!*" she added with a tired smile.

"There is this," Darkwind put in, speaking slowly in his careful, accented Valdemaran. "The notion of you in company with gryphons is so strange that no one would make it up; it is so strange it *must* be believed."

"You don't intend to bring those creatures to Haven!" Cavil exclaimed without thinking.

She started to snap; caught herself, and answered instead, quietly and calmly, "Treyvan and Hydona are not only envoys from the Tayledras and Kaled'a'in, they are mages in their own right. They have offered to teach any Herald with Mage-Gift. Yes, Mage-Gift. They can do that best at Haven, and they are *needed* there. I would be doing everyone a disservice if I insisted they remain here until they were sent for."

The three Heralds exchanged hasty glances, and the one called Shion said, cautiously, "But what of the rest? The other—ah—people?"

A sidelong glance told her that Shion meant Nyara, but she deliberately chose to take her literally.

"Darkwind and Firesong are Tayledras *Adepts,* and they are just as badly needed as the gryphons, if not more so," she replied, "And as for the others, Nyara is Skif's lady, and the *dyheli* and Rris are envoys from their respective peoples. Everyone with me is either a representative of a potential ally, or someone who is practiced in mage-craft and is willing to teach."

At the startled looks she got, she could not repress a chuckle. "It's a strange world out there, my friends," she added. "You can't assume that something that looks like an animal isn't an intelligent person—or that something that looks human is more than a beast. Havens, you should know that from Court duty."

Cavil shook his head, biting his lip in what was obviously a nervous habit. "Lady, this is the single most confusing day of my life," he said at last, with honest bewilderment.

He glanced at the single window in the chapel that still faced the open sky. It was made of thick glass that allowed little view, but enough to show that outside it was black night—except when lightning glared across the sky, turning the window into a patch of white. Obviously the storm had not abated in the least since they had arrived. Here inside thick stone walls, most of the fury of the storm was muffled, but it might very well be the worst storm Elspeth had ever seen.

"It is too late to travel tonight," Cavil said reluctantly. "But in the morning, we must be off. We have taken more time than I like as it is."

That took her a little aback. "In this storm?" she exclaimed without thinking. "The way it's raining, it'll still be going strong in the morning! Can't we wait until it clears, at least?"

Herald Lisha sighed. "It probably won't clear, not for two days at least," she told Elspeth. "Not that I'm a weather-witch or anything, but the weather all over Valdemar has been rotten this year. It got bad around Midwinter, when everyone got hit with that headache, and right before you people popped out of that doorway this storm just blew up out of nowhere. I've never seen anything like it, and I'm not exactly young."

"No one knows what is causing this," Cavil said glumly, "although many people blame Ancar, and a great many more are convinced he has somehow learned to turn the very weather against us. Lisha understates the case, Lady Elspeth. The weather has been simply hellish."

Elspeth noticed that Firesong had been listening intently to this entire conversation, and decided to invite him in on it. "Cavil says the weather has been hellish, that this storm is just one example," she called over to him. He took that as an invitation, and stalked gracefully toward them, his robes flowing about him in a way that made Lisha smile at him appreciatively. "Cavil, Lisha, Shion, this is Firesong k'Treva, another Adept. Firesong, they think Ancar is to blame for the state of the weather. Is this something we need to warn Haven about? Have you any ideas?"

He nodded a greeting to each of the Heralds before replying.

"Of course the weather has been hellish," he said matter-of-factly while Elspeth translated. He understood Valdemaran far better than he could speak it. "There has been a disturbance in the magical currents here, and that *always* makes the weather act up, unless someone is working to balance it. Since you have no weather-wizards and earth-witches working to rebalance the weather, it will continue to be bad."

Lisha's long face was puzzled, Shion's round one thoughtful, but Cavil brightened. "You mean Ancar isn't to blame?"

"In a sense, but it was not deliberate," Firesong explained. He held up a finger. "*First*—that moment when all of you were struck with that blinding headache—that was when a powerful packet of energy was flung up *here* and linked to a physical object in your chief city. That was meant entirely to help you, and indeed you will need it, but it also created great disturbances in the natural order of magic in this land. Weather is influenced by these energy patterns, and so the weather began to turn awry. Now, outside of your land, this Ancar has been mucking about with magic as well, and I suspect without any safeguards at all. That will also stir things up. The forces he has been meddling with are powerful ones, and this has had an effect on the weather over both your lands."

Lisha had the look of a hunter on the track of game. She leaned forward a little. "So what is basically going on is that magic has been like someone rowing across a pond—while the boat is getting from here to there, the rower creates waves and eddies, whether or not he knows it. He maybe stirs up muck from the bottom if he digs his oars in too deep. Yes?"

Firesong's eyes darted from Lisha's face to Elspeth's as she translated, for Lisha had spoken far too quickly for him to understand her. He laughed when Elspeth was done, and nodded vigorously. "Exactly so, and an excellent analogy. Now—we have just opened and closed a Gate in the midst of all this instability, and that has only made things worse. In fact, in this case, it has turned what would have been only a minor storm into a tempest." He shrugged. "*We* do not have these problems, because all Vales have what you call Journeymen and Apprentices balancing the forces while Masters and Adepts work, or doing specific weather-controlling spells to avoid this kind of mess."

He took on a "lecturing" tone, and he might well have gone on in this vein for some time, except that he caught sight of Elspeth's expression. She was directing a rather accusatory glare at him, Darkwind, and Treyvan.

"Why didn't you tell me we'd be doing this to Valdemar?" she demanded, as Firesong broke off, and the three Heralds watched in bewilderment, unable to follow what was going on since she had switched to Tayledras. "Why didn't any of you let me know?"

Firesong shrugged, and crystals braided into his hair reflected flashes of lightning from outside.

"It would have done you no good to know," he pointed out. "What would you have been able to do about it? Nothing. You were a great distance away. Your people have no weather-workers, and until that barrier comes down, you will have none coming in. There was no point in mentioning it."

Shion cleared her throat, her round face telling of her puzzlement and curiosity eloquently. "Please," she said, "What *are* you talking about?"

"The weather," she replied, then took pity on her and gave her a quick translation.

"You mean," she said at last, "It really *is* possible to do something other than complain about the weather?"

She smiled and nodded. "Eventually, we will. But right now, the trouble is that all this wonderful new magic is bringing killer storms down on our own heads."

"*Ke'chara,* you must think of the other side of this stone," Darkwind put in, speaking again in Valdemaran. "Ancar is getting this weather—ah—in the teeth. And he is getting it as much as we; it must be at least as much of a hindrance. Consider how much magic he works, and completely without safeguards."

He sounded positively cheerful about it. Elspeth couldn't be quite that cheerful, thinking of all the innocent folk who were suffering much more from the wicked weather than Ancar was. But still, it was rather comforting to think that some of Ancar's chickens at least were coming home to roost.

"Oh, quite," Firesong said, just as cheerfully, when Elspeth had finished translating. "In actual fact, I would be much surprised if the effect was not a great deal worse over there in his land. He, after all, is the one who has been working the most magic—and it is he and his mages who also care little for the balances of things."

At Lisha's ironic nod of agreement, Firesong sighed, and shook his head a little. "On reflection, I fear that I will have a great deal of work ahead of me, once the current troubles are settled."

Current troubles—as if the war with Ancar wasn't much more complicated than a brushfire.

"It's going to take a lot to 'settle' Ancar," Lisha replied, with heavy irony. "I don't trust the current stalemate, and neither does anyone else in this Kingdom. You'll have your hands full of more than weather before you're here long."

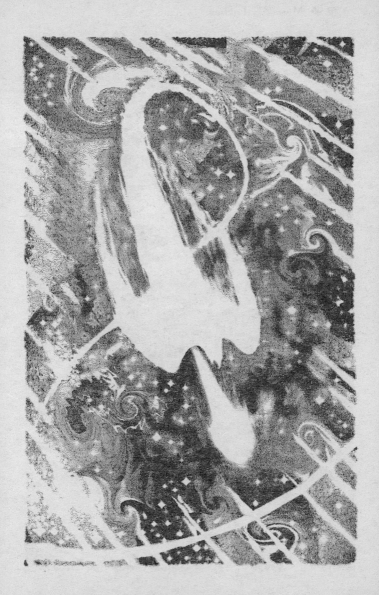

Chapter Nine

Mornelithe Falconsbane stood in the window of his suite, with the shutters flung open wide and a cold wind whipping his hair about his head. He scowled and watched a night-black storm walking toward his "host's" castle on a thousand legs of lightning. As it neared, the light faded and thunder growled a warning of things to come. The wind picked up and sent the shutters to either side of him crashing against the wall, sending dust and the heavy scent of cold rain into his face. He crossed his arms and watched the storm racing over the empty fields beyond the city walls, lightning licking down and striking the earth for every beat of his heart. This would be a terrible and powerful storm; before it was over, crops would be beaten down in the fields, and many of those fields would lie under water.

He had expected nothing less, given what he already knew.

He waited until the last possible moment before closing windows and shutters against the winds of fury; they howled as if in frustration and lashed at the closed shutters with whips of rain. But the shutters were stoutly built. All the storm could accomplish was to rattle the thick glass of the windows behind them.

Thunder did more than rattle the glass; it shook the palace to the cellars, making all the stones in the walls tremble. Falconsbane felt the vibration under his feet as he turned and walked back to the chair he had abandoned at the first hint of the coming storm.

This was the fourth such storm in the last week. Two of the four had brought little rain, but had sent whirlwinds down out of the clouds and hail to damage roofs and break the glass in windows. Falconsbane had seen one of the whirlwinds firsthand, as it had dropped down out of a black cloud, writhing like a thick snake or the tentacle-arm of a demon. It had withdrawn again without touching ground in the city, but other such whirlwinds had made contact with the ground and wrought great damage out in the countryside. Dead animals had been found high up in the treetops, houses had been destroyed, and crops torn up. There had also been marvels—an unbroken egg driven into the trunk of a tree, straws driven through thick boards.

He had been fascinated by the whirlwinds and the wreckage and bizarre marvels they had left in their wake, but otherwise the storms held no interest for him. In fact, this current outbreak had left him fuming with anger, for he only truly enjoyed storms when *he* had called them and was in control of them. The cold and damp made his wounds ache, and all his joints complained and stiffened, reminding him painfully that this body was not as youthful as it looked.

And reminding him that he had not even overcome Ancar's coercions enough to allow him free reign to recreate that youth and renew the spells that had held age in abeyance. If it had not been for those coercions, he would have been able to choose a victim of his own and Heal himself of his damage. One life would give him the energy to cure himself completely. Two would permit him to reverse some of the ravages of age for a time. More than two would permit him to make any changes to himself that he pleased.

And it would be so pleasant if one of those victims could be Ancar himself. . . .

Failing that, he retreated to his favorite chair, the one nearest the fire, and sat warming himself. Daydreaming of revenge and planning his course to obtain it were his only real amusements at the moment.

He probably should be down among Ancar's courtiers, but this had not been a particularly fruitful day, and he had grown bored rather quickly. He had never had much patience with the witless babble of a court even when it had been his own court. In this current body, he had eliminated holding court altogether. When he wished his underlings to hear something, he gathered them together and told them, then dismissed them. When he wished to hear from *them*—which was rarely—he ordered them before him and stripped their minds.

But Ancar seemed convinced that a "court" was necessary, although he no longer held audiences or even permitted anyone below the rank of noble near him. Perhaps for a ruler like him, it was. Even though it was mostly a sham, and he himself never appeared before his assembled courtiers.

Still, a reasonable amount of information could be obtained if one had the patience to listen to Ancar's brainless toadies, and the wit to read real meaning from what the few foreign ambassadors did and did not say. Today, however, had been hopelessly dull. Even Hulda was off somewhere else, leaving him to mouth meaningless pleasantries at fools who could have served far more useful purposes bleeding their lives away in his hands and granting him the power which they could not use.

The very first person Ancar had introduced him to was Hulda, after warning him far too many times about the woman's perfidy. He had been the consummate gentleman. Hulda amused him. She was quick-witted when she cared to be—much cleverer than she appeared. Complacency was her flaw when it came to Ancar; she obviously still believed she ruled him completely, and if anything would bring her downfall, this complacency would be the cause.

She was much wiser in the ways of magic than her pupil; she knew Falconsbane for a Changechild, for she had made some clever remarks about "changing one's nature" when Ancar had first introduced them. He could certainly see the attraction she must have had for the boy when he was still young and malleable. She was lushly ripe—perhaps a trifle overblown, but some folk liked their fruit well-seasoned and their meat well-aged. With her curving, voluptuous lines, good features, long flow of dark hair, and her startling violet eyes, she cut quite an impressive figure.

Falconsbane had bowed over her hand, but had caressed the palm, unseen, before he let it go. He had noted the flare of interest in her eyes, and had smiled, and nodded knowingly as she lowered her lids to give him a seductive glance from beneath her heavy lashes.

She, too, was older than she looked, he knew that instinctively—but she was not as old as he was, not even in this body. Thus far he had managed to avoid more than speaking to her without ever seeming to avoid her, a fact that must infuriate and frustrate her. He intended to play her a while, before he decided how to handle her over the long run. Let her pursue him; let him be the enigma. It would make her concentrate on his physical presence and not on the threat he might be to her power.

She did not connect his presence with the Gate, and at this moment, he preferred to keep it that way. She recognized him for a mage of some kind, but she did not appear to have any way of judging his true abilities. That was all to the good. If he decided to make a temporary ally of her, he would reveal to her what he chose. And at the moment, he did not know if he cared to make her an ally. It might be amusing, especially since his exotic nature patently attracted her, but it might also be very dangerous. She was playing some deep game, and had secrets that young fool Ancar had not even guessed at. Falconsbane wanted to know just what those secrets were before he even began to consider her as an ally.

And mages were notoriously jealous of their power; if she guessed him to be any kind of a rival, it would not take her long to decide to eliminate him. She would try to do so subtly, but she would not be hampered by coercions. Becoming involved in a covert mage-struggle at this stage could only further delay his plans for freedom.

In the meantime, it suited him to pique her curiosity, and to cast little tidbits of information to her designed to make her think—rightfully—that Ancar was intriguing against her and that he was an unwitting part of that plan. The best thing he could do would be to set these two openly at each others' throats. The more tangled this situation got, the better the outcome for him. The more time they wasted struggling for power, the more time he would have to free himself. The more power they wasted, the weaker they would be when he finally succeeded.

He had been looking forward to tangling the situation a bit more, but Hulda had not even put in an appearance at court this afternoon. Falconsbane had quickly become irritated with the inane chatter and had finally retreated to his suite in boredom and disgust. The joint aches warning of an approaching storm had not sweetened his temper in the least

He slumped in his chair, stared at the fire, and brooded. He could not recall, in any of his lifetimes, having been so completely cut off from control. It was not possible to forget even for a moment that he was the one being controlled. This was, in many ways, worse than being imprisoned, for he was a prisoner in his own body.

The flames danced wildly in the changing drafts from the chimney, sometimes roaring up the chimney, sometimes flattening against the logs, but he could not hear the crackling of the fire for the howling of the wind and the continual barrage of thunder. Every time the flames flattened for a moment, it simply made his rage smolder a little more.

His several days in the heart of Ancar's court had made it clear that he had been outfoxed by someone he would not even have had in his employ as a menial. *He* knew how disastrous these storms were, not only to the countryside, but to the energy-fields for leagues around. Even if Ancar didn't care what they did to his land, Falconsbane was going to have to put all this back before *he* could work properly. That was what made him the angriest. He had known that the boy was a fool. He had not known the boy was as big a fool as all this.

He did not hear Ancar come in, and was not aware that the young King was in the room until movement at the corner of his vision caught his attention. The noise of the thunder had covered the sounds of the door opening and the boy's footsteps. That irritated him even more. The brat could come and go as he pleased, even in Falconsbane's own rooms, and the Adept was powerless to prevent it!

He looked up, and Ancar's smug expression simply served to ignite his anger.

"What is wrong with you, you little fool?" he snapped furiously. "Why aren't you doing anything about this storm? Or are you simply such an idiot that you don't care what it means?"

Ancar stepped back a pace, doubtless surprised by the venom in his voice, the rage in his eyes. "What it means?" he repeated stupidly. "What do you mean by that? How can a storm mean anything at all? How could I do anything about it even if it did mean something?"

For a moment, Falconsbane stared at him in surprise so great that his anger evaporated. How could anyone who had gotten past Apprentice *not* know weather control, and how magic affected the world about him?

"Hasn't anyone ever taught you weather-magic?" he blurted without thinking. "Don't you realize what you and those idiot mages of yours have been doing?"

Ancar could only blink stupidly at him. "I have no idea what you're talking about," he said. "I don't understand. What have we been doing that makes you so angry?"

Finally, as Ancar continued to stare at him, Falconsbane gathered enough of his temper about him to answer the boy's unspoken questions.

"Evidently, your teacher Hulda has been hiding more from you than you realized," he replied testily. "It is very simple; so simple that you *should* have been able to deduce it from observation alone if you had ever bothered to *observe* anything. Magical energy is created by living things and runs along natural lines, like water. You do know *that* much, I hope?"

Ancar nodded silently.

He snorted, and continued, "Well, then, like water, it can be disturbed, perturbed, and otherwise affected by meddling with it. If you meddle a little, the disturbance is so minor that no one would notice it if they were not looking for it. If you meddle a great deal, as if you had just thrown a mighty boulder into a pond, *everyone* will get splashed and they most certainly will notice. That is how your Hulda knew you were meddling with a Gate. She sensed the ripples in the magical energies, and knew by the pattern they made that you had created a Gate!"

"I know all that—" Ancar began impatiently.

Falconsbane interrupted him, waving him into silence. "Magic also affects the physical elements of the world," he continued, allowing his irritation to show. "You should have noticed this by now. Hadn't you even seen that some kind of weather change always follows a working in the more powerful magics? The more subtle the element, the more it will be affected. Meddle with a Gate, and even the earth will resonate. Meddle enough, you might trigger an earthquake if the earth is unstable at that point. But the most subtle elements are air and water—which make *weather,* you fool. Changes in magical energy change the weather, as the air and water reflect what is happening in the magical fields. You have stirred up the magical fields hereabouts with your little experiments—and now you are reaping the result. Keep this up much more, and you will either be paying a premium price for imported food, or you will have to steal it or starve next year."

Ancar's mouth hung open a little with surprise, his eyes going a little wider. Evidently this was all new to him. And by the growing dismay in his expression, it was not a pleasant revelation.

Falconsbane smiled nastily. "Any mage who is any good at all makes certain that he calms the fields if he can after he is finished. Any mage with the power to command others need only tell *them* to take care of the disturbances, damping them before they cause any great harm. And any mage worthy of his hire could at *least* steer storms over his enemy's territory! By the time I became an Adept, I could do it without even thinking about it when I worked my magics in freedom. I still could, if I had that freedom to work without hindrance." He folded his arms and slumped back down in his chair in a fit of assumed petulance, staring at the flames and ignoring Ancar.

The boy was a fool, but not so great a fool, surely, that he could not understand what Falconsbane had just told him in so many words. Falconsbane could control the weather as he and his own wizards could not—except that Falconsbane was not free to do so. In order to control the weather, Falconsbane must be freed of the coercion spells.

In fact, that was not quite the case. Ancar need only modify the spells in order to give Falconsbane the freedom to work his will on the weather. But Ancar's education was full of some very massive holes, and one of those seemed to be a lack of shading. Things either were, or they were not; there were no indeterminate gradations. So Mornelithe was hoping that his insulting speech would goad Ancar into freeing him, at least a little—

It worked. As Ancar recovered from his surprise, both at the information and at being spoken to as if he were a particularly stupid schoolboy, his face darkened with anger.

"Well," he snarled, just barely audible above the rumble of thunder, "If you can do something, then *do* it, and stop complaining!"

His fingers writhed in a complicated mnemonic gesture, and Falconsbane felt some of the pressure on his powers easing a little. Only a little, but it was a start . . . a few of the coercions had been dropped. Ancar was not going to release him entirely, but the worst and most confining of the spells were gone.

Without a word, he rose from his chair, and stalked toward the window. Throwing it open with a grandiose gesture, he let the storm come tearing into the room, blowing out all the candles, extinguishing the fire, and plastering his clothing to his body in a breath. He was chilled and soaked in no time, but he ignored the discomforts of both in favor of the impressive show he was creating. Lightning raced across the sky above him, and he flung his arms wide, narrowing his eyes against the pelting rain. A bit of power made his hands glow most convincingly. He didn't need to make his hands glow, of course, but it made Ancar's eyes widen with awe in such a satisfactory manner.

He could have done everything from his comfortable chair, of course, without doing much more than lift a finger or two, but that would not have been dramatic enough. Ancar was stupid enough to be more impressed by dramatics than by results. That was probably why he had ended up with such inferior hirelings in the area of magic. Falconsbane did not need gestures to set his will twisting the forces of magic along the paths he chose. Falconsbane did not even need to close his eyes and drop into trance when the spell he wrought was a simple and familiar one.

Falconsbane sent out his probes, riding the wind until he found the center of the storm, and found the corresponding knot of energy in the ley-lines. He could unknot it, of course, but he didn't want to. Let Ancar's land suffer a little more. Let him see what a weapon controlled weather could be. Seizing the knot of energy, he gave it a powerful shove, sending it farther down the line and taking the storm with it.

Not too far, though. Just far enough from the capital and palace that it would not make his joints ache or interfere with his sleep tonight. He could not actually undo all the things that had *caused* the storm in his present state of coercion, and he did not think that Ancar would be inclined to release him completely just so that he could do so. If the fool asked him why he had not sent the storm into the skies of Valdemar, he would tell the boy that the King's own spells were to blame, interfering with Falconsbane's magic. That might convince him to release a few more of those coercions.

Or perhaps he wouldn't care that his farmers' fields would be flooded, the crops rotting in the sodden earth. It didn't much matter to Falconsbane, except as an example of how short-sighted Ancar was.

The wind and rain died abruptly. As he opened his eyes, he saw with satisfaction that he had not lost his touch. Already the lightning had lessened and the storm was moving off, clouds fleeing into the distance so rapidly that it was obvious something had *made* them change their courses. In a candlemark or two, it would be dry and clear around the palace.

Hopefully, this entire exercise had been showy enough to impress the young idiot. He turned to shrug at his captor. "Well," he said. "There you have it."

Ancar was nodding wisely, his eyes a little wide as he tried unsuccessfully to cover his amazement. "Very good," he said carelessly, still trying to cover his earlier slip. "I can see that you know what you are doing."

Falconsbane simply smiled, then returned to his chair. Now that those particular coercions were off, he relit the candles and the fire with a simple spell. And he noticed, with a twitch of contempt, that Ancar was as impressed by *that* as he had been by how quickly he had sent the storm away.

"I trust that something brought you here other than a wish for my company," he said, carefully keeping any hint of sarcasm from his voice. He gestured at the other chair beside the fire. "Pray, join me."

He was carefully calculating his insolence in being seated in the King's presence to underscore the fact that he *was,* current conditions notwithstanding, the King's equal. And it seemed to be working. Ancar did not say a word about his insulting behavior and, in fact, he took the proffered seat with something as near to humility as Ancar ever came.

"Nothing important," Ancar said airily. It was a lie, of course, and Falconsbane could read his real intentions as easily as if he could read the boy's thoughts. Simple deductions, actually; he knew that Ancar had been reviewing progress—or lack of it—along the border of Valdemar. There had been messengers from that border this very day. Despite Ancar's animosity toward Hulda, in this much he was still of one mind with the sorceress—his hatred of Valdemar. So that particular meeting was probably where Hulda had been this afternoon. It followed that he considered his options to have been exhausted, and now he wanted some help with that particular project from Mornelithe.

"Ah, then since there is nothing in particular you wish to discuss, perhaps you might be willing to satisfy my own curiosity about something," he said, silkily. "This *Valdemar* that troubles you you can tell me something about the land? How did you choose to quarrel with them in the first place?" He studied his own fingernails intently. "It would seem to me that you have been placing an inordinate amount of effort into attempting to conquer them, when so far as I can see, they are fairly insignificant. They have never attacked you, and they always stop at their own border, even when they are winning. Trying to conquer them seems, at least to an outsider, to be a losing proposition."

He looked up, to see Ancar flushing a little, his eyes showing a hint of anger. But the King did not reply.

He smiled. "And if I understand everything I have heard, now you plan to try for them again. What *is* the point here? Are you so addicted to defeat that you cannot wait to give them another opportunity to deliver it to you?" As Ancar flushed an even deeper shade, he continued, taunting the boy with the litany of his failures, gleaned from questioning servants, courtiers, and some of Ancar's other mages. "First you attack them before you are ready, and you naturally suffer a humiliating defeat. Then you attack them without ever bothering to discover if they had found some military allies and suffer a *worse* defeat. Your people are leaking across the border into their land on a daily basis, and you cannot even manage to insinuate a spy into their midst! Really, Ancar, I should think by now you would know enough to leave these people alone!"

Ancar was nearly purple with anger—and yet he held his peace and his tongue. Ancar did *not* want to talk about it. Now that was a curious combination. . . .

And to Falconsbane's mind, that spelled "obsession."

When one was obsessed with something, logic did not enter into the picture.

When one was obsessed with something, one was often blind to all else. An obsession was a weakness, a place into which a clever man could place the point of his wit, and pry until the shell cracked. . . .

As Ancar sat silently fuming, Falconsbane made some rapid mental calculations, adding up all the information he had been gleaning from courtiers, servants, and underling mages. Ancar was a young male, and any young male hates to be defeated, but that defeat must be doubly bitter coming as it did from the hands of *females*. He had failed to conquer Valdemar, failed to defeat its Queen, failed to get his hands on its Princess. He had failed a military conquest not once, but twice.

But that was by no means all, as Falconsbane's probes had revealed. He had tried, with no success whatsoever, to infiltrate a spy into the ranks of the Heralds. The only agents he had in Valdemar itself were relatively ineffective and powerless ones, placed among the lowest of the merchants and peasantry. Mercenary soldiers under yet another female leader had thwarted every single assassination attempt he had made, even the ones augmented by magic.

In short, the Queen and her nearest and dearest seemed to have some kind of charmed existence. They prevailed against all odds, as if the very gods were on their side. Their success mocked Ancar and all his ambitions, and without a doubt, it all maddened him past bearing.

So Falconsbane thought.

Until Ancar finally spoke, and proved to him that in this one respect, he *had* underestimated the young King.

"I must expand," he said, slowly, his flush cooling. "I am using up the resources of Hardorn at a rapid rate. I need gold to pay my mages, grain to feed my armies, a hundred things that simply must be brought in from outside. I cannot go South—perhaps you will not believe me, but the Karsites are the fiercest fighters you could ever imagine in your wildest nightmares. They are religious, you see. They believe that if they die in the defense of their land, they rise straight to the feet of their God . . . and if they take any of the enemies of their God with them, they rise to his right hand."

Falconsbane nodded, a tiny spark of respect kindling for the King. So he understood the power a religion could hold over an enemy? Mornelithe would never have credited him with that much insight. Perhaps there was more to the boy than the Adept had assumed. "Indeed," he said in reply. "There is no more deadly an enemy than a religious fanatic. They are willing to die and desperate to take you with them."

"Precisely," Ancar sighed. "What is more, their priests have a magic that comes from their God that is quite a match for my own. When you add to all that the mountains that border their land—it is an impossible combination. Those mountains are so steep that there is no place to bring a conventional army through without suffering one ambush or trap after another."

"Well, then, what about North?" Falconsbane asked, reasonably. And to his surprise, Ancar whitened.

"Do not even *mention* the North," the King whispered, and glanced hastily from side to side, as if he feared being overheard. "There is something there that dwarfs even the power Karse commands. It is so great—believe me or not, as you will, but I have seen it with my own eyes—that it has created an invisible fence that *no one* can pass. I have found no mage that can breach it, and after the few who attempted it perished, not even Hulda is willing to try."

Falconsbane raised his eyebrows involuntarily. *That* was something new! An invisible wall around a country? Who—or rather, *what*—could ever have produced something like that? What was the name of that land, anyway? Iften? Iftel?

But Ancar had already changed the subject.

"Most of all, I cannot go Eastward," he continued, his voice resuming a normal volume, but taking on an edge of bitterness. "The Eastern Empire is large enough to swallow Hardorn and never notice; the Eastern mages are as good or better than any I can hire, and their armies are vast . . . and well-paid. And they are watching me. I know it."

That frightened him; Falconsbane had no trouble at all in reading his fear, it was clear in the widening of his eyes, in the tense muscles of his neck and shoulders, in the rigidity of his posture.

"At the moment, they seem to feel that Hardorn is not worth the fight it would take to conquer it. They had a treaty with my father, which they have left in place, but the Emperor has not actually signed a treaty with my regime. Emperor Charliss has not even sent an envoy until very recently. I believe they are watching me, assessing me. But if I fail to take Valdemar, they will assume that I am weak enough to conquer." He grimaced. "My father had treaties of mutual defense with Valdemar and Iftel to protect him. I do not have those. I had not thought I would need them."

"Then do not attempt Valdemar a third time," Falconsbane suggested mildly.

Ancar's jaw clenched. "If I do not, the result will be the same. The Emperor Charliss will assume I am too weak to try. They have sent their ambassador here, and an entourage with him, as if they were planning on signing the treaty soon, but they have not deceived me. These people are not here to make treaties, they are here to spy on me. There are spies all over Hardorn by now. I have found some—"

"I trust you left them in place," Mornelithe said automatically.

He snorted. "Of course I did, I am not that big a fool. The best spy is the one you know! But I am also not so foolish as to think that I have found them all." He rose and began pacing in front of the fire, still talking. "One of the reasons I am sure that I have been unable to attract mages of any great ability is that the Emperor can afford to pay them far more than I can offer. I am fairly certain that the mages *I* have are not creatures of his, but there is no way of telling if he has placed mages as spies in my court and outside of it. So long as they practiced their mage-craft secretly, how would *I* ever know what they were?"

Falconsbane refrained from pointing out that he had just told the boy how he would know, that disturbances in the energy-fields would tell him. Perhaps neither he nor his mages were sensitive to those fields. It was not unheard of, though such mages rarely rose above Master. Perhaps he was sensitive, but only when in trance. If so, that was the fault of his teacher.

Ancar abruptly turned and strode back to the window,

standing with his back to Falconsbane and the room, staring at the rapidly-clearing clouds.

"This is something I had not seen before," he said, as if to himself. "And I had not known that magic could wreck such inadvertent and accidental havoc. It would be an excellent weapon. . . ."

Falconsbane snorted softly. It had taken the boy long enough to figure that out.

"Men calling themselves 'weather-wizards' have come to me, seeking employment," he continued. "I had thought them little better than herb-witches and charm-makers. They didn't present themselves well enough for me to believe them. I shall have to go about collecting them now."

"That would be wise," Falconsbane said mildly, hiding his contempt.

Ancar turned again and walked back into the room, this time heading for the door, but paused halfway to that portal to gaze back at Falconsbane.

"Is there anything else you need?" he asked.

Falconsbane was quite sure that if he asked for what he *really* wanted—his freedom—he would not get it. Ancar was not yet sure enough of him, or of himself. Rightly so. The moment he had that freedom, Falconsbane would squash the upstart like an insect.

But perhaps—perhaps it was time to ask for something else, something nearly as important.

"Send me someone you wish eliminated," he said. "Permanently eliminated, I mean. Male or female, it does not matter."

He halfway expected more questions—why he wanted such a captive, and what he expected to do with such a sacrificial victim when he had one. But Ancar's eyes narrowed; he smiled, slowly, and there was a dark and sardonic humor about the expression that told Falconsbane that Ancar didn't *care* why he wanted a victim. He nodded, slowly and deliberately. His eyes locked with Falconsbane's, and the Adept once again saw in Ancar's eyes a spirit kindred to his own.

Which made Ancar all the more dangerous. There was no room in the world for two like Falconsbane.

He left without another word, but no more than half a candlemark later, two guards arrived. Between them they held a battered, terrified man, so bound with chains he could scarcely move. When Falconsbane rose, one of them silently handed him the keys to the man's bindings.

The guards backed out, closing the door behind them.

Falconsbane smiled.

And took his time.

Chapter
Ten

Chilling rain poured from a leaden sky, a continuous sheet of gray from horizon to horizon. Elspeth silently thanked the far-away *hertasi* for the waterproof coats they had made, and tied her hood a little tighter. They rode right into the teeth of the wind; there was little in the way of lightning and thunder, but the wind and sheeting rain more than made up for that lack. The poor gryphons, shrouded in improvised raincapes made from old tents, would have been soaked to the skin if they had not been able to shield themselves from the worst of it with a bit of magic. The rest of them, however, chose to deal with the elements rather than advertise their presence on the road any further. Admittedly, that was less of a hardship for the Tayledras, Elspeth, Skif, and Nyara, with their coats supplied by the clever fingers of the *hertasi*. She felt very sorry for Cavil, Shion, and Lisha, whose standard-issue raincloaks were nowhere near as water-proof as *hertasi*-made garments.

Still, rain found its way in through every opening, sending unexpected trickles of chill down arms and backs, and exposed legs and faces got the full brunt of the weather. "I may have been more miserable a time or two in my life, but if so, I don't remember it," Skif said to Elspeth.

Nyara grimaced, showing sharp teeth, and nodded agreement. "I do not care to think of spending weeks riding through this," she said. "It must be bad for the hooved ones, yes? And does not cold and wet like this make people ill?"

On the other side of her, Cavil leaned over the neck of his Companion to add his own commentary.

"Now you see what we've been dealing with, off and on, for the past six months or so!" he shouted over the drumming rain, sniffing and rubbing his nose. "The—ah—lady is right; every village is suffering colds or fevers. I *hope* that we manage to ride out of the storm soon, but I am not going to wager on it. You can't predict anything anymore!"

Elspeth glanced back at Firesong, who was huddled in his waterproof cape, his firebird inside his hood, just as Vree was inside Darkwind's. *:Isn't there anything you can do about this?:* she asked him. *:Can't you send the rain away, or something? I thought about doing it, but since I've never done it before, I'm afraid to try.:*

:Rightly,: he replied. *:Weather-work done on mage-disturbance storms after the fact is a touchy business. For that matter, weather-work is always a touchy business. I do not know enough about this land, the countryside hereabouts, to make an informed decision. You do not yet have the skill. We do not know what is safe to do with this storm. Anything either of us do to change the weather-patterns could only mean making a worse disaster than this. Ask your friend if this is going to cause severe enough crop damage to cause shortages later.:*

"Is this bad enough to cause measurable crop damage?" she shouted back to Cavil. He squinted up at the sky for a moment, as if taking its measure, then shook his head. "It won't ruin the grazing, and the hay isn't ripening yet," he replied. "Most people around here are raising beef cattle, milch cows, and sheep, not crops. If this were farther south—" He shook his head. "We've been lucky; storms have been violent, but they haven't caused any major crop damage yet."

Yet. The word hung in the air, as ominous as the lowering clouds.

:Then we do nothing,: Firesong said firmly. *:There is no point in meddling and making a bad situation worse! We can endure some rough weather; the worst we will suffer is a wetting and a chill. When I have an opportunity to meet with those who have records of normal weather patterns,* then *I will help reestablish those patterns.:* He sighed. *:I fear I was only too prophetic when I said there was a great deal of work ahead of me.:*

Elspeth shrugged and grimaced slightly, but she could certainly see his point. There was only one benefit the foul weather was bestowing. Cavil could not insist on leaving the gryphons or the Tayledras behind on the excuse that they couldn't keep up with the Companions. He'd said something of the sort just before they left the Ashkevron manor, but his own Companion had told him tartly that no one was going to go racing to Haven in a downpour. In weather like this, even the Companions could not make very good time.

Darkwind and Nyara rode on horses borrowed from Lord Ashkevron, at that worthy's insistence. Those horses were what the Lord had referred to as "mudders;" sturdy beasts that could keep up a good pace all day through the worst weather. They were fairly ugly beasts; jug-headed, big-boned, as muscular as oxen, with rough, hairy hides that never could be curried into a shine. But those heavy bones and dense muscles pulled them right through the mire, and their dun-brown coats didn't show mud as badly as Firesong's white *dyheli* or the Companions—all of which were smeared and splattered up to their bellies.

Well, we hardly make a good show, but that's not such a bad thing, she reflected, shoving a strand of wet hair back under the hood of her cloak. *No one even thinks twice about making a State Visit out of us when they see us. . . .*

In fact, the three times they had stopped overnight so far, their hosts had been so concerned by their appearance that they had simply hurried them into warm beds, and had meals sent up to their rooms. They had been able to avoid State nonsense altogether.

Elspeth had just discovered something about herself, something she had learned after a mere twelve candlemarks in Cavil, Shion, and Lisha's presence. Her tolerance for courtly politics had deteriorated to the point of nonexistence after her stay with k'Sheyna. She just didn't want to hear about it. No gossip, no suppositions, none of it.

At some point during her musing, Skif and Nyara had dropped back as well, leaving her in the lead. Well, that hardly mattered. No one was going to get lost on a perfectly straight road.

Gwena sighed, her sides heaving under Elspeth's legs. :*I will be mortally glad to get to a warm, dry stable,*: she said. :*The Vales spoiled me.*:

The image she sent back included one of both Companions soaking away the cold in one of the hot springs. Elspeth chuckled, a little surprised; she hadn't realized that Gwena and Cymry had made use of the Vale's pools, too.

It made sense, of course, since some things in a Vale had to suit not only humans, but the Hawkbrothers' nonhuman allies. Surely *dyheli* used the hot springs, so why not the Companions?

:*They've spoiled me, too, dear,*: she replied, feeling her own twinge of longing for those wonderful hot pools. The best she could expect would be a hot bath; not the same thing at all. :*We have got to see about creating something like the springs at Haven. Think about coming in for a soak after a freezing rain—*:

:*Like this one? Oh, don't remind me!*: Gwena moaned. :*I can't even warm up by all the shoving through the mud!*:

Elspeth patted her shoulder sympathetically. :*It's almost dark,*: she said, with encouragement. :*It's not that far till we stop. I'll make sure you get something warm to eat, a nice hot mash or something like it, and a fire-warmed blanket.*:

Gwena cast a blue eye back at her, an imploring gaze made all the more pathetic by a soaked forelock straggling over the eye. *:Please. And don't forget just because a dozen nobles pounce on you once you're in the door.:*

Any reply she might have made was interrupted by Shion riding up alongside. "Excuse me, Lady," the Herald said, with a sharp and curious glance at Darkwind. "This man you are with? What exactly is his status?"

Shion and Cavil, both born of noble families, had done their level best to get her to talk—or rather, gossip. They were terribly persistent about things Elspeth considered private matters, asking very prying questions whenever Darkwind was out of earshot. Maybe being with the Tayledras had changed her, but she just didn't see where questions like this one were any of Shion's business.

Elspeth narrowed her eyes a bit at that, but kept her tone civil. And she chose to deliberately misunderstand the question. "I suppose that technically he is my equal," she replied evenly. "He is the son of the leader of Clan k'Sheyna, and an ally in his own right—"

She had a suspicion that this was not what Shion meant, and that suspicion was confirmed when the Herald frowned. "Actually, what I meant was—what is he to you? Why is he here, rather than in his own land?"

Elspeth decided to skate right around the question, and continue to give the answers to the questions Shion did have a right to ask. "He is here because he is one of my teachers in magic, and because he has offered to teach however many of our Heralds who have the Mage-Gift as he can. And yes, he *can* tell who has it. He tells me that I am likely not the only Herald to have it." She nodded as Shion bit off an exclamation. "Exactly. Evidently it was never precisely lost, but it was never used for lack of Heralds who could identify it and teach those who had it." She blinked in surprise as she realized something. "For that matter, I can identify people with it, but I'm not qualified to teach."

:Yet,: Gwena added.

:Hush, you'll undermine my credibility,: she replied.

Shion blinked, and licked her lips. "Do—do I have it?" she asked, as if she hoped to hear she did, and feared it at the same time.

Elspeth Looked for a moment at all three of the Heralds, using that new ability, and shook her head. "Not unless it's latent," she replied honestly. "None of you do, actually. I should tell you it's one of the rarer Gifts anyway. About as common as ForeSight, although that wasn't always the case. People who had it tended to drift out of Valdemar, after Vanyel's time. Most of the time it was identified and trained as if it was FarSight."

She paused for a moment, thinking quickly. "Don't assume I'm something special just because I'm Mage-Gifted. There've been plenty of Heralds who were—and are!—it's just that the Gift wasn't identified as such. Really, the main reason that I'm the first new Herald-Mage is either a matter of accident or divine providence. If a threat like Ancar had come up before, one of the other Heralds with the Gift would have gone outKingdom to get the training. If it hadn't come up now, I would still be sitting in Haven, getting beaten on by Kero and Alberich!"

Shion nodded, looking a little disappointed. Elspeth only chuckled. "Look, I wouldn't worry too much about it if I were you. Any Gift is useful. Any powerful Gift is extremely useful. It's also extremely dangerous to the bearer and those around. Mage-Gift isn't an answer to everything, and sometimes it's less so than mind-magic. What's more, mages don't always think to counter mind-magic. When they do think of it, they don't always succeed."

"That is because they cannot always counter mind-magic," Darkwind said, riding up to join the conversation, as Skif moved obligingly out of the way for him. Elspeth smiled thankfully at him; now maybe Shion would stop prying for a little. Although . . . perhaps she was being too harsh. She *was* the Heir, and what had happened to her in the Tayledras lands did have some importance for the Kingdom. And it was entirely possible that she was overreacting.

Thank Havens he understands our tongue enough to come rescue me!

Darkwind smiled charmingly at Shion. "There are ways to block some kinds of mind-magic, but they also block all other kinds of magic. A mage-shield powerful enough to block Mindspeaking blocks nearly everything else. So if you wish to keep your enemy from Mindspeaking, you also prevent yourself from working magic upon him."

Shion shook her head. "It's too complicated for me," she replied, and dropped back to ride beside Cavil, leaving Elspeth and Darkwind in the lead.

"Your grasp of my language is improving," she teased. He shrugged. Vree's head peeked out from beneath a fold of the hood for a moment. The bondbird looked at the rain in acute distaste, made a ratcheting sound, and vanished back into Darkwind's voluminous hood. Movement inside the hood showed Vree settling back to wait, probably grumbling to himself.

"My grasp of your language is improving because I am taking most of it from your mind, bright feather," he replied, giving her a glance that warmed her in spite of the freezing rain. "I thought perhaps I ought to save you from that too-curious colleague of yours."

"You noticed that, too, did you?" She grimaced. "All three of them are like that. I suppose it's your exotic nature. It makes them terribly curious."

"I don't know. . . ." He stared off ahead for a moment, then switched to Tayledras. "We have been three days on the road now, and it has not stopped, this questioning. Perhaps it is that we Hawkbrothers are more private, but they seem to see nothing amiss with wishing to know *everything* about me. Not only do they wish to know in detail what I plan to do when we reach Haven, they wish to know things that have *no* bearing on our mission. How I feel about everything, what my personal opinions are on such and such a thing, and most particularly, all the details of what you and I have done together. They seem to think they have a right to this information. It is—rather embarrassing."

She shook her head, puzzled and annoyed. "You may be mistaken," she told him, but with a bit of doubt creeping into her voice. If *he* had gotten the impression that Shion was being a little too personal—

But I am the Heir. Maybe she's under orders from

Mother to find out as much as she can about the people with me, and what we might have been—ah—involved in.

"Our cultures are very different, after all," she continued. "What sounds like a question about our personal lives may only be a question about what I was learning with you."

The look he gave her told her that he didn't think that he was mistaken, but he let the matter drop. It wasn't the first time he had complained of the other Heralds' insatiable questioning, but it was the first time he had mentioned their interest in something that could only be fodder for gossip and could serve no other purpose.

"You will probably get the usual greeting when we arrive," he said instead, changing the subject. His eyes twinkled when she grimaced and winced.

"If one more person comes up to me and says 'but I thought you were dead!' I'm going to strangle him," she muttered. "I can't believe people could be so stupid! And what difference would it make if I had been? The twins are perfectly capable, either one of them, of being made Heir. I am *not* indispensable! I'm only another Herald, if it comes right down to that."

"But the rumors made it seem as if you *were* indispensable, *ke'chara,*" he pointed out. "The rumors must have implied that your government was in a panic and trying to cover that panic. That makes me think that the rumors must have been more than idle nonsense; they must have been spread persistently and maliciously."

"Persistent and malicious—" Now that had a familiar, nasty ring to it. "Well, that's Ancar all over," Elspeth replied. "I can't think of anyone who deserves that description more. No doubt where it came from. I don't know what in seven hells he hoped to accomplish, though."

"Enough unrest would suit him, I suspect." Darkwind put a hand inside his hood to scratch Vree's breastfeathers. He had warned Elspeth that he was unused to riding, but he seemed to be doing just fine to her. Of course, it helped that their pace was being held to a fast walk. You had to really work to get thrown at that speed. "He wishes, I think, to make as much disturbance and confusion as possible. The Clans have a game like that, from one created by the Shin'a'in. Artful distraction."

She shook her head, and water dribbled into her face. "I just can't believe that disruption would be enough for Ancar."

Darkwind continued to scratch Vree—which looked rather odd, since he seemed to be feeling around inside his hood for something—and his eyes darkened with thought. "What of this, then," he said, after a moment. "You say that your younger siblings would make good Heirs. But their father is not your father, am I correct?" At her nod, he continued. "What if the rumors of your death were only a beginning—that once it was believed that you were dead, Ancar then planned to add rumors that your stepfather had contrived your death, in order to have his own children take the throne?"

She stared at him, mouth dropping open. "That—that's crazy!" she stammered, finally. "No one who knew my stepfather would ever believe that!"

"No one who *knew* him, you say," Darkwind persisted. "But this land of yours is a very large one, larger than I had ever guessed. So how many of these people out here truly know him? How can they? How many have even seen him more than once or twice, and at a distance?"

It made diabolical sense. Especially given that Elspeth's own father—Prince Daren's brother—had tried to murder her mother and take the throne for himself. People would be only too ready to believe in the murderous intentions of another of the Rethwellan royals.

For that matter, they had been perfectly willing to believe that *she* might plot against her mother, as if betrayal were somehow inheritable.

Ancar was even clever enough to spread two conflicting sets of rumors. One set, that Prince Daren had connived at Elspeth's death, and another, that Elspeth was alive and trying to usurp her mother's throne.

"I hate it," she said slowly, "And you are probably right. Especially since my first destination was Rethwellan, *his* land. People would have been only too ready to believe he'd set something up with his brother to get rid of me."

Darkwind nodded. "And what effect would that have upon the rulers of your land?"

"It—at the very best, it would be a distraction and cause a lot of problems at a time when we don't need either." She clenched her jaw. "At the worst, it would undermine confidence in the Queen and everything she stands for. That snake—he is as clever as he is rotten, I swear! He and Falconsbane are two of a kind!"

"Then we must hope he never achieves the kind of power that Falconsbane had," Darkwind said firmly. "We must work to be rid of him before he does. All the more reason for your friends to be here. We have seen this kind of creature before, and I hope we can second-guess Ancar because of our experience with Falconsbane."

Clouds were too thick for a real sunset, but the light was beginning to fade. Something large and dark, a building of some kind, was looming up in the distance at the side of the road; the rain was falling too thickly for Elspeth to make out what it was, but out here, it was unlikely to be anything other than their next stop, the manor of Lady Kalthea Lyonnes.

Shion looked up and cried, "Look!" in a tone that confirmed Elspeth's guess. They all urged their tired mounts into a little faster pace, and within half a candlemark they were pounding at the gates.

Fortunately, after the trouble at the Ashkevron manor, someone always went on ahead to inform their hosts exactly what was coming. This time Lisha had ridden ahead to warn the Lady and her household about the gryphons; there was a certain amount of trepidation on the part of the servants who came out to meet them, but at least no one fled screaming in fear.

Things were sorted out with commendable haste. The gryphons were conducted off to the chapel—chapels seemed to be the only rooms suitable to their size—the Companions and *dyheli* taken to the stables and a promised hot mash and rubdown. And finally the two-legged members of the party were brought in, still dripping a little, to be presented to their hostess.

"Elspeth!" the Lady cried, clasping Elspeth's hand and

kissing it fervently. "Thank the gods! We heard you were dead!"

Darkwind choked, smothering a laugh, and Elspeth only sighed.

But later that night, after all the fuss was over and everyone had been settled into their rooms, Elspeth sagged into a chair beside the fire and stared into the flames. Perhaps this business of staying with the high-born was a mistake. . . .

On the other hand, no inn would ever accept the gryphons. And at least in this way, word was being spread quickly that she *was* alive and she had returned with some real help against Ancar.

But another little conversation with Shion and with a cousin of Shion's who lived here had just proved to her that Darkwind was right. Shion and the others weren't at all concerned with the welfare of Valdemar—or at least that wasn't their motivation in cross-examining her. They were just plain nosy. They wanted gossip-fodder, and what was more, if she didn't give it to them, they were perfectly capable of making things up out of whole cloth!

Shion's cousin had brought Elspeth her supper, using that as an excuse to ask any number of increasingly impertinent questions. Finally she had concluded, shamelessly, with the question of whether it was true that Hawkbrothers only mated in groups, saying as an excuse that she had read about it in "an old story." And it was pretty obvious that the cousin also wanted to know if Elspeth had been a member of one of those groups.

When Elspeth asked her where she had heard such nonsense, the girl had demurred and avoided giving an answer, but Elspeth already had a good idea who had prompted it. After all, until she had gone delving into the old Archives, there hadn't been more than a handful of folk in Valdemar who even knew that the Hawkbrothers existed. So where else would the girl have heard an "old story" about the Tayledras except from Shion?

Elspeth's jaw tightened. The trouble was, no matter what she said or did, it was likely to make the situation worse. If she dressed Shion down for this, Shion would only be more certain that Elspeth was hiding some kind of dreadful secret. If she forbade any more loose talk, that would only make Shion more circumspect in spreading silly gossip. If she ignored it all, Shion would go right on spreading gossip, and making up whatever she didn't know for certain. There was no way Elspeth could win at this.

Heralds were human beings, with all the failings and foibles of any other set of humans. Shion's failing was gossip—harmless enough under most circumstances. Except for this one, where her fantasies could and would cause Elspeth some problems. . . .

A gentle tap at the door made her look up in time to see Darkwind slipping inside. He glanced around the darkened room for a moment, then spotted her at the hearth and came to join her.

"I do not know whether to laugh or snarl, bright feather," he said without preamble. "And if we had not as many notorious gossips in k'Sheyna as anywhere else, I would probably be very annoyed at this moment."

"I take it you met Kalinda," Elspeth said dryly as he took a seat beside the fire.

"Indeed." His mouth twitched. "I was discussing some trifle with Firesong when she brought us our dinners, then, bold as you please, offered to—ah—'join our mating circle.' I confess that I did not know what to say or do."

Elspeth took one look at his face and broke up in a fit of giggling. That set him off, too, and for the next few moments, they leaned against each other, laughing and gasping for breath. Any glance at the other's face only served to set them off again.

"I—dear gods!—you must have done something. How did you get her out of there?" she choked, finally.

He shook his head, and held his side. "I did nothing!" he confessed. "It was Firesong. He just looked at the girl and said, 'the offer is appreciated, but unless you turn male, impossible.' She turned quite scarlet, and stammered something neither of us understood, then left."

That sent Elspeth into convulsions again because she could very easily see Firesong doing exactly that. The wicked creature!

Her gales of laughter started Darkwind giggling again, and the two of them laughed until they simply had no more breath to laugh with anymore. She lay with her head against Darkwind's shoulder while the fire burned a little lower, and only spoke when he moved to throw another branch into the flames.

"I suppose that will take care of Shion for a while," she said, wiping moisture from the corner of one eye. "I wish I'd thought of that as a solution. But you know, now Shion will probably begin telling everyone that you and Firesong are both *shay'a'chern*. The gods only know what *that* will bring out of the corners!"

"I do not care, dearheart," he replied, stroking her hair. "So long as it saves you grief. And I am certain that Firesong will be positively delighted! I tell you, he is as shameless as a cooperihawk!"

She laughed again, for she had seen the cooperihawks in their rounds of spring matings, which were frequent and undiscriminating.

He chuckled with her and caressed her shoulders, then continued. "I have other confessions to make to you, and none so amusing. I had no idea of the size of your land, of the numbers of your people. I had naively supposed your Valdemar must be like a very large Vale. And I had no idea what your status truly was among your people. And—I now realize that all of my assumptions were based on those ideas."

"My status is subject to change, my love," she replied quickly. "As I told you, I am not indispensable."

"But others believe you are." He held her for a long moment in silence, his warm hands clasped across her waist. "You have duties and obligations, and they do not include a—long term relationship with some foreign mage."

She forced herself to remain calm; after all, wasn't this precisely what she had thought, herself, any number of times? She had known since before she left Valdemar that her freedom was severely restricted. Hadn't she rebuffed Skif with that very same argument?

But she no longer accepted that argument, as she had

not accepted the "fated" path that the Companions had tried to force her to take.

And even though his tongue was saying that he must let her go, his body was saying quite a different thing. He held her tightly, fiercely, as if to challenge anyone who might try to part them.

She must choose her words very carefully. He had opened his heart to her; she must answer the pain she heard under his words. But he would not respect someone who violated all the vows she had made to her own land and people by willfully deserting them, either. The next few words might be the most important she would ever speak in her life.

"I have duties, true enough," she replied, slowly, turning to stare into his eyes. "I never pretended otherwise. I have to find a way to reconcile those duties with what I want and what you want. I think I can, if you will trust me."

"You know I do. With my very life, *ashke*."

His face looked like a beautiful sculpture by the firelight. Time seemed to slow down. Even Vree was stockstill, watching them both unblinkingly. Darkwind held his breath.

"I think I can be true to Valdemar, Darkwind—and to you. I *know* there has to be a way. I refuse to lose either of you—you or my native land and my duty to it. I refuse to let you go."

The last was said so fiercely that his eyes widened for a moment in surprise. "But how can you possibly reconcile them?" he asked at last. "You are your mother's chosen successor. There is very little freedom for you in that role."

"I have some ideas," she replied. "But they hinge on your not knowing what I'm going to do so you can be just as surprised as everyone else. Otherwise people will think that I'm simply acting like a love-struck wench rather than in the best interests of Valdemar."

He held very still for a moment. "And are you a love-struck wench?"

She reached up, grabbed two handfuls of his hair, and pulled his mouth to hers for a long and passionate kiss.

The touch of his lips made a fire build in the core of her. It made it very difficult to hold to coherent thought. "Of course I am," she replied calmly.

Darkwind smiled and stroked her hair. He closed his eyes and pulled her closer, strong and comforting, protecting her as a great hawk would mantle over its young in a storm. His touch against her cheek was as gentle as a feather's, and his sigh of contentment matched her own.

The scent of his body and the smoky warmth of the room blended. She knew she had said the right thing. She had spoken her heart. She had spoken the truth.

The kiss had made her heart race and drove her thoughts into paths entirely foreign to simple discussion. "But I don't want them to know that. Being love-struck doesn't mean my brains have poured out my ears!"

"I hope not," he murmured, "because I am as much in love with your mind as—"

She did not give him the chance to finish the sentence.

Vree watched the two kiss, then tucked his head to sleep. As far as Vree was concerned, whatever came, whatever they faced, wherever they went, all would now be right with the world.

It was a good bonding. Display done. Mate won. Nesting soon. They would fly high together.

At last, they cleared the area covered by the storm, and the final few days were spent riding under sunnier skies. Sunnier—not sunny; there were no cloudless skies, but at least the roads remained less than mud-pits despite the occasional brief cloudburst. The weather was still odd, though; there were always spectacular sunsets and wild lightning storms at night, although these storms did not necessarily produce rain, and the skies never entirely cleared even when they neared Haven.

The city itself sat under a circle of *blue* sky, rather than clouds; a nearly-perfect circle, in fact, and very odd to Elspeth's eyes. When Firesong saw that, he nodded to himself, as if this was something he had anticipated but had not necessarily expected.

At least, when they reached Haven, they were no

longer mud spattered and soggy; they even took a moment to change, when they were within a candlemark or two of the capital. Elspeth had the feeling they were not going to have much of a chance to clean up when they reached the Palace, given the excitement her arrival was generating.

A scant network of signal-towers like the ones in Hardorn had been set up to relay news, although in the foul weather they had been riding through such towers could only be used at night, and often not even then. There were not enough of them to warn their noble hosts that they were coming, but there *were* enough that by now all of Haven knew the approximate candlemark of when they would appear. Once the weather cleared, they had borrowed a cart from one of their hosts, in which the gryphlets and Rris now rode in excited splendor. In every village along the road, even when it was raining, the entire population turned out to see them pass.

Elspeth felt entirely as if she was riding in a circus procession, but she waved and smiled anyway, noting with a great deal of amusement that no one really paid much attention to *her* once they caught sight of the gryphons.

By the time they reached Haven, word had traveled ahead of them by those mirror- and lantern-relays, and as she had expected, the road on both sides was lined with people, four and five deep. It was quite obvious at that point that Elspeth was not the attraction; she was not even a close second. After all, she did not look all that much different than any Herald, and the populace around Haven was quite used to seeing Heralds. The gryphons, gryphlets, and Tayledras were the real attention getters, in that order.

Firesong and Treyvan were in their element, waving genially to the crowd, and occasionally throwing up magical "fireworks" that were insignificant in terms of power, but incredibly showy. They were definitely crowd pleasers. Treyvan would take to the air every few leagues to hover above the procession, while the onlookers ooh-ed and ahh-ed. Hydona simply sighed with patience, and trotted quietly behind the wagon. The gryphlets bounced in the bed of the wagon like a pair of excited kittens, bringing more "ohs" and exclamations of "aren't they *adorable*." As had happened at the Ashkevron manor, the gryphlets convinced the crowd that these mighty creatures were not monsters at all.

Elspeth might just as well not have been along. People cheered her in a perfunctory sort of way, then riveted their attention on the Hawkbrothers and gryphons. When either Treyvan or Firesong performed, she could have stripped naked and done riding tricks on Gwena's back and no one would have noticed.

She had known this would happen. She had rather expected that she might find herself a little jealous. After all, she was used to being the center of attention—the beloved Heir to the Throne, and all of that. She had never been forced to share the focus of all eyes, much less been excluded from that focus.

She was rather surprised when all she felt was relief. And in a way, that simply confirmed what she had been thinking since they had arrived back in Valdemar. She was not really happy being the Heir; she was not truly suited to the job. She had been a lot more comfortable back in the Vale, when no one had treated her any differently than anyone else in the Clan. In fact, with the Hawkbrothers, she was judged only by her merits. She had changed a great deal since she had last seen Haven, and nothing showed that change quite so profoundly as this.

When they reached the outskirts of Haven, the crowd had thickened, to the point where there wasn't room for a child between the fronts of the buildings and the street. The noise was deafening; the mass of folk dressed in their best dazzling to the eye. And for someone who had spent so many months out in the wilderness, the crowds were enough to give one a feeling of being crushed.

She spared a thought and a glance for Nyara, who had probably never seen this many people in all of her life put together. The Changechild was clinging to Skif's hand, but seemed to be holding up fairly well.

:*She's all right,*: Need said shortly, in answer to Elspeth's tentative thought. :*I managed to get her used to something like this by feeding her some of my old memories. She doesn't like it much, but then, neither do you.:*

A good point. Elspeth tendered her thanks, and turned her attention back toward the crowd, watching for ambushes and traps. This would be a good place to hide an assassin, if Ancar had the time to put one in place. People leaned precariously out of windows to watch them pass, cheering wildly, and still paying very little attention to *her.* It felt like a kind of victory procession. She only hoped the feeling would prove prophetic.

In a way, it was kind of amusing, for the merchants and street vendors had taken advantage of the situation and the advance warning they had of it, to do as much impulse business as they might during a real festival. She noted, chuckling under the roar of the crowd, the number of vendors with merchandise they must have made up specifically for this "processional." There were people hawking gryphon and Companion-shaped pastries and candies, cheap flags emblazoned with crude gryphons, hawks, and the arms of Valdemar, toy sellers with carved hawks, Companions, and fat little winged cats with beaks that were undoubtably supposed to be gryphons, and one enterprising fellow with stick-horses with white Companion heads *and* feathered gryphon heads. He was doing an especially brisk business.

She was relieved and pleased to see a number of people in Guard blue mingled in with the crowd. Kero's work, no doubt. In fact, she might very well have called in all of the Skybolts to be on assassin-watch. Trust Kero to think of that.

:I'm watching, too, youngling,: Need said unexpectedly. *:Keep your eyes sharp, but with all of us working, I think we'll get any assassin before he gets one of us.:*

The crowd continued to be that thick right up to the gates of the Palace/Collegium complex. They passed between the walls and onto the road leading up to the Palace, and there the motley crowd gave way to a crowd of people in discrete knots of Guard Blue, trainee Gray, Healer Green, Bard Red, and Herald White. And it appeared that at least a few of the vendors had penetrated even here—or some enterprising young student had turned vendor himself—for here were the flags they had seen out in the city, being waved just as enthusiastically by usually sober Heralds and Guards. There were, perhaps, a few long gryphons and hawks and a few more of the white horses of Valdemar, but otherwise it looked very much the same. The trainees in particular were loud and enthusiastic, their young voices rising shrilly above those of their elders. It was all but impossible to see much of anything past the crowd. Even the Companions were crowded up behind the humans, tossing their manes, their eyes sparkling with enjoyment.

She caught sight of friends at last among the crowd—some of her year-mates, Keren and Teren, retired Elcarth. The noise was such that she saw their mouths moving, and could only shrug and grin, miming that she would talk to them later.

The procession came to an end at the main entrance to the Palace. It ended there by default, that entrance being the only set of doors large enough to admit the gryphons. There those who were riding dismounted, and an escort of Palace Guards in their dark blue lined up on either side of the group to usher them inside.

Interestingly, Shion, Cavil, and Lisha were neatly cut off from the group and taken aside with the Companions and Firesong's *dyheli*. Elspeth was not particularly sorry to see them leave, she only dreaded the gossip that was sure to follow.

The doors opened—and there was Talia, who ignored gryphons, Hawkbrothers, and protocol, and ran with her arms outstretched to catch Elspeth up in a breathless embrace.

They hugged each other tightly, separating only long enough for searching looks, then embracing again. To Elspeth's surprise, she found herself crying with happiness.

"Oh, *stop* it, you'll make me cry, too," Talia scolded in Elspeth's ear. "Dear gods, you look *wonderful!*"

"You look just as wonderful," Elspeth countered over the cheering.

Talia laughed throatily. "More gray hair, dearheart, I promise you. The children are at the age where someone is always plucking them right out of the arms of trouble, usually by the scruff of the neck. I have to warn you. Your mother has called a full Court, Council and all—"

"So she can prove to everyone at once that I'm still alive. I'd already figured she would." Good. That meant that she would not have to wait to put her plan into motion. "Right now?"

"Right now—" Talia sounded a bit uncertain, and it was Elspeth's turn to laugh and put the Queen's Own at arm's length.

"Look at me," she demanded. Talia cocked her head to one side and did. "I'm a little dusty, but I did take the time to change, so we're all presentable. I've survived fire, flood, and mage-storm, almost daily encounters with the nastiest creatures a perverted Adept could create, and daily border patrols. I'm hardly going to be tired out by a mere ride! Bring on your Council—I'll eat them alive!" And she bared her teeth and growled.

Talia threw her head back and laughed, her chestnut curls trembling, and if there *was* more gray in her hair, Elspeth couldn't see it. "All right, you've convinced me. Now go convince them!"

She stepped back and bowed slightly, gesturing for all of them to precede her into the Palace. Gryphons included. Lytha and Jerven trotted in the shadow of their mother's wings, looking curiously all around with huge, alert eyes.

With Talia and the contingent of the Guard bringing up the rear, Elspeth led the procession through the great double doors—for the first time in her memory, both of them thrown open wide—and down the hall that led to the audience chamber. The gryphons' claws clicked metallically on the marble floor, and the bulk of the Palace muffled the sounds of the crowd outside. Most of the cheering had stopped once they all vanished inside, but there was still some crowd noise. And it was more than likely that Shion, Cavil, and Lisha were being interrogated by all their friends about the ride home and the strange people and creatures that the Heir had brought with her.

The double doors at the end of the hall were thrown

open just as they reached them, and a fanfare of trumpets announced them to the expectantly-hushed Court.

And it was an announcement of the full complement, as Elspeth had hoped. It included Firesong and Darkwind, as "Ambassadors of the Tayledras;" Nyara as "Lady Nyara k'Sheyna," leaving the assembled courtiers and power brokers to wonder, no doubt, just what a "k'Sheyna" was; and the gryphons as "Lord Treyvan Gryphon and Lady Hydona and children, ambassadors of Kaled'a'in," leaving the courtiers of Valdemar even more baffled. Poor Rris; he was not announced, although he trotted at the heels of the gryphlets. But he did not seem disappointed as Elspeth glanced back. He was simply watching *everything* with that alert expression that told her he was storing it all up, to become yet another tale in the *kyrees'* oral history. The *dyheli* had been taken off with Gwena and Cymry, but he had never shown much interest in being an envoy anyway; he had made it rather clear to Elspeth that he was there mostly to show to Valdemar that there were other intelligent races allied with the Tayledras than just humans and gryphons.

She paused on the threshold, giving the others a chance to compose themselves before striding into the room full of strangers. The room fell silent, and with a whispering rustle of cloth and a creaking of leather, everybody in the room except the four on the dais bent in a bow or curtsy. She paused for another moment, then moved forward, and behind her she heard the same swish of cloth and creaking of leather; the members of Court and Council rising as she passed. Her own eyes were fastened on her mother and stepfather, both in Whites with the royal circlets about their brows, both standing before their thrones, with Heralds flanking them on either hand, and Guards behind the Heralds. One of those Heralds was Kerowyn, who winked broadly as soon as Elspeth was near enough to see her face; the other was Jeri, Alberich's hand-picked successor. The Guards behind both of them were from Kero's Skybolts. Elspeth relaxed at the sight of all these old friends. *They* would understand what she was about to do, even if her mother didn't.

Selenay's gold hair was clearly streaked with silver;

Prince Daren showed more worry lines at the corners of his eyes and across his forehead. Both of them widened their eyes and frankly stared for a moment at Elspeth before recovering their "royal masks"—she chuckled under her breath, for she was wearing one of her more elaborate sets of *hertasi*-made working-Whites, and while she was clearly garbed as a Herald, it was not a Herald as Valdemar at large was used to seeing one. She could hardly wait until they got a good look at Firesong, who had chosen to contrast his silver hair and the silver plumage of his firebird with Tayledras mage-robes in a startling shade of blue that could never be mistaken for Guard Blue. In fact, she was not entirely certain *how* the *hertasi* had achieved that eye-blinding color. It certainly was nowhere to be found in nature!

The wood-paneled Throne Room was filled to bursting, with every available light-source fully utilized. If the crowds outside had been dazzling, this crowd was dizzying, each courtier in full dress, with as many jewels as possible within the bounds of taste. And some, predictably, had gone beyond the bounds of taste. The place was ablaze with color and light—

:And all of it pales next to Firesong's self-image,: Gwena commented in the back of her mind. Elspeth stifled a chuckle and kept her face perfectly sober.

She smiled broadly as she neared the throne, but submitted demurely to an "official" greeting, as Selenay announced to the room that her beloved daughter and Heir had returned, and made all the appropriate official motions. Even though she longed to fling her arms around her mother as she had around Talia, that would have to wait until they were in private together.

And by then—

She bowed briefly to her mother, then straightened, and took the steps necessary to place her on the dais in her position as Heir. She turned to face the silent Court, and looked out over the faces of new friends, old, and utter strangers. Firesong winked; so did Treyvan. Nyara managed a tremulous smile. Darkwind simply held her eyes for a long breath.

:Hold onto your feathers, my love,: she Mindsent to

Darkwind as she took a deep breath of her own. *:I have a surprise for you.:*

"Thank you, all of you, for your wonderful greetings," she said, carefully pronouncing and projecting each word as she had been taught since she was a child, so that every syllable would reach the back of the room. "I have returned, as I promised, with the help that I went to find—and with more, far more. But with your indulgence, I would like to make an announcement before I introduce our new allies and friends. I, Elspeth, daughter of Queen Selenay and Heir to the throne of Valdemar, hereby renounce my claim to the throne of Valdemar, in favor of my siblings, the Princess Lyra and Prince Kris."

A chorus of whispered comments and oaths came from the courtiers and Guard alike.

"I have been reliably informed by the Companions that both will be Chosen, and thus both are equally suited to the position of Heir to the Throne of Valdemar—as I am *not.*"

The expressions on the faces nearest her—those not in her own party, that is—were so funny she almost burst out laughing. They were utterly, completely stunned; and she had the feeling that her own mother and stepfather wore identical expressions. It looked almost as if someone had run through the crowd, hitting everyone in the back of the head with a board. They could not have been more startled if she had suddenly sprouted wings and horns.

Quickly, before anyone could interrupt, she enumerated her reasons. "As all well know, my blood-father was a traitor and a would-be assassin, and all my life his crimes have hung over my head, clouding confidence in my trustworthiness and ability to rule. With Lyra and Kris there will be no such doubts. I have heard, before I left and as I returned, the same rumors that many of you had heard both before and during my absence—that I was in reality using that absence to plot against my beloved mother. With Lyra and Kris in the position of Heir, no one need worry when I am absent that I may be thinking of taking the throne before my rightful time. The same rumors have always existed outside this Kingdom as well—

and once again, when I no longer hold the position of Heir, the fears that I will attempt to usurp the rule of Valdemar as Ancar of Hardorn usurped his father's throne will be laid to rest. I am not Ancar—and now, no one will ever need to wonder if I could be tempted by the promise of power into following his wretched example."

There, she thought. *Let them think about that, and when they think about it, wonder if those rumors just might have originated with Ancar, since he is so familiar with usurping thrones.*

"But there are additional considerations," she continued quickly, and then surrounded herself in the blink of an eye with a showy glow of magic fires that made everyone gasp and step back a pace. Firesong was grinning and nodding with approval; Darkwind just stared at her, but his mouth was twitching suspiciously. "As you can see," she went on, in ringing, magic-enhanced tones, "I *am* the first of the new Herald-Mages of Valdemar! I am the first and only *trained* Herald-Mage at this moment. There will be others, I promise you, for one of the reasons that I have brought these new allies is to help in the training of new Herald-Mages. And while that is a cause for rejoicing, it is also a cause for concern, for as the sole trained Herald-Mage *and* the Heir, my loyalties and duties are at terrible odds with one another. As Herald-Mage, I must risk myself and my powers in defense of this Kingdom. As Heir, I must *not,* ever, place myself in jeopardy! I have been forced to weigh good against good, duty against duty, and I have concluded that my duty to Valdemar is best served by renouncing the throne and taking my place in the front lines of whatever conflict may come. Valdemar needs my skills and strength far more than it needs me beneath the Heir's coronet."

Now she turned, to see her stepfather beaming with approval, and her mother doing a creditable imitation of a landed fish. Controlling herself carefully, she concluded her speech.

"Therefore, I ask you—you of the Council and Court, and you, Queen and Consort—to accept my abdication and allow me to take my proper place as one Herald among many. I will always be my mother's true daughter, but I no longer wish to be a cause of worry and conflict. And I wish to place my abilities, my life, and my honor fully in the service of my land and people." She looked pleadingly into her mother's eyes. "Will you say me 'aye'?"

Selenay never had a chance to respond, for Prince Daren led the Council and Court in a thundering acceptance of her audacious solution.

It was all over. With weary feet, Elspeth took service corridors rather than the main halls of the Palace. Servants ignored her as just another Herald, although a few stopped to stare at her unique Whites, and one young man paused long enough to whisper, "Herald, that is a *fine* set of Whites!"

She smiled at him and winked. From the look of him, he had a fine sense of fashion himself. Someone had clearly taken a creative hand to his servants' livery. He winked back and hurried on.

But on the whole, Elspeth felt rather as if she had been run through a clothes-wringer in the Palace laundry and hung out to dry. Even after her abdication was a fact, there had still been a hundred things to deal with.

The introduction of the rest of the party, for instance, and the explanations of what, exactly, their positions were, and what they brought to Valdemar's defense. Selenay, still stunned from the abdication, had been taken quite a bit aback by the gryphons, until Hydona had said, quietly, in quite creditable Valdemaran, "I undersssstand herrr Majesssty isss the motherrr of twinsssss?" and at Selenay's nod had uttered a long-suffering sigh and continued, "Then we have a grrreat deal in common."

And since Lytha had chosen that particular moment to bite Jerven's tail, causing him to squall, and Hydona to reach back absentmindedly and separate them both, Selenay had come out of her stunned trance immediately and graced Hydona with a smile that united them at once in a bond of mother-to-mother. Talia had covered her mouth, hiding a grin. So had Elspeth. No one would ever be able to convince Selenay now that the gryphons were "dangerous animals."

Firesong had quite dazzled the Court; he seemed born to manipulate crowds. And by the time Court had been formally ended, he had collected a little court of his own, both he and his firebird posing and preening quite shamelessly. Darkwind went almost unnoticed, and so did Nyara.

Which had probably been Firesong's intent, or at least one of his intentions.

Then there had been the joyful task of greeting all of her old friends, and explaining to them all that she had thought this through very carefully, and *yes,* it was the best solution to the situation. "Ancar has been focusing on me as a target, one that he knows," she had continued. "He doesn't know anything about the twins, and they're children, much easier to guard day-and-night because they have no duties. Mother could even send them off into hiding if she had to."

Of all of them, Kero had understood the best, Kero and her stepfather. But eventually all of them accepted it.

She had made a point of not introducing Darkwind specifically. There was no reason to start up rumors yet, not until after she dealt with Selenay.

Then had come the dreaded confrontation with her mother.

Which turned out not to be a confrontation at all.

She still couldn't quite believe it. At some point during her absence, Selenay had come to accept the fact that Elspeth was grown up now, and capable of making her own decisions. "You will always be my darling daughter," she had said, after a long and tear-filled embrace, "but you are also a wise woman, wiser and braver than I am. You *have* seen the best solution to your divided duties. And while I shall *hate* seeing you go into danger, I can't deny you your right to do so."

That had brought out another freshet of tears from both of them, until Selenay was called to a meeting of the Council. Elspeth, no longer Heir and so no longer required to attend, had gone off to her new quarters.

The rooms were the ones assigned to important and high-ranking guests. She had asked to be installed next to Darkwind, in rooms with a connecting door. She hadn't spent all of her childhood running about the Palace without learning the layout of the place. She had made very sure that she knew exactly where each and every member of her group had been housed. The Seneschal had given her a startled look that turned to a knowing one, and nodded once.

And now she no longer had to worry about what people thought. It didn't matter anymore. She was not the Heir; her liaisons were no one's business but her own.

The feeling of freedom was as heady as a draught of strong wine.

She opened the door, and closed it behind her, letting her eyes adjust to the dim light filtering in through the closed curtains. This should be—yes, was—a suite of two rooms, a public room and a bedroom. She pushed away from the door and sought the latter.

There was a basin and pitcher of water on a washstand in her bedroom; once again she had a twinge of nostalgia for the Vale, but this would have to serve until she could get to the shared bathing room. She splashed some water on her face to wash away the marks of tears, brushed out her hair, and then went back into the sitting room and tapped on the door dividing her rooms from Darkwind's.

He opened it, clearly startled that there was anyone seeking entrance, and clearly *not* expecting her. She took advantage of his startlement by flinging herself at him, and within a heartbeat he had recovered quite enough to return her embrace. It was just as heartfelt and passionate as she had hoped, and he left his mind open to her completely, leaving her no doubt whatsoever of how he truly felt. Profound gratitude and relief, a touch of guilt that despite her speech she might have done this only for him, and love and pride.

She was the first to break off the kiss, reluctantly, but he was the first to speak.

"You were magnificent," he said fervently in his own tongue. "Absolutely magnificent. You made me so proud!"

"Good," she replied, taking his hand and pulling him into her room. "Now, let's get to the serious business, before we do or say anything else."

He nodded quickly, following her inside, and closing the connecting door as he did so. "Of course—you are right, we must make war plans, dealing with this Ancar, and how we can identify and train the new mages—"

"No," she told him, laying a finger on his lips to stop the flow of words. "That's serious, but there's something else that needs settling first. You—and me."

He blinked at her a moment, taken quite by surprise. "Ah—I'm not sure—exactly what—" He blinked for a moment more, then let out his breath as if he had been holding it for days. "You and I. Well. Perhaps the first thing we should do is sit down."

She laughed a little. "Good idea."

The rooms that adjoined one another were deliberately designed so that ambassadors could hold informal court. His would be the mirror image of hers, with a fireplace in the wall the two rooms shared, a desk, several chairs, and a small couch where someone who was ailing or infirm (as many senior diplomats were) could recline at his ease. He led the way to the couch, and she sat down beside him. The light from outside was beginning to fade, but no servant would dare venture in here to light candles until they were called for, which was exactly how she had ordered it. They would be undisturbed until she wished otherwise, for the first time in her life.

"I need to know something right now," she said, as he visibly searched for words to begin the conversation. "What are your long-term intentions and plans? As regards us, our relationship, that is."

He swallowed, and took a deep breath. "I'm taking this all very well, am I not?" he replied, with a weak grin. "Actually, you flung a rock into what had been a quiet and ordered pond. I *was* going to keep myself strictly in the background. I had intended to suborn myself to your needs and wishes, and keep everything so discreet that no one would ever guess what was going on. Firesong and I had even planned on creating the fiction that he and I were *shay'kreth'ashke,* just to throw anyone off the scent. After all, we'd already convinced Shion of that. But now—I suppose I don't need to."

"No, you don't," she replied, then grinned. "In fact, I'd

rather like it if you were as blatant as possible. The more *ineligible* I make myself for the throne, the better. Although I know there is going to be at least one person who would prefer the original plan. Poor Firesong is going to be *terribly* disappointed!" She gave him an arch look. "After all, it was your hair that he wanted to braid feathers into!"

He stared at her a moment longer, then broke into laughter that came within a hair of hysteria but never quite crossed the line. She smiled but didn't join him this time. Her neck and stomach were taut with tension, for he still hadn't answered her question. There was something in her pocket that was burning a fiery hole in her heart.

Finally he calmed, and wiped his eyes. "Well," he said at last, "my intentions are honorable, at least. I should like very much, Elspeth k'Sheyna k'Valdemar, if you would accept a feather from my bondbird."

"I hope you have a spare," she replied, with a chuckle born of intense relief and a desire to shout with joy. "I would like very much to accept, but Vree will never forgive me if you run back into your room and pluck him."

But to her surprise, he reached into an inner pocket in the breast of his clothing and brought out a forestgyre primary—one with a shaft covered in beadwork of tiny crystals hardly bigger than grains of sand. It had a hair-tie of a silver clasp with two matching silver chains ending in azure crystals.

"I have held this next to my heart for the past several months," he said solemnly, "Never thinking you would be able to wear it openly, and not sure you would even be able to accept it at all."

Her vision blurred as he spoke the traditional words that signified a Hawkbrother marriage. "Elspeth, will you wear my feather, for all the world and skies to see?"

She took it from him, her hands trembling; started to fasten it into her hair, but her hands shook too much to do so and he had to help her. Her heart raced as if she had been running fast, and she could not stop smiling—her skin tingled and burned, and she wanted to laugh, sing, cry—all of them at once.

Instead, she took out her own gift. "I don't have a

bondbird," she said. "I don't know how Gwena will feel about this. I can only hope she feels the way I do."

She held out the ring on her open palm, a silver ring with an overlay of crystal. Sandwiched between was an intricately braided band of incandescently white horse-hair, hairs carefully pulled from Gwena's tail, one at a time, so that each hair was perfect. She'd had the ring made up by one of the *hertasi* several months ago, never really hoping she would be able to use it, but unable to give up the dream that she might.

He took it and placed it on his ring finger, and she noticed with a certain amount of pleasure that his hands were trembling as much as hers now. "*Hertasi* work, isn't it?" he asked, rather too casually.

She nodded. He looked at the ring closely.

"In fact—I think I know the artisan. Kelee, isn't it?"

Again she nodded. "I've probably had it as long as you've had the feather," she ventured.

He chuckled. "And the *hertasi,* no doubt, have been chortling to themselves for some time. They are inveterate matchmakers, you know."

She thought about the sly way that Kelee had looked at her when he had given her the finished ring, and could only sigh and nod.

"Well," he said at last, after a long silence. "This is a good thing. I think that my parents and Clan would approve."

Elspeth squeezed his hand and said quietly, "It doesn't matter if they do or not. My feelings would be the same."

Darkwind smiled. "Mine as well."

They embraced again. "Perhaps 'Darkwind' is no longer a proper name for me. You have brought too much light into my life for it to apply anymore. I no longer feel like a lowering storm since joining with you, bright feather."

Elspeth nodded and bit her lower lip. "But . . . there are still storms approaching."

"Yes. We have many plans to make, and many to discard. I think that this is likely to be a very late night. . . ."

* * *

I think that this is likely to be a very late night, Talia thought, motioning discretely to one of the pages near her Council seat. "Go order enough food and wine for all the Councillors, then recruit some of the final-year trainees to serve it and replace the pages," she whispered to him. He was one of the older pages, and nodded with both understanding and relief. He had served the Queen and Council long enough to know how long one of these emergency sessions could last, and while he might have been disappointed at not being able to listen in on the proceedings, the disappointment was countered by the relief that he would not be stuck in the Council chamber until the sun rose.

There was something to be said for having a limited level of responsibility.

As the pages filed out, to be replaced by wide-eyed youngsters in trainee-Grays, Selenay rose to address her Council. The men and women seated around the horseshoe-shaped table fell silent, and lamplight gleamed on jewels and brilliant court-garb. Behind Selenay, the huge crest of Valdemar seemed to glow.

"I am certain that many of you fear that I am going to oppose this abdication," she said, with calm and equanimity. Talia knew better than anyone here that the calm was not feigned, it was real. She and Selenay had spent many nights in Elspeth's absence, trying to find a way to reconcile the conflicts that Elspeth's duties would place her in when she returned, but both of them had assumed that Elspeth would never want to give up her position as Heir. They had both been wrong, and Elspeth's elegant solution to the conflict, while creating several *more* entirely new problems, had solved more than it created.

Selenay locked eyes with each of her Councillors in turn, as Talia assessed their emotional state with her Gift of Empathy. Troubled, most of them, but excited. A bit apprehensive. Afraid that Selenay was going to make difficulties.

"Well," she said, with a wan smile, "Elspeth is wiser than I, and far more expedient. For the moment, although they are not yet Chosen, I am naming Kris and Lyra joint Heir-presumptives. Since they are so very young, being guarded day and night and kept from much public contact is going to do very little harm to them, and given that I am going to assign their safety into the hands of Guardsmen picked by Herald-Captain Kerowyn and Heralds and their Companions picked by my Consort, I think it unlikely that *anyone* will be able to threaten them with such formidable nurses on the watch."

There was overall relief at that, relief so palpable Talia was surprised no one else could feel it, unGifted though they might be.

"It seems to me that the first thing we should do is to ensure that word of Elspeth's abdication spreads as far and as fast as possible," the Queen continued. "This will give her a greater margin of safety, and confuse Ancar completely. And at the same time, we should see to it that the reports of her demonstration of magical powers are as exaggerated as possible." Selenay smiled slyly. "The more Ancar thinks we have, the less he is likely to attempt a sudden attack. Let him believe that Elspeth brought us an army of mages and peculiar creatures, at least until his own spies tell him otherwise. That will give us some breathing space."

Nods and speculative expressions all around the table. Herald-Captain Kerowyn spoke up—and Talia noticed then with some amusement that in the brief time between when Court had been adjourned and the Council had been called, she had managed to change out of her despised "oh-shoot-me-now" Whites. "This is the time to use those night-message relays, Majesty," she said. "Ancar will be sure to read the messages if we make certain that at least one of the towers 'happens' to reflect to the border when they relay on." She grinned. "We can thank him for that much, at least. Companions and Heralds may be invaluable for carrying messages that are supposed to be secret, but the towers are unmatched for relaying anything you *want* your enemy to know."

"See to it," Selenay said with a nod, and Kerowyn frowned with thought for a moment, then scribbled down the message she wanted relayed and handed it to one of the trainees to take outside.

"Now, how can we use this situation to our best advantage?" the Queen continued. "We have the potential to gain a lot of time here, if we use it well." She looked around the table at her Councillors for suggestions. And now the mood had changed, from one of apprehension to one of anticipation and hope.

Talia relaxed further, and surreptitiously gave Selenay the sign that all was well.

For the moment, at any rate. That was all that anyone could count on right now.

Chapter
Eleven

Elspeth knew that Treyvan and Hydona had resigned themselves to some kind of stabling situation when they reached Haven. Instead, somewhat to their astonishment, the gryphons had been housed in the visiting dignitaries' apartments just like the humans. Elspeth was pleased, but not completely surprised. She had recalled a set of two large rooms usually left empty, meant for receptions and the like. When the Seneschal had told her that the gryphons would be treated like any other diplomatic visitor and housed in the Palace, she thought of those two rooms. A question to the pages the next morning confirmed her guess was right. Those rooms were needed often enough that they remained ready and empty at all times; there was no reason why the gryphons couldn't have them. To reach the second room, you had to go through the first, so the arrangement was perfect. The gryphlets could nest in the inner room, and the adults in the outer.

Elspeth, Darkwind, and Firesong went straight to the reception rooms as soon as she confirmed the gryphons were there. The doors—double doors, like the ones in the Throne Room—were standing partially open, as if the gryphons were inviting visitors to come in. The room was completely empty, except for the lanterns on the wall and the adults' nest. She had expected nests of hay and sticks, however, and was greatly surprised to find that instead they had built "nests" of piles of featherbeds, with tough wool blankets over them to save the beds from the punishing effects of sharp talons.

"Featherbeds?" she asked, raising one eyebrow. "My— how luxurious!"

"And why ssshould we make nesssstsss of nassty sssticks when we may have sssoft pillowsss?" Treyvan asked genially, lounging at his ease along one side of the "nest."

"I have no idea," she replied with a laugh that made the feather fastened prominently at the side of her head tremble. "I just wasn't aware that featherbeds were part of a gryphon's natural forests. No one ever told me that there were wild featherbed trees."

"And what made you think we werrre wild creaturesss?" Hydona put in, with a sly tilt of the head. "When have we everrr sssaid thisss?"

"She has you there," Darkwind pointed out. Firesong simply shook his head.

"Do not come to me for answers," the Healing Adept said. "What I do not know about gryphons is far more than what I do know! I cannot help you; for all that *I* know, they could nest in crystal spires, live upon pastries, and build those flying barges that we saw Kaled'a'in use—out of spiderwebs."

"We do not build the barrrgesss," was all that Treyvan would say. "And you know well that we do not eat passstrrriess! But thisss iss not to the point; what isss—we musst find sssomeone who knowsss what has been going on herrre sssince you left, featherrrlesss daughterrr." He gave her an opaque look. "Desspite that all ssseemsss quiet, it isss a quiet I did not trrrussst."

Somehow it didn't surprise Elspeth to hear Treyvan call her that, as he called Darkwind "featherless son." His sharp eyes had gone straight to the feather braided into her hair the moment she and Darkwind had entered the room. Although he had said nothing, she knew *he* knew what it meant. She felt warmth and pleasure at the gryphons' approval. She had Starblade and Kethra's approval of this liaison, but in many ways the gryphons were a second set of parents to her lover, and winning their approval as well made her spirits rise with a glow of accomplishment. That glow of accomplishment faded quickly, though. Treyvan was right. This was the calm before the storm, and there was no telling how long the calm would last. Days—weeks—or only candlemarks. Too soon, whenever the storm broke.

"If there is anyone in this Kingdom who knows everything important, it's Herald-Captain Kerowyn," she said decisively. Of course Kero knew everything; she was in charge of Selenay's personal spies, and she might have a good guess as to when this calm *would* end.

"Now, we have two choices," she continued. "We can bring her here or we can go to find her. The latter choice is *not* going to be quiet. Treyvan, you and Hydona are the most conspicuous members of this rather conspicuous group; would you rather we brought her to you, or would you rather that as many people saw you as possible?"

"*I* would rather they stayed put," came a clear, feminine voice from the door, "but that's my choice, not theirs. On the other hand, here I am, so you don't have to come looking for me."

Kerowyn pushed the door completely open and gazed on the lounging gryphons with great interest. "We can move elsewhere if you want," she continued, looking into Treyvan's golden gaze, "but there isn't anywhere much more secure than this room, if you're worried about prying eyes and nosy ears, if I may mix my metaphors."

It was Treyvan who answered. "Yesss, warrriorrr. I am trroubled with thosssse who may overrrhearrr. But I alssso wisssh to know why you wisssh usss to rrremain in ourr aerrrie. You do not trrussst usss, perrrhapsss?"

Elspeth didn't know if Kero could read gryphonic body language, but Treyvan was very suspicious. He did not know what Kero's motives were, and he was not taking anything for granted. This set of rooms could easily turn into a prison.

Kero laughed and entered the room, her boots making

remarkably little noise on the granite floor. "Simple enough, good sir. You may have convinced the highborn, Heralds, and Companions that you're relatively harmless, but you haven't gotten to all the servants, and you'll never convince some of the beasts. You go strolling about the grounds without giving me the chance to sweep them first, and you'll panic a dozen gardeners, scare the manure out of most of the horses and donkeys, and cause every pampered lapdog that highborn girls are walking in the garden to keel over dead of fright. You don't *really* want angry gardeners and weeping girls coming in here yapping at you, do you?"

Treyvan snapped his beak mischievously. No matter how serious a situation was, he could find something amusing in it. "No," he replied. "I think not." Already he was relaxing; Kero had put him at his ease.

"Excellent." Kero was not in Whites—as usual. She wore riding leathers of a dusty brown, worn and comfortable, her long blonde hair in a single braid down her back. She turned to give Elspeth a long and considered appraisal, lingering over the new Whites. "Well, what is this all about?" she continued. "Trying to set new fashions?"

Elspeth shrugged. "Whatever. I can promise you I can fight in them. Not that I expect anyone to be able to get close enough to me to have to deal with them hand-to-hand."

"Oh, really?" Kero turned away—then lunged, with no warning at all, not even by the tensing of a single muscle.

But not unexpectedly; Elspeth had been her pupil for too long ever to be taken by surprise, especially after tossing out a challenge like that one. Instead, it was Kero who got the surprise, as Elspeth lashed out with a mageborn whip of power and knocked her feet out from under her. Kero went down onto the marble floor in a controlled tumble, and if Elspeth had not been as well-trained as she was, Kerowyn could have recovered for another try at her. But Elspeth was not going to give her that chance. She kept a "grip" on Kero's ankles to keep her off her feet, then wrapped her up in an invisible binding. Kero did not resist, as most Valdemarans would have. Elspeth knew she had seen magic often enough when she led the Skybolts as a mercenary company in Rethwellan and southward. She simply waited, lying there passively, until Elspeth released her, then got to her feet, dusting off her hands on her breeches.

"You'll do," was all she said, but Elspeth glowed from the compliment, and Darkwind winked at her.

"And you have learned much of magic, lady," Firesong observed. "Enough to know not to fight mage-bonds, which is far more than anyone else in this land would know. And I am curious to know how you came by this knowledge."

Kero gave Firesong a long and penetrating look; in his turn, he graced her with one of his most charming smiles. It would have taken a colder woman than Kero to ignore that smile; it would have taken a more powerful wizard than Firesong for that smile to affect her. But in the end, she decided to answer him.

"Simple enough; I'm not from around here." That was in Shin'a'in, not Valdemaran; Firesong's eyes widened a trifle and he gave her a look full of respect. Kero looked around for somewhere to sit, and finally chose the side of the gryphons' "nest" by default. "I was born and grew up in the south of Rethwellan. I was the granddaughter of a sorceress, trained by a Shin'a'in Swordsworn who was her partner, adopted as a Clan Friend to Tale'sedrin, then took a place in a merc company. Eventually I got the Captain slot, and circumstances brought us up here." She shrugged. "We hired on because I knew Prince Daren, we both trained with the same Shin'a'in, and the Rethwellans owed the Valdemarans a debt that hadn't been discharged. The Skybolts were part-payment on that debt. Never guessed when we came riding over those mountains down south, I'd lose all my mages and pick up a stubborn white talking horse."

:No more stubborn than you.:

Every Mindspeaker in the room looked startled at that, with the sole exception of Kerowyn. She only sighed. "That was my Companion Sayvil," she said, apologetically. "She can Mindspeak with anyone she pleases, and she won't pretend otherwise like the rest of 'em. Next thing is I expect her to start Mindspeaking people without the Gift. She's gotten worse about it lately."

:That's because there's been more need for it lately. And speaking of "Need"—:

"I suppose the damn sword decided you didn't deserve it or something?" Kero asked. "Or did you get fed up with it and drop it down a well like I threatened to do?"

"She's with Skif's lady, Nyara," Elspeth began, hesitantly addressing the air over Kero's head. "That's a long story and—"

:You!: came another, and far more excited voice. From the other room bounded a startled *kyree,* trailed by the gryphlets. *:You had Need! You! You must be the youngling trained by my famous cousin Warrl! Lady Tarma's pupil! The one Lady Kethry gave Need to!:*

He bounded over and prostrated himself at her feet for a moment, in the *kyree* imitation of a courtly bow. *:I have heard so much about you! My famous cousin Warrl said you were destined for greatness! You must tell me all of your life so that I may make it into stories!:*

All the time that Rris was chattering in open Mindspeech, Kero's face had taken on an expression that Elspeth had never, ever expected to see.

Completely blank, and slack-jawed. She was, quite clearly, taken utterly by surprise.

She recovered fairly quickly, however. "I don't believe this," she said under her breath, as Rris finished and waited eagerly for her answer. "I mean—what are the odds? Who ever sees *one kyree* in a lifetime, much less two, and for the two to be *related?* I just don't by-the-gods believe this!"

Rris took on an air of extreme dignity, and fixed Kero with an admonishing gaze. *:My famous cousin Warrl used to say that there is no such thing as coincidence, only mortals who have not fought the winds of fate.:*

"Your famous cousin Warrl stole that particular proverb from the Shin'a'in he ran with," Kero countered. "It happens to be about five hundred years older than your 'famous cousin Warrl.' And believe me, I fought so-called 'fate' plenty. I don't believe in fate." She shook her head again. "All right, *kyree*—what is your name?"

:Rris,: he said proudly. *:Tale-spinner, History-keeper, and Lesson-teacher of the Hyrrrull Pack.:*

"All right, Rris, I'll tell you everything you'd like to know, *but*—" she interjected, holding up a hand to stave off the eager creature, "—*not now.* We have a lot to do, and I have the depressing feeling we have a very short time to do it in. It's only a matter of time before Ancar hits us, and right now we can only pray he follows his old patterns, and makes several feints and tests before he decides to *truly* come after us. Now, unless I miss my guess, what you lot want is intelligence, right?" She looked around at the others. "Not only what dear Ancar has been up to, but all the things that have happened since Elspeth left."

Firesong nodded for all of them. "And let me get the last two of our group," he said. "Skif and his lady, the current bearer of your mage-sword. I think you will be surprised at what has become of the blade. It has changed, warrior, greatly changed. We wish this kept reasonably secret—but not from you. You, I think, need to know what kind of an ally Need has become."

He turned before anyone could stop him and went off at a brisk walk, robes flowing behind him. He returned quickly with Skif and Nyara. Skif also wore the *hertasi*-designed Whites—Whites with a number of surprises built into them—and Nyara wore a *hertasi*-made surcoat and light armor—though it would have been very difficult for anyone who was not aware that it was armor to recognize it as such. As always, Nyara carried Need sheathed at her side, but before anyone could say anything to either of them, the sword spoke up, and Need's mind-voice was sharp with shock.

:I know you!:

Kero jumped this time, she was so startled. She stared at the blade, and then swore, fervently and creatively, using several languages that Elspeth didn't even recognize and describing several acts that Elspeth thought were anatomically impossible.

"—bloody *hell!*" she finished with a wail, throwing up her hands in despair, as if in petition to the unseen gods. "Isn't it bad enough that I get a lover who takes over my dreams, a talking horse, and a uniform like a target? Isn't it enough that I go from being an honest mercenary to some kind of do-gooder? Does *everything* in my life have to come back to haunt me and *talk in my head?*"

It took all morning to fill Kero in on everything that had happened to Elspeth, Need, and Skif since they left, but the Herald-Captain refused to impart so much as a rumor before she heard Elspeth's story. Occasionally, Kero fixed the sheathed blade with a sharp glance, and Elspeth suspected that Need was gifting her former bearer with choice comments of her own. They were, in many ways, two of a kind. Evidently Kero began to figure that out for herself, for after a while those pointed glances took on a hint of amusement.

Elspeth was just grateful that *she* wasn't "blessed" with the sword's presence anymore. And she had the feeling that Kero felt the same.

Finally, after a break for a noontime meal, Kero made good on her bargain.

Elspeth had pillows brought in so that they could all sit comfortably, while the gryphons lounged with their forequarters draped over the side of their nest. They sat in a ragged circle, with Kero at one end and the gryphons anchoring the other.

"First of all," she said, playing with the end of her braid as she looked at Elspeth, "I want you all to know that not only do I approve of the way Elspeth handled herself yesterday, but the entire Council still approves of the abdication. It's going to confuse Ancar so much he won't know what to make of it. He'll have to wait to see what his spies have to say about it all before he even begins to plan. He's going to be certain that the abdication was a ruse, until he gets reports that Elspeth really *did* give up all of her power. He's going to be hearing all kinds of rumors, and it's going to drive him crazy. He couldn't imagine anyone *ever* giving up a high position."

"I thought as much," Elspeth said with satisfaction.

"Now I've got a little advice for you and your handsome friend," Kero continued, looking directly and only at Elspeth. "I know you're not the Heir anymore, and who you couple with makes no difference. But there are people who are watching you. Don't make any announcements about pairing up for at least a couple of months; that way no one will think to accuse you of being a soft-headed female who lets her heart overrule her head, all right?"

Elspeth raised one eyebrow. "Does it matter if people think I'm a soft-headed female? As you just said, who I pair with has no real meaning anymore."

Kero gave her *the look,* a scornful expression that had withered sterner hearts than Elspeth's. "It might not to *you,* but you're an example for others, whether or not you realize it. It might seem very romantic to give up throne and duty for the one you love. I'm sure the younger Bards would be thrilled with such a rich topic for balladeering. No one is going to pay any attention to the fact that you're taking on *more* responsibility as the first Herald-Mage in an age. You fell in love, and told your duty to take a long walk, that's how starry-eyed young fluffheads are going to think of it. And while you're at it, think about the hundreds of young people out there who will *use* that as an excuse to abandon responsibilities of their own because they think they are lifebonded! Some chowderheaded young fool who doesn't know the meaning of the word 'duty' is encouraging them to run off to a life of endless love, that's how it would look. Right now, that's the last thing we need."

Elspeth gnawed her lip for a moment, then nodded, slowly. "I can see your point. I'm still someone that people my age look to for an example, and that's not going to change any time soon, if at all. Well, I'm not going to avoid Darkwind, but we can keep from being blatant about things. . . ."

After all, no one knows what the feather and ring mean but the two of us and the folk that came with us. We can make it public knowledge some time later.

"That's all I ask. *Think* before you do something. Always. You may not be the Heir, but you're going to be just as much in the public eye and mind as before, if not more so. You thought being the Heir was bad, I don't think you've thought about how people are going to react

to the first Herald-Mage since Vanyel." Kero smirked
with satisfaction. "Well, now to the business of catching
up. We have agents in Hardorn, Ancar has agents here,
but I'm pretty sure I know who most of his are, and I'm
equally sure he *hasn't* caught most of ours, so we're able
to feed him inaccurate and incomplete information without getting caught in the same trap. His pattern hasn't
changed; whenever he thinks he's found a weak spot in
our defenses, he generally pokes at it for a while before
he actually mounts an attack. He's given up on assassins
for a while, or they've given up on him. Hard to hire people who know the last half-dozen wound up very dead."
She smiled grimly.

"That's good," Elspeth said fervently. "That's *very*
good! What kind of troop strength has he got?"

Kero grimaced. "That's the bad news. It's formidable,
and he outnumbers us about three to two. He has a lot of
regular troops as well as a lot of mages. You managed to
relay that the barrier at the Border was coming down, so
we've been acting as if it wasn't there for about a week
or so, though he hasn't tried anything yet. I take it that it
is down?"

"Probably," Firesong said, tossing his hair back over
his shoulder. "Since one of the signs of that barrier was
an inability to work unhindered magic, and both Elspeth
and I have been able to do so almost from the moment we
arrived, I think we can assume Van—the old spells have
been banished."

Kero licked her lips thoughtfully. "Right. Well, those
mages run test attacks against our Border outposts on a
fairly regular basis, so if he doesn't know the barrier is
gone now, he will soon. I think we can probably take it
as read that he knows *now*. He's learned more caution after getting thrown back twice; he won't rush into an attack right away, I don't think, even after his usual feints
and pokes. The abdication and the appearance of Elspeth
as a mage, as well as tales that she brought more mages
with her, might give him a little more pause. Every day
we make him hesitate, is one more day *we* have to prepare for his next try at us, and if there's one thing I *know*
will happen, it's that he's going to make a try for us."

All of them nodded as Kero finished. "So whatever we can do to confuse him at the moment is going to be of use," Darkwind replied. "Are we waiting for something, ourselves?"

"We are," Kero told him. "When you said you were coming home, I assumed you were going to find some way to get rid of whatever it was that drove Quenten and my other mages off when the Skybolts came north. So I sent some urgent messages asking him to send me as many mages as he could. There are Heralds down in Rethwellan right now, bringing up as many of his White Winds Journeymen and teachers as care to come."

"White Winds is a good, solid school," Firesong spoke up. "It was founded by a *hertasi* mage. We can work with White Winds mages, and I am relieved to learn we will not be the only teachers of Mage-Gifted Heralds."

"Not by a long shot," Kero assured him. "Quenten's White Winds mages will be right up in the front lines, too. They know we're going to have a fight on our hands, and we won't take anyone who isn't willing to work combat-magic. I've got more mages coming, though— and these, I am afraid, are not going to be as easy to work with. Alberich isn't here because he's down south, too. He's bringing back a load of mage-trained Sun-priestesses from Karse."

"He's *what?*" Elspeth gasped. She stared at Kero, wondering for a single wild moment if her teacher had snapped under the strain and had gone quite mad. She had heard about the alliance, of course, but she had assumed all that meant was that Karse was going to present a united front against Hardorn. She had never dreamed that Karse would provide more than that!

"He's bringing back a group of mage-trained Priestesses of Vkandis from Karse," Kero repeated patiently. "I know it sounds crazy, but in case you didn't get all of it from Rolan, this is what happened. There's been a kind of religious upheaval down there, and the Son of the Sun is now a woman, Solaris. Hellfires, that's been going on since before I became the Skybolts' Captain, but it seems that just after you left, this lady organized every priestess and a lot of the Sunsguard, and made her revolt stick. *She* has been watching the situation between us and Hardorn for some time, ever since she was a junior priestess. By my reckoning, that would have been about the time that Ancar usurped the throne. Evidently Solaris decided that Ancar's a snake, old feuds are not worth dying over, and that if the two female rulers of the lands facing his don't drop their differences and decide we're all girls together, Ancar is eventually going to have *both* for lunch." Kero shrugged. "Sounds like the kind of lady I can get along with. So, that's contingent one and two, both on the way. Contingent three is just now getting organized; Daren got in touch with his brother, and the King of Rethwellan is deciding how many of his court mages he can spare, and how many can be trusted to be of real help. He asked us if we wanted him to recruit, but Daren turned that idea down, since there'd be too good a chance a lot of them would be plants from Ancar."

"That's all very good news," Darkwind observed.

But Elspeth frowned. "It is good news, so why are you worried?" she asked Kero.

The Herald-Captain sighed. "Because even with all that help, we're still outnumbered head-to-head, both in mages and in troops, and that's just the troops we know about."

Elspeth thought back to the last conflict, and the mage-controlled troops Valdemar had faced.

"He can take the peasants right out of the fields and throw them into the front lines," she said slowly, her heart sinking.

Kerowyn nodded grimly. "That's right. Ancar doesn't *care* if his country falls to pieces, so he can conscript as many men to fight as he wants to. He doesn't care if they're decent fighters or not; they're fodder, and he can keep throwing them at our lines until they wear us down."

"You are sssaying that he will rissk ssstarrving hissss own people that he may win hisss warrr?" Hydona said, astonished.

All Elspeth and Kero could do was nod.

But Kero wasn't finished with the bad news. "Last of all, he's got some new mage with him; this one just turned up at Ancar's Court fairly recently, and this one worries me." She bit her lip, and looked from the Tayledras to the gryphons and back. "The fellow is so odd that I'm wondering if you lot can't tell me what we can expect out of him. He looks more than half cat, from what my agents tell me, and he keeps pretty much to himself. Only one of them has seen him, and just for a moment. We don't even know his name for certain—just a guess, Falcon's Breath, Falcon's Death, or something like that."

Falcon's—oh, gods. No.

Elspeth felt as if she had taken a blow to the stomach, and Nyara looked stricken. Firesong bit off an exclamation, and Darkwind a curse. The gryphons both jerked bolt upright. Skif looked quite ready to kill something.

Kero looked around at all of them and raised her eyebrows. "I take it you know this person?"

Darkwind was the first to recover. "You could say that," he replied dryly. *"Will we never be rid of the Beast?"*

The last was half-snarled, and Skif's nostrils flared as he nodded in agreement. Firesong shut his gaping mouth with a snap.

"That sincerely annoys me. I can only ask myself what dark demon holds the Beast in high esteem, that he keeps returning," the Healing Adept said after everyone turned to look at him. He bestowed a look full of irony on Kerowyn. "Twice already he has escaped from situations that should have finished him," Firesong continued, "and the next time I shall not believe he is dead until I burn the body, and sow the ashes with salt!"

"I may assume, then, that this is not good news?" Kero asked mildly.

It was Treyvan who answered that question.

"No, warrriorrrr," he growled, crest and hackles up. His voice was so full of venom that Elspeth hardly recognized it. "Thisss isss not good newsssss."

By nightfall, they had a basic plan. Firesong would first find the place where the new Heartstone lay and fully activate it. Then he would roam the Palace with Jeri, looking for the old magic workrooms and any artifacts or

books that might still be in existence and stored somewhere other than the Archives. Once the rooms were
identified and the artifacts found, he would help Jeri get
them properly cleaned and restored to their original func-
tions. He did not expect that to take very long. As soon
as the workrooms were ready, Firesong would begin
training the strongest of the new mages.

The gryphons would identify any Heralds here at the
Collegium that had obvious Mage-Gift and begin their
basic training if they were not of such potential that they
needed Firesong's attention. If there were any doubts
whether or not a Herald had Mage-Gift, Darkwind or
Elspeth could pass judgment. Need could as well—but
the blade opined that it would be better to keep the fact
of her existence as an intelligent personality very quiet. A
sentient sword would be certain to attract attention, and
all of it the wrong kind.

"This group is strange enough without adding a talking
sword," Kero agreed. "Good gods, I don't know how I'm
going to explain some of you!"

Meanwhile, until the mages from outKingdom arrived,
Darkwind and Elspeth would work with Firesong and the
new Heartstone, and search the Archives for "lost" books
on magic. *She* was certain that there were books they
needed hidden in there, and that only the prohibition on
magic had kept her from finding them in her earlier
searches. Now that the prohibition was gone, she should
be able to locate them. While books would not replace a
real teacher, they could augment what teachers could do.
And they might offer spells none of the Tayledras knew,
and clues to what Ancar might muster.

Good plans, all of them. Now they would have to see
just how long those plans lasted. The worst of their nightmares was now real. Ancar and Mornelithe Falconsbane
appeared to be allies. Add in Hulda, and however many
mages Ancar had recruited—and Valdemar was racing
against time and the most furious of mage winds.

Only Mornelithe and Ancar knew what they were going to do next. Despite what others said about true mages
not guarding against mind-magic, Ancar had long ago
learned many of the limits of Heraldic abilities. ForeSight

or FarSight, neither worked well against him; all they could do was try to outthink him.

:What have you learned for us?: Dawnfire asked An'desha, as Falconsbane dozed in his chair beside the fire. *:Is there anything new?:*

She had appeared in the flames of the fireplace itself; if Falconsbane happened to wake, it would be very easy for her to hide herself and her power away. The Avatars often appeared to him in the fireplace now; with Ancar so on edge, he could and did burst into Falconsbane's rooms at any time, waking the Adept, and An'desha did not dare to be away from the body if that happened. An'desha had learned to manipulate Falconsbane's mind and body to make him more aware of his fatigue. The Adept slept most of the time he spent in his rooms, but he was not aware that he was spending a truly inordinate amount of time in slumber. An'desha saw to it that he ate and drank and cared for himself; the rest of that time An'desha spent in rummaging through Falconsbane's memories.

:I have more of Falconsbane's memories,: he replied, and then, with pardonable pride, added, *:and I have been convincing Falconsbane that the defects and faults in his thinking that I cause by accident are truly caused by Ancar, deliberately, to hamper him. It makes him very angry, and less inclined to aid Ancar willingly.:*

Dawnfire was joined by Tre'valen; a pair of graceful forms of gold and blue, with whitely glowing eyes. This time they had both appeared as hawks of flame, rather than in human form. An'desha found their chosen forms oddly comforting, for they were very clearly vorcel-hawks, and they made him think of home every time he saw them.

:Excellent!: Tre'valen applauded, and An'desha flushed with pride. *:Open your thoughts to us, little one, and we shall search through those new memories of yours. Then tell us what else you have learned as we sort them through.:*

That was done quickly; it was a pity there was so little of substance in the memories. This time An'desha had gotten access to the sculpting and training of Falconsbane's daughter Nyara. He could not think of Nyara as *his* daughter; he had not engendered her, and he certainly had nothing to do with her upbringing. He did, however, feel a kinship to her. It seemed to him that they were siblings of a kind; they had both suffered from Falconsbane's whims, and in similar ways. He could empathize and sympathize with her as no one else could.

But the Avatars found more of interest in those pain-filled memories than he had thought they would. *:Oh, this is excellent,:* Tre'valen applauded. *:We shall be able to help Nyara with this. She will never look entirely human again, but there is much that can be undone, now that we know how it was wrought upon her.:*

He hadn't thought of that! The thought that he might be able to help Nyara, even a little, gave him a great deal of pleasure. There was so little he had been able to do for her, and nothing to save her.

:Falconsbane now moves about the court freely,: he reported, as Dawnfire and Tre'valen sorted through the memories they had taken from him. *:He does little but observes much, and I am able to watch what he thinks.:* For all of his myriad faults, Falconsbane was no fool, and his observations were always worth making note of. *:He has concluded that Ancar is something of a younger, much clumsier, and stupider version of himself. Ancar rules as he did, by fear. Other than those he thinks are valuable, which are mostly great nobles, no one is truly safe from Ancar's mages or his magic.:*

Tre'valen turned his burning white eyes on An'desha. Strange, how he had no trouble telling the two Avatars apart. *:Why is it that Ancar does not molest his great nobles?:* the shaman-Avatar asked sharply.

:I can only tell you what Falconsbane thinks,: he said hesitantly. *:The Adept believes that Ancar himself does not know. He thinks in part that Ancar still fears the power those nobles hold, even though he could eliminate them if he chose—it is a fear from the time when he was still the Prince and had little power but that which he stole. And he believes that in part it is because most of them are still his allies, and he knows that if he betrays them, no one will trust him.:* He hesitated again, then

added, *:And Falconsbane thinks he is a fool; if he fears the power of these nobles, he should eliminate them quietly, in ways that seem accidental. This is what he would do.:*

Dawnfire's form writhed and distorted. *:Somehow I am not surprised,:* she commented.

An'desha continued. *:He sees that this is how he himself ruled, but he feels that Ancar is being extremely stupid about it. While Falconsbane could have conquered every one of his own underlings, singly or together, if they had chosen to revolt, he would have had sabotage in place already to destroy them and all they held dear. Ancar would not be able to muster a sufficient defense if all of his underlings attacked at once. So he thinks that Ancar is being very foolhardy.:*

Indeed, Falconsbane's thoughts had been far more contemptuous than that. He felt Ancar should eliminate every risk, and saw his failure to do so as a sign of weakness. An'desha had not been so certain. It seemed to him, after watching Ancar among his courtiers, that the young King felt as long as he kept the *threat* of retaliation before his underlings, but only made examples of those few he did not need, he would succeed. People were often like rabbits; frighten them, and their minds ceased to work. And An'desha was by no means as certain as Falconsbane that the Adept *could* have taken all of his underlings if they had chosen to mass against him. Look what one broken Clan, a pair of gryphons, a couple of Outlanders, and his own daughter had managed to do! Twice, it had only been the intervention of the Goddess and her Avatars that had saved him! No, another sign of the damaged state of Falconsbane's mind was this insane overconfidence, this surety that if only Ancar released the coercions, Mornelithe Falconsbane could conquer any obstacle.

Not that he was aware of what the Goddess had done, nor the gaps in his own reasoning, which surely was the cause for his own foolish bravado.

:You have learned much of this Court. What of Ancar's mages?: Tre'valen asked. *:How do they judge their master? Is there any likelihood they will rise up?:*

An'desha considered the question carefully. *:Hulda is*

the most powerful,: he said at last. *:She seems to think that Ancar will never escape her influence, and does not realize that he already has done so. The other mages have a hierarchy of their own—the most powerful is a Blood Mountain sorcerer, Pires Nieth. Falconsbane believes that one has ambitions to rule, himself. He comes of a noble family, possibly is of royal blood by bastardy. Falconsbane thinks that if Hulda and Ancar were both to fall, Pires would attempt to seize the throne for himself. But he is only a Master, and not as learned or powerful even as Ancar, and although he rules the other mages, he lives in fear of both Ancar and Hulda.:*

The Avatars communed silently with each other for a moment; the flames danced and hissed about their fire-winged forms. *:Would he intrigue, do you think?:* Dawnfire asked. *:If you revealed yourself to him, could he be counted upon to help you and aid you in getting rid of Falconsbane?:*

An'desha hesitated, then replied, *:I do not know. Falconsbane considered him as a possible ally against Ancar. The Adept would not trust him, so how could we?:*

Tre'valen nodded. *:A good point.:*

:Besides,: An'desha continued, *:He is a blood-path mage. Ancar will have none about him who are not blood-path mages. These men—they are all men, but Hulda—are evil, foul, and the only reason they are not as foul as Falconsbane himself is because they have fewer years, less power, and less imagination. Willing sacrifice is one thing—:*

:You have no argument from me, youngling,: Tre'valen said, hastily. *:You are right; we cannot trust or foster blood-path mages. It would be obscene.:*

An'desha wished he had some way to make notes of what he wished to tell the Avatars; he always had the feeling he was going to forget something important!

:There is only one other thing,: he said finally. *:Falconsbane would never do anything to aid either Hulda or Ancar because he hates them both, so he is fostering the friction between them. I have been trying to make him think this is a good idea. Am I doing rightly?:*

This time Tre'valen chuckled. *:Anything you can do to*

bring confusion to this nest of kresh'ta *will be welcome, youngling. You are doing rightly, indeed.:*

The fire popped loudly, and Falconsbane stirred uneasily. He was about to wake.

:Farewell!: Dawnfire said hastily—

—and the Avatars were gone, in the space of an eyeblink.

An'desha withdrew as well, to watch and wait.

Falconsbane stirred as the fire popped again, sending a coal onto the hearth. He opened his eyes, and the coal glared at him from the hearthstone, a baleful fiery eye. He was vaguely aware that there had been something else that had disturbed his sleep but was unable to identify it.

With what had become a habit, he cursed his captor for the clumsy, too-restrictive spells that were making it harder and harder to think or react properly. If that idiot Ancar were only half the mage he thought he was —!

And as if the thought had summoned him, footsteps in the hall heralded Ancar's arrival.

As usual, he burst through the door with no warning and no consideration, as if Falconsbane, like the rooms themselves, was his own personal property. And as usual, he squinted against the perpetual darkness that Falconsbane cloaked himself and his apartment in, a darkness that Falconsbane enhanced with a touch of magery. If the little brat could not learn to announce himself, then Falconsbane would not make it easy for him to fling himself into the suite at will!

"Falconsbane?" Ancar said, peering around the room, and looking, as usual, for a form in one of the hearthside chairs. "Ah—there you are!"

Mornelithe sighed, as Ancar flung himself into the other chair. At least the child didn't have the nerve to order *him* to stand! "I am very fatigued, Majesty," he said, making no effort to mask the boredom in his voice. "What is it that you require of me this time? I fear that no matter what it is, I have little energy to spare for it."

In fact, he was lying; after disposing of a pair of Ancar's political prisoners, he was very nearly at full strength. Granted, he did seem to be sleeping a great deal, but that could be accounted for by the damages he had taken and the coercions he was under. Those things affected the mind and the body, and he did not wish to spare the energy needed to fight the coercions when he might use that same energy to break Ancar.

So far as pure mage-energy, rather than physical energy, was concerned, he felt confident that there was very little he *couldn't* do—if he had not been so hedged about with Ancar's controlling spells.

But he was certainly not going to tell Ancar that.

"I just received word from the border with Valdemar," Ancar blurted, in a state of high excitement. Falconsbane was taken aback by the level of that excitement, the tight anticipation in Ancar's voice. The youngster was as taut as a harpstring! "The barrier against magic is *gone!* I am calling a council of mages; how long until you to feel up to joining it?"

Gone? That unbreakable, stubborn barrier was *gone?* Falconsbane's interest stirred, in spite of himself, and his attempt to maintain a pose of indifference and exhaustion. "Not long, a matter of moments—" he began, cautiously, trying to collect his thoughts.

"Good. Come along, then. The walk will wake you up." Ancar sprang to his feet, and Falconsbane fought being pulled out of his chair. Not physically, but via magic, as the young King used his spells to attempt to make Mornelithe rise and follow him. Both the exercise of the coercions and Falconsbane's resistance were automatic. Like the response of a plant to light, or the strike of a snake at prey.

Then he abandoned his struggle, and permitted the King to force his reluctant body to obey. After all, what was the point? He wasted more energy in fighting than he could really afford, and there was no telling when Ancar might send him another prisoner. At the moment Ancar was so wrought up by the news from the border that he wasn't paying a great deal of attention to anything else anyway. Falconsbane wasn't going to make a point of resisting if the King didn't even notice what he was doing.

As they left Mornelithe's rooms, three pairs of guards that had been waiting on either side of the door fell in behind them. The Adept raised a purely mental eyebrow at that. Evidently either Ancar feared attack in his own halls, or else he was not taking any chances on Falconsbane's willingness to come to this "council" of his.

Interesting, in either case. Could it be that he sensed his own coercions weakening, and now was ensuring his captive's compliance with more physical and tangible means?

Ancar led the way out of the guest quarters and down a staircase into a series of dark, stone-faced halls in a direction Falconsbane had never taken. There were no servants about, but several times Falconsbane thought he smelled the scent of cooking food wafting down from above. It must be nearly dinner time, then, and not as late as he had thought.

Finally, Ancar stopped and stood aside while one of his guards opened a perfectly ordinary wooden door, revealing a room that was not ordinary at all.

It was swathed from ceiling to floor in curtains of red satin, and the only furniture in it was a single, large table, with a thronelike chair at one end (currently empty) and several more well-padded chairs on the other three sides. One of those chairs, the one at the throne's right hand, stood empty.

Hulda, looking extremely alert, impeccably and modestly gowned, and without any trace of the sullen sensuality she normally displayed, sat to the throne's immediate left. Her violet eyes fastened on Ancar and Falconsbane, and her lips tightened slightly. More people—all male, mostly the same age as Ancar, and presumably some of his best mages—occupied the other chairs. Most of them Falconsbane recognized; others he had never seen before. All of them wore the same expression of baffled and puzzled excitement, mixed, in varying degrees, with apprehension.

Ancar went straight to the throne and sat down, leaving Falconsbane to make his own way to the sole remaining seat and take it. He did so, taking his time, cloaking his displeasure in immense dignity, wondering if that right-hand seat had been left vacant at Ancar's orders, or not, and what it might mean that it had been left unoccupied. Was it simply that no one else wished to be that close to Ancar, or was Ancar giving a silent but unmistakable sign of Falconsbane's status among the mages by ordering it to stand empty until the Adept arrived?

Ample illumination came from mage-lights hovering above the table; a frivolous display by Falconsbane's reckoning, but there were a few of Ancar's mages who were fairly useless, and could easily be spared to maintain them. It did eliminate the need for servants to come in and tend candles or lanterns, and if this chamber was used for magical purposes, it was best that only a few people ever had access to it. Ancar waited until Falconsbane had taken his seat, and complete silence fell across the table. There was not so much as a whisper.

He did not stand, but he held all eyes. He waited a moment longer, while the silence thickened, and then broke it.

"I have heard from my mages in the West. The barrier that prevents magic from passing the border with Valdemar is down," he said, his voice tense with excitement and anticipation. "It appears to be gone completely. My mages at the border assure me that we can attack at will."

From the stunned looks on the faces of every other mage, including Hulda, Falconsbane concluded that he was the only one besides Ancar to whom this did not come as a revelation. There was a moment more of silence, then all of them tried to speak at once. Hulda was the only one that maintained a semblance of calm; the rest gestured, shouted, even leapt to their feet in an effort to be heard.

The cacophony was deafening, and Falconsbane gave up on trying to understand a single word. Ancar watched all of his mages striving for his attention, each one doing anything short of murder in order to have his say, and the King's face wore a tiny smile of satisfaction. He was enjoying this; enjoying both the fact that the barrier was down and his will would no longer be thwarted, and enjoying being the center of attention.

Then he held up his hand, and the clamor stopped as

suddenly as it had started. His smile broadened, and Falconsbane suppressed a flicker of contempt. Pathetic puppy.

He pointed at Hulda, who alone had not contributed to the clamor. She frowned at him, presumably at being designated to speak with such casual disregard for her importance. But that didn't prevent her from speaking up immediately.

"We should be careful," she said, looking cool, intelligent, and businesslike. "We should test the waters first, many, many times, before we even make any plans to attack, much less mount an actual attack. We don't know how or why this happened, but in my opinion, this is very likely to be a trap. Every weakness we have seen in the past has proved to be a trap, and if the pattern holds, this will be as well. The Valdemarans are treacherous and tricky, and this could be just one more trick in a long history of such things. It would be only too easy for them to lure us across their border, then close the jaws of such a trap on us." She shrugged. "They've done so often enough, and they've eaten away at our strength while losing little of their own."

Falconsbane smiled, but only to himself, at the idea of Hulda calling anyone "treacherous and tricky." Then again, it took a traitor to recognize one.

"Precisely!" the mage Pires Nieth cried out before Ancar could designate another to speak. He jumped to his feet, his disheveled hair and beard standing out from his face, making him look like an animal suddenly awakened from a long winter's sleep. "Hulda is right! That was exactly what I wished to say! This requires extreme caution; the Valdemarans have tricked us before by pretending to know nothing of magic, yet turning it on our own troops, and—"

The clamor broke out again, but from what Falconsbane could make out, the consensus was that all of the mages were for caution. Interesting, since from what he had observed, the mages were usually divided on any given subject except when Ancar had previously expressed his own opinion. And from the faint frown on Ancar's face, this did not suit his intentions at all. But there were also signs of hesitation there. Falconsbane guessed that this was an old argument, and that it was one those in favor of caution generally won.

As they babbled on, each one more vehement than the last in urging restraint, Falconsbane analyzed his observations and began to formulate a plan. One thing in particular surprised him, and that was the reaction of Ancar's mages. Apparently, whatever had brought this "barrier" down, it was none of *their* doing. And what truly amazed him was that none of them had the audacity or the brains to claim that it was!

Well, if they would not, Falconsbane would make up for their lack of will and wit. This was another opportunity to impress on Ancar what he could do—and imply he might be able to accomplish far more, if given a free hand. Perhaps this time Ancar might be impressed enough to actually do something.

He let the other mages talk themselves into a standstill, while Ancar's frown deepened, until they began to notice his patent disapproval of their advice. The voices faded, and finally died altogether, leaving an ominous silence. Not even the curtains moved.

Into this silence, Falconsbane dropped his words, cool stones into a waiting pool.

"I am pleased to learn that my tireless efforts upon King Ancar's behalf have not gone unrewarded," he said casually, as if it were of little matter to him. "The cost to me in fatigue has been inconvenient."

There. Now he had a plausible explanation for spending so much time asleep in his rooms, as well as riveting Ancar's attention and gratitude—such as it was—on him. And he had just established himself, not only as Ancar's foreign ally, but as a more potent mage than any in this group. Given the combination of events and the fact that he could now, easily, take on anything covert Hulda would dare to try against him—if she did dare—he felt fairly secure against the woman's machinations.

Ancar's head snapped around, and the King stared into his eyes, dumbfounded. Clearly, this was the very last thing he had expected from his tame Adept.

"*You* broke the barrier?" he blurted. "But—you said nothing of this!"

"You woke me from a sound sleep, Majesty," Falconsbane said smoothly. "I am hardly at my best when half awake. I have labored long and hard in your aid, and I am simply pleased to learn that those labors have borne fruit. It seemed to me that there was no reason to raise your hopes by telling you what I was attempting, when the barrier was at such a great physical distance and I was laboring under so very many handicaps. I never promise what I cannot deliver."

That, in light of the many wonders he had heard Ancar's other mages promise and fail to perform, was a direct slap at most of them. As they gaped at him, he continued, "I dare say that there is no reason to be overly cautious in the light of this development, since it was our doing and not some plot of the Valdemarans. I will be able to do far more for you when I am under less constraint, of course. . . ."

He hoped then that Ancar would say or do something, but his rivals in magic were not about to accept his claims tamely.

Again all the other mages began talking at once, pointing out that there was no way of knowing for certain that it had been Falconsbane who had broken the barrier, each of them eager to discredit him. Mornelithe himself simply ignored their noise, smiling slightly, and steepling his hands in front of his face. It was better not to try to refute them. If he looked as if he did not care, Ancar was more likely to believe he really *had* worked this little miracle.

Or, as one of his long-ago teachers once said, "Tell a big enough lie, and everyone will believe it simply because it is too audacious not to be the truth."

Finally, Ancar brought it all to a halt by raising his hands for quiet.

Silence fell over the table, immediate and absolute. Ancar had his mages firmly under his thumb, that much was certain.

"It does not matter if Mornelithe Falconsbane proves to you that he broke the barrier or not," Ancar said sternly. "It does not even matter to you if I assume that he did.

Nothing among the lot of you has changed. The essential fact is that all of *you* have worked in vain to take it down. Now, it is down. And I intend to do something to take advantage of that fact!"

At that, every one of the mages at the table, except for Hulda, looked both chastised and as if he wished he was somewhere else.

And given Ancar's record in the past, perhaps they had reason to wish just that. He had lost more than one of his higher-ranking mages to the Valdemarans during the last two attempts to take their border. Right now, they were probably recalling that and wondering what they could do to keep them from being singled out to "test" whether or not that barrier was really gone. None of them had any wish to risk his precious skin against the Valdemarans. All of them would welcome some idea that would save them from that fate. They licked dry lips and glanced nervously about, and it was fairly obvious that they were unused to really thinking for themselves, or coming up with plans on the spur of the moment.

Once again, it was Falconsbane who broke the thickening and apprehensive silence. This should earn him the gratitude, and at least the temporary support, of every man at this table. Yes, and the woman, too, if she could see a way to profit by it.

"My lord," he said, addressing Ancar directly and ignoring everyone else, "do the lives of common folk in your foot-troops mean anything to you? Are they valuable? Have you any shortage of conscripts? Can you swell your ranks again if they die by the company?"

Ancar stared at him as if he had been speaking Tayledras or Shin'a'in; completely without understanding. Perhaps the concept of valuing the lives of fighters was foreign to him. It would have been foreign to Falconsbane as well, except that he had been in a situation or two where the troops he had were all he would get. At that point, by definition, those lives had value. But finally, Ancar answered.

"Of course not," the King said impatiently, as if only a fool would ask such a question. "I have an endless supply of peasant boys from women who whelp them like puppies. I have mage-controlled troops, and it does not matter if they are real fighters, boys, or graybeards. They will obey and fight as I please, and there are always plenty of peasants from the same source to conscript when they fall."

He did not mention that he had tried armed force before, and failed. Instead, he was giving Falconsbane the compliment of assuming the Adept must have a different plan than the one that had failed.

Falconsbane smiled. "Ah, good," he replied, genially. "That is, on occasion, a concern. If there happens to be a shortage of fighters, or there is no way to make reliable fighters of peasantry, then one must be careful of how the troops are disposed. But in your case—there is your answer. If the lives of troops are meaningless, my lord, then *spend* them."

Ancar shook his head. "Spend them?" he repeated, baffled.

Falconsbane leaned forward over the table, underscoring his intensity with his posture, and the nearest of the mages drew back a little before the avid hunger in his eyes. "*Use* them, my lord. What does it matter if this is a trap? Throw lives at a weak point until you seize it! Their controlling spells will hold past the border now, you have no need to fear that they will no longer obey you once you cross it. So throw them at the border, at one spot, in numbers too great for the Valdemarans to counter." His smile broadened. "I would venture to say that the Valdemarans have a witless concern over the loss of their fighters. That can be used against them, and it is a potent weapon in your arsenal. Throw your troops at the border, march them over the top of their own dead. Take a position, hold it, fortify it, and use it to take another position. Take *land,* my lord, and eat into their side as a canker-worm eats a rosebud. Ignore losses, ignore other targets. Take land, and cut Valdemar in half. If lives do not matter, then use them up to your advantage."

Ancar stared at him, eyes wide, but now it was with an unholy glee, and he drank in the words as a religious zealot would drink in holy writ. Falconsbane mentally congratulated himself. Ancar had known that he was valuable for what he knew. Now the boy knew he was valuable for his intelligence as well.

"Morale is no question when dealing with controlled troops," he added, "but it will be for the Valdemarans. And that is a weapon, as well. Think of how their hearts will quail, when they see the enemy continuing to come, grinding the bodies of their own dead beneath uncaring boots. Think of how they will falter and fail—and finally, flee."

"Yes!" Ancar shouted, crashing his fist down on the table and making his mages jump nervously. "That is precisely what we should do!" He began drawing an invisible diagram on the table with his finger, but only about half his mages bent to follow it. That was the half that Falconsbane needed to keep an eye on, the ones that might, possibly, prove dangerous. "We keep the mages in the rear, where they can be protected by the entire army—and we throw the mage-controlled troops at the border! That is the perfect use of our resources! And when Selenay—"

"No, my lord," Falconsbane interrupted, quickly. The boy was obsessed with the Valdemaran Queen, and now was not the time to permit him to fall into that trap. "Do not make the mistake that has haunted you in the past. Ignore the monarch, ignore your personal enemies. You will have time enough and leisure enough to work your will on them when you have conquered their kingdom. *Land,* my lord. Concentrate only on taking *land.* Capturing and holding large pieces of Valdemar itself. Nothing else."

"This will require a great deal of energy," Hulda interjected. From the expression on her face, thoughtful, and now a little alarmed, Falconsbane judged that she had finally been shaken out of her complacency. She was thinking fast, and did not want to be left out of this, with Falconsbane taking credit not only for breaking the barrier, but for coming up with a battle plan as well. "But it will grant us a great deal *more* energy to replace it!" She turned a brilliant smile on Ancar, but one that was as bloodthirsty as it was broad. "Think of all of the troops, both ours and theirs, dying, and in their deaths, supplying a great crimson stream of blood-magic! Sacrifices, by the hundreds, thousands! We will get back twice the power we expend to control the troops. This is a brilliant plan—"

She smiled brightly at Falconsbane, a smile poisoned with malicious hatred. Falconsbane only raised his eyebrow a trifle.

"—and it is one that, properly managed, will gain us more than we could possibly lose even at the worst case." She settled back in her chair, serene in her confidence that she had at least added her own direction to the flood tide.

But Falconsbane was not yet done.

"In addition, my lord," he continued, seeming to watch only Ancar, but keeping a stealthy eye on Hulda as well, "I would like to add something else for your contemplation. There is another consideration entirely. You have an envoy from the Eastern Emperor here at your court."

Hulda sat bolt upright and fixed him with a hard stare. Ancar nodded cautiously. Obviously he did not see where this was going.

Falconsbane held on to his patience. If this had been a child of his, he'd have had the youngling whipped for stupidity a hundred times over by now.

"You need to give this man information to send his master. You need it to be information of a certain kind. You must show him that you are a powerful ruler. By displaying this kind of—initiative—I think you will give this envoy a great deal to think on. By showing that you know the best way to use your resources, I think you will impress him with your ability to take advantage of any opportunity you are given." He narrowed his eyes a little, and pointed a finger at Ancar. "But most of all, by displaying a ruthless hand toward your own troops, you will prove to him and to his master that you are not to be trifled with."

Ancar smiled broadly, and Hulda's face had become an unreadable mask.

What Falconsbane had suspected, Hulda had just confirmed, although he doubted that Ancar realized this. Hulda was either an ally of the envoy, or a spy of the Emperor. Whether this was an arrangement of long standing or a recent development, it did not matter. The interests of Hulda and that of the Empire were the same, and Ancar was a fool not to have seen it.

This would give him another source of friction between the two of them. Things were looking up.

"You show another side of your powers that I had not expected, Mornelithe Falconsbane," the King replied, unable to keep the glee out of his voice. "And your reasoning is sound. I should have added you to my councillors long ago."

He looked at Hulda. She kept her face as smooth and expressionless as a statue.

"Very sound," Ancar repeated, with emphasis.

He stood up, and looked down at all of them. No one disagreed this time.

"So be it," he said. "We are agreed on a strategy. I will issue the orders immediately. Fedris, Bryon, Willem, you will go with the first contingent of troops to control them. More will follow. Do not risk yourselves, but make certain you drain every bit of blood-magic energy that comes from their deaths."

He looked around the table once again, and his smile did not fade. Nor did Falconsbane's.

"You may leave," King Ancar said, and the smile he wore was the mirror of Falconsbane's.

Chapter
Twelve

"So this is the Heartstone?"

Elspeth sneezed; the dust still in the air even after the room had been cleaned was thick enough to make her eyes water. Even Firesong's bondbird looked dusty—and not at all pleased about it. "Our little gift from V—ah— You Know." She was a little uneasy about mentioning her ancestor. You never knew who might be listening.

"Indeed, and although I assume You Know made it, I truly have *no* idea how this one was made in the first place," Firesong replied ruefully. He appeared to feel the same as she did about saying Vanyel's name out loud. "I seem to be saying that a great deal lately."

The firebird tipped its head sideways, giving him an odd look. He laughed a little, and Elspeth grinned a little, despite the undercurrent of unease she had felt since she got up this morning. "Well, now you have some idea of how much there is that you don't know," she told him, with mockery in her voice. "You can start feeling like the rest of us mortals. Trust me, you'll get used to it."

She turned her attention back to the large globe of crystal on the table in front of her, rubbing her nose to make it stop itching. It didn't work, and she sneezed again.

This Heartstone did not look much like the one she had seen in k'Sheyna Vale. *That* had been a tall, tooth-shaped piece of rough stone set in the center of an open glade, alive with power, but with a cracked and crazed surface and a definite feeling of *wrongness* about it. Not a neatly spherical piece of crystal the size of her head, swirled with hints of color, sitting in the middle of a stone table.

In fact, this room did not look much out of the ordinary at all. It was a direct copy of one on the ground floor of the Palace, one that was probably right above it, if Elspeth had reckoned her distances and angles right. Or maybe—no, probably, this room had to be *much* older—that room was a copy of this one. Why copy it? Perhaps to throw off enemies who were looking for it; this, if she had understood Vanyel correctly, was the physical link to the Web of power that bound all Heralds and all Companions together. Or perhaps the room had been copied because of the magic-prohibition; something like it was needed, but people kept "forgetting" this room existed. Certainly the servants had been surprised to discover a door behind the paintings stacked against it, despite the fact that the door was clearly visible in bright lantern light.

The room itself was not very large; just barely big enough for the round table in the middle and the padded benches around it. The table itself would seat four comfortably, and eight if they were very good friends. A single lantern suspended above the center of that table gave all the light that there was, and that wasn't much; it had been designed to leave the room in a state of twilight, even when the wick was set at its brightest. And in the middle of the table, a globe of pure crystal sat in isolated splendor. Just exactly the same as the room upstairs.

But that was where the similarities with the other room ended. That one was used often for FarSeers, when they needed to exercise their Gift in an atmosphere of undisturbed quiet so that they could concentrate. The crystal globe in the center of the table was used to help them focus that concentration, and it could be picked up and moved, although with difficulty. The globe was very heavy, and the center of the table had a depression carved into it so that the globe could not be moved by accident. That sphere of crystal *was* disturbed often enough that there were a few chips in it, from times when it had rolled off the table and fallen onto the floor. When there were too many chips, someone would take it to one of the jewelers to have it polished smooth again.

The table here was stone, not wood, as were the benches. A lot of the dust had come from cushions that had disintegrated, cushions that Firesong had already replaced. It would take an earthquake that leveled Haven to get *this* globe of crystal to move, and Elspeth was not certain even that would do it. The globe was fused somehow into the stone surface of the table, and the stone pillar supporting the table fused with the stone of the floor.

Firesong assured her that the stone of the floor at that point was fused with the very bedrock the Palace rested on. This arrangement was quite literally a single piece of rock now, and even if the Palace was demolished, that pillar of stone would probably still stand.

No, she decided, it would take more than a mere earthquake or human clumsiness to move *this* crystal stone!

"No one in my knowledge has ever *created* a Heartstone like this one," Firesong told her. "Normally, we simply choose an appropriate outcropping in our Vales— one that goes down to bedrock—and make it into the Heartstone. I don't know of anyone who has ever fused several disparate pieces of stone with the bedrock." The firebird jumped off his shoulder to the table, and stalked over to the crystal globe to examine it with immense dignity from all sides. It even pecked the surface once or twice, but Elspeth did not for a moment assume it was being "birdlike." A bird's eyes saw the world very differently than a human's, and it was entirely possible that Firesong's bondbird was examining the crystal for his bondmate.

The stone itself glowed, very faintly, even to normal sight. The servants had seen that, and commented about it, as they were lighting the lamp. Interestingly, the glow didn't alarm them as Elspeth had assumed it would. There was something very welcoming about this room, very comfortable. One immediately felt at ease, calm, and ready to work.

The visible glow was dim, but to anyone with Mage-Sight, the stone pulsed with power, brightening and dimming with a steady rhythm that Elspeth could only liken to a heartbeat, though one much slower than any human's. Little chasings of sparkles danced across it from time to time.

The other way this room differed was not only in age, but in *feeling*. Aside from the atmosphere of welcome, there was also an atmosphere of detachment and isolation. Outside sounds were muffled in the room above this one, so that the ringing of the Collegium bells could only be heard faintly. In this chamber, they could not be heard at all. Once the door closed, the Palace seemed to fall away, and as she stood here, the very silence took on a presence, as if every other human being was hundreds of leagues away.

"It is shielded," Firesong said. "The room, I mean. It is shielded as heavily as if it were a mage's workroom, although it appears that you and I and Darkwind have been given the key to those shields. They are powerful, layered, and very old; this room should be able to contain anything. As it must be, if it is to contain a Heartstone and yet be in the center of a populous area. The people of Haven are clearly not prepared to live with the energies of such magics." He raised a snow-white eyebrow at her. "For that matter, I do not know what such magics would do to those who are not Tayledras. There might be problems that one would never encounter in a Vale."

Elspeth licked her lips, and nodded. "I agree with you," she said. Those energies were very real to her; she felt them on her skin, like warm sunlight. They were not unpleasant, not at all, and she had Vanyel's word that she would come to no harm from them, but they were nothing she would want an ordinary person exposed to. These energies might not harm, say, a woman with child—but what if that woman were not a mage? Mages automatically took in energy and incorporated it into themselves, but what if it was not incorporated? All Tayledras were, at least to a tiny extent, mages. It was *born* into them, a gift from their Goddess. What would not harm them might harm someone from outClan.

Mage-energies radiating from the globe made her grateful that Firesong had thought to shield the servants before he allowed them in here to clean. This was like basking in warm summer sunlight! Now she really *knew* why working with this kind of magic bleached the Hawkbrothers' hair and eyes to silver and blue. Firesong had told her that working with node-energy did the same to all Adepts, but living with a Heartstone made it happen more quickly to Tayledras. And for those who actually worked with a Heartstone—well, he claimed his hair was white by the time he was ten. She believed him now. She wondered how long it would take hers to make the change, for when she had looked in the mirror this morning, there had been streaks of silver as wide as her thumb running through her hair, and her eyes were already lighter than they had been. Actually, she had rather liked the effect.

At least when her mother looked at her now, she would never again be haunted by her resemblance to her late and unlamented father.

Actually, maybe it was seeing all the silver hair that made her realize I wasn't her baby anymore. . . . Hmm. Maybe seeing the silver hair was what convinced the Court and Council that I knew what I was doing! People tended to listen more closely to someone their eyes told them was old enough to have attained some wisdom. There could be unexpected benefits to this bleaching business!

"The last of the workrooms is clean," she told the Adept, who had taken a seat on one of the benches and was staring into the Heartstone with a little smile of bemused content. "We moved things that were being stored up into the attics, and the few people who were using them for living places or offices have gotten space elsewhere. They're ready to use, as soon as you have a student you think is dangerous enough to need them."

"Ah, good," he said, proving by his immediate answer that he wasn't as entranced as he looked. "We will be ready for them soon enough. Within a day or two, I think. At the moment you are the only Adept among the Heralds, but that could change at any time. With so many out in the field, one never knows what may ride in."

She nodded. "I think if there really *is* an Adept-potential riding circuit, he or she will be coming in within the next couple of days, Firesong. Remember, the Web holds us all, and the Web 'knows' we need all the strong Mage-Gifts that are out there. Strongly Gifted people are not going to have a choice; *something* will bring them in."

Firesong tilted his head to one side to look at her, and tucked the curtain of his hair behind his ear absently. "Interesting. Very useful." He returned his gaze to the globe of crystal for a moment, as if he might see a vision of those Heralds in its depths. "And have you located all of the books and manuscripts on magic and the histories of Herald-Mages?"

She nodded, as he looked up again. "I think so," she said. "At least, if there are any more, they're hidden in shielded places I can't sense. Thank you for pointing out that books used around magic would pick up some contamination and be visible to Mage-Sight. I never would have found most of them if you hadn't mentioned that."

He simply smiled. "Then let me borrow a single moment of your time. I believe the Stone and I are in full accord now. I know that it is completely active. So there is only one more thing to do, so far as you are concerned— the little triggering I told you of."

Time for him to introduce me—us—to it. Despite Firesong's assurances that the Stone was quite safe, she shivered a little. Her only experience with a Heartstone was with the damaged rogue in k'Sheyna Vale, the "parent," as it were, of this one. It had not been in the least pleasant. On the other hand, if she were going to work as a full Tayledras-trained Adept, she must be able to use not only node-energies, but the powers of her Heartstone. The latter would give her the power to set magics that would outlive her, something few mages ever succeeded in doing. This Heartstone *seemed* "friendly." Yet it had come from a Stone that had tried to kill more than one of the Tayledras she knew, and had succeeded with those she hadn't known.

But she trusted Firesong. He said this Stone was not only safe, but it *must* be keyed to her, even as the shields around this room were keyed to her, so that she, in turn, could key it to other Adepts. Not just her, but Gwena as well—magically speaking, she and Gwena were bonded as closely as a lifebonded couple. So, with some trepidation, she opened herself completely to Gwena, then put her mental "hand" in Firesong's and closed her eyes.

Suddenly, she was enveloped by light and welcome; and a sense of something very, very old, and at the same time, very, very young. The age of stone, the youth of pure power, both were part of this thing that took her into itself.

:Oh, my—: she heard Gwena exclaim, and knew that her Companion had encountered the same feelings. And this was nothing she had expected. There was intelligence, of a sort, but not a "mind." At least, it was nothing she recognized as a mind. Fortunately, it was also utterly unlike the angry, unstable "intelligence" of the k'Sheyna Stone. This intelligence, whatever it was, had a far different view of "time" than she did, and if it had thoughts, they were so alien she could not even begin to grasp them.

But it was alive, there was absolutely no doubt in her mind about that. It recognized the two of them, and it welcomed her and Gwena both and would do so in the future. They "belonged" now. It would give her whatever power she needed, so long as she was in reach. That was what it was supposed to do.

Here was the moment of truth that made her Tayledras; a Heartstone's power was meant for the good of the Clan as a whole—which in her case, was all of Valdemar—and not to be used for an individual's needs. The shielding and the Veils that protected a Vale, the power to sculpt the rocks and create the springs, the force that grew the trees that supported up to a dozen *ekeles* apiece, all this came from the Heartstone. Excess energies were cleansed and stored there, for the use of all.

And for the moment, all that she wanted it to do was

to help her create a mage-shield around Haven. For the protection of all. She sensed Firesong's approval as she began.

Not too much protection, for that would block Mindspeech and other Gifts, but about the same as the Vales had when they were not under siege. Firesong understood what she wanted, and lent his own expertise, guiding her, but letting her set her own pace. He had done this before and cheerfully encouraged her as he showed her exactly what needed to be done. But *she* needed to do the actual work; this was her land, her "Vale," her Heartstone.

To her surprise, she discovered that most of what was needed was already in place; either Vanyel's work, or Firesong's, or both. Much of it had a feeling of great age about it. It was possible that there had been mage-shields here before, and they had simply faded with time, leaving behind a framework for her to invest with the new power at her disposal. All she needed to do, really, was to give the shield its proper shape, and define her protections. . . .

When she opened her eyes again, she was sweating with exertion and very tired, but Firesong nodded at her with the satisfaction of a teacher who has just seen his student complete a lesson perfectly. "Good!" he said. "Excellent! Now, since that shield is linked with this Heartstone, and not to *you*, it will hold even after you are gone or dead. That is the advantage of a Heartstone; the magics linked to it are perpetuated long past the death of the caster. Any other spells fade when the caster becomes depleted or dies. Distance can weaken the magic, too. That is why, when an Adept creates a Great Work, he tries to remain with it as much as possible—or else he does it in concert with others of his school and links it to their collective powers. That way the burden can be shared, or even passed on to students. The White Winds and Blue Mountain mages work that way, for instance."

That made sense. She wiped her forehead with a handkerchief and nodded. "I can see that—but there *are* magical devices and artifacts. I distinctly remember Need showing us that she used one to make spell-impregnated swords. Doesn't that imply that some magic *can* be put into things permanently?"

Firesong made a face, and shrugged. "Surely. But *I* do not know how to do so. Perhaps, at some point, that so-stubborn blade may be willing to show us. Until then I must go on as I have."

Well, that made sense, too. She changed the subject. "Should we go see how the gryphons are doing? Treyvan said his batch might be able to start doing something about the wizard-weather today, and I'd like to be there when they start."

"So they are come along that quickly?" Firesong said, with pleasure and surprise. "Wonderful! I should like to see this as well, and select those who might need extra tutoring. We cannot begin teaching them combative magics soon enough. Every hour we gain against the Beast must be used."

Together they left the room, closing the door behind them and blowing out the lantern beside it. Elspeth was surprised at how well the gray wood of the door seemed to fade into the gray stone of the wall in the half-light of the corridor, and Firesong winked at her. "Camouflage of a sort," he told her. "Those who do not need to find this room, probably will not be able to, even though they will no longer 'forget' it existed. This is not a spell, just good building. That was, in part, how it managed to remain overlooked all these years."

They took the steps up to the ground floor, then found one of the corridors leading to a door into the gardens. Treyvan was teaching his "fledgling mages" in an old building in the gardens, a storage shed that had been built in the form of an ornamental tower, complete to being made of stone. It was only three stories tall, but it had a good flat roof and a fine view of the countryside on clear days. It had been placed in a grove of dwarf trees and proportioned to them, so that it appeared to be much taller than it really was. On a clear day, one could see every detail of Elspeth's old pottery shed from its rooftop.

This was not a clear day, however, and the view from the top could be a perilous one in ugly weather. And it had been ugly, ever since the new Heartstone came to rest here. That should change over the course of the next few days; it would take a while to get the local patterns to return. Now the Stone was properly activated, properly shielded, and under supervision. Firesong had done a little about the mage-born storms plaguing the capital, but he had been too busy to learn as much as he needed to about the countryside, so he had erred on the side of caution, refusing to do very much. Another storm had threatened all day without breaking, bringing high winds and moisture-filled clouds in from the east. The wind whipped their clothes around them; Firesong had dressed for working in the dust of the Heartstone room, wearing relatively subdued grays and greens, but his costume was still that of a Tayledras mage, and as the wind caught his sleeves and hems, it made him look as if he were being attacked by his own clothing. The firebird narrowed its eyes to slits and clung to the padding of his shoulder, hunching down and practically gluing itself to his neck. His hair streamed out behind him, a creature of a hundred wildly whipping tentacles.

:I would not want to have to comb out that hair,: Gwena commented. Elspeth agreed; when the wind got through with it, he'd probably spend hours teasing out all the knots. No wonder the scouts wore theirs short!

:Oh, he'll find someone who's willing to comb it out for him, Gwena,: Elspeth responded cheerfully. *:I've heard rumors of a lovely young Bard!:*

Elspeth smelled rain as another gust hit her face, and winced. The grounds were already sodden, and another drenching would turn the gardens into a swamp. Well, maybe Treyvan would be able to do something about this before it did more than *smell* like rain. The farmlands north of here were parched; if they could just get some of this precipitation up there, the farmers would bless them for the rest of the season.

She and Firesong hurried along one of the gravel-covered paths to the tower. It was easy to see even at a distance a pair of golden-brown wings waving energetically at the top. The rest of the gryphon—and all of his pupils—lay hidden behind the stone coping around the tower's edge.

:Treyvan's in fine fettle,: Gwena said, with an excited laugh. For the moment, even Gwena had put the lowering threat of Ancar out of her mind. *:I'm down below the tower, but I've been able to follow the whole lesson, except while you and I were "talking" to the Heartstone, of course. He's just about ready to have the new mage-trainees try out their weather-working, but I told him you were coming, so he's waiting for you. He wants you and Firesong to see them at work, I think. These are very cooperative students, and they work well together.:*

They rounded a hedge that had been hiding the base of the tower, and there was Gwena, with two other Companions beside her, all of them looking with interest at the tower top. One of those Companions was Rolan; Elspeth recognized him immediately. But she couldn't make out who the other was. Even for a Herald, it was sometimes hard to tell Companions apart.

:I'm Sayvil, dear,: came the dry mind-voice she had heard a time or two before. *:And interested to see how the new teacher was coming. I didn't know gryphons could be mages, although* kyree *can, and you know about* hertasi *and* dyheli *mages, I presume. He's doing a fine job; I wouldn't change a thing.:*

Oh, so Sayvil was another one of those Companions who knew something of magic? Wasn't *that* interesting. . . .

Was that why she Chose Kero? Or was there some other motivation? It would certainly help to have a Companion who knew about magic in charge of someone who had come riding into your Kingdom wearing a magic sword!

Well, that could wait. There were too many other things that she needed to know. *:I'll let him know you approve, my lady,:* she replied, just as dryly, and got an amused chuckle for her pains.

The bottom stories of the tower were used mostly for storing gardening implements, and the top for storing seeds and bulbs, and wintering dormant plants. The whole building had a pleasant earthy smell about it although it was terribly dark, and she and Firesong had to grope after the ladder. The tiny windows in the sides of the tower were proportioned to make it look as if it were twice the size it actually was, and since the stone walls were a handspan thick, they let in very little light. The "ladders" here were an interesting cross between a ladder and a staircase with alternating steps, made so that they could be climbed by someone with both hands full. Not that Elspeth would want to, but the gardeners scampered up and down them all day without thinking twice about it.

There was more light from the open hatch to the roof, and that made the last of their climb a bit easier. They poked their heads up through the open hatchway cautiously, just as a couple of fat drops fell with identical *splats* onto the wood beside their heads.

"You are in good time, younglingssss," Treyvan said. "You have ssssaved usss frrrom needing to worrk in the wet." The male gryphon took up half of the roof space; the rest was occupied by two youngsters in trainee Grays, and three adults in Whites. Elspeth didn't recognize any of them. Of the three adults, one could not have been more than twenty at most; the other two were somewhere around thirty. The young one was blond and had the look of a Northerner about him; the other two, male and female, both with brown hair, had the stocky build of the folk on the Rethwellan border. The two trainees were probably in their last year; one was thin and very dark, the other plump and fair.

"I will make introductionsss when we arrre finissshed," the gryphon added hastily, as another set of raindrops joined the first. "Ssstudentsss, you may begin."

Elspeth was a little surprised to see, as they looked at each other and immediately meshed their powers, that he must have directed them to work as a group rather than separately. On the other hand, since the object was not just to train these people, but to actually do something about a bad situation with the weather, his strategy made sense.

The older of the two trainees handled the wind; he began to leech energy away from the weather system that had created this storm in the first place, an odd knot in the sky to the east of Haven. Elspeth couldn't quite see the point of this particular tactic; the wind *did* begin to die down, but that left the storm simply sitting there, right over the capital itself, ready to dump rain on them at any moment. But then the youngster passed the energy he had taken to the oldest of the Heralds, and that lady, rather than trying to change the direction of the existing wind, used the power to start another system north of Haven. Elspeth closed her eyes, and saw what they were Seeing, a "landscape" of weather, exactly like the sculptured terrain in a sandtable. The trainee was taking "sand" from a "hill" in the east and giving it to the woman. She was putting that "sand" in the south, creating another hill, there, while the second trainee began to scoop "sand" from the north and pass it along to the woman as well. The air made a kind of thin "liquid" flowing over the sand, too light to move it, but forced to move according to the way it had been sculpted. Where there was a slope, it "flowed" downhill, picking up force. So now there was a new wind that blew in from the south, heading north—

Which, by all reliable reports, could really use the rain that had been dumped uselessly on the capital for the past several weeks. Two more of the Heralds added something else, sculpting the "sand" further, one pulling the air to the north, and one pushing, out of the south. But these two had added something new, to create that push and pull. The one in the north was making things cool and wet, and to the south warm and dry. Elspeth opened her eyes, and saw that the storm really was moving in a new direction; by concentrating, she Saw that "sandtable" as an overlay on the "real" world.

When she had finished making her depression, the second trainee simply held the water in the clouds until they began to move into the north and west and, finally, out of sight.

Firesong smiled; Elspeth "watched" what they were doing using her Mage-Sight and "outer eyes" at once, completely enthralled by the clever way they were accomplishing their goal together. Now she saw why Firesong didn't want to work any weather-magic without knowing the land around them. It was something that could all too easily go wrong.

On the other hand, this was an application of fairly minor Gifts with major results, and she could well imagine what kind of havoc such weather control could wreak on or before a battle. Bring in a really major storm, and dump a month's worth of rain at once on a battlefield, and you created a quagmire. Force the enemy to come to you across it, and he was exhausted before he reached your lines.

"Well done!" Treyvan said, as the last of the clouds disappeared into the north, leaving behind a warm, cloudless blue sky without even the scent of rain. With a sigh of relief, the five new mages released their hold on the storm, certain now that it was going to behave, and turned to their strange teacher with glowing faces full of the pride of accomplishment. They deserved that glow; even among the Tayledras, Elspeth had never seen mages work together that well. That alone was an accomplishment of major proportions.

"Very well done," Firesong put in. "Fine control, good judgment, and the systems you set up should hold long enough for the rain to travel to where it should have gone in the first place. You are learning quickly. That you work together is a wondrous thing—all of you together can do far more than one of you alone."

One of the Heralds, clearly quite exhausted, sat down on the coping around the edge of the roof. "I'll admit that I was disappointed when my Mage-Gift proved to be just as minor as my FarSight, but now," he shook his head, "I'm not certain I'm ever going to call *any* Gift 'minor' anymore. The idea of actually steering a storm around the sky—in the wrong hands, something like that could be devastating. I don't want to think of someone hitting fields before harvest with hail. You could starve the whole country that way."

:Good man,: Gwena said from below. *:He's thinking, and in combat terms.:*

"You're right, and think about hitting a line of foot-soldiers with hail, while you're at it. FarSight and Mage-Gift are a good pairing," Elspeth told him. "You can use the first to make certain you *don't* dump a storm where it can harm someone, or at least someone on your own side, and just now you saw what you can do with the second."

:Kero would tell you that there is no such thing as a "minor" mage, only a mage who doesn't know how to make the best use of what power he has,: Sayvil observed from below, making all of them start. *:Most of her mages were what they call "earth-witches"—mages of similar power to you. But they knew all about holding what you have in reserve until you are in a position where a little application of magic will bring a big result. Think of it as waiting until your enemy is off-balance, then pushing.:*

The three Heralds exchanged glances, and nodded; the two trainees just looked very solemn and a little frightened. Elspeth couldn't blame them. They were very young to be thinking of going into battle—only partially trained, and with a new Gift they had no appreciable experience in using—but that was just what they were going to be doing, and soon.

"Listen, we ought to introduce ourselves," the Herald who had spoken said hastily, perhaps hoping to avoid another unsolicited comment from Sayvil. "I'm Herald Rafe—this is Brion and this is Kelsy."

"We're Anda and Chass," said the first trainee shyly. "You're Elspeth, right? Is this the Hawkbrother friend of yours? The one who is a warrior and a mage?"

She nodded. "I'm Elspeth. This is Firesong, not Darkwind. Firesong has never been anything but a mage, but we don't hold that against him!"

Firesong made a face at her, and his firebird gave an audible snort, something that made all five of the students stare and chuckle.

"Darkwind is going through some old books right now, looking for some charts. I'm sure you'll meet him some time soon." She smiled impartially at all five of them. "Actually, my only purpose at the moment, besides watching what you were doing, was to bring Firesong up here to introduce you to him."

Quickly she turned to the Healing Adept and explained in Tayledras what the differences were between a Herald and a Trainee. Then she switched back to speech the others would understand. "So what you have here is a very mixed group of ages and experiences. I'm amazed that they work so well together."

Firesong nodded. "I wish to take these for a day or so, as I think you were hoping. If they can add their powers to work the weather, they can surely add them to shield."

"I have no objection," Treyvan said, cocking his head to one side. "You know more of thisss than I. Gryphonsss are sssolitarrry magesss, mosssstly."

"Thanks, both of you." Elspeth turned back to the group. "He'll be another of your mage-teachers, for a couple of specific lessons, probably within the next couple of days."

"In fact, at the moment, we are fairly disorganized," Firesong concluded, granting them all one of his dazzling smiles. "I pledge you, we will do better soon!"

"I sssurely hope sssso," Treyvan hissed wryly. "But Firesssong, if you would ssstay here for a moment, I ssshould like you to begin now, and explain sssomething to thessse ssstudentsss forrr me."

That was clearly a dismissal, and Elsbeth ducked back down through the trapdoor. By the time she reached the ground, only Gwena remained of the Companions that had been watching from below.

:One of these days, Sayvil is going to frighten someone right off a roof,: Gwena said, shaking her head and mane vigorously. *:Honestly! Oh, Treyvan's group wasn't the only one doing weather-work today; Hydona had her lot working in the morning, but since they're much stronger, she had them working at a distance. Off to the west a ways, doing something about that horrible Gate-storm we triggered when we came home.:*

Elspeth sighed with relief. "Thank goodness. I was feeling terribly guilty about that mess. Darkwind said that at this point, what with all the new energy-patterns around, there are probably storms over every major node in this Kingdom. Gods, I can't believe the mess we've got."

:I hope he also pointed out we can't take care of them all,: Gwena said with resigned practicality. *:There aren't enough of us, and there isn't enough time. The only reason we can deal with any of it is because it's a way to train our new mages.:*

"He did." Elspeth took a moment to hoist herself up

onto Gwena's bare back. "Dearheart, I need a ride. Darkwind said when he finished with the books, he was going to go consult with Kero a bit more and I should meet him at the salle." She stifled a yawn. "There just aren't enough hours in the day. This calm is so deceptive—but under it all, I feel like we can't get everything we need done taken care of fast enough. Ancar is *going* to get us, and only he knows when."

:*Right*.: Gwena set off at a brisk trot, without a complaint. Elspeth took the brief respite to try to force the knotted muscles of her neck to relax. Before being "introduced" to the Heartstone, she had spent the morning going over the newest set of trainees, testing them for Mage-Gift, then giving them a rush course in the basics of magic. She had an advantage over Darkwind, as a teacher; she *knew* what the mind-magic lessons were like, and she could tell her students exactly how mind-magic and true magic differed. Once they were proficient in those basics, she turned her group over to Hydona.

Then she had gone off to the archives, and the crates and boxes of books she and Darkwind had discovered late last night, all of them with fading traces of long-ago mage-energies on them. Most of them were handwritten, were either original bound manuscripts, or handmade copies of even older manuscripts. Fortunately, all her delving into the archives had made her uniquely qualified to sort through them, and determine which were real books teaching magic and which were only contaminated by proximity. Then she had handed the mage-books over to those Heralds that Herald-Chronicler Myste felt could translate them into more modern terms. There had been a few clearly written in Tayledras, which had given Darkwind a bit of a shock, and a couple in no language either could identify. Darkwind was planning to take those to Kerowyn, once he determined if there was anything worth their time in the Tayledras books.

Both of them were running themselves ragged. Her day had started before dawn, and it would last long past midnight. There just weren't enough hours; the peace of the Palace was *so* deceptive. Even with the violent weather plaguing them, it didn't seem as if they were about to be invaded. In fact, things weren't really much different than they had been when she'd left. It was easy to be fooled into thinking there was nothing wrong here, but Ancar was planning something, she knew it. . . .

For that matter, he might well be *doing* something, right this very minute. With all those storms on the borders, the relay-towers were useless except when the weather cleared a bit. At least she had a barrier over Haven now, and Firesong would return to the Heartstone when he was done with Treyvan's students, and use her shield as a model to set other protections in place, as many as he had time and strength for.

And tomorrow, before dawn, it would all begin again.

That was why Gwena was not scolding her for riding the short distance to the salle. Not when riding was quicker than walking, and not as exhausting as running.

She slid off Gwena's back at the door to Kerowyn's domain, and hit the ground at a trot. The salle, a huge, wooden building, with clerestory windows and mirrors on two of the walls, was full of trainees being supervised by Jeri, Kero's assistant, and a Herald who had been hand-picked and personally trained by Alberich, the absent Weaponsmaster. Jeri looked up when she caught Elspeth's reflection in a mirror, nodded at her, and pointed with her chin toward Kero's office, all without missing a command to her line of young, clumsy sword wielders.

Elspeth skirted past the youngsters in their worn practice armor, moving along the wall with the benches between her and them, and avoiding the piles of practice gear strewn in her path. She tapped on Kero's door at the other end of the room, using her own code without thinking twice about it.

It was a good thing she did. The door opened a mere crack, just wide enough for an arm in brown leather to snake out, grab her by the wrist, and pull her inside.

As soon as she cleared the doorway, the reason for Kero's action was obvious. Darkwind was with her, sitting cross-legged in the corner, but so was another man, a stranger, filthy and travel-stained, dressed like a peddler. He had half-risen from his stool at Elspeth's entrance, taking a wary stance and perfectly ready to defend himself.

One of Kero's spies—probably one of her old mercenary company, the Skybolts. That was the only thing he could be. Her heart sank. The man would not be here unless he had some word on Ancar, and from his grim expression, it was probably more trouble.

"I'm glad you're here," Kero said, with a nod to the stranger, and a quick hand-sign Elspeth recognized as being the Skybolts' hand-language for "all clear." He sank back down onto his stool again, and picked up a towel from a pile on the floor next to him. "You and Darkwind know the most about Falcon's Breath, and Ragges here actually managed to see him. He's been describing the man to Darkwind. I want you both to hear what he has to say."

"Bright feather, I fear it really is Falconsbane," Darkwind added. "Ragges has described him perfectly; it could be no other."

Elspeth sat down quickly on another stool, with an explosive sigh. After twice thinking Falconsbane was gone for good, then hearing he had escaped yet again, her reaction to hearing this confirmation that he lived was, oddly enough, simple exhaustion. "Damn. Damn, damn, damn. I didn't really think there was any chance of a mistake. I wish that Beast would just *die*."

"Don't we all," Kero said, leaning up against the door with her ear near enough the crack that she would be able to hear anyone approaching on the other side. "Well, go on, Ragges. Anything you know for a fact could be more important than either of us would guess."

Bleak depression settled over Elspeth as the spy continued his report.

"This Falconsbane is not only advising Ancar, he seems to be very high up in Ancar's mage-ranks," the stranger said, wiping his face vigorously with a towel. As he rubbed, Elspeth realized that what she had taken for dirt and the man's own swarthy complexion was actually makeup or dye. Underneath it he was far paler than he looked. "Rumor had it, literally just as I left, that he is claiming *he* has taken down some kind of protective barrier that keeps magic out of Valdemar. There were so many rumors that war was at hand that I fled the capital, hoping to outrun any army Ancar might mount."

Darkwind looked sardonic. "He would claim anything he thought he could convince folk of," was all the Hawkbrother said, his lips twisted with distaste.

"Well, Hulda is not long for her spot of 'favorite mage' if she can't find a way to counter his influence," Ragges told them, picking off bits of hair and things that counterfeited moles perfectly, which had been glued to his cheeks. "At the moment his star is rising pretty quickly. But there's another player in this little game now, and I have no idea what *he's* about. There's a new envoy at Ancar's court, wearing badges and livery from some lord *I* don't recognize. And mind, most of the allies Ancar picked up in the beginning have pretty well deserted him by now, so whoever sent this lad must be fairly certain there's no way that Ancar can turn on them." He fished a bit of pencil and a scrap of paper out of his pocket and made a quick sketch. "This is the badge, and the man seems to be great friends with Hulda. She does her best not to be seen coming and going, but she spends a great deal of time in his suite. She's so busy watching for spies from her rivals she never noticed me."

Kero gave the sketch a cursory glance, and shrugged. "Nothing I know," she said.

"Let me see that," Darkwind said, suddenly, urgently. She handed it to him, and he frowned over it for a moment.

"I have seen this somewhere—within a day," he said, his brow creased as he stared at it. "No—I saw it today, this very morning. In a book. No, not *in* the book, I remember now!"

He reached down to the pile of books at his feet and looked just inside the covers of each of them in rapid succession. Finally he exclaimed, "Here!" and held up the book for all of them to see.

"That's the device, all right," Ragges said decisively. Kero shrugged again, but Elspeth took the book from Darkwind and leafed through it. It was in Valdemaran so archaic she had taken it for another language entirely until this very moment. But she had not noticed the very first page before, which looked a great deal more modern. She went back to that first page when she simply could not puzzle out any of the script. As she had hoped, in a modern, scholar's hand, she found a history of the book itself. This was a copy, not the original, but the scribes had faithfully reproduced every handwritten marginal note and scribbled diagram.

For this was a copy of a very important tome; one of the books brought to this land before it was a Kingdom, before it was even a nation.

By the Baron Valdemar, who became, by declamation, King Valdemar the First.

"According to this," she said, slowly, puzzling out the words and feeling cold fear growing in the pit of her stomach, "the device inside the cover of this book is that of the former owner—the one that King Valdemar 'borrowed' the book from, when he ran west with his people."

No one would ever have anticipated this; no one could have.

Kero frowned. "I have the sinking feeling I'm not going to like what you're going to tell me."

"It's the personal arms of the ruling family of the Eastern Empire," Elspeth said, her throat closing until her voice was hardly more than a harsh whisper. All her life she had heard tales of the horrors and injustices that the Emperor wrought on his subjects, and always the refrain had been "be glad the Emperor is too far away to notice us." Valdemar had run for *years* with his people before settling here, but the memories of what he had escaped still haunted every scholar's nightmares. There was no name for the Eastern Empire; it didn't need one. It covered the entire Eastern coastline, a monolithic giant from which not even rumors escaped. "The Emperor of the East himself has sent an envoy to Ancar's court—"

"The Emperor's personal envoy is playing footsie with Hulda?" Kero exclaimed, her voice rising sharply. "Old Wizard Charliss? The Emperor of the East? Bloody *hell!*"

Whatever else she might have said was lost as someone pounded urgently on the door. "It's Jeri!" said Kero's assistant, with strain audible in her voice. "There's been a relay-message from the east, and they sent a page out here to get you. They need you people in Council right now! Ancar's troops are attacking our border!"

"Bloody *hell!*" Kero cried again, then snatched open the door and headed out at a dead run, with Elspeth and Darkwind right on her heels.

The ax had fallen, and it was worse than Elspeth had feared. Nightfall brought three more messages as soon as lanterns could be seen from relay-tower to relay-tower, with word that a Herald with more detail was on the way.

But the messages, although they were clear and concise, made absolutely no sense.

Elspeth rubbed her eyes and fought back the urge to sleep; no one in the Council chamber had slept for three days. Right now Selenay was reporting what little the Council knew to her chief courtiers while Prince Daren held her seat. Elspeth was trapped between exhaustion and tension. There was no time for sleep; there was no time for anything, now. A trainee put a mug full of strong, hot tea discreetly by her hand; she took it and emptied it in three swallows.

Ancar's forces had crossed the border shortly after noon on the first day of the attack. As Kero and Elspeth had feared, they seemed to be more of his magically-controlled conscript-troops, and they continued to remain under control long past the point when spells had lost their effectiveness in the past. So the barrier was down, just as Vanyel had warned.

What was insane was that they had overrun the first garrison in their path, and had lost at least half their men taking it. Now they were fortifying it and holding it against a counterattack, while more of Ancar's troops came in over the border at their back—and given the rate at which they were losing men, in a day or two they would have to replace the *entire* force that had mounted the attack in the first place!

"This isn't like Ancar," Kero said tiredly, as she and the Lord Marshal shoved counters around on a map in response to every message from the border. "He just doesn't *fight* like this. That garrison is of no value whatsoever; there's no one of any importance there, there's nothing valuable there, it's just one more place on the border. It isn't even *strategically* valuable. He just doesn't go after targets that aren't worth anything—he *certainly* doesn't continue to hold them afterward!"

"I'd say he'd gone mad, except he already was," the Lord Marshal agreed, running his hand through his thinning hair. "I have never seen Ancar strike for anything that did not have a substantial value to it. That was why we didn't bother to fortify that town all that heavily."

"Someone else is dictating his tactics," Darkwind said suddenly, sitting up straight.

All eyes turned toward him. "He's never let anyone dictate his tactics before this," Kero replied skeptically. "That's one reason why we've held him off for so long. He's very predictable, and bad losses have always made him give up. He *always* follows the same pattern; he tests us until he loses his test force, then he falls back. Resist him strongly, and he gives up."

"That was so in the past, but it is not so now," Darkwind replied emphatically. "He has given over his main strategy to someone else, and *we* know who it is that spends the lives of underlings like sand, and leaves a river of the blood of his own people in his wake."

He looked significantly at Elspeth, who nodded. "Mornelithe Falconsbane," she said.

"The *mage?*" was Kero's incredulous reply. "Since when does a mage know anything about tactics?"

"Are these sound *tactical* decisions?" Darkwind countered. "No. But they *will* win the war for Ancar. All he needs do is keep driving his troops in, and they will overwhelm you. He will conquer by sheer numbers. Recall, neither of them care at all for the state either land will be in when the war is over. Falconsbane would as soon both lands were decimated, and he could very well have prodded Ancar until he cares only for revenge."

The rest of the Council stared at him, appalled. Elspeth felt her gut knot with cold fear. This was what she had felt, but had not been able to articulate, probably because she had not wanted to believe it. But now, hearing it spoken aloud, she did believe it.

"No one can win against something like that—" one of the Councillors faltered.

Darkwind only nodded grimly, and Elspeth seconded him.

"Then we are doomed. It is only a matter of time—" The Seneschal did not wail, but he might just as well have. His words, and the fear in them, echoed the feelings of everyone around him.

Black despair descended—eyes widened with incipient hysteria—and the High Council of Valdemar was only a heartbeat away from absolute panic.

"Not if we do something completely unexpected," Elspeth heard herself saying, and she marveled absently at the calm she heard in her own voice. "Something atypical. That was how Darkwind and I defeated him before. We figured out what he thought we would do, and we did something that he couldn't anticipate."

"He'll assume panic," Darkwind put in. "He'll assume that you will mount a rearguard action and attempt to hold a line while the rest of your populace flees, becoming refugees. He will expect you to go north and south, I think; he will try to cut you off from Rethwellan, and count on the mountains to trap you. I would guess that once he panics you, he will come in from a southerly direction to drive you."

Kero studied the map. "That fits," she said at last. "That cuts us off from our allies, although he probably doesn't know about the new alliance with Karse."

"We have an alliance with *Karse?*" squeaked someone to Elspeth's left. Kero ignored whoever it was. "So he's going to be expecting some kind of digging in, a defensive line, you think?"

"Isn't that what logic dictates?" Darkwind replied. "A large defensive attempt. Fortification. So, what is *not* logical? How can we strike at him in a significant way that he will not anticipate?"

Kero stared at him for a very long time, then transferred her gaze to Elspeth. "A dagger strike," she said slowly. "A very small counterattack, inside his own stronghold. We cut off the snake's head. Kill Ancar, Hulda, *and* Falcon's Breath, and the whole thing falls apart."

Darkwind nodded, his mouth set in a thin line, his lips gray with tension and fatigue.

Silence around the Council table, although Elspeth saw her stepfather nodding out of the corner of her eye. Prince Daren knew something of expediency.

"That's murder—" faltered Lady Elibet.

"That's *assassination,*" said the Lord Patriarch sternly. "Coldblooded, and calculated. A deadly sin by any decent man's moral code."

"Oh, it's a moral dilemma, all right," Kero replied, grimly. "It's murder, it's cold-blooded, it's wrong. If you face an enemy, you should give him a chance to defend himself. Hellfires, killing is wrong. I'm a *mercenary,* my lords and ladies, and I will be the first to tell you that there is no nice way to kill. But what choice do we have? If we try to run, we either abandon *everything* to him— and may I remind you, at least half of our population has no means to escape—or we find ourselves running into a trap he's set for us. So the half that *runs* gets slaughtered, too. If we make a stand, his numbers overrun us and destroy us. And while *we're* dying, so are his own troops. Remember them? They're poor mage-controlled farmers, graybeards, and little boys! In fact, once he starts taking *our* land, he'll start turning our own people against us! *Do we have a choice*?"

Kero looked into the eyes of each Councillor in turn; some returned her stare for stare, and some only dropped their gazes to the table in front of them, but one and all, they only shook their heads.

Elspeth cleared her throat when Kero's gaze reached her. Kero nodded; since she was no longer the Heir, she had no real place in Council, but habit would make them listen to her anyway.

"We can baffle him with strike-and-run tactics," she said. "That will delay him while he tries to take ground. If he is expecting either all-out panic or a defensive line, while the special forces are getting into place, we can puzzle him by not playing either of the games he expects."

Kero nodded cautiously at that. "Is there a plan behind this?" she asked.

"One he wouldn't think of—evacuation," Elspeth replied. "Strike north and lead him up while you evacuate to the south. Then strike from the south and lead him into scorched-earth while you evacuate in the west. That way we can get everyone out—and Captain—no one is going to like this—but if people won't leave, pull them out and burn their houses and fields. They won't stay if there's nothing to eat and nowhere to live."

Someone gasped in outrage, but the Lord Marshal nodded, his face a mask of pain. "We have to think of the people first," he said, "And if we deny Ancar any kind of sustenance, he will be forced to march far more slowly than if he can loot as he goes."

"But how can we destroy our own land?" Elibet *did* wail. "How can we simply give him our Kingdom, and lay waste to it ourselves? How can we do this to Valdemar? And how can we explain this to the people?"

Elspeth did not stand, but held herself proud and tall. "Tell them this," she said. "Valdemar is not grainfields, or roads, or cattle; it is not cities, it is not even the land itself. It is people. Grain will grow again—herds can be bred—houses can be rebuilt. It is the lives of our people that are at stake here, and we must preserve them. *That* is what we must fight for, every precious life! There is no book that cannot be rewritten, no temple that cannot be rebuilt, so long as those lives are preserved. So long as the people live—so does Valdemar."

She looked around the table as Kero had, meeting the eyes of every woman and man on the Council.

"There is not a Herald in Valdemar who will not stand between those people and Ancar's forces—even if the only weapons he has are those of his mind and bare hands," she continued. "That includes me—for, my lords and ladies, I will be the first to volunteer for the group that goes into Ancar's land. You know how much he hates me, personally, and what he will do if he takes me. Every Herald will defend our people to his last breath and drop of blood, and lament that he has no more to give. Tell your people that—and remind them that the Heralds have no homes, no belongings, and never have. All that Heralds have comes from the people—and it will all return to their service, first to last, until there is no more to offer."

Chapter
Thirteen

Kero sent the trainees out of the Council Chamber—more for their protection than from the need to keep secrets from anyone Chosen. The trainees were as trustworthy as their Companions, but there were a lot of them. It would be difficult to protect all of them from enemy agents if word somehow got out that they knew the contents of a secret plan. Searchingly, she looked at each of the members of the Council in turn. "From here on, nothing leaves this room," she said emphatically. "And I mean *nothing*. If I had a way, I'd put a spell on you people to keep you from even thinking about this when you're outside this room."

Darkwind coughed politely, and Kero's head swiveled like an owl's. Her eyes met his, and he nodded, once. "Don't tell me; you *can* do that," she hazarded. "I should have guessed."

Darkwind shrugged. "It is called a spell of coercion," he offered politely, "And we do not use it except in times of greatest need. We prefer not to use the version that makes one forget something important, unless we think that an enemy may also be a strong Mindspeaker. It can be broken, but the person in question must be in the physical possession of a mage stronger than the one who set it, at least in the areas of mind-magic. It can be worked around, but again, the person must be in the physical possession of a countering mage, and it takes a great deal of time. A Tayledras must also have the consent of the one it is placed upon; others are not so polite about it."

Like Falconsbane, Elspeth thought grimly. She recalled, all too vividly, what Starblade had endured to have his coercions broken.

The other members of the Council, including Heralds Teren, Kyril, and Griffon, stirred uneasily, and there was more than a shadow of fear in some eyes. *Magic;* that was the problem. Mind-magic they knew, but this was different, alien, and fraught with unpleasant implications. About the only times any of them had encountered true magic, it had been in the hands of an enemy.

:Now they know how the unGifted sometimes feel around them,: Gwena commented ironically.

Prince Daren simply looked interested; after all, he had seen magic at work often enough in his days as his brother's Lord Martial. "I'd heard of coercions, but before today I'd never met any mage who could set them," he said. "It was said that the Karsite Priests of Vkandis could set coercions, though, and some things Alberich told me from time to time seemed to confirm that."

Talia, who sat secure in the knowledge her Gift of Empathy gave her, that Darkwind would sooner cut his own arm off than harm *her* or any other Herald, nodded gravely. "I can see where such a precaution would give our force a great deal of protection from slips of the tongue."

"This would be for your protection as well as my team's," Kero said flatly. "What you can't tell, no one can extract from you, even by using drugs. I don't think we need to fear Ancar sending agents in to kidnap any of you, but please remember that illusions work here now. He *could* get someone in to impersonate a servant, drug your food, and get you to babble anything you know, before leaving you to sleep it off. With the right drugs, you'd never even know it had happened."

Talia paled, and rightly. Both she and Elspeth recalled how even when the magic-prohibitions had been in place, Hulda had managed to get in place as an assistant to Elspeth's nurse and drug that nurse so that it was Hulda who issued the orders.

Lady Kester blanched. "You're not serious—" she began, then took a second look at Kero's face. "No. You are. Dear and precious gods. I never thought to see Valdemar in such a pass that Councillors could not be protected in Haven."

"Nor did I," Prince Daren sighed, "But let me be the first to agree to such a spell being set upon me. We are many and the servants here are more numerous still. We have not enough mages to check for the presence of illusions at all times." He raised an eyebrow at Darkwind, who bowed a little in response. "I trust this little spell of yours will be *limited* in scope?"

"If I set it now, and lift it when the discussion is ended, it will be limited to that time period," Darkwind replied. He looked around. "There is this; if any of you feel truly that you cannot bear to have such a spell set upon you, there is always the option to leave and have no part in the decision."

It was an option no one really wanted to take. In the face of Daren's acceptance, and Talia's, which followed immediately upon his, the other Councillors could do nothing else but accept. No one wanted to be left out of the decision, nor did they care for the idea of giving up any of their responsibilities.

Darkwind was exhausted, but he was also an Adept; he was not dependent on his own personal energies to set this spell. Elspeth sensed him fumbling a little in his attempt to find the nearest node; she solved his problem by linking him to it herself. His brief smile was all the thanks she needed.

It was a sad irony that coercive spells were some of the easiest to set. Darkwind was done before half of the Councillors even realized he had begun.

"There," he said, letting his link to the node go and slumping back in his chair. "Now, none of you will be able to speak of this outside the Council chamber, nor with anyone who is not of the Council."

"We won't?" Father Ricard said wonderingly, touching his forehead. "How odd—I don't feel any different—"

"Which is as it should be." For the first time, Firesong, who was sitting behind Elspeth, spoke up. "A coercive spell is an insidious thing. One set well should not be noticed at all. As none of you ever noticed that you could not speak of magic, nor remember its existence, except as an historical anomaly." His lips curved in gentle irony as they started. "Yes, indeed, speakers for k'Valdemar— your land has been under a coercive spell for long and long, and you had never noted it. Such is the usage of magic in skilled and powerful hands. You should be grateful that your last Herald-Mage was a man of deep integrity and great resourcefulness."

:And had a lot of Companions to help him,: Gwena added smugly, confirming Elspeth's suspicion that the Companions had been involved in keeping true magic a "forgotten" resource.

Kero let out a long, deep sigh. "Well, now that we've some assurance we can keep this out of Ancar's hands, we need to put together our team. Ordinarily—I beg your pardons, but ordinarily this is covert work, and none of you would ever hear about it, much less help me agree whom to send. You *might* have heard about the results, if Selenay, Daren, and I agreed that you needed the information. There have been a number of operations you've heard nothing of, and there will be more."

The Lord Patriarch smiled, a little grimly. "We had assumed that, my lady."

Kero coughed. "Well. I had hoped you had. But this time, I *need* that agreement from you, because if we are going to succeed, we must send mages against mages, and we'll be taking those mages away from the direct defense of Valdemar. They're going against Ancar, Hulda, and a mage we *know* is a dangerous Adept, and that means sending in the best we have. So we must accept Elspeth's offer."

"Must we?" Talia asked, but without much hope.

"Speaking as a strategist," the Lord Marshal said unhappily, "I must agree. She has volunteered, and she is a Herald—she knows her duty. And again, it is the last move that Ancar would ever expect."

"The last that Falconsbane would expect, as well," Darkwind put in. "He will be anticipating that every highborn that can will be fleeing to safety in Rethwellan. He cannot conceive of willing self-sacrifice. *If* he knows that Elspeth is here and not still in k'Sheyna, he will expect her to do the same as he would, to try to escape him and not fly into his reach. After all, she could seek asylum with her kin and be accepted gladly, and she has all the mage-power she needs to escape his minions easily."

"If you send Elspeth, you must send Skif," Lady Kester said firmly. "Whether you will admit it or not, *I* am perfectly aware that he has done this sort of thing before. Send an experienced agent with her, one who has been working with her."

"If I go," Skif replied, from behind Darkwind, "then Nyara comes as well. Cymry backs her to come along. She is clever and skilled, a trained fighter, she has a score of counts to settle with Falconsbane, and she knows him as no one else does."

Kero gave him a long look, transferred it to Nyara, then caught Elspeth's gaze, and did something she seldom resorted to with anyone but her lover, Herald Eldan. She used Mindspeech.

:Family resemblance, kitten?: she asked.

Elspeth nodded, very slightly. There was no point in going into excruciating detail at this point. Let Kero simply assume that Nyara was trying to make up for the perfidy of a relative, and perhaps, to extract revenge for something Falconsbane had done to her. That was something Kero could understand.

:Ah,: came the reply. *:I'd wondered.:* And she left it at that. Kero was nothing if not expedient. And she trusted Skif's judgment as she trusted her own.

"By the same token, I must go with Elspeth," Darkwind put in. "We have worked together successfully, I am the more experienced mage of the two of us, and as Nyara knows Falconsbane, so she knows Hulda. That will give us four agents to target them, two of them mages and Adepts."

"But you and Elspeth would strike first at Hulda and Ancar," Firesong pointed out. "There is some urgency for *our* people in ridding the world of the Beast, and only an Adept is likely to be able to counter his protective magics. That being the case, I should go with you as well. If you divide, two to target the Hardornens, and two to target the Beast, Skif and Nyara should have an Adept with them. There is no point in dividing those who have worked together."

Kero nodded. "I have to admit that Falconsbane is not a priority for us—"

Firesong shrugged. "He should be—believe me, even more so than the Hardornens. So, let us plan a two-bladed attack upon *him*. That gives you an Adept that Falconsbane *does not know* to work upon him, and an Adept each for Hulda and Ancar, Adepts who are also well-trained as fighters. I am by no means certain that an Adept can take the Beast; I suspect I will accomplish more by distracting him, making him think I am his only enemy. This means that the physical attack, which he will not anticipate, can come from Skif and Nyara."

:*And me*,: Need said quietly, for Elspeth's ears alone. :*But the boy will be damned useful. I think I'm going to have to be awfully close to Falconsbane to do any good.*:

Elspeth tried not to look surprised at the Healing Adept's speech, but she had not expected Firesong to volunteer for this. She glanced back at Darkwind, who shrugged.

:*He is unique*,: Darkwind said wryly. :*With his own will. He does have the mind-set of the Healing Adept, and that means he would not care to see Falconsbane working his twisted will on lands that* had *been Cleansed. And I suspect that your mutual ancestor may have impressed some kind of sense of responsibility for your continued health upon him. I certainly would not turn his aid away! But for predictability—I would look upon Firesong as a benevolent trickster.*:

"What are we going to do for mages if you're all leaving?" Lady Kester asked, a little desperately.

"You have the gryphons," Darkwind pointed out. "They are both Masters. You have Heralds and trainees with Mage-Gift, currently being schooled in combative magics."

"Ah. . . ." Kero leaned back in her chair, and hooded her eyes with her lids. "We won't be depending entirely on the gryphons. Since this is all under the rose—I have a surprise for you all. There are more mages coming, and I expect them to start arriving any day now."

As the Councillors turned as one from watching Elspeth and her group to staring at Kero, she revealed to them the news of the three groups of mages currently being brought at top speed toward Haven, riding pillion behind Heralds and trainees released from the Collegium for the duty. She had virtually denuded the Herald's Collegium of all but those Mage-Gifted and first-year students.

"*That's* why you sent all those so-called 'training groups' off!" exclaimed the Lord Marshal. Kero nodded.

"So, we will have mages. Will they be Adepts?" She shrugged. "I can't tell you. I don't know what they're sending us. What I *can* tell you, since I used mages in my Company, is that a mage is only as good as the tacticians he works with, and his willingness to really use his talents to the fullest. Just because someone is an Adept, that does not mean he is going to be effective."

"I have, in my time, seen a few completely ineffective Adepts," Firesong put in. "I have seen a *Journeyman* defeat one of them in a contest. Kerowyn is correct."

"So there you have it. Are we all agreed on the team?" Kero spread her hands to indicate that she was ready to call a vote on it.

The vote was unanimous, though it was fairly clear that there was some reluctance to place the only Adepts Valdemar had access to, and its former Heir, in such jeopardy.

"Fine." Kero nodded. "Then as far as I am concerned, this meeting can close. We all have things we need to do. I have to find a way to insert these folk into Hardorn. You have things you need to tell your people. Ladies and lords, you will be in charge of the physical defenses and the evacuations. You should consult with the Lord Marshal about that, and how to organize them to coordinate with his strike-and-run raids. I'll join you as soon as we come up with an insertion plan." She raised an eyebrow at Talia, Elspeth, and Prince Daren. "You three have a task I really don't envy. The Queen is not going to like this."

Talia and Elspeth exchanged a knowing glance and a sigh. Daren shook his head.

"Perhaps," he suggested gently, "I should be the one to break the word first to Selenay. I shall remind her of how sad the little ones would be to become half-orphaned; I hope then she will not slay the father of her children out of sheer pique."

Elspeth and Talia waited nervously in the rather austere antechamber to Selenay and Daren's private suite, but it seemed almost no time at all before Daren was back, beckoning to both of them to come with him. They followed him into Selenay's private office, and Elspeth's heart ached to see how drawn and worn her mother's face was. And to add to that burden of grief and worry—

But Selenay only came straight to her, held out her arms, and embraced her tightly but not possessively. Her body shook with tension but not with the tears that Elspeth had feared.

Finally she released her daughter, and held her away at arm's length, searching her face for something although Elspeth could not tell what it was. Her eyes were narrowed with concentration, and Elspeth saw many fine worry lines around her eyes and creasing her forehead that had not been there when she left.

"Good," she said finally. "This isn't something someone talked you into. You know exactly what you're doing. You thought of this yourself?"

Elspeth nodded. Her mother had pulled her hair back into a no-nonsense braid like Kero's, and like Talia, she was wearing breeches and tunic, her only concession to rank being a bit of gold trim on the tunic hem and her coronet about her brow. Her sword and sword-belt were hanging from the chair beside her desk, and knives lay on top of a pile of papers. Although she had seen her mother in armor and on a battlefield, this was not a Selenay that Elspeth had ever seen before, but she rather expected that anyone who had fought with her mother and grandfather in the Tedrel Wars would find this Queen very familiar. Selenay had pared *everything* from her life that was not relevant to the defense of her land. Valdemar was in peril, and the Queen was ready for personal action.

"I thought about trying to be a commander, but I'm not a tactician, and not even a particularly good fighter. No one knows me to follow me as a charismatic leader," Elspeth said slowly. "In the lines, I would be just one more warrior. Yes, I *could* help with magic defenses—I could even coordinate the mages—but I would be *your* daughter, and the ones from outKingdom would always expect me to favor Herald-Mages and their safety over those from outside. Such suspicion could be fatal. Kero always taught us that you don't stand off and fling sand at a fire from a safe distance; you go in and cut a firebreak right in its path."

"Kero taught you well." Selenay rubbed her eyes with her index finger, and blinked hard against tears. "The Queen agrees with you; the mother—what can I tell you? I hate the idea of sending my child off into this kind of danger, my heart wants to hold you back and keep you safe. But you are a woman grown, Elspeth. You are responsible for your own safety and I can't protect you anymore. Besides, there is no safety anywhere in Valdemar, not now. Elspeth, I am so *proud* of you!"

Elspeth had never expected to hear that last; it caught her by surprise, and her heart swelled and overflowed. She flung herself into her mother's arms again, and this time they both gave way to weeping. Talia, and then Daren, joined them in a fourfold embrace, offering comfort and support. This was sorrow both bitter and sweet, sweet for the accomplishment—bitter for all that accomplishment meant to all of them. Nothing would ever be the same again, even if they all survived this.

When both of them got control over themselves again, they separated, slowly and reluctantly, with tremulous smiles.

"Thank you, Mama," Elspeth managed. "That is the

most wonderful thing you have ever said to me. I've always been proud of you, too, but never more than to-day. . . ."

"When you were such trouble—before Talia came—there were times that I despaired of ever seeing you act like a responsible adult, much less make me so very proud that you are my daughter," Selenay said at last, with a grateful glance at Talia who only blushed. "No one could ever ask of you what you have just given to Valdemar."

Now it was Elspeth's turn to blush. "I don't know if Papa told you about my rather florid speech in there about saving the people rather than the land," she said. "But being with k'Sheyna and the Hawkbrothers is what showed me that. The way they simply give up their homes and move on when it's time—but mourn the loss of every hawk and owl, *hertasi* and human—that showed me where we should be putting our effort. Let Ancar grab land; the people of Valdemar ran and survived before, and they can now. And if we five can pull this off, they'll have something to return to."

Selenay shook her head in wonder. "You've grown up. And you're wiser than I ever will be—"

Elspeth laughed shakily. "No, just knowledgeable in different things, that's all. Mama, I have to get back to Kero; the sooner we get out of here, the better for all of us."

"If you can spare me for a moment, I'll go with her," Talia added. "I think I have a contact that will give them a way to move across Hardorn quickly."

Selenay nodded. "I will need you in about a candlemark, to help me calm some hysterical highborns when I tell them they are in the path of an invasion we can't stop, but not until then."

Selenay took Elspeth into a quick embrace. "If I don't see you before you leave—remember you take my love with you," she whispered into Elspeth's ear. "And you take my respect and hope as well. I love you, kitten. Come home safe to me. Come home, so I can celebrate your handfasting to that handsome young man who loves you so."

Elspeth returned the embrace fiercely, then fled to resume her duty before Selenay could see that tears threatened to return.

"So. Name everything in this room that can be used as a weapon," Kerowyn grinned at Elspeth.

"Your breath, Firesong's clothes, and that awful tea," Elspeth replied to the old joke. Darkwind and Firesong cracked smiles.

Once again, they all had gathered in Kero's office. Talia was explaining to Kero her link with the secretive and close-knit "clan" of itinerant traveling peddlers. Elspeth had heard it all before, but it was still fascinating, for Talia seemed the last person in the world to keep up an association with the "wagon-families," as they were known. Very often they were regarded as tricksters and only a short step above common thieves. It had been one of the wagon-men who had taken word of her imprisonment out of Hardorn when she had been captured and thrown in a shielded cell by Ancar.

"—so I've kept in constant contact with him, and I've tried to help him get his people out of trouble, when I could," she concluded. "Quite frankly, they can go places we can't, and it occurred to me that it would be very useful to have their cooperation if we needed to get someone into Hardorn, so I've been building up a lot of favors that they owe me."

Kero nodded thoughtfully, tracing little patterns on the table top with her finger. "The gods know I've tried and failed to get an agent in among them. They're very close-mouthed and insular."

Tiredly, Talia ran her fingers through her hair. Elspeth wondered if she would get any sleep at all, or if she'd go on until she collapsed. "Ancar hasn't got any friends among them, I can tell you that. He's taken whole families; I don't care to think what he does with them, but once his men take a wagonload, the people are gone without a trace. Since that started happening, only single men and a few women, all without families, have dared to operate over there—and only in groups, so a single wagon can't just vanish. They've taken to putting together wagon-groups of entertainers and peddlers, and putting on movable fairs. But here's what I think my contact will offer, if I ask him, as the payback for all my favors. I think he'll set our group up with a bigger carnival, give them genuine wagons and things to sell, and basically see that his people protect ours from discovery by outsiders."

Kero made a skeptical face. "Entertainers? Carnival showmen? Gods, I don't know ... I'd thought of something a lot more, well, secretive."

Elspeth snorted. "And how do you propose to hide Nyara or the bondbirds?" she demanded. "The minute anyone gets sight of her *or* the birds, we'd be in trouble, if we were trying to pass ourselves off as simple farmers or something! How many farmers own large exotic birds, or even a hawk? And we'd never pass ourselves off as Hardornen nobles."

"My point exactly," Talia said. "You *can't* hide them, so make them just one more very visible set of entertainers in a sea of flamboyance. After all, where *do* you hide a red fish?"

"In a pond full of other red fish," Kero supplied the tagline of another Shin'a'in proverb. "All right; contact the man. Don't tell him anything until you get his consent to the general idea, and Darkwind can slap one of those coercion things on him."

Talia nodded, and rose from her seat. "I'll have him here by dawn," she said firmly, and left.

Firesong looked highly amused. "Carnival entertainers?" he repeated, "Entertainers, I understand, but what is a carnival?"

After Elspeth explained it to him, he looked even more amused. "You mean—we shall cloak the fact that we are working genuine magic, that we have mage-born creatures, by performing entertainer tricks?"

"*And* selling snake-oil," Kero added, and had to explain the concept of *that* to him as well. By the time she had finished, he was laughing, despite the seriousness of the situation.

"But this is too perfect!" he chuckled. "Oh, please, you *must* let me play a role. The Great Mage Pandemonium! I shall never have another opportunity like this one!"

"I don't know how we could stop you," Skif said dryly. "And your bird is the harder to hide of the two."

Vree cocked his head to one side. *:Tricks, I,:* he offered. Then, to everyone's astonishment, he jumped down onto the table, waddled over to Firesong, and rolled over like a dog, his eyes fixed on the Healing Adept. *:Tricks, I, with Aya. Together.:*

"I think he wants you to have a trick bird act with himself and your firebird," Darkwind said, his eyes still wide with surprise. "I keep thinking he has a limited grasp of abstract concepts, but every once in a while he astonishes me. It would be a *very* good way of explaining the presence of both birds."

"I could assist you, Firesong," Nyara added shyly. "And dance. Falconsbane made me learn to dance, seduction dances, which would be popular, I think. You could say I was your captive."

"And everyone who saw you would be certain *her* looks were due to costume and makeup, and the birds to dye or bleach." Kero nodded. "I like it. You know, I can even show you some things that will make it look as if Nyara's—ah—attributes *are* all makeup and costume. We could shave thin lines of her body-fur to look like seams."

"And I shall dress as flamboyantly and *tastelessly* as Skyseeker k'Treva!" Firesong crowed. "We call him 'Eye-burner' to tease him, for he has *no* taste! A pity I cannot dye Aya a brilliant pink as well—"

The look the firebird gave him, of purest disgust, only sent him into another fit of laughter.

Darkwind shrugged. "For that matter, there's not a reason in the world why we can't bring the *dyheli* along as another one of your 'captives.' There isn't anyone in all of Hardorn except Falconsbane who'd recognize a bondbird, a *dyheli*, or Nyara, and Falconsbane isn't likely to be patronizing a carnival."

"Also an excellent point." Kero pondered a bit more. "But there is the problem that you are all going to have magic associated with you ... hmm. Can any of you lot do what Quenten could—layer illusions?"

Elspeth nodded quickly. "All of us can, it's really very simple."

Kero smiled slowly. "Good. Then here's what we'll have. You—" she pointed at Firesong, "—are a very *minor* mage, too minor for Ancar to recruit, but able to cast illusions. You put them on the Companions, the *dyheli,* and possibly yourself. Only you layer the Companions; top is a pair of glossy matched bays, under that is what any other mage will think is the reality, an illusion of a pair of nasty, old, spavined geldings. You layer the *dyheli* the same way; top is the way it really looks, under that is a donkey. You leave Nyara alone—"

:I can make certain anyone who casts a true-sight on her will see a misshapen girl in cat makeup,: Need supplied. *:And the assumed presence of an illusion will account for the presence of magic around us.:*

"Right, that was exactly what I was going to suggest." Kero was grinning. "Gods, we are a deceitful bunch! It's a damn good thing we're honest, or no one would be safe!"

Firesong looked supremely content. Elspeth reached for Darkwind's hand under the table, only to find his seeking hers. They exchanged a quick squeeze as Vree, with a very self-satisfied gurgle, returned across the table and leapt back up to Darkwind's shoulder.

"Once you get into Hardorn, you'll have to make it up as you go along," Kero said. "But the way I'll get you across I think can be pretty simple. The bastard can't watch the whole border, but drop a lot of what he thinks are Heralds in one place, and you *bet* he'll watch that spot pretty closely! So I'll turn out a bunch of the Skybolts in fake Whites—send them someplace that looks as if it might be strategic, and you cross wherever else you want. Put what looks like a million Heralds *anywhere,* and Ancar will be certain something is up. Hell, I might just give him something—"

Now *she* began to laugh, wearily, but after a moment, Elspeth realized it was not out of hysteria.

"What is it?" she asked.

"Oh, just something that occurred to me. I'll get one of the Blues to build me some kind of complicated war engine out of broken bits, something that can't possibly work but looks impressive enough to take out a city wall with one blow. I'll have my pseudo-Heralds escort *that* to his fortification, and let him take it. He'll spend forever trying to figure the thing out!" She wiped her eyes with the back of her hand, as the others began to chuckle. "Oh, gods, it is *such* a good thing for the world that we're honest!"

"Speak for yourself!" Firesong replied, with mock-indignation. "I intend to persuade as much coin from the pockets of the unsuspecting as possible!"

The firebird only snorted and resumed its preening.

Falconsbane sipped at a goblet of fine spiced wine and sat back in his chair with a wonderful feeling of pure content. Or, at least, as content as he could be while he was still someone else's captive. Everything was proceeding as it should, and completely in accordance with his plans.

His strategies on the border had succeeded so well that Ancar had sent him several more prisoners to dispose of, by way of reward. He had managed to determine that it was not the coercive spells that were keeping him from access to the local nodes and ley-lines, but a set of complicated keying spells that led back to—surprise!—Hulda. And those spells were keeping Ancar away, too, without a doubt. The only real power that Ancar would be able to touch, other than that derived from the death of underlings, would be through Hulda now. The keying spells would even make it difficult for Falconsbane to access those nodes were he not under coercions.

That made him all the more determined to rid himself of the bitch. He certainly didn't need her, and her overblown and overripe charms had long since lost any attraction for him; her promiscuity was appalling. She *could* have offered him the key; she had not. Therefore, she had no plans to share her power with anyone.

This put Ancar's inability to access power outside himself in another light altogether. If Hulda had locked that power away from him, he might not be altogether incompetent after all.

She was playing some kind of deep game, that one.

Falconsbane was not going to play it, either by her rules or anyone else's.

A slight tap on the door signaled another small triumph. That was Ancar, and Falconsbane had finally convinced him to announce himself before he came barging into Mornelithe's suite. Respect; the boy needed to learn respect, and he might even be worth saving and making into an underling when all this was over.

Meanwhile, the bitch needed to learn a little lesson, too.

"Enter," he said aloud, and Ancar's ever-present escort opened the door silently. Two of the guards entered first, followed by the King, who joined Falconsbane beside his fire. The guards took their positions, one on either side of the door; Falconsbane found their presence rather amusing. Evidently the boy took no chances; he protected himself physically even in the presence of someone he—relatively—trusted. What did he do when he took a wench to his bed? Drug her so that he knew she was harmless? Feh, he was so unappealing, that was probably the only way he would get a bedmate.

Ancar poured himself a cup of wine from the pitcher on the hearth. For all that he took no chances, he was prone to acting very foolishly. Falconsbane was a mage; he could have changed the content of that wine without having any access to poisons. Or didn't Ancar know that was possible?

Falconsbane waited for him to speak first, since it was obvious from the King's manner that nothing urgent had brought him here. But from Ancar's faint frown, something displeased him enough to make him seek Mornelithe's counsel.

Finally, the young King spoke. "I have tried to take power from those lines of energy you spoke about, which seem to be the same thing that Hulda called ley-lines. Something has blocked me from them." His frown deepened. "Although I could never use the nodes you spoke of because they were too powerful for me, I have been able to touch those lines in the past. But now I cannot, and I do not know why."

So, access to the ley-lines had been keyed very recently. Perhaps when Hulda realized that Ancar had attempted a Gate. She knew he was experimenting and had chosen this way to place a limit on what he could do.

"It is none of my doing," he pointed out. "But I had noted this myself; I, too, have been blocked. It is one of the reasons why I can do so little to help you, other than offer advice. I think, however," he added slyly, "that if you would trace the spells that keep you at a distance to their origin, you would find it to be Hulda."

Ancar sat upright. "Oh?" he replied, too casually. "Are you very certain of that?"

Falconsbane only shrugged. "You may see for yourself, Majesty. You certainly have the Mage-Sight to do so. There is nothing preventing you from tracing magic back to its originator."

Ancar sank back into the embrace of the chair, his frown deepening. "She overreaches herself," he muttered to himself. Mornelithe guessed that he had not meant to speak that aloud.

But Falconsbane chose to take the comment as meant for his ears. "Then give her a lesson to put her properly in her place," he said quietly. "Which of you rules here? Will you let her block you from the use of power that is rightfully yours? The coercive spells you have placed upon *me* have certainly worked well enough. Set them on her! Let her cool for a time in your prison cells. Let her see the rewards of thwarting you. Tame the bitch to your hand and muzzle her that she not bite you."

Ancar's jaw clenched and his hands tightened around the goblet. "I do not know that those spells will hold her," he admitted, reluctantly. "She is at her full strength. You were weak when I set them upon you."

Falconsbane laughed aloud, startling him so that his hands jerked, and a few drops of wine splashed out of the goblet. "Majesty, the woman is a bitch in heat when she sees a handsome young man! Lay a trap for her, then bait it with one such, and you will have her at a moment of weakness as great as mine! Only choose your bait wisely, so that he will exhaust her before you spring it."

Ancar brushed absently at the droplets of red on his

black velvet tunic, and considered that for a moment. "It might work," he replied thoughtfully. "It might at that."

"If it does not, what have you lost?" Falconsbane countered. "You are something near to a Master mage, and that should suffice that you can set those spells subtly enough that she does not notice them until she tries to act against your interest. Such things are either tough or brittle. If they do not hold, they will break. Few can trace a broken spell if she even notices that the attempt was made to coerce her. If they do hold, then you will have her."

Ancar smiled at him over the edge of the goblet. "You are a good counselor, Mornelithe Falconsbane, and a clever mage. That is *why* I do not lift the spells on you, and do not intend to until I have learned all that you can teach me."

That came as something of a shock to Falconsbane, although he hid his reaction under a smooth expression. He had not given the boy credit for that much cleverness.

He would be more careful in the future.

Ancar left Falconsbane's chambers with a feeling of accomplishment. So, *that* was why he had been denied the power he needed lately! The traces that led back to Hulda were easy enough to see when you looked for them—exactly as Falconsbane claimed. He had not thought she would dare to be so blatant in her attempts to keep a leash on him.

The Adept was right. It was time to teach her a lesson; time to put the leash on *her*.

And he knew exactly the bait for the trap. Hulda was tiring of her mule driver (in no small part because she was using him to exhaustion), but Ancar had anticipated that and had found a replacement a week ago.

This one, a slave—Ancar regretted that his tastes ran to women, and had set his agent to looking for a female counterpart to him—was altogether a remarkable specimen. The agent claimed he had been bred and schooled, like a warhorse, for the private chamber of a lady of wealth from Ceejay. She had met with an accident—quite remarkably, it was a real accident—and the agent had acquired the slave from the innkeeper to whom her lodging-monies were owed. It was then that he had discovered the young man's talents, when he found the boy in bed with his wife. . . .

He was, fortunately for Ançar, a man of phegmatic temper and a man with his eye on the main chance. He had realized at once that this was an incident of little import. His marriage was one of convenience. The boy was a slave—whom would he tell? And who would believe him if he did speak? The woman would not dare to speak, for she would be the one disgraced if she did. The merchant's reputation was safe enough, provided he rid his household of the boy and sent him far, far away. All he needed to do would be to find a buyer—and he knew he had one in Ancar.

He persuaded his wife that she would not be punished and received such a remarkable tale of the lad's skill, training, and prowess, that he had sent a messenger to the King straight away. Ancar had bought the boy immediately, sight unseen, on the basis of that report, and had set him to work on one of the chambermaids, spying on the two to see if the reports were true.

They were more than true, and Ancar had come very close to envying that fortunate chambermaid. When the lad was through with her, she literally could not move, and she slept for an entire day.

Since then, the boy had been schooled as a page and kept strictly celibate. Reports had him frantic to exercise his craft. He should be quite ready to please Hulda now.

Ancar put the plan in motion, beginning by ordering roughly half of Hulda's staff replaced that very hour, and slipping the boy in with the replacements. The rest would follow, for the slave had been conditioned that *any* female he called "mistress" must be pleased. Hulda would not be able to resist his fresh, innocent fairness, especially in contrast to her swarthy muleteer. She would set out to seduce him, and by the time she realized that the seduction was the other way around, she would be enjoying herself so much she would not think to look any further than the pleasures of the moment.

Ancar waited until his spies told him that Hulda had retired, and not alone. He reckoned that four candlemarks would be enough to give them together, and timed his spells accordingly. Her chamber was guarded against combative magics, but not against this. Then again, she had never dreamed he would be audacious enough to use controlling spells against her.

The spells fell into place, softly as falling snow. Ancar waited a candlemark or two more, then moved in with his escort of guards.

No one tried to stop him; the guards at her doors were all his. But he did not come bursting into her chambers—no, he had the doors opened slowly, carefully, so as not to startle the boy.

After all, he might have use for such a talent some other time.

The boy awakened instantly, and looked up from the wild disarray of the bedclothes, his long blond hair falling charmingly over one sleepy, frightened blue eye. Ancar put his finger to his lips, then motioned to the boy to take himself out of the room.

The slave slipped out of the bed so quietly that he did not even stir the sheets. He did not even stop to gather up his garments; one of the guardsmen, flushing a little, stopped him long enough to hand him a robe before he escaped back to the servants' quarters. Ancar made a mental note to reward the man; a naked page skittering through the halls might cause some awkward comment. Quick thinking deserved a reward.

Ancar motioned to his guards to take up positions around the bed. Then he cleared his throat noisily.

Hulda reacted much faster than he had expected her to. She came up out of the bed like an enraged animal, fully attack-ready, her face a mask of pure anger.

"You!" she spat, seeing Ancar standing at the foot of her bed. "How *dare* you!" And she lashed out at him with her magic, as she would at a disobedient brat that needed a severe correction.

Tried to, that is. Ancar's controlling spells stopped her in mid-strike.

He had expected her to be dumbfounded, perhaps to

make another attempt. He had never thought she would go from "correction" into an all-out attempt at attack.

He stepped back a pace as he felt his spells shuddering under the impact of her attempt to break them—break through them, and break *him*. One look at her expression told him that she *knew*—

Knew that her control of him was over. Knew that he now intended to make an obedient servant of her. He was now the enemy, and she would destroy him if she could.

And in that moment, he realized just how tenuous his hold over her was. Suddenly, he was overcome with terror. She could, at any moment, break loose from his control. And when she did—she would go straight for his throat.

He was no match for her.

"Take her!" he shouted at the guards. They did not hesitate—and one of them had been around mages long enough not to give her any chance to turn her spells on *him*. The moment that Ancar snapped out the order, the man seized a rug from the floor and flung it over Hulda's head, following it by flinging himself on her and the rug together. She had a fraction of a breath to be enveloped, realize she was trapped, and start to fight free. By then, he was on the bed, and coolly rapped her on the head with the pommel of his dagger. She collapsed in a heap; he gathered her up, rug and all, bound the entire package with a series of sashes and bedcurtain cords he snatched up from around him. He got to his feet, picked her up, and laid her at Ancar's feet, and then stood back, presenting the "package" as a well-trained hunting dog presented his master with a duck.

Ancar grinned. "Well done!" he applauded, noting that the man was the same one who had given the page a robe. He *would* have to see the man was rewarded well. Perhaps with the page?

Well, that would have to wait. It was not safe to leave Hulda anywhere in the palace proper; the place was rife with her power-objects. But there was one place that would be perfectly safe.

And perfectly ironic.

Long ago, he and she had worked together to make one

particular cell completely magic-proof. It had held the Herald Talia for a short time, and Ancar and Hulda both had been determined that once they recaptured the woman, she would become a return visitor to that cell, this time with no means of escape. The cell was so well shielded that not even mind-magic could escape it. The shields were a perfect mirror surface on the inside and would reflect any magic cast right back into the teeth of the caster.

And since Hulda had not been able to follow through on her promise to give him Talia, it was only fitting that she herself should test her handiwork. The irony was that although she herself had set the shields, from the inside she would not be able to take them down. Delightful.

He signed to the guard who had captured Hulda to pick her up again, and noted with approval that the man took the precaution of administering another carefully calculated rap to Hulda's skull before picking her up. He was taking no chances—and Hulda would have a terrible headache when she woke.

The page was standing just inside the door to the pages' quarters as they passed, still wrapped in Hulda's fine silk robe, but with his long blond hair now neatly tied back, and his fair young face flushed. The guard carrying Hulda looked at him briefly and flushed, but it was not a blush of embarrassment. Ancar suppressed a smile of amusement.

Yes, he would certainly reward the man with the page. One night with the boy, and the guard would probably die for his lord out of purest gratitude.

With one guard leading, and the man with the Hulda-bundle following, he led the way down into the dungeons.

On the way, he ordered some servants' livery to be brought along. He would leave nothing to chance, allow nothing from her chambers to enter the cell. If she wished to remain naked rather than clothe herself as his servant, that was her choice. If she chose to clothe herself—well, perhaps the lesson would be taken. If he could only *control* her, she could still be a useful tool. . . .

Almost as useful as Mornelithe Falconsbane.

* * *

Falconsbane did not move from the chair when Ancar left. He was fairly certain the boy was going to take his advice. He was also fairly certain the boy would succeed.

Temporarily.

Hulda was a powerful Adept. The boy had never actually fought any mage head-to-head, much less an Adept, before this moment. When she recovered her strength, she would be perfectly capable of breaking anything that held her and quite ready to kill the one that had ordered her humiliation.

It might take a great deal of time—but she would do so, eventually, and she would devote every waking moment to the task. Hadn't Falconsbane? And Hulda would not be hindered by physical weakness or unfamiliar surroundings.

The only question in Falconsbane's mind was whether or not Ancar would succeed in killing her before she broke free of his control entirely.

The situation was perfect. He sipped his wine, and smiled.

One way or another, whether Ancar won or lost—*he* would be free, and both Hulda and Ancar would die. If Hulda killed Ancar, the coercions would go with him, and Hulda would be weak enough to destroy.

Falconsbane did not intend to leave an angry Adept on his backtrail when he left. The woman might make the mistake of trying to take him for herself.

If Ancar killed Hulda, he would have to devote everything he had to the attempt, and Falconsbane could break free as soon as the last bit of Ancar's strength and attention went to the struggle. He might even help Ancar, a little and unobtrusively.

Then when Ancar lay completely exhausted, Falconsbane would kill *him*. Sadly, it would be so swift he would not gain much blood-magic power from it, but not all things in the world were ideal.

And then—he would have to flee. Either westward or southward; things should be chaotic enough with both obvious leaders gone that he could get back into territory he knew without recapture. If he had to cross Valdemar— well, he could simply cloak himself in the illusion of a simple human peasant, fleeing the war. He could feign being simple-minded to cover his lack of the language.

He toyed briefly with the notion of staying here and attempting to take the kingdom over—but no. Firstly, Ancar had laid waste to it in his foolish warring. At the moment, it was not worth having. There would be two hostile forces inclined to move in, at least, and perhaps more. He did not know this land, and all it would take would be one lucky fool at a moment of his own weakness to kill *him*. No one native to this place would ever suffer his rule willingly.

No, he must return home, pick up the pieces, build his power back to what it had been, and see what had happened to the Hawkfools in his absence. There were still the artifacts under the Dhorisha Plains to acquire—the permanent Gate beneath the ruins near k'Sheyna to explore—and revenge to be taken. His daughter was still loose, somewhere. And that most desirable mage-sword.

And gryphons. . . .

Gryphons. . . .

Chapter Fourteen

Falconsbane drifted off into sleep, dreaming of gryphons in torment. Some were faded memories, some were fancies of his, a few cruelties he hadn't yet tried. The dreams were as tortured as the man was twisted, and An'desha could hardly wait for them to fade into the formlessness of deep sleep. When Falconsbane slept, An'desha relaxed and waited for the Avatars to appear. If he'd had a stomach, it would have been twisted with nerves; if he'd had a body, he would have paced. That was one of the problems—there was a body, but it was no longer his.

The last time the Avatars came to him, they promised him that they had found his outside allies on the way, and that he would be able to Mindspeak with one in particular directly—and very soon. They warned him that this would only be possible while Falconsbane was deeply asleep and An'desha could walk the Moonpaths, but the prospect of actually having someone who could speak to him and help him in a real and physical way was so wonderful that it had not mattered. One person, at least, would know his secret and would work to free him.

As Falconsbane's breathing slowed, the fire on the

hearth flared for a moment, and a pair of glowing eyes in a tiny human face winked into existence. It was Tre'valen; he spread his arms there in the flames for the briefest of moments. The halo of transparent hawk wings shone around them.

:Come,: he said, and beckoned. An'desha did not need a second invitation; nervous energy catapulted him from this world into the next. As Tre'valen passed from the fire to the other worlds that held the Moonpaths, An'desha followed in his now-familiar wake.

He flung himself after Tre'valen with heart and will, going *in* and then *out*—

And, as he had so many times before, found himself standing beside the Avatar, on a pathway made of pearlescent light, surrounded by luminescent gray mist. Once again, he walked the Moonpaths with the Avatar of the Star-Eyed. But next to the Avatar was, not Dawnfire, but someone entirely new.

The newcomer was an old woman, but strong and built like a fighter, with knotted muscles and face and arms burned brown by the sun and toughened with work in all weathers. She wore strange garments made of dark leather, simple breeches and an odd cape-shirt that seemed to have been made of an entire brain-tanned deerhide. Her hair was cut off at chin length and was as gray as iron and straight as grass. She stood beside Tre'valen with her hands on her hips, and although her face was seamed with wrinkles that indicated a certain stern character, he caught a kindly twinkle in her black eyes.

He liked her instinctively; if *this* had been his Clan shaman, he might never have tried to run away.

"So this is the boy," she said, and reached out to seize his chin so she could peer into his eyes. He had the distinct impression that she was weighing and measuring everything he was and had ever been. "Huh. You need some shaping, some tempering, and that's for certain. You're not pot-metal, but you're not battle-steel either, not yet."

He traded her look for look, sensing that shyness and diffidence would win nothing from her but contempt. "I haven't exactly had an opportunity for tempering, Wise

One," he replied. "My experiences have been limited by circumstance."

Tre'valen laughed silently, his star-filled eyes somehow seeming more human than usual, and the old woman's lips twitched as if she were trying not to laugh herself. "And why is that, boy?"

"Because—" he faltered for a moment, losing his courage as he was forced to actually *say* what he was. Or rather, was not, anymore. "—because my body belongs to Falconsbane, and any moments that I live I must steal from him."

She raised an eyebrow, as if she did not find this to be so terrible. "Oh, so? And I suppose you feel very sorry for yourself, eh? You feel the fates have mistreated you?"

He shook his head. "Yes. No. I mean—"

"Ha. You don't even know your own mind." She lifted her lip in a faint sneer and narrowed her gaze. "Well, this fellow here has told me all about you, and I'll tell you what *I* think. I *could* feel sorry for you, but I won't. I've known too many people with hard lives or harder deaths to feel sorry for you. And what's more, if you indulge yourself in self-pity, I'm gone! I don't waste my time on people who spend all their time pitying themselves and not doing anything. You want out of this situation, boy, you help make it happen!"

The words stung, but not with the crack of a whip, or as salt in a wound, but rather as a brisk tap to awaken him. He lifted his chin and straightened his back. For all the harshness of her words, there was a kindliness in her tone that made him think she really *did* feel sorry for him, and would help him the best way she knew how.

And she was right; was Nyara's lot not much harder than his own? And any of Falconsbane's victims had perished in pain that surely exceeded anything that had happened to him! "Yes, Wise One," he said, forthrightly. "Tre'valen has already explained all this to me. If I am to take my body and my life back, I must earn the aid to do so. I was a coward, Wise One, but not a fool. Or rather, I was a fool before, but I am no longer one, I hope."

She snorted, but the smile was back and the sneer was gone. "Piff. A brave man is simply someone who doesn't let his cowardice and fear stop him. Hellfires, boy, we're *all* cowards at some time or another. Me, I was afraid of deep water. Never did learn to swim."

He had to smile at that. Oh, this was a crusty old woman, but she had a good heart, and a keen mind that must make her a kind of shaman among her own people. And she *did* want to help him, he knew it now as well as he knew his own predicament. Somehow her will to help him made him more confident than the Avatars' promises. They were otherworldly and uncanny, but she was as earthy and real as a good loaf of bread. As the Shin'a'in proverb went, "It is easier to believe in grain than spirits."

"I should rather think that the water would fear *you*, Wise One, and part to let you pass," he said, greatly daring but feeling she would like the attempt at a joke.

She did; she laughed, throwing her head back and braying like a donkey. "All right, Tre'valen, you were right, he'll do. He'll do."

:I said so, did I not?: Tre'valen countered, amused.

She turned serious, all in a moment. "Now listen, boy. You remember those people Falconsbane wanted to get his claws into so much? The daughter, the girl in white, the Hawkbrother boy? The ones Tre'valen told you were going to be coming this way to do something about Ancar and Falconsbane?"

He nodded. Nyara he knew too well. The girl of the white spirit-steed was one that Falconsbane had coveted, and had never even touched. The Hawkbrother— *Darkwind,* he remembered—was the son of Starblade, the Hawkbrother mage Falconsbane had gleefully corrupted.

He winced away from the memories that name called up, and not just because they were unpleasant, but because there had been moments of pleasure there, too. Falconsbane was an Adept at combining pleasure and pain, as well as an Adept mage. And he had taken pleasure *in* the pain, and used the pleasure to *cause* pain. That was what made An'desha so uncomfortable with those memories ... that was what felt so ... unclean. Falconsbane knew so much—and to use what he knew in the way he did—that made him all the worse, for he could have used it to such good ends had he wished. The Avatars did, and this woman had power. And the others—

"Well, those three are coming. To Hardorn, here. They are on the way right this very moment. They intend to get Ancar and Hulda—and Falconsbane; eliminate them completely, before Ancar can destroy Valdemar. What we—you, me, and the Avatars—want to do is see if they can't get Falconsbane without getting *you*. Do you understand what I'm saying?" She cocked her head to one side and regarded him carefully.

"Somehow we have to find a way to kill Falconsbane without killing my body, so I can have it back." He shook his head, feeling a sudden sinking of spirits. Put baldly, he could not see how they could manage this. "I am no mage, Wise One, but that seems an impossible task," he faltered.

She snorted. "Hellfires, boy, I've seen less likely than that come to pass in my time. Improbable, maybe. What's impossible is how he has managed to flit from body to body, down all these years," she countered. "We don't know how he's done it. If you can find that out for me, we have a chance."

His spirits soared again. She had a point! Falconsbane *had* to have a way for his spirit to remain intact down all the centuries. And she was clearly a mage, so perhaps once she knew how the Adept had done this, perhaps she could see a way to force him out again.

He nodded with excitement, and she smiled. "Right," she said. "Now, there are actually five people coming in on this, and three of 'em are Adepts, so among all of us, I think we have a pretty good chance of coming up with an answer for you. Say—" she added as an afterthought. "You want to see what they look like right now? I tell you, it's worth seeing, you will not believe what they're doing."

"Oh—yes, please," he replied, eagerly. Tre'valen had shown him these people once, but he was starved for another sight of them. One, in particular. . . .

A circular section of the mist between her and Tre'valen brightened—and then suddenly it was as if he were staring out a round window onto a road.

There were three riders framed in that "window," riding side-by-side. First was that incredibly handsome young man, this time with his long hair bound in a single braid down the back of his neck, and dressed in a motley of robes that would have been, separately, breathtaking and striking, but worn together presented a vision of the most appalling bad taste that An'desha had ever seen in his life. Around his neck, the young man bore a jangling tangle of cheap and tawdry jewelry, and surmounting his head was a—

Well, An'desha could not call this "creation" a "hat." It was turbanlike, but so huge that it made his head look as if he were the stem of a mushroom, with a huge, scarlet cap. It, too, was covered with tinsel and jewelry, and rising in moth-eaten splendor in the front was a cluster of the saddest plumes ever to have sprung from some unfortunate bird.

His mount was a *dyheli*, but one with gilded horns, ribbons woven in his tail, and mismatched bells jangling all over some kind of harness as bright and tasteless as the rider's robes. The *dyheli* seemed to find this as amusing as the rider did.

And perched on his shoulder, in a state of resigned disgust, was a white firebird, wing-primaries and tail-feathers dyed in rainbow colors, with a huge ribbon-cluster tied onto its head, and ribbon-jesses trailing from bracelets on its legs. It was most definitely *not* amused.

An'desha smothered a giggle.

"Makes quite a sight, doesn't he, our young Firesong," the old woman said, grinning. "Now, looking at *that,* would you ever guess him to be a Tayledras Healing Adept?"

"Never," An'desha said firmly. "Nor would I take him to be other than a charlatan."

"Most wouldn't take him at all," she said dryly, "for fear his clothes might stick to them."

It was hard to turn his attention away from Firesong—for even done up in all that laughable "finery" he made An'desha ache with odd longings. He did look away, though, for the other two riders would be just as important to him as the handsome young Hawkbrother.

They rode a pair of glossy, matched bays, but were otherwise completely unremarkable. They were just another pair of shifty-eyed toughs. Under the slouches and the skin-dye, the oily hair, the sneers and the scuffed leather armor, he *could* see that the two were that Elspeth and Skif he had also seen before, in Tre'valen's vision. But it would have taken the eye of someone who knew them to see a pair of fine young Heralds in these two ne'er-do-wells. He guessed, from their postures, that when they walked, Skif would swagger, and Elspeth would slink. He would not have trusted either of them with a clipped coin, and he rather fancied that when they entered a place, women rushed to hide their children.

The vision shifted, and it was clear that the three were riding in front of a wagon, drawn by mules. And there was Nyara, beside the driver, wearing practically nothing at all, with a collar and chain holding her to a huge iron ring beside the wagon seat. She did not seem in any distress, however; in fact, she had draped herself across the seat in a languorous and seductive—and very animalistic—pose. Beside her, wearing a less flamboyant version of Firesong's motley, was Darkwind. He slouched over the reins, his posture suggesting that he was both submissive and bored. His hawk sat on his shoulder, looking around alertly, with ribbon-jesses like the firebird's, but without the ribbon-hat.

But the collar and leash on Nyara bothered him, and made him worried for her. What would she do if some toady of Ancar's attempted some kind of attack? "The collar snaps right off," the old woman assured him, evidently reading his mind as easily as the Avatars did. "She can be rid of it any time she likes. They're playing at being entertainers, with a traveling Faire. Firesong's a magician with a trick-bird act, Darkwind is his assistant, Nyara is his 'captive cat-woman.' She does a dance where she takes off most of her clothes, too; I tell you *that* makes the hair on these villagers curl. The other two are selling a bogus cure-all that Firesong supposedly makes. It's spiced brandy with some good herbs in it, which is more than I can say for most quack cure-alls, and they price it about the same as a bottle of brandy, so people are willing to buy."

An'desha stared at Nyara, not because he found her seductive, but because an idea was slowly beginning to form in his mind. "Wise One," he offered, hesitantly, "You do know that if Falconsbane should hear rumors of a cat-woman, he would be eager to know more. He might even try to see her for himself. He does not know it was Nyara who smashed his crystal and flung him into the Void."

"He doesn't?" the old woman replied, her eyes brightening with interest.

"No," An'desha said firmly. "I know his mind, and I know that he never knew that. At the moment, he believes that she fled into the East. He could readily believe she came far enough to be caught by these folk. And *he* does not know *how* far to the East he truly is from his home."

"Really?" The old woman's eyes narrowed in sudden concentration. "Now isn't that a bit of interesting thought! I'll pass that on, and we'll see if we can't build on it, eh?"

He smiled shyly back at her, and was about to ask her where she was in this caravan—and then felt the tuggings that meant Falconsbane was about to awaken.

"I must go!" he said—and plunged away.

The sparse crowd on either side of the road was quiet. In Valdemar they'd have been cheering.

But this wasn't Valdemar, and these people had little energy for cheers.

:*You don't deserve me,*: Cymry said to Skif, with a chuckle in her mind-voice.

:*So long as it's mutual,*: Skif replied. From anyone besides Cymry, he'd have taken offense, but such jabs between close friends were amusing, in a situation where little else was. He was worried about Nyara, wondering if she had overestimated her ability to cope with her role of sexual object. The stares of the men made her tenser than she admitted, and the strain of the dancing-show left her trembling with fear after every performance.

He scowled at the townsfolk, who stood outside their doors and stared at the passing wagons, a bit of interest coming into their otherwise sad and bleak-eyed faces. He didn't really want to scowl, and it made him sorry to see the fear in their eyes when he gave them that unfriendly look, but the scowl fit the persona he wore. Hardorn had gotten worse since the last time he had been through it, and things hadn't been all that good then. Most of the people had lost all hope, and it showed, in the untended streets, in the threadbare clothing, in the ill-kept houses.

:I know I don't deserve you, but what brought that on?: he asked her.

:There's a young man over there with a bad leg—see him?: she replied, pointing with her nose to the road just ahead. *:He was in the cavalry, got hurt, and got kicked out, and he thinks you stole me—and he knows you don't deserve me. He's got some rudimentary Mindspeech, so I can hear him.:*

And from the frown on the young man's face, he was resentful enough to make his thoughts heard to anyone unshielded. It was fairly easy to see why he'd gotten the boot from the cavalry; he'd broken his leg and no one had bothered to set it properly, so it had healed all wrong. He could use it, but not well and he needed a cane; the leg jutted at a crooked angle that must have made walking an agony. Skif grimaced; that sort of thing would never have happened in Valdemar. It would never even have happened in Kero's Skybolts, or any other good merc company.

It appeared that the rotten weather was plaguing Hardorn just as badly as Valdemar, and Ancar had not even bothered to try to do anything about it. The town was between storms at the moment, but the streets were deeply rutted, as muddy as a river, and the skies were overcast.

But Firesong would make certain the bad weather held off so that the troupe could hold its entertainments as soon as they set up. *They* traveled under cloudy but rainless skies, thanks to him, Darkwind, and Elspeth.

The traveling Faire needed that break in the local weather, if they were going to make any money; that had been part of the bargain Kero and Talia had made for the protection of the wagon-folk. Wherever the carnival went, the weather would be as close to clear as they could manage, so the tents would go up without hindrance, and the performers' shows could go on without a downpour. And, as usual, Nyara would be one of the most popular acts in the carnival.

He thrust down his surge of jealousy and anxiety at that thought, his hands tightening on Cymry's reins. And he vowed, once again, that he would not take that jealousy out on her. She was doing her part—she didn't like what she was doing any better than he did. She had told him it made her feel greasy, as if the men watching her had been running their hands on her and leaving oily marks behind. It frightened her although she would never admit it to anyone but him. And he was afraid it called up old, bad memories as well.

That didn't make the jealousy go away, but it made it a little easier to live with and control. Perhaps simply thinking about it was giving him more control over it. He hoped so, because Nyara's exotic beauty was likely to bring the attraction of men wherever she went, even if she wore the robes of a cloistered sister.

There had been some muttering about Nyara's popularity as an act among the rest of the troupe after their first stop and her first performances. That muttering had ended when he and Nyara distributed the "take" among the rest of the entertainers. That had been Nyara's idea, and he was glad she had suggested it, for it had turned what might have become an ugly situation into a pleasant one. Now everyone watched cheerfully as their tent filled for Nyara's show, for the bigger the audience, the more there would be for all to share. Their cover story, of searching for lost relatives with a view to extracting them from Hardorn, was holding water, given more credence by the fact that among the troupers, they were making no attempt to conceal the fact that they had no interest in making a profit.

As Talia had warned, there were no families with this

troupe; only single men and a very few women. Most of those women were actually as hardened and tough as Elspeth looked to be. Only people willing to risk everything for a fast profit would make such a journey. There were no real Faires in Hardorn anymore, and no single peddlers providing the country folk with goods. This might be the only entertainment these people would see for the next year—and it would certainly be the only chance they'd have to spend a coin or two on something besides day-to-day necessities. Ancar might be grinding his people into poverty, but there were still youngsters falling in love and wanting love-tokens; still pretty girls wishing for something bright to attract someone's eye; still loving husbands wanting a special little gift for a new mother. Ordinary life went on, even while war raged over the border, and Ancar despoiled his own land. . . .

The houses ended, and the road came out on the village common—high ground, thank goodness, and not as sodden as the last place they'd played. Ahead of him, the other members of the troupe had begun to form the rows of wagons that became the carnival. Every wagon had its particular place; closest to the village, the food sellers and the trained beasts. Next, the folk with fairings and other goods to sell. Farthest away, entertainment tents. There were reasons for the placement, based on how people spent their money; Skif didn't pretend to understand any of it, but he followed the wagon-master's waved direction, and led the way for Darkwind to bring the wagon up beside the one with the contortionist and jugglers. They were, as always, the last in the row, since Nyara was the most popular of acts. Anyone who wanted to see her had to make his way past the temptation of every other peddler, vendor, and entertainer in the carnival.

Firesong didn't even pretend to be an "act" anymore; his show was strictly to attract people to the tent between Nyara's shows, so that Skif and Darkwind could try and sell them bottles of cure-all. He was having the time of his life. He combined sleight-of-hand with genuine illusions, ending with bird tricks, which Aya suffered through and Vree positively bounced through. There was one trick, however, that all of them enjoyed—

—the one where Aya would sail out into the audience, and pick out particularly impoverished-looking children, bringing one back to his bondmate. Then Firesong would pluck gilded "coins" from the child's ears, hair, pockets—any place he could think of—until the child's hands were overflowing with the bounty of what appeared to be gold-painted mock-coins. Then he would send the little one back out to his or her parents, who were always indulgently pleased with the little one's "treasure," assuming it to be as tawdry as Firesong's jewelry.

Of course, the next day, when the illusion wore off and the coins proved to be real copper and silver, their reaction would probably be something else entirely. Every member of the assassination team wished they could see that moment. There was something redeeming about doing small acts of kindness while they faced their necessary task with varying measures of reluctance.

The wagon slowed and was parked. Elspeth and Skif left their Companions to join Darkwind in readying their show.

Elspeth unhitched the mules and picketed them. Skif went to the back of the wagon and jumped up onto the little porch there, reached up to release a latch at the top, just under the roof, while Darkwind did the same at the front.

Skif watched Darkwind, reflexively analyzing his weak points and noting his handyness. Skif had been going over parts of his past during this trip, and remembered the knife-edges of resentment he had suppressed while Elspeth and Darkwind grew closer. He remembered analyzing Darkwind for the quickest elimination many times, in case he became a threat to Valdemar or Elspeth. Now, though, there was no animosity toward him—it was simply habit.

Darkwind stepped back and signaled. Carefully, they brought what had appeared to be the side of the wagon down on its hinges; this was the stage. This would be where Firesong would work his magic; behind the stage-platform was the real side of the wagon, and there were racks of "Magic Pandemonium Cure-All" in scarlet bottles, built into the recess the stage had covered. The stage itself was hinged its entire length, and he and Darkwind dropped it down onto four stout legs they pulled from under the wagon to support its weight.

While he and Darkwind set up the stage, Elspeth and Nyara crawled under the wagon to take the tent and tent poles from the rack beneath. By the time the stage was set up, they had the tent spread out on the other side, ready to erect. He and Darkwind pounded stakes into the soft earth at each corner, ready to take the guy ropes.

Another stage dropped down from this side of the wagon, but this one had a curtain behind it and was the actual wagon wall. Nyara would appear and retreat into the wagon itself, which doubled as their living-quarters. The wagon formed the back wall of the tent, with the canvas forming the other three walls and roof. It only held about ten people crowded in together, but the stage was high enough that no one could reach Nyara without encountering either him or Elspeth. Lanterns on either side of the curtain gave enough light to see most of Nyara's performance.

Ten was as many people as they wanted to have to handle, just in case anyone decided to try to get more out of Nyara than a dance. Darkwind provided the "music" she danced to—a drum—and Skif and Elspeth stood guard over the stage while Firesong guarded the outside. If the men ever got to the point where swords weren't deterrent enough, Darkwind or Elspeth would hit them with true magic to get rid of them.

The canvas was heavy and unwieldy; he and Firesong—who had shed the hat and most of the robes to help with the work—took one side, while Darkwind and Elspeth wrestled with the other, and Nyara crawled inside to set up the tent poles. He sneaked a look at her receding—anatomy.

The first few times they'd done this, it had taken so long that the other wagon-folk had given them a hand so that the carnival could open before dark. Now they were only a little slower than the rest, which was fine, since they were at the end of the line anyway. They would be set up by the time people actually got here.

He sniffed; there was hot oil and spice from the food-vendors, who sold grease-fried bits of salty dough and other things, cups of sweetened water with vegetable dyes in them, and very cheap beer. He knew better than to eat anything from the vendors; one of the reasons that "Pandemonium Cure-All" made money was that it had stomach-soothers in it, and the Great Mage Pandemonium could usually effect a cure or two right on the spot. The vendors shrugged and said philosophically that Faire-food was always pretty awful; if you wanted a good meal, you ate at home. But given the hungry stares some of the people of Hardorn had, Skif had to wonder if this *was* good food now, to them. Gods, that was a frightening thought.

The center of the tent rose to a peak; Nyara had gotten the middle pole up. She always had a knack for that. A moment later, the two corner poles went in. Skif and Darkwind pulled the corner ropes as tight as they could, then tied them to the stakes they'd pounded into the ground. The canvas by the wagon bobbed as Nyara tied it to the top of the wagon from inside. He dusted off his muddy hands on his breeches and went around to the front to join the others.

Darkwind and Elspeth were already at the edge of the outer stage, and a moment later, Firesong emerged from the back of the wagon, his dubious finery back in place and a grin on his face. His firebird stretched its wings by flying to the front of the carnival and back, causing cries of excitement from the gathering townsfolk as it flew overhead, streaming ribbons. Vree did the same, indulging in some aerobatics to make up in showmanship what he lacked in appearance.

"We've got everything well in hand," Darkwind said, as he looked around for something to do. "Why don't you go into the wagon and spend a little time with Nyara before the first show? You two have little enough time with each other."

It was a suggestion Darkwind didn't have to make twice. Skif ran up the set of stairs at the tail of the wagon and joined Nyara.

She was putting on little bits of makeup and rabbit fur to make her look as if she was wearing a costume. They included a preposterous pair of artificial ears that she could have used as sails, if they'd had a boat.

She was holding them with an expression of distaste. "I do not like these," she sighed. "They do not fit well, and they are very itchy!"

He chuckled and took one for her, carefully fitting it over her own, delicately pointed ear. "If you wouldn't be so impatient, and wait for me to come and help you, they wouldn't itch as badly," he told her, carefully gluing it in place along her cheek.

She smiled wryly, and handed him the other one to put on for her, then began to add cat-stripes to her forehead and cheekbones. "I wish we did not have to do this," she said pensively. But behind the pensive expression, he sensed real strain and fear. Was there more strain there tonight than last night?

"I do, too," he told her, his voice husky with the effort of holding back emotions. She turned, then, and quickly laid the palm of her hand against his cheek, staring up into his eyes.

"If you dislike it so greatly that it hurts you—I will stop—" she faltered, searching his face for his true feelings. "We could—I could be displayed in a cage, perhaps—"

But that notion clearly made her more afraid than the dancing did. He shook his head, his stomach in turmoil, and captured her hand in his own. "No," he told her. "No, this is the best and fastest way to get Him to hear about you. We need that. But—I worry about you," he continued, his throat feeling choked and thick. "I know that this could be hurting you, all these men, staring at you, and thinking the way your father did. I worry if you think *I'm* thinking that, too, if you wonder if that's the only way I see you, as something to use—to own—"

She licked her lips and swallowed. "Yes," she admitted after a long moment. "Yes, sometimes I do wonder that. And sometimes I wonder if that is the only real worth I have—"

He started to blurt something, but she laid her finger against his lips, and smiled, a thin, sad smile but a real one. "But then," she continued, "you say something like you just did—or Need tells me to stop being a stupid little kitten and get *on* with my job, and I know it is not true."

She took her finger away, pulled him close, and locked him in another of her impossible, indescribable embraces.

When she released him again, she said only, "I love you, Herald-man."

He kissed her gently, but with no less passion. "I love you, too, cat-lady."

She laughed at the grease-makeup that smeared his face and delicately touched a clawed finger to the tip of his nose.

And then Darkwind began to beat the drum for Firesong's first turn, and there was no time. . . .

Treyvan narrowed his eyes, and regarded a scarlet-clad Sun-priestess with what he hoped was a predatory expression. "I agrrree with you that Rassshi isss a young idiot," he said carefully, "and he isss likely mossst difficult to worrrk with. He isss ssscatterrrbrrrained."

The priestess nodded, her mouth forming a tight, angry line.

"But," he continued, "you will worrrk with him. He knowsss the ssspellsss that you do not, and you need to know them. Morrre, you need to learrrn how to worrrk with thossse you do not carrre forrr."

The priestess tossed her head; he had been warned about her. She was formerly from a noble Karsite family, and she was very conscious of her birth-rank. She had made trouble before this, during her training as a Priestess. Rashi, besides being scatterbrained, was the son of a pigkeeper. But he was kindhearted as well, and he knew a series of protective spells that no one else here had mastered—and whether she liked it or not, Treyvan was determined that Gisell *would* learn them, and would learn to work with him.

Treyvan rose to his full height, and towered over her. "You will worrrk with him," he repeated. "A mage who will not cooperrrate isss a dangerrr to all of usss. And I am *not* of Valdemarrr, Karrrse, orrr Rrrethwellan. I do not *carrre* about you orrr yourrrr alliancesss. I will be gone when thisss warrr isss overrr. I do thisss asss a perrsssonal favorrr to Darrrkwind. And I will sssnap the ssssspine of anyone who makesss thisss tasssk morrrre difficult!"

Her face went blank, as she picked his words out of the tangle of trills and hisses, and then she paled. He snapped his beak once, loudly, by way of emphasis, a sound like two dry skulls crunching against each other.

"I have younglingssss to feed," Hydona added suggestively, looking over Treyvan's shoulder. "Meat-eaterrrsss. They *do* ssso love meat of good brrrreeding."

The priestess swallowed once, audibly, then tried to smile. "Perhaps Rashi simply needs some patience?" she suggested meekly.

"Patiencssse isss a good thing," Treyvan agreed, lying back down again. "Patiencssse isss a jewel in the crrrown of any prrriessstesss."

The priestess bowed with newly-born meekness, then turned to go back to poor young Rashi, her assigned partner, who probably had no idea the young woman had come storming up to Treyvan to demand someone else. The trouble was, there *was* no one else. The priestess had alienated every Herald and most of the Rethwellan mages except dim but good-natured Rashi.

Gisell was only half-trained, but would certainly be Master rank when she finally completed her schooling. Rashi was only a bottom-rank Journeyman, a plain and simple earth-wizard, and never would be any more powerful than that—but his training had been the best. His instincts were sharp, and his skills were sound.

This was the essence of all the pairs, triads, and quartets that Treyvan and Hydona were setting up. Powerful but half-trained mages were partnered with educated but less powerful mages, with the former working *through* the latter, as Elspeth had worked in partnership with Need. To the knowledge of any of the fully-schooled mages, no one had ever tried this before. All the better. What had never been tried, Ancar could not anticipate.

Some of these teams were already out with the Guard or the Skybolts—and there had been, not one, but *two* Adept-class potential Heralds among the two dozen or so that had come riding in, responding to the urgent need sent out on the Web. Both of them had been paired immediately, one with the single White Winds teacher young enough to endure the physical hardships of this war, and one with the Son of the Sun's right-hand wizard, a surprisingly young man with a head full of good sense and a dry sense of humor that struck chords with Treyvan's own. They were doing a very fine job of holding Ancar's progress to a crawl, simply by forcing Ancar's mages to layer protections on the coercive spells controlling his fighters. Ancar had, in fact, been forced to send in the Elite Guard, putting them immediately behind the coerced troops to supply a different kind of motivation to advance.

Treyvan and Hydona were in complete charge of Valdemar's few mages and mage-allies, simply because they *were* the most foreign. Their ongoing story, at least so far as anyone other than Selenay and her Council were concerned, was just what Treyvan had told that young priestess. They were doing this as a favor to Darkwind; they were completely indifferent to Valdemaran politics, external or internal. Add to that their size and formidable appearance ... thus far, no one had cared to challenge any of their edicts. When they needed to coordinate with Valdemar's forces, they went through subcommanders Selenay had assigned.

Treyvan turned his attention back to the trio he had been working with before Gisell interrupted. "Yourrr parrrdon," he said, thinking as he did so that at any other time and place, these three would have been at such odds that there would probably have been bloodshed. Not that they weren't getting along; they were cooperating surprisingly well. But a south-border Herald, a red-robed Priest of Vkandis, and a mage who had once fought Karse under Kerowyn ... it could have been trouble.

The priest shrugged, the Herald chuckled, and the merc mage shook his head. "Gisell always difficult has been," the priest said, in his stilted Valdemaran. "Young, she is."

"Just wait until she gets out on the lines, she'll settle down," the Herald advised. The mage, an older man, bent and wizened, nodded.

"They gen'rally do," he said comfortably. "Either that,

or they don' last past their first fight." He glanced at the other two. "You, now—I kin work with the both of ye."

"Query, one only, had I," the priest said, looking at Treyvan, but with a half-smile for the old man. Treyvan waited, but the priest, oddly, hesitated. Treyvan wished he could read human faces better; this man's expression was an odd one. It looked like his face-skin was imploding.

"Red-robe, I am not, truly," he said after a moment. "Black-robe am I. Or was I."

He looked from the Herald to the other mage, who shrugged without comprehension, and sighed.

"Black-robe, the Son has said, no more to be. Black-robes, demon-runners are." And he watched, warily, for a reaction.

He got one. The old mage hissed and stepped back a pace; the Herald's eyes widened. It was the Herald who spoke first, not to Treyvan, but to the priest.

"I'd heard rumors some of you could control demons," he said, his eyes betraying his unease, "but I never believed it—I never saw anything to make me believe it."

"Control?" The priest shrugged. "Little control. As—control great rockfall. Take demon—send demon—capture demon. The Son likes demons not; the Son has said: 'Demons be of the dark, Vkandis is all of the light.' Therefore, no more demon-runners."

"So she demoted you?" the mage demanded. "Uh—took your rank."

But the priest shook his head. "No. Rank stays, robe goes, and no more demon-runners." He turned back to Treyvan. "Question: demons terrible be and all of the dark. Yet them do we use now, here?"

Treyvan lidded his eyes, thinking quickly. How he wished this man's superior was here! "Jussst what doesss he mean by 'demonsss'?" he asked the Herald, who seemed to have some inkling of what the priest was talking about.

"There've always been stories that some of the Vkandis priests could control supernatural night-creatures," the Herald replied. The priest followed the words closely, nodding vigorously from time to time when the Herald hit precisely on the facts. "They're supposed to be unstoppable—they keep whole villages indoors at night for fear of them, and they are said to be able to take individuals right out of their beds in locked homes, with no one the wiser. What these things are, I don't know—though from what you and Jonaton there have taught me so far, my guess is they're from the Abyssal Plane, which would mean they aren't real bright. Basically, you haul them out, give them a target or an area to patrol, turn them loose—and try to stay out of their way."

The priest was nodding so hard now that Treyvan was afraid his head would come off. "Yes, yes," he said. "Yes, and terrible, terrible."

Treyvan's own magic was of the direct sort; he had little experience in using or summoning creatures of any of the Planes. The closest he had ever come was in calling an elemental or two, like a *vrondi*. This sort of thing was usually undertaken by a mage with little mind-magic and a fairly weak Mage-Gift, but with a great deal of trained will. A focused and trained will could accomplish a great deal, even when the sorcerer's own powers were slight, provided the sorcerer had a known source of energy. Unfortunately, when a mage's own abilities were poor, the most certain source of energy was that of pain and death. Which was why most of the mages summoning other-Planar creatures were blood-path mages.

This priest seemed to be the exception to that rule; he was somewhere on the border between Journeyman and Master, and he certainly didn't *need* demons to help him. He seemed very sincere, and very anxious that they know both that he *could* call demons, and that they were pretty dreadful creatures.

"Terrible, terrible," the priest repeated. "But Ancar terrible is. Yes?"

Ah, so what he was saying was that the demons were a dreadful weapon, but they were a weapon Ancar might deserve to get in his teeth.

Now here was a dilemma, if ever there was one. A terrifying weapon, an evil enemy. Did the one deserve the other?

Treyvan ground his beak, frustrated. He had flown out

to the front lines once, and it was a damned mess. It had
Falconsbane written all over it; there was that kind of cal-
lous disregard for life. The carnage could not have been
described. Ancar was driving his troops over ground so
thick with the bodies of the dead that there wasn't a handspan of dirt or grass visible anywhere. If a soldier lost a
limb, he could bend over and pick up a new one.

To use the weapon, or not?

"Could Ancarrr take yourrr demonsss, once you
loosssed them?" he asked the priest urgently. "Could *he*
ussse them?"

The man looked very startled, as if he had not considered that question. Then, after a moment of thought, he
nodded slowly.

Treyvan let out a growling breath he did not realize he
had been holding in. So much for the moral question. You
do not fling a weapon at your enemy that he may then
pick up and use.

Or, as the Shin'a'in said, "Never *throw* your best knife
at your foe."

"No demonsss," he said firmly. "We do not give
Ancarrr demonsss he can sssend back." The priest
looked relieved. The Herald and old Jonaton definitely
looked relieved.

"Now," he continued, "Let usss once again trrry thisss
messshing of sssshieldsss. . . ."

The gryphlets and the two royal twins were playing a
game of tag. Of all of them, Hydona reflected, it was the
children who were affected the least. For as long as Lyra
and Kris had been alive, there had been war with Ancar
and danger in Valdemar. For as long as Lytha and Jerven
had been alive, they had nested in a perilous world. For
both sets of twins, the danger was only a matter of de-
gree. And the tension their parents were under was offset
by the joy of having a new set of playmates.

For the two human children, having the fascinating
Rris as a new teacher and nurse only made things better.
And as for the gryphlets, they now had a brand new play-
ground, and an entire new set of toys and lessons. For the
four of them, life was very good.

The youngsters all lived together during the day in the salle. Lessons at the Collegium had been canceled for the duration, and the trainees set to running errands—or, if they were about to graduate, were thrown into Whites and put under the direct tutelage of an experienced Herald. The salle had only one entrance, and that could be easily guarded—and was, not only by armed Guardsmen but by every unpartnered Companion at the Collegium, in teams of four pairs. Inside, ropes could be strung from the ceiling for young gryphlets to climb, practice dummies set up for them to wrestle, and a marvelous maze of things to climb on, slide down, and crawl about in could be constructed for both species. All of these things were done. They caused twice the noise of a war themselves when they were in full swing.

When the children tired, there was always Rris or the two human nurses—a pair of retired Heralds—who were ready to tell stories or teach reading and writing—well, reading, anyway. The gryphlets' talons were not made for holding human-sized pens. The nurses also instructed the youngsters in the rudiments of any of the four languages now being spoken on the Palace grounds.

Already it was a race to see if the human children picked up more Kaled'a'in, or the gryphlets more Valdemaran, just from playing with each other.

Hydona sighed, thinking wistfully how much she wished she could join the little ones, if only for an hour. But at least she had them when the day was done . . . and Rris was the best teacher anyone could ever have asked for. It was a truism that those who provided support were greater heroes than the ones who fought the wars, so Rris was as much a hero as his "Famous Cousin Warrl."

She knew that Selenay felt the same, but Selenay spent far more time away from her little ones than Hydona did, for Selenay's day did not end when she and a set of pupils were exhausted. The Queen and Kerowyn coordinated everything from the War Room in the Palace.

And it could not be done, save for the Mindspeakers among the Heralds.

Valdemar's greatest advantage remained its communications. Tactics could be put hand in hand with strategy from the Palace, thanks to Mindspoken dispatches, read in condensed battle-code, from field scoutings. Valdemar's second advantage was knowledge of the land; Heralds on circuit for so many generations had kept precise maps. Whether the land was high or low, wet or dry, resources could be moved rapidly with a minimum of waste.

Ancar had taken a bite from the side of Valdemar; Selenay and Kerowyn were ensuring that he did not find it an easy bite to digest. Treyvan's mages harried his mages, concentrating all their power on simply disrupting whatever spells had been set, by targeting the mages for specific, personalized nuisance attacks as well as attempting to break the spells themselves. This, evidently, was a strategy no one had used here. Ancar had not anticipated that FarSeers could identify his mages at a distance, and pass that information to mages who could then tailor their spells to suit. It did seem to be helping. And the Guard and Skybolts ran constant hit-then-run-away attacks against his lines, never letting Ancar's troops rest quietly, and doing their best to disrupt the supply lines.

The good news was that the civilian evacuation was working. There were a minimum of civilian casualties, those mostly too stupid or stubborn to leave when they were told to. This was something Hydona could not understand. How could humans be so attached to *things* and *property* that they would lose their lives simply to stay with those things? Nesting for the deranged.

She watched the youngsters a moment more, her heart aching with the need to cuddle them, human and gryphlet alike. But they had not noticed her, and she would not disturb their moment of joy for the world. Too often, the appearance of a parent meant the bad news that the parent would be away for a while. And while the younglings were amazingly resilient and seemed able to play no matter what, there were dark fears lurking beneath their carefree exteriors. When Mummy or Daddy came to say they would be "away," there was always that fear that "away" would mean far away, like Teren and Jeri, and Darkwind and Elspeth—and they might not come back again. . . .

Hydona slipped out again, with a nod of thanks to the

Guard and a feather touch for three of the Companions. Her pupils were ready for the front lines; soon all of the mages would be with the troops, and it *would* be time for that dreaded "going away." Treyvan and Hydona would have to leave the little ones, to take personal command of the mage-troops.

But as she neared the Palace, she saw a horse being led to the stables, and took a second, sharper look at it.

Rough gray coat; dense muscles; huge, ugly head—

It was! It was a Shin'a'in battle mare!

She spread her wings and bounded a few steps, taking to the air to fly the rest of the distance to the Palace. As she neared, she saw someone—one of the gray-clad trainees—waving frantically to her.

She backwinged to a landing, trying not to knock the poor child off her feet, as the girl braced herself against the wash from her wings.

"There's some 'un t' see ye, Lady," the girl said. "What I mean is, she's seen th' Queen, now she wants t' see one o' ye gryphons."

"Do I go to herrr, orrr doesss ssshe come to me?" Hydona asked logically.

"I come to you, Lady," replied the black-clad Shin'a'in Swordsworn, who emerged from the door behind the trainee. To Hydona's amazement she used Kaled'a'in, not Shin'a'in or Valdemaran.

This plethora of tongues could get to be very confusing, she thought fleetingly as the Shin'a'in sketched a salute.

"It would, of course, be far too difficult for you to enter this door," the woman continued. "I bring greetings, Lady, from your kin—"

Then before Hydona could say or do anything, the woman closed her eyes in concentration and began to rattle off a long series of personal messages, messages that were, unmistakably, from Hydona's kin and friends still in the Kaled'a'in Vale. There were something like twenty of them, and the poor trainee simply stood there in bafflement while the Swordsworn recited.

Hydona simply absorbed it all, lost in admiration. "Rrremarkable. How did you do that?" she asked when the Shin'a'in was done.

The woman smiled. "I was shaman-trained before the Star-Eyed called me to this," she said simply. Hydona nodded. Since half of the shamanic training required memorization of verbal histories, twenty messages would be no great burden.

Then Hydona noticed something else. The woman was not black-clad, as she had thought, but was garbed in very deep blue.

Well, at least she is not here on blood-feud! That would have been a complication no one needed right now.

"I am here," the woman said, answering Hydona's unspoken question, "for the same reason that you are here. I am the emissary from my people to k'Valdemar, and in token of that, I brought the Queen a true alliance gift. And I see no reason why you should not know it, since shortly all will." She smiled widely. "It is good news, I think, in a time of bad. Tayledras, Kaled'a'in, and Shin'a'in have united, and are holding open safe exit routes upon the Valdemar border to the west and south. Those places will stay in safe hands. Should all fail, the people of k'Valdemar can do as they did in their past— retreat, and find safe-havens. We, our warriors and yours, shall stay and survive, and work to set all aright."

Hydona felt limp with relief. That had been her unvoiced, worst fear—that somehow Falconsbane would raise the western border against Valdemar, and trap everyone between an army of his creatures and Ancar's forces.

And—k'Valdemar? So, the Kingdom of Valdemar was being counted as one great Clan. And by all the Clans. . . ?

Shin'a'in, Tayledras, and Kaled'a'in . . . Hydona could guess at only one thing that could have pried the Shin'a'in out of their Plains, or the Tayledras from their forests—

She sent a glance of inquiry at the woman, who nodded significantly and cast her eyes briefly upward.

So. *She* had sent forth an edict, had She? Interesting. Very interesting. It made sense, as much as anything did these days—and after all, Treyvan and Hydona had been part of bringing it all about. Of course, it was also entirely possible that the Star-Eyed was being opportunistic.

She could be claiming responsibility for events that simply *happened,* as if it were part of a great Cosmic Plan. Most of this uniting of the Clans and People could have been dumb luck. Still, for whatever reason it happened, there it was, and it was a relief indeed.

This Shin'a'in must have ridden day and night to get here as fast as she did, even with Tayledras Gating to get her to the Vale nearest the Valdemar border!

"Yourrr parrrdon," Hydona said, as she read the signs of bone-deep, profound fatigue that the woman's control had hidden with fair success. "I am keeping you frrrom a rrressst that isss sssurely well-earrrned."

"And I will accept your pardon and take that rest," the woman said, with a quick smile of gratitude. "And when you meet me later—I am called Querna, of Tale'sedrin." Then she turned to the poor, baffled trainee, who could not have been much older than twelve or thirteen, and spoke in careful Valdemaran. "My thanks, child. I have discharged the last of my immediate duties, and I will now gladly take your guidance to the room you spoke of."

"Thank you, warrriorrr! Rrressst well!" Hydona called after her. How many languages did these people know? Hydona felt a moment of embarrassment at her growling accent. Ah, but accents were unimportant as long as words were understood. And those words! Treyvan would be so pleased!

She hurried to find her mate, to give him the good news, with a lightness of step she hadn't felt in a long time.

Now, if their tactics of mistake and harassment would hold, if the innocents could escape, if they could only hold Hardorn's forces long enough for their real weapon to find its mark, *then* they could celebrate. All the People and their friends together, and the children....

Chapter Fifteen

Firesong rode in front of Skif and Elspeth, telling himself that there was no reason to give in to depression. Things were no different now than they had been when this journey began, but giving himself encouraging lectures did not really help. For the past several days he had hidden his growing and profound unhappiness, feigning a careless enjoyment of his role. There was no point in inflicting any further strain on the others, who had their own worries and stresses.

But this land was appalling. The farther into it they came, the worse it got, as if the closer they went to Ancar's "lair," the worse his depredations on his land and people.

Firesong had grown up around the gray and brown of lightbark and willow, sighing-leaf, loversroot and sweetbriar, but the overcast and mud of Hardorn were different, even if the colors were the same as those Vale plants and trees. The grays and browns of Hardorn were those of life departed, not the colors of the life itself. The colors of his robes that had seemed so outrageously bright in Valdemar were sullen and sad. It felt like life had seeped away into the ever-present mud, and he had faded like the colors.

Intellectually, he knew that he had not been prepared for the experience of so many people living together in their cities and towns, and for the problems that caused. Tayledras simply did not live like that, giving each person in a Vale a reasonable amount of space and privacy—and outside their Vales, the land was always wild and untamed in every sense. However, he fancied he had come to grips with the way folk lived here, and certainly he had even come to appreciate some of the advantages.

But that had been in Valdemar, not Hardorn. This was *not* just his reaction to seeing folk crowding themselves like sheep in a pen, and not only his reaction to the joyless and uncreative lives most of them led. That, in itself, was quite bad enough. For most of these folk, their days were an unending round of repetitive labor, from sunup to sundown, tasks that varied only with the season, and not much even then. A dreadful amount of time was spent simply in obtaining enough food for themselves and their families. The "wizard-weather," as folks called it here, had been hard on Valdemar, but it was only a small part of what was destroying Hardorn.

There were better ways, ways to make an ordinary man's life more fulfilling—he had seen that much in Valdemar—but Skif told him that the ruler of this land wanted things this way. A hungry man is concerned with the filling of his belly and not with attempts to free himself from a vile overlord. Being forced to toil to exhaustion each day left no one any time to think of aught but how the next day's toil could be endured.

In Valdemar, at least, while the poorest folk did labor mightily to feed themselves, they also had some leisure, some time to devote to things outside that round of work. Time to make things purely for the sake of ornament, time to talk, time to sing and dance.

But here . . . here there was no escape from grueling labor, for before one could even work to gain one's bread, one must labor in the service of the King. Only after much work was put in—tilling the King's fields, mending the King's roads, minding the King's herds—could one return to one's own tiny holding and work for one's own self. And this went on, every day, week in, week out, with never a holiday and never a day of rest.

And meanwhile, the very land itself suffered. Firesong had never seen anything like this, and had only heard of it from his own teachers. Few mages, even those following dark and blood-stained paths, ever did this to the lands they claimed, for they planned to use those lands and took thought not to use them up.

All things living produced tiny amounts of mage-energy which gathered like dew and flowed down into the ley-lines and thence to the nodes. There was some energy available at the sources, weak, but easy to tame, and accessible to a Journeyman. There was more to be had from the lines, though it was stronger, and took a Master's hand. And the magic of nodes, of course, was something only an Adept could ever hope to control. All this power flowed naturally, in good time, and as both King and mage, Ancar should have husbanded those resources. But Ancar was not content with that. His magics forced the energy from the land, taking the life with it. Small wonder that folks felt drained and without hope! Ancar was stealing their life-force away from them, from their children, from their crops and their animals!

Ancar was a study in malicious negligence, who had risen to power by gradual theft overshadowed by visible force.

The only bright side to all of this was that what Ancar was doing was relatively easy to cure. Even the cure itself was the essence of simplicity.

Dispatch the monster. Get rid of him, and he would no longer be a leech on the side of this land. His lingering spells would decay, ley-lines would drift back to normal, and things would, in time, return to normal.

Even Ancar's wizard-weather was not as violent as it could have been. He had not been creating any great pools of power to disturb weather patterns as had happened purely by accident in Valdemar, as the Haven Heartstone in turn woke other long-dormant places. Those wells of power had collected without the kind of control and supervision there would have been if there had been a Vale of Tayledras in charge. The weather over Valdemar was steadying now, and centuries'-worth of aged power, steeped into the rocks and trees, was unfolding like a fresh flower-bloom.

Once Ancar was dead, the weather in *his* land would also return to normal.

But this place made him itch to have the job done and be gone. The despair here spread like a slow poison into his own veins, and made his muscles tight. The sooner they were all gone from here, the sooner he would be able to get back to Valdemar and begin Healing the damage there. He could nudge the land into some kind of magical order, so that Elspeth and her Heralds could work their magics properly. Despite the arrogant poses he kept, mainly for his own amusement, Firesong knew he could only influence the natural order, not control it. Healers, hunters, artists, and farmers knew that.

They passed a knot of farmers in their fields, filthy and mired, stooping over a plot of tubers, half of which were already rotting in the ground. Their threadbare, shabby clothes were nearly the same color as the mud they labored in. Their faces were blank and bleak, with no strength wasted on expression. He shuddered and turned away.

This place was cancerous. Its slow death was palpable, and came from the capital, enforced by marauding soldiers, steel-handed police, and insidious magics. Falconsbane was not much better, but he had never drunk up the life of his land the way these fools were.

The mood of the place had infected Firesong enough that things that had been amusing in the beginning of this trek no longer seemed clever. He had ceased to ask Aya to wear his ribbons, although when the firebird made his flights to attract the customers, he carried his trailing ribbons in his claws rather than wearing them. And he himself no longer donned that silly turban or bright robes until just before they came to a village. There was nothing to distinguish him from Darkwind, save length of hair.

Soon, he told himself. *It will be over soon.*

All that really gave him pleasure was to brighten the

hearts of the children with his magic tricks, and to know that they were going home with enough money to buy their families a few days of decent meals.

If there were any food to buy.

That might be enough to hold them in hope until help really came, for the carnival was within a few days of the city where Ancar held abode.

Soon. Soon.

He fretted about Nyara, about her ability to handle what was surely the most onerous position in this little band, and about her mental stability, given her background. He would have fretted more, if not for Need. The sword spoke to him often, as often as he wished; they had spoken together of this more than once. He believed Need when she assured him that she could hold Nyara if the strain became too much to bear and she snapped beneath it. She had more than once proved herself equal to the task of controlling an adult mage; he had no doubt she could control Nyara if she had to, at least physically. Firesong, as one familiar with Healer-skills, recommended that Nyara's body could be influenced to calm or comfort her. Need understood.

He had confidence that between them, Skif and the blade could bring Nyara back to her senses if something went horribly wrong. But none of that would be good for Nyara, or help her own sense of self-worth in any way, and he prayed that it would never come to a testing.

There was one source of personal irritation that he could do nothing about. He had not had a lover since they left Valdemar—and for Firesong, who had not slept alone for any length of time since he was old enough to send feathers to suitors, this was an irritation indeed. There had been that charming young Bard in Haven ... but that had been all. Nothing in Vanyel's Forest, of course. Nor on the road between the Gate and Haven. And from Haven to this moment, nothing again. No one in the carnival had even approached him.

He would not, even for a moment, consider Darkwind. Not that Darkwind wasn't devastatingly attractive. It simply would not be fair. Elspeth did not understand all the nuances of Tayledras courting-play or customs, and she might well be hurt and unhappy if Firesong—

Besides, Darkwind had not reacted in any way as if he was interested in Firesong, which was irritating in itself, though Darkwind could hardly be faulted for personal tastes. Still. There it was. Even if Elspeth could be persuaded it was all completely harmless, Darkwind was simply not going to play.

There was Skif, however . . . Skif had not shown any interest either, but that could be for lack of opportunity.

He considered that for a bit longer. Nyara had such a warped childhood that there was *nothing* she took for granted. If he made it clear to her that there was nothing in this but a kind of exchange between friends—

She would still feel badly. I would damage her self-esteem. She would be certain that she is worthless to Skif if he "must" go elsewhere for a partner. I cannot do that to a friend. And to do that to someone already under as much as she is—would be as if I plunged a blade into her back.

Nothing came without a price. There was no hope for it. Unless someone else in this carnival approached the outsiders, he would just have to remain chaste.

Horrid thought.

But there it was.

The bonds between Skif and Nyara, as those between Darkwind and Elspeth, were simply too new and too fragile to disturb. Those love-bonds were like blood-feathers; if he touched them, they might break, and if they broke, the birds would bleed—if not to death, certainly to sickness. Their relationships were too important to jeopardize, and their friendships too valuable. He would survive his longing. But even once. . . .

No, and no, and no.

He sighed, and Skif looked at him curiously. He indicated the farmers with a jerk of his head, and Skif grimaced. Evidently the young Herald also felt some of the sickness affecting this land, even if he had no mage-senses.

And amidst all the more serious troubles in this unhappy land, amidst all the dangers and uncertainties of this mission, his lack of partners was hardly more than trivial.

But as Skif turned away, he caught himself admiring the young man's profile. Not his usual type, but variety was the essence of life, and—

Oh, Firesong, he scolded himself. *Do grow up. Try to treat this as a serious situation! Your needs are certainly not the only ones in this world!*

Odd, how one never noticed a need, though, until it was no longer being filled.

Or until it was being discovered.

Darkwind listened to Nyara stirring about restlessly for a moment, before she settled on a bunk. She had chosen to hide herself away; now they needed to keep her appearances as secretive as possible, so that only rumors of her existence would reach Falconsbane. He might dismiss them, but if he didn't, she could be the bait in a trap designed to bring the Beast to them, to their choice of ground. It would depend on what his spies told him; whether they were convinced that her appearance was all sham, or whether they thought, given that they knew Falconsbane was real, that this might be another of his kind. It was just one plan of several, but it was the plan that had the greatest potential.

There was another reason to keep her out of sight, a very ugly reason. The nearer they got to the capital, the more of Ancar's Elite Guards there were, prowling about and helping themselves to whatever they wanted from the cowed populace.

So far there had not been more than two or three at once, either riding patrol along the road, or apparently stationed at the villages. They had taken note of Darkwind, Skif, and Elspeth, measured them with their eyes, and evidently concluded that the cat-girl was not worth a fight with skilled mercenaries.

Better to keep Nyara out of their sight as much as possible, however, and keep the trouble to a minimum. It was like the mercy of hooding a skittish hunting-hawk in a strange environment, too—she would not have enjoyed being outside to see the land anyway.

It was relatively easy to deal with the men when they were in the tent audience; the one time there had been four willing to start some trouble, he and Elspeth had used a spell they had devised between them to take the troublemakers under control and make them forget what they wanted. They did this in such a way that seemed, later on, to have been nothing more than intoxication. It was a combination of mind-magic and true magic, and it took two to work it; once again, he and Elspeth were proving themselves as a partnership. Nyara had never even known there had been potential trouble; that was how skillfully Elspeth had worked with him. He would not have her know, either. These days, Nyara was a fragile thing; he would not allow anything to crush her.

That meshing with Elspeth though—so effortless, and so seamless, despite the danger—had matched anything they had done together outside of the bedchamber for sheer intoxicating pleasure. Magic had been like that before, when he was younger. Thanks to Elspeth, it was now that way again. It made for a tiny bright spot in the gloom of tensions that surrounded them all.

He knew that Skif was worried, for they had hurried this plan through, and it was not as well-thought-out as Skif liked. Skif fretted about the other members of the carnival, and how much they could be trusted. He had a point, too—there were too many pressures that could be brought to bear on one of these folk if Ancar's men got wind of something wrong and decided to haul someone away for questioning. And now that they were within a few days of the capital, he knew that Skif and Elspeth both had another overwhelming fear. They had been gone for a long time—long enough for a war to be won or lost. Although news of a real, stunning victory would surely have reached even their carnival, there was no way of telling what was truly happening on the front if the victories were small ones. The word in Hardorn would be the same for small victories, small defeats, or stalemate—the same bombastic assurance that the war was going well, and victory was assured. What was going on back home? What was Ancar doing to their beloved land? Were the tactics they had sketched out working? Could

Treyvan and Hydona handle all those varied mages? How much of Valdemar had been lost already?

The Companions refused to contact others of their kind any more than absolutely necessary, and then only briefly, for fear of detection. Elspeth told Darkwind with unhappy certainty that her mother would misinform the team about how the war was going if it was necessary. It did nothing to ease his worries.

In fact, all of them were acting as if they were preoccupied and fretting about something, with nerves on edge and tempers short. It didn't take any great wizard to understand why. They *all* wanted this done, for good or ill, and over with. They were taking action, pursuing the best solution they could come up with, using what resources and fortunes they had. As always, they had hope—and each other.

Some of the members of their troupe were already expressing misgivings about forming this carnival, and not because the Valdemarans were with them either. Every one rode with weapons near to hand, for Ancar's Elite Guard had already made trouble at the last two stops. At the first, they had tried to force one of the women-contortionists to give them pleasure; that time he and Elspeth had worked their magics and sent them all into a deep sleep, implanting memories of a great deal of ale and a bet on who could drink the most. At the second, a group had overwhelmed one of the peddlers who had been alone for a moment, taken all his money, and scattered his goods into the mud. Darkwind was not looking forward to tonight's performance.

He checked back with Nyara, and found she had fallen asleep. He envied her that escape. No doubt, Need had a great deal to do with it. In this situation, the blade was not above imposing her will on the girl.

This must be purest hell for poor Skif, who had less trust in Need—and the rest of the world—than Darkwind had.

Thanks to the gods for a partner who is strong enough to bear as much as I. The sheer relief of knowing that Elspeth could and would take not only an equal share of the load, but would take up the slack if he faltered, was something Skif could not enjoy. It was another tiny source of pleasure in this perilous situation.

The task—the danger—the tension—

It was hard to concentrate on performing with everything else that was going on in his mind and heart, and he knew the others felt the same pressures. And yet, if they did not perform well, they would stand out among the others. Being drab among the other peacocks could be fatal.

For that matter, giving a bad performance could easily bring another kind of attention; that of Ancar's men, who could decide to take out their disappointment on the performers.

:Darkwind.:

The gravellike mind-voice could only be Need, and despite his worries he smiled. He was beginning to like the old creature. She had a good sense of humor, and what was more, she was just as ready to tell a joke at her own expense as at anyone else's. With Need along, he did not fear for Nyara's physical safety; however, he worried for her mental safety. If Need had not been with them, it would have been a different story entirely.

She had waited until Nyara slept to speak with him.

:Yes, Lady?: he responded immediately.

:I have some news that may cheer you up.:

:Please, Lady, tell.:

:I have an informant inside Ancar's Court.:

He could not have been more stunned if Nyara had risen from her bed and clubbed him with a frying pan.

Need had an informant? In *Ancar's Court?* How in the name of—well, all the gods at once, had she managed that? The blade sounded very smug, and well she should be!

His spirits rose immediately—just, no doubt, as she had assumed they would. But if he had not been Mindspeaking, he surely would have stuttered his reply, he was that flabbergasted. *:Lady, that is excellent, incredible news indeed! How does this happen?:*

:Let's just say I have my means.: She chuckled. *:And my methods. This is a good source, trustworthy, and most unlikely to be uncovered; he's got mind-magic, and he's*

close enough to the Beast that he can, if he's very careful, not only find out what is going on with Falconsbane, but influence him as well.:

His elation to turned to alarm. An informant was one thing—and he had to assume that this person had Mindspeech—but to use that mind-magic on Falconsbane? That was more peril than he himself would have cared to undertake! *:Lady, do either of you know how dangerous that is?:* He could think of any number of things that could go wrong, *particularly* with an outsider trying to influence Falconsbane's thoughts. The Beast had very little Mindspeech, if any at all, and much less in the way of tolerance. There was always the chance that he would detect anyone who touched his thoughts. He had not gotten as far as he had by being stupid—and what was more, Darkwind *knew* that Mornelithe was skilled at shielding against mind-magic. How could even an expert hope to touch his mind undetected?

:Steady on. We're not dealing with the Falconsbane you knew,: she said so calmly that it made his spinning thoughts slow down and calm. *:Hear me out before you panic.:*

As he kept a fraction of his attention on the road, she detailed what had happened to Mornelithe Falconsbane from the time after he was lost in the Void and up to this very day.

In some ways, he was forced into a reluctant admiration, simply for the Beast's ability to survive. But all that punishment had taken a toll on Falconsbane. And she was right; from all she described, he was a very depleted, mentally damaged individual, and one who did not even realize the extent of his handicaps.

:So, you see,: she concluded, *:he's damaged goods, so to speak. But he's not aware of the fact. Between the coercions that Ancar has him under, and the fragmenting of his own personality, he's just not up to noticing anything subtle. For that matter, he often doesn't notice something blatant, so long as it doesn't make him act against his own best interest.:*

Darkwind ground his teeth a little. It sounded too good to be true. Was it? Or was there a great deal that Need had eliminated in the name of an expedient explanation? She had known what they were going to do from the very moment they had begun planning it. She had even taken part in the discussions. But that did not prevent her from running her own schemes to augment theirs. *:Let me contemplate this for a moment before I answer you,:* he hedged.

The sword sounded amused. *:Contemplate all you like. We've got the time, as long as you don't take a week. I know this is sudden, but I didn't want to break it to you until it was a reality. I'm the last person to tell you to rush into anything. I'm awake now.:*

The mules flicked their ears at him as his hands tightened on the reins. If it had been anyone else telling him all this, he would never consider it seriously. Everything hinged on being able to trust someone they didn't know, had never seen, would not be able to contact directly. Someone they had never even dreamed existed.

But it was not just anyone claiming all this. It was Need. She was caution personified. She never trusted anything or anyone entirely—even less than Skif. If his instincts said to check something twice, hers would move her to check it a dozen times. She simply did not rush into anything; she left that to her bearers.

It followed, then, that she had already done far more about this "informant" than she had told him. Perhaps that was why it had taken her so long to report it. She had said that she had not wanted to tell him of this before it was a reality—and she had plenty of time and opportunity, if distance was no great deterrent to this contact. When it came right down to it, he had no idea what her abilities really were. So.

He weighed everything he knew about Need and her ways and decided to ask two questions.

:How long have you been cultivating this contact?: he asked. *:Is there more about him you can't tell me yet?:*

She chuckled, as if she had expected those very questions. *:That's what I like about you, Darkwind. You're a suspicious one. To answer your questions, there's quite a bit I can't tell you about him yet, and I've been in one form of contact or another with him for some time. My in-*

*direct contacts started even before we crossed the border.
I can't tell you how it all came about, but I can promise
you that those who put me in contact with him are trustworthy entities.:*

Entities? An interesting choice of words. One could
describe the Companions as "entities." Were the Companions behind this?

*:Not exactly, but something very like the Companions.
Someone you would trust if I could tell you:*

Something—oh—like the Swordsworn, then? The
Kal'enedral had certainly been helpful in the past with regard to Falconsbane.

Need laughed. *:Persistent, aren't you? And a good
guesser, too.:*

He nodded, and his hands relaxed. In that case—it
must be *leshy'a Kal'enedral;* that would explain a great
deal. What the spirit-Kal'enedral were doing in Hardorn
he had no idea, but poor Tre'valen had said that She had
told him the interests of the Shin'a'in were now carrying
beyond the Plains. Perhaps this was one of the things She
had meant.

*:Do I take it that you are bringing this through me and
not through Nyara to spare her distress?:* He could well
imagine what unhappiness receiving any information
about her father at this moment would cause. She didn't
enjoy being used as bait for him, but it was the one useful
thing she could think to contribute. He suspected that a
burning desire for revenge held her steady in the day-to-
day strain of being "staked out" like a stalking-horse.
And as for actually seeing Mornelithe face-to-face
again—he was certain that Nyara tried not to think of
that. She probably tried not to think of him at all. This
would not help her precarious peace of mind.

:Precisely.: Need seemed very satisfied with his sensitivity. *:Ah—have you noticed that on the whole she is
looking and acting more—human? One of the things my
time with her has accomplished is that I am able to find
the memories of what the Beast did to her. Knowing that,
I can do some things to reverse his changes.:* Need
sounded smug again. He did not in the least blame her.

:I'm no god or Avatar, but there are a few things I can still do.:

:I had noticed. My plaudits, Lady. You may not call yourself Adept, but you cannot be far from one.: He smiled at her raspy chuckle.

:So, can I count on you to break this to the others? If you want to make it sound as if you've been in on this from the beginning, that's fine, if it makes the rest more inclined to trust the information.: Need apparently felt that she required his support on this; very well, she would have it. He assented readily. This was too great an opportunity to allow anything to spoil it.

:There is one small blessing in Nyara's lack of confidence in herself, Lady,: he pointed out. *:Poor little thing, she has been so used to thinking of herself as useless that it will not even occur to her that you might have brought this word to her, and not me.:*

He sensed something like a sigh from her. *:Sad, but true. Well, Skif and I are working on that. And if all of this falls out as best as possible, she'll have a boost in that direction.:*

The next village was coming up; he saw the huddle of buildings through a curtain of trees just beyond the first wagon. He could deal with all of this later. Right now there was a persona to keep up, a show to stage, and hopefully there would be no trouble from Ancar's men to complicate matters.

However, on that last, the odds weren't with them, and he knew it only too well.

The carnival-wagons drew nearer the cluster of buildings, then entered the edge of the town. He and Elspeth both sensed the tension as they drove through the village. The townspeople did not even gather to watch them as they passed through; instead, they watched furtively from their windows and doorways, trying to be as unobtrusive as possible. Their faces were even more haggard than was usual in Hardorn.

As the procession reached the common, the reason for the tension became clear.

More of Ancar's Elite, some in armor and some only in uniform, were gathered outside a large building on the edge of the common to watch them pull in. It looked as if there were about twenty or thirty of them. He had no idea what so many of the Elite were doing here in this tiny town; it seemed that they were garrisoned here on a permanent basis, but there didn't seem to be a reason for a garrison. No one in the last town had bothered to warn them about this—and it was something new since the last time any of the wagon-folk had been here.

Whatever it was that caused the Elite to be here—well, the carnival was running a risk in setting up tonight. The Elite always had money and few enough places to spend it. But one of the reasons that they always had money was that they were in the habit of taking whatever they wanted. They seldom needed to actually buy anything, and when they did—well, there were always plenty of people to steal more money from under the guise of "donations for the troops."

Still, it was difficult to force a good performance out of an artist. A frightened musician forgot words and music; a terrified dancer would move like a wooden doll. A juggler under duress dropped things. And no one could give any kind of a performance with a sword at his throat, or a knife pointed at a loved one. The effect of terror on a performer would only be funny for a limited number of times before the amusement began to pall. If luck was with them, some of these men had figured that out by now.

The routine was the same as always, but the tension had spread to everyone else in the troupe by the time all the tents and wagons were set up. Darkwind's stomach was in an uproar and his shoulders a mass of knots before they even set up the tent. And before the customers began to trickle in, word was passing among the wagon-folk; sensible word, by Darkwind's way of thinking.

Ancar's men were to be *given* anything they expressed an interest in. Free food, free entertainment, free drink. Smile at the nice soldiers, and tell them fervently how much you supported them. *Encourage them to toss coin in a hat if you must have it, but do not charge them,* ran the advice. *If we get out of here whole, that will be enough.* He passed on the advice to the others, who agreed fervently. There was no point in antagonizing these men, and if they were in a good mood and remained so, they might even avoid more trouble later.

"Hoo, I'll *give* them bottles of Cure-All if they'll take it!" Firesong said fervently. "In fact ... hmm ... that's not a bad idea. They'll be stuffing themselves from the Mystery Meat sellers. All that grease would give a goat a belly-ache. I'll prescribe Cure-All to the ones that look bilious. It's a lot stronger than anything they're used to gulping down, and given all the soothing herbs in it, it might make them *pleasant* drunks. If nothing else, it will knock them out much more quickly than the ale."

That was a notion that had a lot of merit. "Mention it has a base of brandy-wine in your selling speech, Firesong," Darkwind advised. "That will surely catch their interest. Something like—ah— 'made of the finest brandy-wine, triply distilled, of vintage grapes trodden out by virgin girls in the full of the moon, and laden with the sacred herbs of the forest gods guaranteed to put heat in an old man and fire in a young one, to make weeping women smile and young maidens dance—' How does that sound?"

"You know, you are good at that." Firesong gave him a strained, ironic half-smile.

"Perhaps I should consider making an honest living," Darkwind replied with heavy irony.

"Sounds good enough to make me drink it, and I made the last batch," Skif observed, coming around the corner of the tent. "And I've got an idea. Nyara *doesn't* dance. It's too dangerous; maybe we can hold four or five armed men off her, but we can't take on thirty. And if ten of them are in the tent, that's twenty somewhere outside where you can't see them. Tonight, the performance in the tent is you, the birds, and Darkwind. Nyara stays hidden. They don't know she's here, so let's not stretch our luck by letting them see her."

"I wish this," Nyara said from the dark of the wagon, her voice trembling in a way that made Darkwind ache with pity for her. How many times had her father made her perform in just such a way for his men? "I greatly wish this. What need have we of showing my face here and now? And there will be no one expecting shared monies tonight, yes?"

"Quite true," Elspeth said firmly. "After all, the last thing that anyone in this carnival wants is to give these men any cause at all to make trouble, and one look at Nyara will *make* trouble. In fact, I'm going over to the contortionists' tent and advise all their women stay out of sight, too."

It seemed to be a consensus.

While they readied the tent for the shows, Darkwind related everything Need had told him. The news was enough to make everyone a little more cheerful, so when the Elite did show up, Firesong was able to give them a good performance.

At first, only one of the Elite would accept a bottle of the Cure-All. From the grimace on his face, he had eaten far too much of what Firesong called "Mystery Meat," and far too many greasy fried pies. He took the Cure-All dubiously, with much jibing from his friends—

Until he downed the first swallow, and came up sputtering. His face was a study in astonishment.

"That bad, eh, Kaven?" one of them laughed.

"Hellfires *no,*" the man exclaimed, wiping his face on the back of his arm and going back for another pull. "That *good!* This here's prime drink!" With one bottle at his lips, he was already reaching toward Firesong, who divined his intention and quickly gave him a second flask. He polished off the first bottle, and got halfway through the second, with his mates watching with great interest, when the alcohol caught up with him. He took the bottle from his mouth, corked it carefully, and stowed it in the front of his tunic. Then, with a beatific smile on his face, he passed out cold, falling over backward like a stunned ox.

Firesong ran out of Cure-All immediately, but he made certain that every man of the Elite got at least one bottle. After that, they could fight it out among themselves.

Some of them did, in fact; brawling in the "streets" between the wagons in a display of undiscipline that should have shamed them, but which seemed, from the lack of intervention by the officers, to be standard behavior.

Thereafter, they wandered the carnival, bottles in one hand and whatever had taken their fancy in the other, moving from one entertainer to the next. While they were sober, Firesong and Darkwind took pains to make certain that they never repeated a trick from one show to the next—and in desperation, they were using small feats of real magic instead of sleight-of-hand. But once the men were drunk, it made no difference, for they could not remember what they had just seen, much less what they had seen in the show before. The small size of the tent was a definite advantage now, for only ten of them could crowd in at a time, which meant they never had the same audience twice in a row. But the alcohol fumes were enough to dizzy the birds, and the stench of unwashed bodies was enough to choke a sheep.

As darkness fell, the aisles between the wagons were both too crowded and too empty. The Elite filled it with their swaggering presence. There were *no* townsfolk brave enough to dare the carnival; the Elite held it all to themselves. By now all of the Faire-folk were knotted with fear and starting at any odd sound. This was horribly like being under siege. Darkwind wondered grimly why they had not helped themselves to the women of the town, as they seemed to help themselves to everything else, but Skif had an answer for that when he murmured the question out loud.

"Any attractive women that have relatives out of town are probably gone to those relatives," Skif told them. "Those that are left are being very careful never to be where one of the Elite can grab them without a lot of fuss. These men aren't totally undisciplined, and even if Ancar doesn't care what they do, their local commander knows that if they take their excesses beyond a little bullying and petty pilfering, the whole town will revolt. He doesn't want that; he has a quota of goods or food he has to meet, and he can't do that without the local labor. But we're outsiders, so we're fair prey. No one here will care if anything happens to us."

A good reason for the women of the carnival to stay out of sight. . . .

At that moment, shouts and pain-filled cries rang out

above the noise of the peddlers and entertainers—exactly what Darkwind had been dreading, yet expecting.

Thirty-one bodies lay unconscious in the middle of the carnival, laid out in neat rows; two of the peddlers were bringing in the thirty-second and last. Virtually all of the rest of the wagon-folk were getting their animals from the picket lines and hitching up.

These two men, a pair of burly drivers, hauled him by wrists and ankles. They let him drag on the ground, taking no care to be gentle, and flung him down beside the rest.

Every one of these men had collapsed where he stood, within moments of the first cry. Most of them had been within a few feet of the victim.

Firesong knelt at the end of one of the rows, his face gray with exhaustion. He was responsible for the mass collapse, and it had taken everything he had; an ordinary and simple spell of sleep had been made far more complicated by the need to target *only* the Elite, and to strike all of them at once. This was more complicated than either Darkwind or Elspeth could handle, and he had acted while they were still trying to organize themselves. Firesong's spell had taken long enough to set up that some of the damage had already been done.

The victim of the attack was one of the peddlers; not a particularly feminine-looking lad, but beardless and, most importantly, alone at the moment when four of the Elite came upon him, completely alone, in between two sets of deserted stalls. At this point, the Elite had all realized that there were no females anywhere in the carnival; that there would be no sexual favors here. His stock-in-trade, ribbons, were something none of the men wanted, but they *did* serve as a reminder that there were none of the easy—or at least, accessible—women they had anticipated getting their hands on.

As Darkwind understood it, the only warning the young man had was when the first four soldiers began an argument with him, claiming they had been cheated. Since he hadn't given away a ribbon all night, much less sold any, he hadn't the faintest notion what they meant and had tried to back his way out of the situation.

Then they had surrounded him, informed him that what they had been cheated of was *women,* and told him he'd just have to make it up to them.

By then, there were ten, not four, and he hadn't a chance. By the time the first four had pushed him to the ground, there were even more.

One man, at least, had beaten the lad before Firesong's spell took effect.

This had all been an incredible shock to Firesong, who had spent all of his life in the Vales. Darkwind was not foolish enough to think that molestation was unknown among his people—but it was *very* uncommon, given that most women *and* men could very well defend themselves against an attacker. As a scout, he had seen the worst possible behavior on the part of Falconsbane's men and creatures and had some armoring against what had come. Firesong had no such protection; Firesong was a rare and precious commodity, a Healing Adept, and as such he had been protected more than the ordinary Hawkbrother.

He had never seen anyone victimized like the boy. Others, who had MindHealing skills, would have dealt with such cases, which would probably have involved an enemy from outside the Vale. It was the attack itself that had him in shock, far more than the drain on his resources.

Darkwind had never thought to feel pity for the handsome Adept—but he did now, and he longed to be able to give Firesong some comfort in the name of clean and uncomplicated friendship. But there was too much to do, and no time for such niceties.

Darkwind laid a hand gently on Elspeth's shoulder. "Are you ready?" he asked. "It's our turn now."

She nodded, her mouth in a tight, grim line.

"I don't like this, you know," she said conversationally, although he sensed the anger under the casual tone. "If it were up to me, these bastards would all wake up eunuchs—if I let them wake up at all. I'd rather get rid of them altogether. Permanently. Let their gods sort them out."

"If it were my judgment, I would agree with you." He shook his head and sighed. If this were home, he could do as she preferred without a second thought. But it was not; they were not alone, they could not fade into the scenery and vanish. More importantly, however, neither could the people of the carnival and town.

If these men were maimed or killed, retribution would fall, and swiftly, on both the wagon-folk and the village. The only people who had even a chance to escape that punishment would be the Valdemarans, who had magic that would help them get away. Assuming that Ancar's mages did not try to track them. To put the villagers and Faire-folk into such danger would be an act of unforgivable arrogance.

No, there was no real choice in the matter; he and Elspeth would simply follow the plan they always used. These men would sleep walk themselves back to their barracks. They would wake up tomorrow with no memory of the molestation, and no memory of being struck down as they either participated, watched and cheered, or waited their turn. They would only remember that they had a good time at the carnival, that they drank more than they should of that drink of dubious origin, and that they had crawled back to their quarters and passed out.

"At least let me give them the worst hangovers they've ever had in their lives," Elspeth begged fiercely. "And make them impotent while the hangovers last!"

He sighed, not because he didn't agree with her but because it seemed far too petty a punishment, but it was all they dared mete out.

"I wish we could do worse to them," he said. "I wish we could fix everything. Our best chance at that is to do what we came here to do. Get rid of Ancar, Falconsbane, and Hulda."

She nodded grimly but softened as she meshed her mind and talents with his. In a few moments, it was done, and the men began to rise woodenly, stumbling to their feet and bumbling in the direction of their barracks. Their faces were blank, their eyes glazed, and they looked altogether like walking corpses.

"I'd like to give them plague," Elspeth muttered, staring after them. "I would, if I didn't think the townsfolk would catch it. Maybe some lice or social disease. Genital leprosy?"

As the last of them rose and bumbled off, Firesong stood up, slowly, looking a little better, but still drained and sickly. The last of the wagon-folk were gone, too, and from the sounds all over the encampment, they were getting ready to leave. There were two torches stuck into the ground that gave fitful, sputtering light. "It is hard on a mage to cast magics when there has been no time to prepare for them," he murmured, his expression open and vulnerable and showing much of the pain he must be feeling. And also some guilt. "Had to push it through with personal power, and damp it all down, so we wouldn't be discovered." Firesong rubbed his eyes. "Still. I feel I could have prevented this if I had only acted sooner."

"You need not feel guilty," Darkwind said quietly as Elspeth nodded, trying to put some force into his words so that Firesong would believe him. "You were faster than we were. And you did the best you could."

Firesong looked down at his hands. "But it was not enough," he said unhappily, the strain in his voice betraying how deeply he ached over this. "Where is the poor lad? Liam was his name? I do not like to think of him being alone—"

"Gerdo has him," Elspeth said. "He carried him off to their wagon."

Firesong looked astonished at that; Darkwind was a little surprised himself. Gerdo was one of the contortionists, and if he'd spoken a dozen words to Liam in all the time they'd been in Hardorn, Darkwind, at least, didn't know about it. They were, at best, casual acquaintances.

"He said Sara would understand," Elspeth continued, "since she was attacked herself. And he said something else, that he knew how Liam felt, sort of, because the same thing happened to him when he was a boy. He said they could at least tell Liam that it wasn't his fault. Maybe if they tell him often enough, he'll start to believe it."

"I feel I must go apologize," Firesong said after a moment.

Darkwind nodded, and sensed Elspeth's agreement and Gwena's gentle urging. "Do you mind if we join you?" he said simply

There was no rest for them that night; the entire carnival packed up and moved in the dark. They did not stop until the next village that did *not* have a garrison of Ancar's men. Darkwind, Elspeth, Nyara, and Skif took turns driving the wagon and sleeping in it. The poor Companions and the *dyheli* had no such luxury; they had to make their way on their own four hooves. Firesong spent most of that day and night with Gerdo, helping with Liam. Darkwind was not surprised at that; Firesong was a Healing Adept, after all, even though he was not a body-Healer *per se*. He had the ability to do Liam a great deal of good—and Liam's plight could do Firesong an equal amount of good.

Firesong was talented, Gifted, beautiful, and arrogant. In many ways, he had seen himself as above everyone else in this mission, even his fellow Tayledras. Nothing had really touched him except the damage done to the land; he had, for the most part, ignored the damage done to the people. Up until this moment, the pain of these people had been mostly an abstraction to the Adept— something to be deplored and kept at a distance, but nothing that really affected him. *Now* it had hit home. He had seen willful, cruel violence close at hand. Firesong had opened himself to pain and could not avoid it any more.

Firesong returned to his fellows late in the afternoon, uncharacteristically sober and silent, but with a certain amount of weary satisfaction on his face. When Liam finally appeared as the wagons were setting up for the shows, Darkwind understood the expression.

Liam appeared to have found a kind of peace and support. He was ready to get to work, and could look his fellows in the face. The young man had come through the immediate crisis well; while he would bear scars, they would not be as devastating as they might have been.

And Firesong seemed to have learned a great deal, too. When he looked about him, his beautiful face radiated empathy and compassion for those people who felt pain.

He no longer wore a mask of any kind, frivolous or haughty. "Saving the defenseless" appeared no longer to be a meaningless phrase spoken as any other platitude, but rather a goal to be understood as a way of life. Real pain had been touched and understood; Healing was no longer simply a mental exercise for Firesong.

That night, Need finally conveyed to them what she had learned from her "contact."

Darkwind wished devoutly that he could go to bed early, but he had done with less sleep in his life, and this was more important. They wanted things to look as normal as possible, though, and "normal" meant that the wagon should at least *look* as if they were all asleep. So the five of them sat on two of the beds, heads together, whispering into the darkness of the wagon.

:Firstly—we've all had some ideas about who was the real power in Hardorn, the one who's responsible for the way things have gone to pot around here,: Need said. *:We all thought it was Ancar, but it wasn't. He isn't more than a Master, if that. It was Hulda.:*

Elspeth choked. "Hulda?" she whispered urgently.

:That's right. She is an Adept.:

"But—the protections that were on Valdemar when she was there—how could she have been an Adept?" Elspeth sputtered.

:Apparently she never used any magic while she was there, child, so she never invoked the interest of the vrondi. *She knew what she was doing, and understood the nature of the protections. Anyway. She set up this draining effect that's been pulling life-force out of this land; Ancar's been getting all the loot, all the gold and the pretties, baubles to keep the baby happy, but she's been hoarding the power for herself. What she's done with it, though—I don't know, and neither does Mornelithe. Falconsbane thinks she was courting the Emperor's envoy; they use magic over there, so maybe she was sending them the power. If she was, it's the first time I've ever heard of people being able to do that sort of thing.:*

Darkwind shook his head, feeling nauseous. That had to be one of the strangest and most perverted things he'd ever heard. "So Hulda has been deliberately wrecking this land?"

:Pretty much. Encouraging Ancar to do what he wants, without ever giving him any real power or training past a certain point. Huh. Maybe I do know what she was doing with all that power. Those magical attacks, coercive spells on the troops—all of that is far too powerful for the mages Ancar has in his employ to be able to successfully invoke—unless someone was feeding them the energy to do it. Interesting idea.:

"That makes a great deal of sense," Firesong agreed, his voice flat with exhaustion. "More sense than that she would be making courting-gifts of mage-power. So Ancar has been the puppet, and she the manipulator?"

:Until lately. She's been sloppy, and he's been chafing at the constraints she put on him. She made the mistake of promising him more training and not delivering. So he started experimenting on his own; that's how he got Falconsbane. Put up half a Gate without knowing what he was doing or what it was for, wished desperately for an Adept to get him out of it before he got eaten alive, the Gate took the wish for the destination, and delivered Falconsbane with a bow on him.:

Firesong bit off an exclamation. Darkwind could only sit and shake his head with weary astonishment. "Either he is the stupidest lucky man in the world, or the luckiest stupid one," Darkwind said at last. "I would not have given him the chance of a dewdrop in an inferno of surviving such a blunder."

"And Mornelithe has the luck of a god, I swear it." Firesong snorted with a little more energy.

:He put Falconsbane under coercion while still magically naked and helpless—for once in his life, the Beast couldn't fight or break what was put on him. So; now Ancar has an Adept, he starts to feel as if he can do without Hulda. Falconsbane has been encouraging this, figuring on setting both of them against each other and running out while they get rid of each other. Except that Ancar managed to catch Hulda in a moment of weakness, and right now he has her inside a mage-mirrored prison

cell she helped create. So she's out of the way, for the moment.:

"So, what we have is the three powers at the top, who should be working together, who we've assumed have been working together, are actually fighting each other?" That was Skif, and he sounded incredulous despite his own weariness. "We might yet be able to pull this off!"

:Before you get too confident, let me give you the details,: Need said dryly.

The details were many, and often baffling. Only by assuming that Need's assessment of Falconsbane was accurate could Darkwind even begin to understand how the Beast had made so many fundamental blunders. It was incredible, impossible, insane. But, he realized, that described Falconsbane perfectly.

Still, it was terrifying to think what would happen if Falconsbane should happen to change his mind about cooperating with Ancar. The damage that had been wrought without that cooperation was terrible. And the number of successes the army of Hardorn had against Valdemar without Falconsbane's real help was even worse. But *with* it—

And Falconsbane was capricious. He could change his mind at any time. *Their* only chance was to strike for him while he was still Ancar's captive, for if he became Ancar's comrade before they reached the capital—the odds in their favor were not good.

The odds for Valdemar would be even worse.

Chapter
Sixteen

An'desha waited on the Moonpaths; alone this time, for Dawnfire had appeared only long enough to summon him and then had left him. That might mean the old woman wished to speak with him, then. That was good, for An'desha had been keeping Falconsbane annoyed with Ancar, as she had asked him to do, and at the moment it would be more likely for a pig to stoop on a hawk than that Falconsbane should become Ancar's willing helper.

Still, the Adept was a slippery and unpredictable creature. An'desha had been forced to play fast and loose with Mornelithe's mind to stave off the thought that it *might* not be such a bad thing to cooperate with the King. He'd had to remind Falconsbane of the coercions, and the King's own word that he had no intention of taking them off.

The trouble was that Hulda was still incarcerated. The protections she herself had put on the cell were better than Falconsbane had given her credit for. There was no sign that she was going to come bursting out of there and finish Ancar off any time soon, and the Adept was growing impatient.

He heard footsteps—real footsteps, on the Moonpath to his right. He turned to peer into the glittery fog. It had to be the old woman, for the Avatars had never made the sound of footsteps, and she was just contrary enough to create a sound in a place where such things were superfluous.

The old woman emerged out of the fog; from the set of her jaw, she had much to tell him.

"Well, boy," she said, stopping within a few paces of him, and looking him up and down as if to take his measure, "I hope you're as ready for this as your friends think because this is where we gamble everything."

"Friends?"

"The Avatars."

A chill of anticipation mingled with fear threaded his veins, for all that his "veins" were as illusory as the old woman's footsteps. "I can only try," he said carefully. "I have kept Falconsbane at odds with Ancar. He was beginning to think it might be good to ally with King Ancar after all."

She nodded brusquely. "That's good. You've done very well, boy. But this is going to take a surer, more delicate touch, and constant work. I mean that. We've come to the real turning point, and there's no way back now. You won't be able to leave him alone for a heartbeat, and you'll have to be absolutely certain he doesn't know you're playing with him. My people aren't more than a day away."

An'desha felt very much as if he had been suddenly immersed in ice water, but his voice remained steady. "So, whatever we do, it must be done soon. You have a plan, and its success depends upon my performance. If I fail, we all will lose."

"Exactly." She gave him another of those measuring looks. "This is where we see if you can really come up to what we're going to ask of you. You're going to have to create memories for Falconsbane from whole cloth, boy—memories of one of the servants telling him about the carnival, and that there's a captive cat-woman dancing in one of the tent-shows there. We want him to hear about

Nyara, we want him to come after her. We intend for him to walk into ambush. Can you do that?"

Create whole memories . . . he had been making fragments, adding to things Ancar truly had said so that they could be read as being insulting, for instance. Falconsbane had no idea his memories had been tampered with. An'desha had plenty of memories to use to make this one, memories that featured the servants talking. Was there any reason why he couldn't do this?

"I believe I can, Lady," he replied, trying to sound confident.

She smiled for the first time in this meeting. "Good. Then I'll leave you. You're going to need a lot of time to do this right, and I'm only wasting it."

And with that, she turned and walked off into the mist, and was gone.

Part of the plan, however, was not going to work. Having a servant tell Falconsbane about the carnival was simply not believable, no matter what the old woman thought. *No*, he thought, *as he examined Falconsbane's sleeping mind and all the memories of servants in it. No, I cannot have a memory of a servant telling him something. They do not speak to him unless they need to, for they fear him. But a memory of him overhearing them— yes, that I can do. There are plenty of those, and they will be less obtrusive, for he listens to the servants speak when they do not think he can hear them.*

The memory, he decided after some thought, should be just a little vague. Perhaps if Falconsbane had been sleeping?

He selected something that had happened in the recent past, a recollection of a pair of servants coming into Falconsbane's room to tend the fire, and waking him. That time they had been gossiping about Ancar and Hulda and had not known he was awake. It was a good choice for something like this; Mornelithe had been half-asleep, and had only opened his eyes long enough to see which of the servants were whispering together. It was another measure of how damaged he was that he didn't think of the servants as any kind of threat. The old Falconsbane would never have been less than fully alert with even a single, well-known person in the same room with him, however apparently helpless or harmless that person was.

He took the memory, laid it down, then began to create his dialogue. It wasn't easy. He had to steal snippets of conversation from other memories, then blend them all in a harsh whisper, since Hardornen was neither his native tongue nor Falconsbane's. He did not *think* in this language, so he had to fabricate what he needed, making his dialogue from patchwork, like a quilt.

He kept Falconsbane sleeping deeply as he labored through the night. If he had been able to sweat, he would have; this was hard labor, as hard as horse-taming or riding night-guard. It was so much like weaving a tapestry—like he imagined the legendary history-tapestries were. But at last it was done, and he watched it himself, to examine it as a whole with a weary mental "eye." He was so weary that even his fear was a dull and distant thing, secondary to simply finishing what had been asked of him.

The two servants entered the room; the memory of this was only the sound of the door opening and closing. They were whispering, but too softly to make out more than a word or two—"show," and "faire," and some chuckling. Then—a bit of vision as if Falconsbane had opened his eyes and shut them again quickly. A glimpse of two men-servants, one with logs and the other with a poker, silhouetted against the fire.

". . . what could be worth going back there?" asked one, over the sound of the fire being stirred with the poker.

"There's a dancer. They call her Lady Cat, and she looks half cat. I tell you, when she's done dancing, you wish she'd come sit on your lap! When she moves, you can't think of anything but sex. She's supposed to be a slave; she's got a collar and a chain, but she doesn't act much like a slave, more like she owns the whole show."

Another laugh, this one knowing. "I'll bet she does! I'll bet she does things besides dance when the show closes, too!"

"Well, that's what I mean to find out—"

Sounds of logs being put on the fire, then of the servants leaving the room and closing the door behind them.

It looked good, what vision there was behind it. It sounded good, solid and real. *Well, now to wake Falconsbane up, and make him think the little conversation has just now occurred.*

He woke the Adept with the sound of the door closing, and a little jolt, then left the memory out in Falconsbane's mind where it was the very first thing he would "see."

And it worked! The Adept thought he had actually witnessed the entire conversation!

He watched as Falconsbane mulled it over, wondering if this so-called "Cat Lady" was a carnival fake, created because of his own growing notoriety, or was real—

Oh, no—oh, no. She can't be a fake—he can't even think she might be a fake. Quickly An'desha shunted that thought away, guiding Falconsbane's sleep-fogged mind in the direction *he* wanted.

No, of course the cat-woman wasn't a fake. No one would dare counterfeit a Changechild, much less counterfeit Falconsbane; his own reputation would frighten anyone who dared to try it! No, it had to be real, and if it was real, there was only one creature it could be.

Nyara, An'desha whispered, keeping his own terror of being caught under tight control.

Nyara. Falconsbane's claws tightened on the bedclothes, piercing holes in the cloth. She had run eastward, after all! Probably she had started running when he had escaped death at the hands of the cursed Shin'a'in, and had not stopped until she had been captured. Now was his chance to catch her and make her pay for her treachery!

But I must hide her existence from Ancar, An'desha prompted.

But of course he would have to hide her very existence from Ancar. He would have to slip out of the palace, go alone and unobserved, and take her himself. If Ancar learned about her, he would want to see her, and the moment he saw her he would know she was Falconsbane's handiwork. Ancar was not the fool Falconsbane had thought—although a fool he certainly was—and he would certainly use Nyara as an additional hold over his captive

Adept. Falconsbane had invested a great deal of power in making Nyara what she was, and any mage higher than Journeyman would know that using her he could control the creator. The old law of contamination. Any mage left some of himself along with his power, even an Apprentice knew that. There was the likelihood that even Hulda's old toy knew it as well.

Going to this carnival alone and unobserved, though— that would take some creativity. There were always guards at his door, and more guards throughout the palace. He would have to find a way to avoid them, and a time when Ancar was occupied elsewhere. This would take a great deal of advance preparation, and no small amount of power to come and go without detection.

Why else have I been storing up mage-energy? An'desha asked.

But then, why else had he been storing up mage-energy? Even with the coercions, he could still work spells that would make him ignored by anyone who set eyes on him. He could even work a true spell of invisibility for a short period of time. He could stun the guards for as long as he needed, and he had certainly picked up enough information from the servants' gossip to know the easiest clandestine ways in and out of the palace. If he picked a time when Ancar was busy with the war plans, he could be down to the carnival and back with no one being the wiser.

And as for Nyara—once he had her, even though her death would of necessity be rushed, he could make it seem an eternity to her. Perhaps—perhaps he could enhance all her senses, and stretch her time perception, so that every tiny cut seemed to take a year.

Such a sweet reunion it would be. . . .

Falconsbane began to plan what he would do to his daughter when he finally had his hands on her. An'desha shuddered but did not pull back into the familiar corner of his mind.

Skif couldn't help but notice the air of relaxation all through the carnival this afternoon. Wagon-folk all over the carnival had breathed a sigh of relief as they set up just outside the walls of the capital, at the gate nearest the palace itself. Ancar might permit his men to do as they willed anywhere else, but here they were as restrained as good, disciplined troops in any other land. Pairs of Elite Guards with special armbands patrolled the streets, and today while running his errands, Skif had seen one man hauled off for public drunkenness, and another for robbing a street peddler.

Skif only wished that he and the others could share in the general feeling of relief. For the Valdemarans and their allies, the dangers had just increased exponentially.

The general consensus among the wagon-folk was that it would be well worth staying a week or so, here, and safe enough to let the women come out of hiding. There were good pickings to be had in this city. Many of them had constructed clever hiding places in their wagons for a small hoard of coins in anticipation of a good run.

No one among the wagon-folk knew what the Valdemarans were really up to; their story—which still seemed to be holding under the pressure of passing time—was that they were going into the city; that they had found out that their missing relatives had last been heard of here, and they were going to get them out, if they were still alive. Missing relatives was a common enough tale in Hardorn these days, and if the wagon-folk wondered about the odd group, they had so far kept their speculations to themselves.

Skif had gone out into the city to get the lay of the land; now he returned to the carnival with the provisions he had been "sent" for, and a great deal of information. Last night Nyara had danced in three shows; and his every muscle had been tight with strain at each one, wondering if she would be able to continue the charade. This morning there were at least a few people in the marketplace talking about her. If Falconsbane would just hear about her and come looking. . . .

Already townsfolk threaded the aisles of the carnival, looking, fingering, and sometimes buying. He pushed his way through them until he came to "Great Mage Pandemonium's" stand. At the moment it was closed; the five of them had decided it would be better only to perform after nightfall, and to keep the use of magic to a minimum. Nyara was only a draw to the adult crowd, anyway, and the day-goers seemed to be families and older children.

The rest should be in the tent, relaxing; the wagon was too cramped for anything except sleeping. And *just* sleeping; he was far too shy to do anything with Nyara in company, and Elspeth and Darkwind felt the same. They'd been making it a habit to eat, lounge, and carry on the things that had to be tended to, day-to-day, in the larger area of the show-tent.

He had expected the atmosphere to be tense when he entered the tent, but he had not expected the set of peculiar expressions on the faces of his friends as they turned toward him. They were seated on makeshift stools of whatever equipment boxes happened to be handy. Even in the dim light beneath the heavy canvas, they looked as if they were suffering from sunstroke. Stunned, and quite at a loss.

"Our sharp friend has handed us a complication," Darkwind said, his own expression swiftly changing from irritation to apprehension and back again as he glanced at the sword at Nyara's side.

"It seems that Falconsbane isn't really Falconsbane."

What? "An imposter?" Skif blurted, that being the only thing he could think of. "We've been chasing an—"

"No, no, no," Elspeth interrupted. "No, that's not it at all! But—the Beast is not exactly *alone*."

Now Skif was even more bewildered, and he shook his head violently, as if by shaking it, the words would make some sense. "What in Havens are you talking about?"

:Damn it, you're all missing the point,: Need said with irritation. *:Except Firesong, but I've been talking to him all morning. Here, let me show you.:*

Then, without even a "by your leave," Skif found himself inside the thoughts of some *other* person entirely, just as Need had once flung him inside her own memories when she had first awakened, to explain what she was by showing him. But this was not Need's memory; this person was young, male, and seemed to be Shin'a'in—

:*Halfbreed*,: Need interrupted. :*Trust me, it made a difference in how things came out.*:

He watched, a silent observer, as the boy discovered his mage-powers, determined to run away to the Hawkbrothers, got lost in the Pelagiris Forest, tried to light a fire—

—and the entity that called itself Mornelithe Falconsbane—in *this* lifetime—came flooding in to take his mind and body and make them his own.

Abruptly, Need flung Skif out of those memories, and he found himself back in the carnival tent, blinking, the others shaking their heads as they, too, recovered from the experience. "I wish you wouldn't do that without warning a man," Skif complained, hitting the side of his head lightly with the heel of his hand. "It—"

:*It saves time,*: Need replied testily. :*Well, now you know.* That's *who my informant has been.*:

"The boy?" Skif chewed his lip a little. "And presumably he still lives within Falconsbane's body. Forgive me, but I don't see how that changes anything."

:*He lives inside his body. Falconsbane has stolen it. What changes everything is that the boy found out how Falconsbane's been doing this. An'desha's body is far from the first he's stolen. Unless we stop Falconsbane in a way that keeps him from taking his spirit off to hide again, it won't be the last. People, this has been happening since the time your folk call the 'Mage Wars.' All he needs is a body out of his bloodline, with Mage-Gift. And trust me on this; he spent a lot of time back then making certain he'd have a lot of descendants. Usually he does the same any time he's had a body for a while.*:

After a moment the sense of that penetrated, and Skif cursed softly. "You mean if we take him the way we had planned and kill him, we might be facing him *again* in a couple of years?"

:*If he finds somebody else with his bloodline, yes. Or takes over Nyara's children. You see, he had another motive for trying out all his Changes on her, first. Mage-Gift will always breed true in her children now, and if and when she decides to have them, despite the lies her father told her, she'll be very—ah—prolific. Catlike in more than looks, it seems.:*

Skif froze in place, his body and mind chilled, as his eyes sought Nyara's. She nodded unhappily. "I could not fight him, Skif. Need could help me, but she cannot be everywhere, at all times, and what are we to do? Insist that our grown children stay with us all their lives?"

:Even if you don't have children, there are always more where An'desha came from. His *father was out spending his seed all over the south. Sooner or later, Falconsbane will be back.:*

"We can't capture him—we can't kill him—what in the nine hells *can* we do with him?" Skif demanded, his voice rising. He threw his hands up in the air, exasperated. "What are we here for? Why don't we just give up? Why are we even trying?"

Firesong gave him a look that shut him up abruptly. "We can kill him, Skif," the Healing Adept said calmly, his face an inhuman mask of serenity. "Need and I have been discussing this since you left. We can be rid of him, forever, *and* in a way that will allow An'desha to reclaim his body. But it will take four of us working together; you, Nyara, Need, and myself. Possibly even your Companion. It will take superb timing and equally superb cooperation. And it will not be silent."

"By silent, you mean that it is going to take some very obvious magic?" Skif hazarded. This time it was Darkwind who nodded.

"That's why Elspeth, Vree, Gwena, and I will not be here. *We* will have to strike after Ancar takes the backlash of this magic or detects it in other ways, but before he has a chance to act on that knowledge. Since Falconsbane bears a great many of his coercion spells, slaying the Beast should snap them, and they will recoil on him like snapped bowstrings." Darkwind rubbed one temple, then moved his hand up higher to scratch Vree. "More timing, you see. There will be a moment when he is very stunned, and that is when *we* must strike. Firesong will give us a signal when Falconsbane is gone. First we will take out Ancar. Then we will deal with Hulda."

After all the time it had taken to get to this point,

things seemed to be cascading much too fast, one plan running into the next like an avalanche. But so far as Skif was concerned there was still one question to be asked.

"If you can kill Falconsbane without killing the other fellow, wouldn't it be easier to kill him straight off and not worry about this boy?" There, it was out. He didn't like it, but how could seeing her father's body walking around do Nyara any good? And why complicate matters? It was very nice that this An'desha fellow had helped them, but sometimes you had to accept innocent casualties. . . .

The realist and the Herald warred within him, and the realist looked to be winning, but it was not making him feel anything other than soiled, old, and terribly cynical.

"We could, and it would be simpler," Firesong admitted reluctantly. "But it is something I do not care for. On the other hand, one less complication might increase our chances for surviving this." It looked to Skif as if he were facing his own internal struggle, and didn't care for the realities of the situation either.

Skif nodded; Elspeth looked uncomfortable and distressed, but nodded also, for she had learned long ago to accept that the expedient way might be the best way. But to Skif's surprise, it was Nyara who spoke up against the idea.

"Need has given me a sense of what An'desha has dwelt within, all these years," she said slowly. "What Falconsbane did to me is nothing to what he has done to this boy. He has helped us at risk of real death—and he has done so knowing we might decide not to help him. *I* say it would reflect ill upon us all our days if we were to pretend he did not exist. I say we should save him if we can, and I put my life up for trying."

She looked at Skif as if she were afraid he would think her to be crazed. He did—but it was the kind of "crazed" that he could admire. He crossed the tent and took her in his arms for a moment, then turned to the others.

"Nyara's right. It's stupid, it's suicidal, but Nyara's right and I was wrong." He gulped, shaking all over, but feeling an odd relief as well. "We have to help this boy, if we can."

:And that is why you were Chosen,: Cymry said softly, into his mind.

"All right, Great Mage Pandemonium," he said. "Then let's do this all or nothing. After all—" he grinned tautly as he remembered his old motto, the one he had told Talia so very long ago. "—if you're going to traverse thin ice, you might as well dance your way across!"

Night fell, and Falconsbane's preparations were all in place. They were in for another bout of wizard-weather, this time an unseasonable cold, and as far as he was concerned, that was all to the good. Bad weather would make it easier for him to disguise himself.

There was a very convincing simulacrum of himself in the bed, apparently sleeping, in case anyone came in while he was gone.

Ancar was in his war-room, a large chamber with a balcony overlooking the courtyard of the palace. Hulda, of course, was still in her cell, and showing no signs of breaking free. The other mages were all with Ancar, but the King did not trust Falconsbane enough to allow him access to the actual battle plans unless things had unraveled to the point that there was no choice.

The servants were mostly elsewhere. Rumors of what Falconsbane had done to the prisoners Ancar had given him insured that, except when he was known to be sleeping. There were two guards at his door, however. . . .

Falconsbane moved soundlessly to the doorway, and placed his hands at head-height on either side of the doorframe. This would be very tricky; he had very little mind-magic, so this would all be true spellcasting. Difficult, when one could not see one's target. . . .

He gathered his powers; closed his eyes, concentrating, building up the forces. And then, at the moment of greatest tension, let them fly, arrows of power from each hand that pierced the wall without a sound.

He opened his eyes. There was no noise, no hint of disturbance, on the other side of the door.

He reached for the voluminous cloak he'd had one of the servants bring him this morning and swirled it over his shoulders. It fell gracefully to his feet in heavy folds he pulled the hood up over his head, using it to cover his face, so that nothing showed but his eyes. As cold as it was tonight, no one would think anything wrong, seeing a man muffled to the nose in a cloak. Likely, everyone else on the street would be doing the same thing and hoping that it would not rain.

He opened the door. The two guards still stood there, at rigid attention. Perhaps—a trifle too rigid?

Mornelithe chuckled and waved his hand in front of their glazed eyes. "Hello?" he said, softly, knowing there would be no response.

Nor was there. Ancar had not thought to armor the guards he had on Falconsbane against spell-casting, trusting in the coercions to keep Falconsbane from doing anything to them. But Mornelithe was not doing anything against Ancar's interests, no indeed. . . .

"Just going for a little walk, men," Mornelithe whispered to the unresponsive guards in a moment of perverse whimsy. "I'll be back before you miss me, I promise!"

He closed the door carefully and set off down the hallway in a swirl of dark fabric. He was not worried about the servants seeing him; if they caught sight of him, they would never imagine the stranger was Falconsbane, and Mornelithe's authoritative stride was enough to make most of them think twice about challenging his presence in these halls. Ancar had a great many visitors who did not wish to be seen or challenged, and people who were foolhardy enough to do so often disappeared. In a few moments, the two men he had bespelled would wake from their daze, quite unaware that anything had happened to them. He would bespell them again on his return.

It was Ancar's other guards and soldiers Mornelithe wished to avoid. He hoped there would be none of them to challenge him, but the best chance of avoiding them lay in getting outside quickly.

He could bespell more guards if he had to, but then he would have to find a way to dispose of them. They might be missed. That would be awkward, and not as much fun as he'd prefer.

He continued down the hall without meeting any more

men in Ancar's uniform, but as he rounded a corner and drew within a few feet of his goal he heard the distinctive slap of military boots on the wooden floor. Four sets, at least.

He gambled; made a dash for the door leading to the staircase and wrenched it open. He slipped inside just before the guards came into view, and ran right into a young servingman, just as he closed the door and turned on the landing.

The boy opened his mouth. Falconsbane seized him by the throat before he even managed to squeak. There was no time for finesse; he simply choked the boy so that he could not make a sound. He then wrapped them both in silence, drained the servingboy of life-force, and left him on the landing.

Let whoever found him figure out how he had died.

The staircase led directly to the public corridors of the palace. Here he was even less likely to be challenged, and he opened the door at the bottom with confidence, striding out into the corridor and taking a certain enjoyment in the way people avoided looking at him directly. Anyone who walked in such a confident, unhurried manner in *Ancar's* palace must be powerful and dangerous . . . both attributes belonged to people that the folk here would rather avoid. Especially if the strangers took pains to hide their faces.

Unhindered, he passed out into the chill and darkness and paused for a moment on the landing above the courtyard. The guards at the doors did not even look at him; after all, they were there to keep people out, not in. He trotted quickly down the steps to the courtyard, casting a covert glance as he did so to the room behind the balcony immediately above the main doors. Lights were still burning brightly, and shadows were moving about inside. The war-council was still going strong.

Good. Let the children play.

There were more guards at the various gates he had to pass to get to the city itself, but once again, they were there to keep people out, not in, and they ignored him. On his return journey, he would come in through another way, via the gardens, and an ingenious series of gates with locks that could be picked with a pin or latches that could be lifted with a twig, holes under walls, and trees with overhanging limbs. This was the route that the servants used to slip in after a clandestine night in the town. Pity it only worked to get *in* by, but overhanging limbs that permitted a drop *down* were not very useful when the reverse was needed. He was a mage, not an acrobat.

He passed the last gate and a squad of very bored, very hardened soldiers who looked as if they would have welcomed an intruder just so that they could alleviate their boredom by killing him. Then he was out in streets of the city, and free.

For one, brief moment, he was tempted to just keep walking. Forget a cat-woman who might or might not be Nyara; forget that he might be hundreds of leagues from his own territory. He was free—he could take that freedom and just walk away from here.

But as he thought that, he suddenly felt the jerk of the coercions on him, a chain jerking a dog back to its kennel. The force was sufficient to make him stagger. And he snarled inside the shadow of his hood.

No, this breath of freedom was an illusion after all. And he could not simply walk away. Ancar's coercive spells were set too well, and the King had evidently planned against this very possibility. He had the freedom of the city—but that was all.

At least, until Ancar was dead.

Very well. Let him see if this Lady Cat was indeed Nyara. And if she was, he would use her death to fuel his own powers, taking back into himself all that he had used to make her.

Then he would return to Ancar's palace . . . and lay some new plans.

An'desha was very glad that his link with his physical body was so tenuous that as long as Falconsbane was awake it might just as well have not existed. If he—or rather, his body—had broken into a sweat of nervous fear, Falconsbane would *certainly* have noticed something was going on!

That moment when Falconsbane had thought to simply

walk off—An'desha had taken a gamble and given the Adept a jolt he *hoped* Falconsbane would interpret as Ancar's coercions. The gamble had worked, but the old woman had been only too correct when she had warned that this was going to take every bit of cleverness and concentration he had. The Adept had come within a heartbeat of bringing down all their plans.

The die was cast. Whatever happened would follow from this, win or lose.

Falconsbane moved swiftly through the darkened, noisome streets to the city gate. His nose wrinkled in distaste at the odor of offal in the gutters, an odor even the bitter cold could not suppress. And this was supposed to be one of the better parts of this city! An'desha could not for a moment fathom why anyone would want to live in one of these hives. He felt a pang of longing as sharp as any blade for his long-lost Plains, or even the Pelagir territory Falconsbane had taken for his own. *Wilderness,* he thought achingly, as a vision of the endless sea of grass that was the Plains in late spring danced before his mind's eye. *Shall I ever see it again?*

On the other side of the gate in the city wall, the Faire spread out on the long slope of a meadow, inclining away from the city. Lighted stalls, wagons, and tents showed that the carnival was in full swing, and streams of people going to and from the faire proved that folk still craved entertainment. Perhaps they craved it even more, under Ancar's repressions.

Falconsbane made his way through the crowds; most folk ignored him or avoided him, but he hardly noticed. His eyes searched out and dismissed every occupant of every stage. He passed a wealth of jugglers, musicians, conjurers, salesmen of every sort of strange brew and device—

And finally, where the crowd was thickest, he found what he sought.

He could not get too near the wagon-stage in question, for the people were piled ten and twenty deep around it. The performance he had heard so much about was just ending, but Falconsbane saw more than enough to make his heart race.

Dancing provocatively to the throbbing of a drum, posing and twisting in positions that rivaled the contortionists on the next stage, was Nyara.

Even with the foolish and patently false ears and tail she wore, and the peculiar makeup that added stripes to her face, it was clearly Nyara, dressed in a few veils and a singlet—

And a collar and chain-leash.

She posed once more, dropped a veil, and whisked around the corner of the wagon, to what was obviously a performance tent—where, presumably, she would remove more than a single veil.

A fellow in an impossibly gaudy costume began chanting something to that effect, inviting the crowd to see "more of her," in just a half candlemark. Then he followed after Nyara, presumably to ready the stage inside the tent.

And after the initial shock and elation, Falconsbane could only think of one thing.

This is a trap.

An'desha panicked. To have come so far, and to have Falconsbane flee on the threshold—no, it could not happen! There had to be something that would push him past this, to the place where caution didn't exist! To the point of madness, of obsession—

Yes! There was!

Quickly, even as Falconsbane completed that thought, An'desha added another, praying to the Star-Eyed that he would not notice An'desha's "voice" in his head.

She was with the gryphons; they must have the gryphons with them!

Falconsbane's field of vision narrowed and tinged red with a rush of rage that sent a flood of blood to his head, and burned along his veins.

:Good boy! I'll warn the girl,: came a harsh whisper to An'desha, as the mere mention of gryphons triggered Falconsbane's powerful, ancient obsession. Now it did not matter to Falconsbane that this might be a trap. Nothing mattered—except that there might—no, *must*—be gryphons, the two gryphons who had twice escaped his path. Maybe the little ones, too!

An'desha felt a new fear now as he realized that his thoughts and Mornelithe's were intertwining the more he manipulated the Adept's thoughts. He was inserting thoughts and ideas so much quicker than before—what if Mornelithe left this body and took *An'desha's* consciousness with him, instead of abandoning the body to its rightful owner?

Then that is the price I must pay, An'desha thought, with smothered despair, and spurred Mornelithe forward. *Either way, may the Goddess ensure Mornelithe is done for.*

Quickly, Falconsbane shoved his way through the crowd, ignoring protests and return shoves, working his way to the end of the row where he could get to the back of the tents. There, if anywhere, would be the gryphons. They were too big to hide anywhere else.

He shoved his way into clear space and darkness, out of the reach of the torches illuminating the public areas of the carnival. He had squeezed his way between two of the wagons, and was now in an area of the carnival meant only for the Faire-folk. There were at least a dozen large tents here, all in a neat row, most glowing softly from within. Beside one, a horse was grazing quietly. It screamed to his mage-senses of illusion; he looked below the illusion—to see a poor old, broken-down nag where the glossy bay was standing.

Amusing. Typical trickster's chicanery.

And even as he got his bearings, he saw the shadow of a gryphon, briefly, against the side of one of the tents.

Falconsbane took in that shadow, those waving wings, and went quite mad—a madness like a deadly storm, built over the course of centuries.

Falconsbane's hands blazed with power, ready to strike. He rushed at the tent, screaming at the top of his lungs in anger, burning the canvas away as he neared, and came to a halt—

And saw Nyara; she held a sword as if she actually knew how to use it! Behind her, a young, curly-haired man was using a lantern to make clever shadow-shapes with his fingers against the canvas.

It *was* a trap! But he would trap *them!* This had become absurdly funny. He—

Something dark loomed up behind him and struck like a lightning bolt before he could twist to evade it. He fell forward with a shock onto—

The point of the sword.

Held by Nyara.

But—there were no gryphons—

Falconsbane felt his rage ebbing, along with his power, and a great surge of bitter disappointment, just as the first wave of pain hit him.

No—

Firesong waited in the shadows of the back of the tent.

—when suddenly Nyara cried out desperately. "A gryphon! Somebody make a gryphon, one he can see! He's about to get away!"

Taken by surprise, with no illusion ready, he could only fumble after a bit of power to obey her.

Oh, please, don't let everything fall apart now—

Skif thrust his hands up in front of the lantern, as if he were doing a shadow-puppet play, and writhed his clever fingers into something that cast an amazingly lifelike shadow of a nodding gryphon on the back wall of the tent. The lower mandible opened and closed in a remarkable imitation of a gryphon talking, and his fingers made wingtips.

But would it be enough to fool Falconsbane?

He got his answer a breath later, as something—someone—shrieked with towering rage, then terrible power burned through the canvas and Falconsbane stood there—hands blazing, eyes afire with madness, teeth bared in an animalistic growl as if he would rend them apart like a beast of the forest or one of his own monsters.

He faced Nyara, his hands aglow with raw power; she brought Need up into a guard position. From the way her stance changed, Skif knew she had given control of her body over to the old woman.

But magic does not need a blade to strike, and can kill

from afar. Only Need had the ability to destroy the Adept.
But if Falconsbane did not find a target other than his
daughter, she might not survive to close with him.

Fear acted on him like a drug, sharpening his own re-
flexes, and making it seem as if everyone else moved at
a crawl while he ran. Firesong was only now bringing up
his hands to strike at the Adept, and he would be too late
to stop the first attack on Nyara unless Skif redirected it.

He reached for his own blade, knowing he stood no
chance against Falconsbane—but at least he could defend
Nyara. Even if he died doing so—

:*No, Chosen!*: There was an equine scream and a flurry
of hoofbeats. Cymry loomed up out of the darkness and
rushed into Falconsbane. Mornelithe stumbled forward,
face gone blank with surprise.

To meet Nyara, standing with Need braced, ready for
him.

They had expected a combat, with Firesong taking on
Falconsbane's magic, and Nyara striking at a moment of
distraction.

Cymry evidently had other ideas.

She continued her rush right into the tent, and shoved
the Adept right up onto the blade, impaling him on its full
length.

Somehow, Nyara held steady, under the double impact
of his body and the surprise that their clever foe had been
so incredibly *stupid*.

Mornelithe gathered his power, instinctively grasping
after the one thing he still controlled.

The witch-horse danced backward, neighing with triumph.

Nyara braced herself against him, but even so, she
staggered back. He was half again her weight, after all.
The force of the shove had carried him halfway up the
blade; he stared stupidly at her, face-to-face. Pain took
him as a triumphant conqueror, and death beckoned. His
eyes flitted to the blade as his power ran away along with
his own life-force and his red, red blood, flowing into the
ground before him.

His magics failed, aborted by the trauma to his body.

His power was draining away, and so was his life. This body was dying, very quickly.

He could use what was left to have revenge on them—or he could escape and get his revenge another time.

He chose as he had always chosen, laughing in spite of the terrible pain that wracked this latest body he had stolen.

An'desha felt Falconsbane gather the last of his energies, and leap—

—and now, completely in control, he stared down with his own eyes. Pain seized him as a dog would seize a rag doll, and shook him, and he screamed as his vision failed and darkness came down around him—darkness, and despair—

But as the darkness descended, he saw light—

The Moonpaths! It was the old woman, standing on the Moonpaths, with a black abyss between him and her. She held out a hand to him.

"Here!" she said. "To me!"

He hesitated.

"Do you trust your Goddess?" she said. "Jump to me!"

A thousand thoughts flitted through his mind, but uppermost was that *this* must also be an Avatar of the Goddess, one that had cloaked Herself in the seeming of an old woman—yes, that made sense, for how else could he have spoken with Her? No human woman could have touched his mind on the Moonpaths!

—yes, and wasn't the last face of the Goddess that of the Crone? She who gave life and death?

Wasn't She the Goddess?

He *must* trust Her!

He leapt; She caught and held him—

And She clung to him, and held him out of the abyss even as it opened up under his feet.

Skif caught the crumpling body, lowering it to the ground *far* more gently than he would have if he hadn't seen that ghost of a frightened child looking out of the eyes just before the body fell. Nyara's eyes were closed, her face a wooden mask of concentration.

:Hold onto him, son. I'll be leeching a lot of your energy for this. Keep him steady. Nyara is going to have to pull me out a hair at a time.:

He stared at the wound; at the ashen face of what had been Falconsbane. Surely, Need could not save anything this time!

:Hush, fool. I have to Heal it all in my wake, but I can do it. I've Healed worse, once, and I wasn't even awake at the time. 'Course, I did have help. . . .:

He had to close his eyes; a wave of dizziness came over him and did not pass, but only got worse. It felt like that moment, years ago, when he and Cymry had gotten washed over that cliff, and fell, and fell—

He was going to die like this, falling forever!

Panic—

:Chosen—touch me—:

It was Cymry; he caught her presence and held her, even as he was holding Falconsbane—

:An'desha, Chosen. Never Falconsbane again. Don't worry, I can hold you forever, if I must. My strength is yours. Take whatever is there for your own. With you always.:

The dizziness steadied, ebbed, faded. He opened his eyes.

Nyara stood beside him, leaning on the blade, panting as if she had just run for miles. There was no sign of the wound except the dark slit in An'desha's shirt, and the blood soaking into the ground. The chest rose and fell with full, even breaths, and under his hand the pulse was strong and steady. And even as he stared down at the miracle in his arms, the eyes opened, and looked up into his.

Innocent. Vulnerable. Terrified.

And no more Falconsbane's eyes than Nyara's were.

An'desha looked up into the face of the stranger, the one who had been making shadow-gryphons with his fingers, and who now held him carefully, with no sign of the hatred he must feel toward Falconsbane. He looked over at Nyara, who leaned heavily and wearily on a sword but took a moment to smile encouragingly.

They *did* know who and what he was!

And he looked at the sword. Which, he now realized, *was* the old woman.

:You lied to me!: he wailed, as he started to shake, still held in the terror of near-death.

:I never told you I was your Goddess,: came the tart reply. *:I only asked if you trusted Her.:*

Firesong was hot on Falconsbane's trail, flying through the spirit-realms, a silver falcon. The traces faded with preternatural speed, and Firesong poured even more of his own life into tracing Falconsbane back to the little pocket of the Nether Planes where he had made his hiding place, his place of refuge, where death and time could not touch him. Through the swirling colors and chaos of the paths of power, he followed the spark that was Falconsbane, until he watched it dive into a pocket of blackness, an opening into a greater darkness. Small wonder he had not gone mad when trapped in the Gate's greater Void! He had practice, after all, in coping with such things.

Falconsbane reached the shelter of his refuge, fled inside, and sealed it up from within. If you had not seen the rabbit dive into its warren, you would never have noticed it. Clever, clever Falconsbane, to have seen that the Void held all in stasis, and to realize that in the shifting swirls of the paths of power, no one would ever notice a little flaw, a seam, where none should be.

But Firesong *did* know. And what was more, he knew how to get into it.

Death was about to keep a long-overdue appointment with Mornelithe Falconsbane.

He paused for a moment, then allowed himself a grim smile. He *had* told Elspeth and Darkwind that there would be a sign when it was time to attack Ancar. And here was all that energy, so much, in such a tiny and compressed package. Granted, it was blood and death energy, and too tainted for a Healing Adept to actually use. But it would be a shame to get rid of Falconsbane and allow it all to go to waste, drifting back into the currents of energy and fading away. . . .

And fire purified. Wasn't that why his use-name was "Firesong?"

So it was, and it was time to sing. He seized the shelter in fiery hands—talons—of energy.

As he tore open the walls Falconsbane had built, he sensed an instant of surprise, followed by pure panic.

But that was all he allowed time for.

In passion, he took on the aspect of his firebird, and used every last bit of his powers to sink talonlike fingers and sharp, silvery-white beak into Falconsbane, shelter and all, tearing them into motes and ribbons and sparks, flinging them across the sky of Hardorn in a burst of fireworks that would be seen for leagues—

Every mote, every ribbon, every spark, he personally and completely purified with his own soul's fire while he sang in triumphant ecstasy. He wiped it all clean of every sickening memory, every jot of personality, and scattered it far and wide into the bitter night air.

If he ever comes back again, it will be as a cloud of gnats!

Firesong burned away the last little bit of the shelter within the Void, released the magical "ash" of it into the flow of the Void, and then sank back into his own body.

He opened his eyes to find himself on the ground, with Nyara propping him up, and Skif and Fal—no, *An'desha*—staring at him intently. It *was* An'desha; Falconsbane would never, ever have had traces of tears on his cheeks. Falconsbane would never have Nyara's hand resting on his shoulder in a gesture of protective comfort.

It was An'desha who broke the waiting silence, as outside, people still exclaimed over the fading fireworks.

"Is he gone?" An'desha asked tremulously.

Firesong nodded wearily but with immense satisfaction.

An'desha stared at him for a moment, and then, unexpectedly, began weeping again; hoarse, racking sobs of long-pent and terrible grief.

Sobs that sounded uncannily like the ones Liam had made. . . .

Firesong hesitated for a moment. Was there anything he could offer this poor boy? Would he believe comfort coming from another Adept such as his tormentor had been? Yet—oh, how he *wanted* to offer comfort and have it taken!

:*You're a Healing Adept, boy,*: Need reminded him, gruffly. :*But you don't need magic to Heal. Just words. And kindness, and care.*:

Firesong shakily levered himself up off the ground, knelt beside An'desha, and offered his arms tentatively.

An'desha folded into them as into a haven of safety. Firesong cradled the boy carefully, murmuring into his ear.

"It's all right, An'desha. It's all right now. He can never hurt anyone again. You beat him. You are safe now, and we will always be here to help you. *I* will always be here to help you. . . ."

Chapter Seventeen

The sky overhead erupted into a garden of fiery flowers. Darkwind jerked up his head like a startled horse, and he stared at the odd-colored flashes, showers of sparks, and soundless lightning playing across the sky and lighting up the clouds.

"Damned showman," he muttered under his breath. "That 'Pandemonium' persona is rubbing off on him!"

:Time to move, ashke,: he sent to Elspeth, who nodded.

Darkwind was on a horse he'd stolen from the stable of an inn; the horse, if not the current rider, belonged to Ancar's Elite. Elspeth was on Gwena, still cloaked in her illusion. Both of them were in stolen uniforms, with Elspeth's hair tucked up under her uniform hat, and her breasts bound flat, so that she looked like a very slender man. The uniforms hadn't been very difficult to get; there were plenty of troopers getting drunk in the city taverns, and if two of them woke up in the morning to find themselves stark naked, bound and gagged—well, it probably wasn't the first time something like that had happened. And by then, he and Elspeth would either be long gone, or no longer in a position to worry about the consequences of being identified.

He had cobbled together something that looked enough like a messenger pouch to pass at a distance, supposedly containing dispatches from the front lines. That had gotten them as far as the courtyard; they were about to dismount, when the fires in the sky began, and the currents of power around them bucked and heaved like a herd of startled *dyheli*.

To anyone with a scrap of mage-sense, it was distressing. He had never felt quite so violent a disturbance in the energy-currents before.

:Ancar can't possibly miss this!: Elspeth "cried," as they both tried to look as if everything was normal—except for the fireworks, of course—she shouted and pointed upward as all the ordinary people on the walls and in the courtyard were doing. *:And I can feel a mage-storm building* very *fast. People are probably getting nosebleeds all over the city—:* Even now, a huge anvil-shaped cloud was boiling up over the city seemingly from nowhere.

And now every man guarding the walls and the gates, every servant that heard the cries of surprise, and every stableboy came running out to gape at the skies like a parcel of fools. Their cries brought others.

And, unbelievably, *Ancar!*

He could hardly have missed the upheavals in the magic-currents, and given how many spells he had tied into Falconsbane, he must have been knocked metaphorically head-over-arse when they snapped back on him at the Beast's death. But they had never, in all their wildest hopes, imagined he would come running out onto the landing in front of the main doors of his palace like any other fool, just to look up at the sky!

And no one, *no one,* was paying any attention to Elspeth and Darkwind in the middle of the courtyard.

They didn't even pause to think; as one, they drew strung bows and a pair of arrows from the cases on their saddles. As one, they nocked and fired and followed the first arrows with a second, then snatched for a third while the first two were still in the air.

Ancar was a mage; he was likely to be shielded against a magical attack, but not necessarily a physical one ...

So they hoped, anyway. It was the best chance for a physical attack that they were likely to get. Darkwind watched the arrows arc toward the oblivious King and held his breath, not even daring to mutter a prayer for success, his whole being straining after the streaking shafts.

All four arrows hit the edge of a mage-shield set against physical attacks, and disintegrated in a shower of sparks.

Well, that certainly got his attention, he thought fleetingly as Ancar spotted them.

Ancar's eyes slid right over Darkwind and fixed on Elspeth. And even from halfway across the courtyard, there was no doubt in Darkwind's mind that he *recognized* Elspeth. There was an instant of frozen shock, and his lips moved as his eyes widened. *He knew.* Somehow, through disguise and illusion, he knew *who* it was who came to kill him wearing the cold mask of diamond-pure Vengeance. Elspeth was an arrow of justice sped from the hand of the Queen and the bow of Valdemar.

Ancar seemed to go mad then, his eyes blazing with anger. His hands flared up in an instant with blood-red mage-energy. Rather than stunning him, the shock of recognition seemed to galvanize him into sudden action. Darkwind and Elspeth both dropped their useless bows; Darkwind ducked over his horse's neck and kicked free of his stirrups, just as Ancar let fly a mage-bolt that passed through the space where he had been and shattered the pavestones, making Darkwind's stolen horse buck and jump sideways. The Hawkbrother rolled out of the way, shoulder against the hard stone.

Elspeth tumbled in a more controlled manner off Gwena's back. Darkwind reached out an ephemeral "hand" to her; the two of them meshed powers with the ease of long practice, joining shields, just as a second mage-bolt crashed into their united defenses.

They were not given a chance to breathe—bolt after bolt of raw power crashed into them, burning away outer shields and forcing them to devote all of their attention to defenses. . . .

Nor was that all; the death of Falconsbane, the battle, all these had tipped the precarious balance over Hardorn's capital. For too long Ancar and his mages had worked their magics without regard for the world around them, throwing it further and further out of balance.

Now something had thrown it too far, as Firesong had warned might happen. Nature went as berserk as the King.

As Ancar cast his deadly bolts of power, another equally deadly bolt lanced down out of the clouds overhead and struck somewhere in the back of the palace. It hung, shattering the night as it lanced from the skies and lingered, momentarily deafening and blinding them, signaling the worst lightning-storm Darkwind had ever seen. It easily surpassed the storm they had triggered over Ashkevron Manor with their Gate for sheer fury.

Twice, as they bowed beneath the battering of Ancar's mage-bolts, lightning hit the palace itself, setting fires on the roof. Ancar seemed oblivious to it all, intent only on pounding the two of them into red dust on the cobbles of the courtyard.

Then a third bolt struck the doors behind the King. The bolt's thinnest tendrils—enough to split huge trees— licked Ancar's shields, then the charred, exploding doors knocked Ancar to the courtyard itself. It left his clothes singed, but it didn't seem to affect his concentration; he came to his feet immediately and resumed his attack, even as Darkwind was still trying to clear his vision from the flash. Vree and Gwena were nowhere to be seen.

He *could not* imagine where Ancar was getting all this power! The man couldn't be more than a Master—how was he holding off two Adepts?

"He's mad!" Elspeth cried out, as another bolt of lightning struck and exploded the wall above the metal gates, scattering bricks and bodies down onto the pavement below. Another bolt followed it, and by its light, Darkwind caught a good look at Ancar's face.

He realized that she was, literally, right. Ancar had bitten through his own lip and hadn't even noticed. He *was* mad; mad enough to burn himself out, crazed enough not to care, using himself up in a prolonged version of a mage's final strike. What was more, the King was insane enough to use the lightning-power. Darkwind felt his skin prickle, his only warning of a bolt coming in the next instant. He leapt to catch Elspeth's wrist, and jerked her aside only to see a bolt of lightning sear the stones where they had just been.

And Ancar laughed, a high-pitched cackle that held nothing of sanity in it, his eyes so wide that the white showed all around, reflecting hellish-red from the blazing mage-energy of his hands. He pointed his finger at them; this time it was Elspeth who shoved Darkwind, and once again they evaded a lightning-strike by no more than a few arms' lengths.

Ancar pointed again—in the flash of a secondary strike behind him, Darkwind saw all of Ancar's hair standing on end as he absorbed the chaotic power of the storm. His aim was improving with every strike, and this time they were both flat on the ground. They would never get out of the way in time!

Two ghostly shapes moved on the scene. One fell from the sky, pale compared to the lightning, but almost as swift.

Vree!

Gwena reared up out of the shadows of the staircase where she had been hidden. Vree dove at Ancar and struck, clawing the King's face to distract him, tearing huge furrows in his scalp and forehead to keep him from seeing the Companion.

Ancar shrieked with pain and his blazing hands rose to engulf the bird.

Gwena came down on Ancar with all the force of her powerful body behind her forehooves and knocked him to the ground. The bones of his shoulders shattered audibly even above the thunder.

Ancar screamed again, first in pain and anger, then in sheer terror, as he saw the hooves coming down on him where he lay.

A single blow of those silver hooves to his head would have killed him instantly, and with a malicious intent

Darkwind would never have credited if he had not seen it himself, she deliberately avoided such a blow. No—perhaps it was to avoid striking Vree, who struggled from where he'd bound to Ancar's scalp and flapped away, wing-wrenched and upset, but alive. In a frenzy of rage nearly as mad as Ancar's, Gwena trampled him, dancing on him with all four hooves until the screaming stopped, and he was nothing more than red pulp seeping into flagstones.

:That!: Her mind-voice was a scream, and she was still pounding the inert meat with her wet, red hooves. *:That! That's for Talia! That's for Kris! That's for—:*

"Laugh now, horse!" came a shout from the palace, and a mage-bolt took Gwena in the side, lifting her right off the ground with the force. Gwena hit the ground, hooves slipping beneath her, and landed on her side with a *thud.*

Darkwind's gaze snapped up, to the balcony above the doors.

Hulda!

That was the only person it could be, even though the woman was dressed in servants' livery, and was as wild-eyed as Ancar had been.

"Go ahead and laugh at *this*—" the woman cried, raising her hands for another blow. Darkwind erected hasty shields over Gwena, who moved her legs feebly and flailed her head as she tried to rise.

Behind Hulda, a man grabbed her arm, distracting her for a moment. "Don't be a fool!" he shouted in oddly-accented Hardornen over the roar of the thunder. "We have to get out of here! Leave these idiots!"

She pulled away from him and started to build power for another attack—but once again he pulled her away, this time succeeding in drawing her back inside.

Darkwind was *not* going to let her escape—and there was no sign that anyone was going to interfere at this point. The mage-storms and lightning had driven everyone out of the courtyard and off the walls.

He scrambled to his feet and ran up to the sundered stairs, then hooked his fingers around stonework, climbing to reach the balcony. *:Go!:* he shouted at Elspeth, *:Get inside and cut them off from below!:*

This kind of climb was nothing to a Tayledras. As Elspeth dashed into the doors below him, his hand reached the balcony itself, and he pulled himself up and over the railing.

And just as he burst into the ravaged room, he felt the unmistakable shivering in the power-currents of someone building a Gate nearby. . . .

They had all studied the plans of Ancar's palace until they could have walked the place blindfolded. Elspeth remembered a stair going right up into the hallway above, just inside the main doors. The place was deserted; everyone had either gone off to fight the fires or fled in terror when the mage-battle began. She ran up the stairs two at a time, and as she reached the top and the corridor that it led to, she heard the sound of a fight on the other side of the second door along the corridor.

She didn't stop to think; she just gathered power and blasted, disintegrating the door and running through the hole while the dust was still raining down.

And she stumbled to a halt as she hit something that felt like a web, a net that closed around her in a heartbeat and held her immobile.

But her eyes still worked, and the very first thing she saw, by the white light of pure power, was the man that had pulled Hulda inside.

The man, who bore a distinctive device on his tunic— *Dear gods—the Emperor's envoy!*—

—was building a *Gate!* He already had the framework up. He wasn't even using a real door as his anchor, he was simply building the thing in midair!

How much of what's happened has been his *doing?*

Darkwind knelt on the floor, beside the shattered doors to the balcony, cringing beneath his shields as Hulda rained blow after fiery blow down on him. So far, Hulda hadn't even noticed *her*. The hinged splinters of the balcony doors slammed against the wall, as the rainless mage-storm raged outside, whitening the room in flashes from the lightning. Thunder roared, drowning out any other sounds, and smoke crept in the window from the fires outside.

Elspeth fought the bonds that held her, frantically seeking a weak spot.

Suddenly, the darkness in the Gate brightened—and became a hole in the air, a hole leading to a brightly-lit room somewhere, filled with furnishings in a sinuous style Elspeth had never seen before.

The man turned toward Hulda. "Are you coming?" he snarled. "Or are you enjoying yourself too much to leave?"

Elspeth realized his lips had not moved with his words. He had projected them in open Mindspeech so strong that anyone, Gifted or not, would have Heard him. As his attention wavered for a moment, split between the Gate and Hulda, so did the bonds holding her. She freed one hand, and shook a knife from her sleeve down into it—her old, reliable, predictable, *material* knives. *No pottery to hurl this time. . . .*

As Hulda turned to answer him, Elspeth cast the knife, knowing that if the envoy went down, the Gate would go with him.

He was not expecting a physical attack; the knife caught him in the throat. It buried itself to the hilt. Blood spurted from a severed artery, a fountain of ebony-red in the hellish white light. The envoy's face convulsed; both hands clutched at his throat. He staggered backward, across the threshold, and through the Gate itself.

The Gate collapsed as he fell through it.

The bonds holding her faded away. And *now* Hulda saw her.

There was no recognition in Hulda's eyes, but there was plenty of pure rage.

Elspeth readied a mage-bolt of her own, but Hulda was faster. And Hulda was trapped, with nowhere to escape to; Darkwind was between her and the balcony, Elspeth was between her and the hallway. So she fought with all the desperate strength of any cornered creature, and with the stores of energy she had drained from the land of Hardorn for all these past years. . . .

She was an Adept, easily the equivalent of Falconsbane—and she was not handicapped by having an agent in her own mind, or by a disintegrating personality.

Within moments, Elspeth knew with rising panic that stole her breath that she was in trouble, trying to hold eroded shields against a barrage of mage winds, each of them geared to a specific energy, that began to eat their way down through her protections. They circled her in a whirlwind that caught up papers, bits of wood, shattered glass, and other debris, pelting her with physical as well as magical weapons.

But panic made her mind clearer, and a sudden memory matched the whirlwind. *Firesong—the lesson—*

She spun her shields until they mated with the whirlwinds; then reached through them, and began to absorb the energies of the attack into her own. But the instant Hulda realized that she had found a counter, the woman set the winds on Darkwind, and attacked Elspeth with—

Demons!

Creatures of shadow and teeth boiled up from the floor, and a hundred taloned hands reached for her. Fear sent arcs of cold down her limbs. Elspeth backpedaled and came up against the wall; for a moment, she was lost in panic. She had no counter to *this*—

Panicked, until in the next heartbeat, she remembered that these might be illusions. Illusions vanished if challenged! She pulled her sword, forgotten until now, and swung.

The "demons" vanished without a sound. Hulda then flung a wall of fire at her. Her confidence increased. *This* she could handle! Perhaps Hulda was not so formidable after all!

She countered it by absorbing it—took another step toward the woman—

And then Hulda recognized her. "You! The Brat!"

"The *Adept*," Elspeth screamed back defiantly. "Your better, bitch!"

Hulda's reply was drowned out by another thunderclap; there was a trace of real fear in her eyes, and her face was like a stone mask. Elspeth laughed hysterically. Hulda was *afraid!* Afraid of *her!* They could take the bitch, they could!

But Hulda evidently decided that if *she* was doomed, she would take her enemies with her.

Hulda reached out with her powers in a thrust that knocked Elspeth back into the wall again, and with great shudders of power that shook her body as they shook the walls, she began to tear the building down around them.

The walls and ceiling screamed with the shrieks of tortured stone and wood. Elspeth dodged a falling chandelier that brought a quarter of the ceiling down with it—

—just in time to see Darkwind falling beneath the outer wall, going down under a cascade of stone and burning wall-maps that buried him completely in an instant.

"*No!*" she screamed, reaching for him with mind, heart, and powers, forgetting her own peril—

Only to receive, not an answer, but a flood of energy. Energy that felt—final, as if it was all he had.

Her heart convulsed, but her body acted.

She shook her arm and felt her other knife fall into her hand. She screamed again, a wordless howl of rage and anguish; invested every last bit of power in the second knife—and threw it.

The knife cut through the air and ripped through Hulda's shields.

Hulda collapsed in a boneless heap, her howling winds collapsing at the same instant, leaving behind an echoing silence filled only by thunder, and the crunch of an occasional brick falling. A glittering knife-hilt shone from her left eye socket.

She was dead, but she had taken Darkwind with her.

Elspeth turned and stared at the heap of broken stones, her throat choked with grief so all-consuming that she could not think, could not even weep. She stumbled a step or two toward the pile—

And Vree came winging in out of the darkness, through the gaping, broken wall. He landed beside the stones, and hopped over to them—to the only part of Darkwind that she could see, his hand. He nibbled the fingers, as if to try to coax life into them, and Elspeth's grief overflowed into scalding tears that blurred her vision. Her throat closed, and she sobbed, then moaned with pain.

He was gone. She was alone. Hulda had won, after all. His loss was an ache that would never be healed.

:Damn . . . bird.: A whisper in her mind.
What?
:Elspeth . . . ashke . . . .:

Grief turned to hysterical joy, all in a heartbeat. He was alive!

She shook her head, frantically wiping at her eyes to clear them, then ran to the pile of stones and began to pull them off of him. Vree hopped excitedly beside her, making odd creaking sounds, as she managed to clear his head and shoulders of debris.

He looked terrible; bruised and bleeding from a dozen small cuts, and she trembled to think how many bones might be broken. But he was alive!

:Gods.: He opened his eyes for a moment, then closed them. *:I feel . . . awful. Like . . . a wall . . . just fell on me.:*

Her heart overflowing, she resumed pulling stones from his body, ignoring splitting nails and sharp edges that cut her hands, thankful that the winds had snuffed out the earlier fires. Finally she came to a thick slab of wood—a strategic map, showing invasion plans. A map of Valdemar.

It had protected Darkwind from the heaviest of the stones, prevented his lungs and ribs from being crushed. Paint flaked from the board as she twisted it free of him, and troop-counters fell like rain from the "Losses" box she found propping up one end of it. She kept having to shake her head to clear her eyes of tears as she pulled debris away from him, trying to figure out how badly he *had* been hurt.

:Wait. Check Gwena. . . .: he began, his thoughts coming to her from a haze of generalized pain.

:No need,: Gwena said weakly. *:I'm going to live. And there's no one down here to bother me while I decide if I still want to. No bones broken, I don't think—some burns, and bruises that go to the bone. Keep him from fading, I'll call Cymry. And you send Vree for him, in case I can't reach him!:*

Although that was somewhat confused, Elspeth had no trouble figuring out which "he" Gwena meant. *:Vree,:* she said intently, turning to the falcon, concentrating on trying to impress him with her urgency. *:Vree, we need Skif. Find Skif. Bring him here quickly!:*

Vree bobbed his head once, then nibbled Darkwind's finger, spread his wings, and flapped heavily off into the darkness again.

:He's ... a horrible night flyer, ashke. *Hope he ... doesn't hit anything.:*

"Just stay with me," she said aloud, fiercely, starting with that hand to check for broken bones, since it was the piece of him least likely to cause problems if she accidentally moved it. Or held it. "Don't pass out on me."

:I'll try. . . .:

"Stop that!" she snapped, still rubbing away tears. "Stay awake, stop fading! Or—or I'll tell you Hawkbrother jokes! How many Hawkbrothers does it take for a mating circle?"

:No ... not that ... anything but that. . . .:

"Only one, but he has to be flexible!"

:I'm doomed. . . .:

When Skif arrived, he brought Nyara and Need with him, and his expression betrayed his relief at finding the situation nowhere near as desperate as he had feared from Gwena's weak Mindcall. He told Elspeth that he'd seen worse injuries than Darkwind's out in the field, when miners or builders had been trapped under collapsing walls. Darkwind would not only live, he would do so with all organs and limbs intact. . . .

That gave her some measure of comfort and calmed her shattered nerves a little. And although at some point she would be mad with impatience to hear his side of the story, and the confrontation with Falconsbane, at the moment there was enough on her plate to worry about. They still had to get out of here.

They laid Need down beside Darkwind with his hand on the hilt—she complaining the whole time that she had done enough Healing for one day—and carefully lifted the last of the stones from Darkwind's back and legs. By the time they finished, people were drifting back into the palace, and coming to stare curiously at the wreckage in the room.

But Elspeth and Darkwind still wore their purloined uniforms, and when Elspeth turned and barked "Out!" at the onlookers, they quickly found something else to do.

They limped their way out of the building without being stopped, carrying Darkwind on the map that had saved him, using it as a stretcher. Skif did pause long enough to look down at Hulda and make a *tsk*ing sound.

"A knife," he sighed. "How—predictable."

She thought about hitting him, but she was just too weary—mentally, emotionally, and physically.

He reached down for the offending object, cleaning it on his none-too-clean sleeve and handed it back to her. "Where's the other one?" he asked, as she slipped it into her arm sheath and pulled her sleeve back down over it.

"In the throat of the Eastern Envoy—who is, I suppose, back in his Master's domain," she replied. "He was building a Gate, I got him with the knife, and he fell through it."

Another curious onlooker peeked in the door but vanished before she could even snarl at him.

"Falling dead, with a knife bearing the crest of Valdemar on the pommel-nut," he said dryly. "Very subtle, Elspeth. Couldn't you have sent a more direct message to the Emperor? Like, perhaps, 'Your father won the Horse Faire. Your mother tracks rabbits by scent. Love and kisses, Elspeth of Valdemar.' "

A bit of the ceiling dropped, breaking the silence, followed by the sound of someone picking his way across the floor upstairs. She growled at him, at the end of her patience. "I didn't exactly have much choice," she pointed out. "And if we're going to get out of here before someone names us the assassins of the King, we'd better move now!"

"A good point," he acknowledged, and picked up his end of the board holding Darkwind. "Need—Gwena's rather handicapped at the moment. I don't suppose—"

:*Gods. Can't you people do anything for yourselves?*:

"We are not Healers," Nyara pointed out sweetly. "You are."

:*Right. Bring logic into this.*: Elspeth could have

sworn that the sword sighed. :*All right. Bring on the horses.*:

:*I am not*—: Gwena snapped, :*a horse!*:

Skif helped Darkwind up into Cymry's saddle. Gwena's worst injuries were mostly to muscle, and easily within Need's purview; Darkwind's to bone, which took several days to Heal, and the best Need could do was set them and hold them in place. With Gwena Healed enough to carry her own weight, Elspeth elected to put Darkwind on Cymry's back and walk, with her on one side, steadying him, and Nyara on the other.

"I'll catch up with you," Skif told them. "You get back to the carnival and warn everyone that—let's see—" He thought quickly. "Falconsbane and Hulda tried to kill Ancar; he got both of them, but not before they called up a demon that mashed him to a pulp. Anyway, tell them all that, and tell them it's going to be hell around here when everyone realizes all three top people are gone. They may want to get out."

"They may want to stay and loot," Elspeth pointed out, tilting her head at the number of people trickling out of the palace carrying things—and the growing stream going in, unhindered by threat of fire, lightning, or remaining guards.

He shrugged. "Doesn't bother me; they'll just be getting back some of what Ancar's been taking, indirectly. There's just a few things of Ancar's I want to make sure don't survive."

Elspeth looked at him curiously, one hand on Darkwind's leg, supporting him. "What, documents? How could you know where—" Then she shook her head. "Never mind. I don't want to know how you know. We'll get ourselves ready for fast travel and meet you at the camp."

Cymry started forward, through what was left of the main gates. Gwena limped along behind.

Skif took himself into the palace.

By the time he slipped back out of the doors, there were people looting already—running through the hall, grabbing whatever they could carry, and dashing back out again. Most of those people wore the uniforms of Ancar's Elite Guard, which didn't surprise him in the least. None of them offered any kind of hindrance to him, once they saw *he* wasn't carrying any choice bits of loot. And every once in a while, he saw one of the political prisoners or kidnapped girls he'd just freed from the dungeons making for the city, some bauble or valuable in hand.

Behind him, one room and all its contents were burning merrily. One more small fire among the other three or four started by the lightning, anyone would assume. It was likely that looters would add to those fires before the night was over.

He stopped long enough at the royal stables to steal a pair of strong, fast horses, and a small carriage; they'd need both for An'desha and Darkwind. Some of the stable hands seemed to have had the same idea, for the really fine horseflesh and the royal carriages were all gone. As an afterthought, he stopped long enough in the courtyard to pitch a kind of souvenir into the back of the wagon he'd appropriated—the map that had saved Darkwind. He thought Elspeth would like to have it.

And as he passed through the gates, he was already making plans for the fastest route out, one that passed through the fewest number of towns that might hold garrisons. Getting to the border was going to be tricky.

Getting across was going to be even more fun. . . .

Maybe we ought to see if old Firesong has one more trick in him. Or maybe Elspeth? A Gate into Valdemar would be damned useful about now. . . .

Pires Nieth settled himself gingerly into Ancar's throne. To say that he was exhausted was understating the case, but he dared not allow that to show. He had only taken control of the chaotic situation by the thinnest of margins, and only because the commanders of the Elite were more afraid of mages than they were greedy. His illusions of demons alone had been enough to convince them that he held all the power of his late master; if he'd had to produce more than illusions, he'd have been in desperate trouble.

Fortunately, the commanders had taken the illusion for the real thing, and had brought *their* men back under control. Now the palace was completely cleared of looters, the city was rapidly being pacified, and *he* was the man who was going to inherit Ancar's rather damaged crown. Once anyone thought to contest him for it, well, it would be too late.

Hardorn was not what it had been—but it was more than he had ever owned before.

The throne was mostly intact, a few semiprecious stones missing. The throne-room itself was smoke-stained and bore the muddy footprints of looters. But it was still a throne and an audience chamber, and there were plenty of servants to repair both.

Oh, you've done very well by yourself, Pires, he congratulated himself as his cowed and frightened sheep—ah, *courtiers and mages*—gathered to pay him their homage officially. *You have done very well by yourself, and all by being clever, watching everything, knowing when to play your hand—*

A commotion at the end of the room made him frown. The courtiers swirled like little fish disturbed by the passing of a larger, hungry fish. What now?

A battered and disheveled messenger came pushing through the crowd, his eyes wild, his face sweat- and dirt-streaked. "The border!" he panted, frantically. "An attack on the border!"

Damn—the Valdemarans—well, I have no quarrel with them, I can simply make a truce— "What are the Valdemarans doing?" he asked. "Who's the commander in charge? How quickly can he retreat from—"

"Not the *western* border!" the man wailed. "The *eastern* border! The towers just relayed a message from the eastern border! There's an army there, a *huge* army, it outnumbers us by a hundred to one, and it's rolling over *everything!*"

It was at this time that Pires Nieth realized his throne might not be valuable for very much longer. And he tried to think of who he could go to that would trade Ancar's flattened crown for a fast horse.

* * *

Treyvan mantled his wings over the youngsters, cradling gryphlet and human alike. The salle was warm and bright, but the little ones took no notice of the sunlight, nor of the toys piled all around them. All four were distressed, for all four knew that their parents were going away, and where they were going, people got hurt.

He was making soothing little sounds, when suddenly his feathers all stood on end, and he felt the unique trembling in the forces of magic that signaled a Gate forming in this very room.

His first thought was that Falconsbane had found a way to build a Gate here, to attack the children. He shoved them all behind him, turning with foreclaws outstretched, building his shields and his powers to strike at anything that struck at him. His action took the two Heralds on guard entirely by surprise, but they reacted with the speed of superbly-trained fighters, drawing their weapons and facing the direction he faced.

A haze of power shimmered in the doorway to the salle. Then—the door vanished, to be replaced by a meadow of sad, yellowed grasses—

A meadow?

And Firesong and Elspeth came stumbling through, followed by Nyara and Skif, the *dyheli,* the birds, and the two Companions, one of whom carried Darkwind on her back, and dragged a slab of wood. The other Companion carried someone else, wrapped up in so much cloth as to be unidentifiable.

The Gate came down immediately. So did Firesong, collapsing where he stood. Darkwind looked none too good either.

"Get a Healerrrr!" Treyvan snapped; one of the Heralds sheathed her blade and took off at a dead run before he even finished the sentence. The other joined him at Firesong's side.

"What happened?" the young man demanded. "Is—"

"We got Falconsbane, Ancar, and Hulda, in that order, yesterday," Elspeth replied, helping Darkwind down off Gwena's back. "All hell broke loose over there. We'll probably see the effects of it on the border, in a day or a week, depending on if anyone thinks to use the relay-towers to get word to the front lines. There was rioting in the city as we left, and we traveled just long enough for Firesong to get back the strength to Gate us home. The unrest was spreading faster than we could move."

"What isss the wood?"

Darkwind chuckled weakly, still clearly in some pain. "A trophy. A lifesaver of a trophy."

Just then, the first Herald returned with not one, but three Healers, and right behind them were Selenay and Prince Daren and their bodyguards, followed by a runner from one of the Valdemaran relay-towers. It looked as if the man had been bringing an urgent message, had seen the Queen and her consort running like *dyheli* for the salle, and had followed them instead of going to the Palace.

He nearly got skewered by the bodyguards until he flung up both hands, showing himself weaponless, and panted out, "Message from the border!"

"Ten to one it's starting—" Treyvan heard Skif mutter to Nyara, who nodded wisely, as she aided the unknown down from the second Companion's saddle. He, she, or it also simply slumped down to the floor, but not until Firesong had gotten to his (her?) side with one of the Healers.

Skif was right. The message from the border was of chaos.

Some of Ancar's army—the Elite—continued to attack. Most were fleeing. Even Ancar's mages were no longer a factor, for they were actually fighting among *themselves*.

"We need to get out there," Selenay said, immediately. "All of us. Companion-back it shouldn't take that long."

Elspeth shook her head. "I'm still in good shape, Mother. I can build a Gate for you. The only reason Firesong brought us here was because of the distance; it isn't even half that far to Landon Castle, and that should be right near the front." She grinned wanly. "I certainly saw enough of *that* place the last time Ancar hit us to put a Gate in the chapel door."

"Done," Selenay said instantly, and turned to Treyvan. He waved a claw at her. "Fearrr not, Lady. We shall be rrrready. Hydona and I can deal with sssuch magessss asss may get thisss farrr."

"Be here in a candlemark with whoever and whatever you want to take with you," Elspeth said, and looked at Darkwind. "I should go, too."

Selenay shook her head. "No, love, not really. Daren and I will go because there will be decisions on what must be done with Hardorn, but now—this is hardly more than a matter of cleaning up."

Darkwind nodded agreement. "The danger will not be to you. The dangers are all in a disorderly retreat, to keep the forces from hurting each other. Your people know you; you are the one in charge. And they no longer need an Adept out there."

"My thoughtsss exactly." Treyvan nodded.

Selenay was not going to waste time or words; she and Daren hurried back out, trailed by guards, messengers, and Heralds.

Selenay and Daren returned with their Companions, all armed and provisioned, and a guard of six Heralds and six Royal Guardsmen. They were ready, Elspeth was ready—Treyvan was very proud of his young human pupil, who was showing her true mettle. He gently reminded her of how the Gate Spell worked, and stood ready to guide her "hands."

Elspeth took *her* place before the salle doors to create her very first Gate.

Treyvan watched her with the critical eye of a teacher but could find nothing to criticize. She had not needed his aid at all; she had done her work flawlessly. The portal filled with the image of a dark, ill-lit, stone-walled room.

"That old miser never will buy enough candles to light that great barn properly," Selenay muttered, covering her amazement with the rather flippant remark. Treyvan thought it rather brave of her, when she did not ask "Is it safe?" but rather, "Is everything ready?"

A chorus of "ayes" answered her, and the Queen herself, with her Companion, was the first one through the Gate. Two by two, the entourage went through.

Elspeth dissolved the Gate—and sat down herself, abruptly. Treyvan was expecting it, however, and helped her to sit, waving away the Healer who had been tending Firesong. "It isss wearrrinesss, only," he assured the woman. "Gate-enerrrgy."

He bent over Elspeth. *:Silly child,:* he chided, mind-to-mind. *:You have all of the Heartstone to regain your energies! Use it! Firesong assuredly is!:*

:Oh,: she replied sheepishly. *:I—ah—forgot.:*

And only then did the Healer tending the unknown persuade her (him?) to remove the cloak swathing his face and body.

Treyvan flashed into "kill" stance, shoving the youngsters behind him with his outstretched wings.

:Falconsbane!:

Then, before anyone could do or say anything, he looked deeply into the creature's eyes and saw there, not the ages-old tyrant, but a young and vulnerable boy.

He relaxed, flattening his feathers, and tucking his wings in with a flip. "Ssso," he said, "And who isss thiss, that wearrrsss the body of ourrr old foe?"

It was Firesong who answered, with one hand protectively on the boy's shoulder. "This is An'desha, old friend. And—"

:And he has earned more than the reward he sought.:

The mental voice boomed through his head, resonating in his bones. Every feather on Treyvan's body stood on end, as he felt the stirrings of energies deeper and stranger than the local mage-currents. Light filled the room, a warm and sourceless light as bright as sunlight on a summer day. A faint scent of sun-warmed grasses wafted across the salle—

The light collected behind An'desha; more light formed into an identical column behind a very startled Nyara. The columns of light spread huge, fiery wings over the two; Treyvan's skin tingled and Darkwind and Firesong gasped.

:These twain have given selflessly. It is the will of the Warrior that what was stolen from them be returned.:

A female voice this time—and Darkwind reached toward the pillar of light behind Nyara as if he recognized it, and soundlessly mouthed a name. Treyvan realized that, no, these were not winged columns of golden light, but a pair of huge golden birds, shining so brightly that Treyvan squinted and the humans' eyes watered. But the birds had human eyes—eyes as black as night, but spangled with stars.

:*So let the balance be restored.*: Both voices called, in glorious harmony, a peal of trumpets, the cry of hawks—

The light flared, and Treyvan cried out involuntarily, blinded, deafened, able to see only the light and hear only the joined and wordless song of those two voices, which went on, and on—

And was, as suddenly, gone.

He blinked, his beak still agape. The light was gone, and with it the two huge hawks of light—

Then his beak gaped even farther as he looked down at what had been An'desha/Mornelithe.

A young, bewildered, and clearly *human* man sat there now; as he looked up in shock and wonder at Treyvan, his golden skin betrayed his Shin'a'in blood, although his golden-brown hair spoke of an outClan parent somewhere. His eyes were still green-gold and slitted like a cat's, and there was still a feline cast to his features; his build was still powerful and his fingernails still talonlike—but no one would ever look askance at him in a crowd now.

Treyvan looked quickly to Nyara, who was staring at An'desha, and saw that similar changes had been made to her. She looked down at her hands, at skin that no longer bore a coat of sleek, short fur—and burst into tears.

It took a while for Skif and Treyvan to understand her distress, and longer for Skif to persuade Nyara that he still *would* love her now that she was no longer so exotic. Treyvan advised the blade Need to stay out of it; wisely, she did.

An'desha was simply overjoyed. He had never expected to look human again—he had only wanted *a* body back, not necessarily the original body Mornelithe had taken. It was from him that they learned what the two fiery birds were—"Avatars of the Shin'a'in Warrior"—and who—"A shaman of my people, Tre'valen, and his lady, Dawnfire."

Darkwind nodded as if he had expected something of the sort; he and Elspeth shared a warm and secret smile of pleasure. Firesong looked as if he had gotten a revelation from the gods. The gryphlets and children, who had been quiet witnesses to all of this, simply watched with wide, delighted eyes.

Finally, they packed themselves back up to the palace, silent, awestruck youngsters and all. Treyvan was simply afire by then with impatience. "I *mussst* know!" he exclaimed as they settled into the gryphons' rooms, and another small army of Healers and servants descended on them. "I ssssee that thisss An'desssha isss not Falconsssbane, but how, *how,* did he become Falconsssbane? Orrrr did Falconsssbane become him?"

Firesong had his arm about the young man's shoulders, in a gesture both protective and proprietary. "Falconsbane became him, old bird," the Adept replied. "And how he got there is a very, very, long story."

:A long story? A long story?: Rris came bounding up at last, dashing in from the hallway, ears and tail high. *:Knowledge is good! History is better! Tell me! Tell me all!:*

Treyvan grinned to himself. Once the *kyree* discovered what he had missed witnessing, they were never going to hear the last of it!

Firesong laughed tiredly; An'desha stared at the *kyree* in utter fascination, and Treyvan only shook his head and sighed at Rris' unbounded enthusiasm.

"We will have time enough to tell you all you wish, Rris," Firesong said. "An'desha and Darkwind and I are the most weary of this company, and I think—"

"If you think that we're going to order the lot of you to stay here and recover, you're right!" snapped one of the Healers. "You're in no shape to go haring around on a battlefield." He turned back to An'desha, muttering something about "Heralds."

"Well, Rris," Elspeth said with a smile, getting up off the floor to go sit with Darkwind. She leaned gingerly into his shoulder, "It looks as if you're going to have a of us at your disposal for some time."

:*Yes!*: Rris replied, bounding in place. :*Yes! I will make histories of all of it!*: And he abruptly settled, fixed Darkwind with his direct and intelligent gaze, and demanded, :*Now. You, Darkwind. Begin at the beginning, and leave nothing out.*:

Darkwind slowly picked up the battered map of Valdemar and threatened Rris with it.

Elspeth burst into laughter, laughing until tears came to her eyes. "Don't kill him, *ashke;* he's a Bard and has immunity here."

"Impudence, you mean," Darkwind muttered. Then smiled, and gently put the map back down.

"It all began," he said, as if he were a master storyteller, "on the day we left home."

Rris cocked his head to one side, curiously. :*K'Sheyna?*: he asked, puzzled.

"No," Darkwind replied, his eyes on Elspeth and not the *kyree.* "Home. Valdemar."

Treyvan thought that the blinding light of the Avatars could never be matched. But it was challenged and eclipsed then, by the light in Elspeth's eyes.

Author's Note

No one works in a vacuum; a creation can only reach people with the help of more than merely the creator. In the case of a book, the reader seldom sees all those people, often never knows that they exist.

At DAW Books, it all began with tireless First Reader, Peter Stampfel, a fine musician in his own right (catch him and his group, the Bottle Caps, when you're in New York). He is the man who reads hundreds, if not thousands, of manuscripts every year and picks out those he thinks the editors would like to see. One of the ones he picked out was *Arrows of the Queen,* for which I owe him eternal gratitude.

Then comes Editor in Chief, Elizabeth Wollheim, whose critique has made what had been good books into much, much better books, and who also has taken the courageous steps of publishing a trilogy with a *shaych* hero and of putting illustrations back into books. No one could ever want a better editor; no one could ever have an editor who was easier to work with. Without her, Valdemar would never have been what it has become. Without her, I would not be the writer I am today. A good writer never stops learning, and I could have no better teacher than Elizabeth Wollheim.

Also entering the fray, in the times when Betsy was juggling too many red-hot pokers to manage another, is Sheila Gilbert. This is the lady who has been bringing you the fine work of Tanya Huff as well.

Of course I can't fail to mention Elsie Wollheim and her late husband Don, without whom there would not be a DAW Books, and very likely would not be a Heralds of Valdemar series. Elsie and Don discovered far too many science fiction talents to ever list here, and with their unfailing honesty and determination to "do right" by their writers, have won the admiration and love of so many of us.

The stalwart centurion of the copy editing line, Paula Greenberg, makes certain that all my capitalizations and spellings match and imparts as much consistency as anyone can to someone as chaotic as I am.

The patient Joe Schaumburger ensures that none of us forget anything, keeping track of it all, occasionally proofreading, reminding us that we haven't sent our proof corrections, and a million other things, all at once. I can only conclude he has a monumental memory, as well as a charming personality, and it is always a pleasure to hear from him.

Out in the "field" are all the booksellers—the independents, who start so many careers, and the chains, who nourish careers. We have the American Bookseller's Association to thank for the fact that there is scarcely a town in the United States that does not have a bookstore, which was *not* the case when I was a youngster. We have the ABA to thank for crusading tirelessly against those who would have books taken off the shelves, censored, and banned.

And we have the American Librarians' Association, who make certain that those who can't afford to buy *all* the books they want can still read them!

On the home front, I have my personal set of High Flight folks to thank, and very first and foremost is Larry Dixon. A talented artist and writer, he also is my "first editor"; everything he has touched has always been immeasurably better for it. He is the best partner anyone could want; he has also become my husband which makes it even better! Interestingly, we began with a working relationship, he as artist, I as writer. It was a collaboration begun the first weekend we met, called "Ties Never Binding." It evolved into the "Winds" trilogy.

Another co-writer, Mark Shepherd, is our secretary in addition to being my protégé. He is the one who keeps track of fan mail, release-forms for fan-fiction, insurance papers, correspondence, schedules, and all the rest. Without his help, we would be in a far greater mess than we are!

And riding tail-guard at the Aerie is Victor Wren, Larry's assistant and computer guru extraordinaire. It is Victor's expertise that makes it possible for us to bring you the images you have seen in this book; Larry's pencil drawings are scanned into their computer imaging system, Larry and Victor retouch them there, add special effects, then print them out as camera-ready halftones.

We have had the help of fellow wildlife rehabbers, fellow members of NAFA (North American Falconry Association), and others who devote themselves to preserving the wild for future generations.

There are our friends in the field—Andre Norton, Marion Zimmer Bradley, Anne McCaffrey, Ellen Guon, Holly Lisle, Josepha Sherman, Martin Greenberg, Mike Resnick, Judith Tarr, Esther Friesner, Lisa Waters, Ru Emerson, Tanya Huff, Elizabeth Moon, C.J. Cherryh, Terri Lee, Nancy Asire, and many others.

Last, and surely the best, are the fans. "Herald House-Mother," Judith Louvis, who runs the fan club "Queen's Own," all of the editors and contributors of the fanzines, the folk in "Queen's Own Online—Modems of the Queen" on GEnie, and all of you who have enjoyed these stories and keep asking for more. This is a heartfelt acknowledgment and sincere thanks to all of you. We will be writing of Heralds and Companions, Shin'a'in, Tayledras, and Kaled'a'in, the past and future of Valdemar—oh yes, and the Eastern Empire—for as long as you care to read the stories.

Zhai'helleva!
Mercedes Lackey

Mercedes Lackey

The Novels of Valdemar

THE MAGE WARS (with Larry Dixon)
- [ ] THE BLACK GRYPHON (hardcover0   (UE2577—$22.00)

THE LAST HERALD-MAGE
- [ ] MAGIC'S PAWN: Book 1   UE2352—$4.99
- [ ] MAGIC'S PROMISE: Book 2   UE2401—$4.99
- [ ] MAGIC'S PRICE: Book 3   UE2426—$4.99

VOWS AND HONOR
- [ ] THE OATHBOUND: Book 1   UE2285—$4.99
- [ ] OATHBREAKERS: Book 2   UE2319—$4.99

KEROWYN'S TALE
- [ ] BY THE SWORD   UE2463—$5.99

THE HERALDS OF VALDEMAR
- [ ] ARROWS OF THE QUEEN: Book 1   UE2378—$4.09
- [ ] ARROW'S FLIGHT: Book 2   UE2377—$4.99
- [ ] ARROW'S FALL: Book 3   UE2400—$4.99

THE MAGE WINDS
- [ ] WINDS OF FATE: Book 1 (hardcover)   UE2489—$18.95
- [ ] WINDS OF FATE: Book 1 (paperback)   UE2516—$4.99
- [ ] WINDS OF CHANGE: Book 2 (hardcover)   UE2534—$20.00
- [ ] WINDS OF CHANGE: Book 2 (paperback)   UE2563—$4.99
- [ ] WINDS OF FURY: Book 3 (hardcover)   UE2562—$20.00
- [ ] WINDS OF FURY: Book 3 (paperback)   UE2612—$4.99

THE MAGE STORMS
- [ ] STORM WARNING: Book 1 (hardcover)   UE2611—$21.95

DAW

A note from the publishers concerning:

QUEEN'S OWN

You are invited to join "Queen's Own," an organization of readers and fans of the works of Mercedes (Misty) Lackey. This appreciation society has a worldwide membership of all ages. Nominal dues are charged.

"Queen's Own" publishes a newsletter 9 times a year, providing information about Mercedes Lackey's upcoming books, tapes, convention appearances, and more. A network of pen friends is also available for those who wish to share their enjoyment of her work.

For more information, please send a business-size SASE (self-addressed stamped envelope) to:

"Queen's Own"
P.O. Box 132
Shiloh, NJ 08353

(This notice is inserted gratis as a service to readers. DAW Books is in no way connected with this organization professionally or commercially.)

Melanie Rawn

THE DRAGON PRINCE NOVELS

☐ **DRAGON PRINCE: Book 1**   UE2450—$5.99
He was the Dragon Lord, Rohan, prince of the desert, ruler of the kingdom granted his family for as long as the Long Sands spewed fire. She was the Sunrunner Witch, Sioned, fated by Fire to be Rohan's bride. Together, they must fight desperately to save the last remaining dragons, and with them, a secret which might be the salvation of their people. . . .

☐ **THE STAR SCROLL: Book 2**   UE2349—$5.99
As Pol, prince, Sunrunner and son of High Prince Rohan, grew to manhood, other young men were being trained for a bloody battle of succession, youths descended from the former High Prince Roelstra, whom Rohan had killed. Yet not all players in these power games fought with swords. For now a foe vanquished ages ago was once again growing in strength—a foe determined to destroy Sunrunners and High Prince alike. And the only hope of defeating this foe lay concealed in the long-lost Star Scroll.

☐ **SUNRUNNER'S FIRE: Book 3**   UF2403—$5.99
It was the Star Scroll: the last repository of forgotten spells, the only surviving records of the ancient foe who had nearly destroyed the Sunrunners. Now the long-vanquished enemy is mobilizing to strike again. And soon it will be hard to tell friend from foe as spell wars to set the land ablaze, and even the dragons soar the skies, inexorably lured by magic's fiery call.

THE DRAGON STAR NOVELS

☐ **STRONGHOLD: Book 1**   UE2482—$5.99
☐ **STRONGHOLD: Book 1** HARDCOVER   UE2440—$21.95
☐ **THE DRAGON TOKEN: Book 2**   UE2542—$5.99
☐ **THE DRAGON TOKEN: Book 2** HARDCOVER   UE2493—$22.00
☐ **SKYBOWL: Book 3**   UE2595—$5.99
☐ **SKYBOWL: Book 3** HARDCOVER   UE2541—$22.00
A new cycle begins as a generation of peace is shattered by a seemingly unstoppable invasion force which even the combined powers of High Price Rohan's armies, Sunrunners' magic, and dragons' deadly fire may not be able to defeat.

DAW

Tad Williams

Memory, Sorrow and Thorn

THE DRAGONBONE CHAIR: Book 1
☐ **Hardcover Edition**   0-8099-003-3—$19.50
☐ **Paperback Edition**   UE2384—$5.99

A war fueled by the dark powers of sorcery is about to engulf the long-peaceful land of Osten Ard—as the Storm King, undead ruler of the elvishlike Sithi, seeks to regain his lost realm. And to Simon, a former castle scullion, will go the task of spearheading the quest that offers the only hope of salvation . . .

STONE OF FAREWELL: Book 2
☐ **Hardcover Edition**   UE2435—$21.95
☐ **Paperback Edition**   UE2480—$5.99

As the dark magic and dread forces of the Storm King spread their evil across the land, the tattered remnants of a once-proud human army flee in search of a last sanctuary and rallying point, and the last survivors of the League of the Scroll undertake missions which will take them from the fallen citadels to the secret heartland of the Sithi.

TO GREEN ANGEL TOWER: Book 3
☐ **Hardcover Edition**   UE2521—$25.00
☐ **Paperback Edition, Part I**   UE2598—$5.99
☐ **Paperback Edition, Part II** *(July '94)*   UE2606—$5.99

In this conclusion of the best-selling trilogy, the forces of Prince Josua march toward their final confrontation with the dread minions of the undead Storm King, while Simon, Miriamele, and Binabek embark on a desperate mission into evil's stronghold.
